# Seventeen Wishes

## ROBIN JONES GUNN

**BETHANY HOUSE PUBLISHERS**
MINNEAPOLIS, MINNESOTA 55438

*Seventeen Wishes*
Revised edition 1999
Copyright © 1993, 1999
Robin Jones Gunn

Edited by Janet Kobobel Grant
Cover illustration and design by the Lookout Design Group

This story is a work of fiction. All characters and events are the product of the author's imagination. Any resemblance to any person, living or dead, is coincidental. Text has been revised and updated by the author.

A Focus on the Family book published by
Bethany House Publishers
A Ministry of Bethany Fellowship International
11400 Hampshire Avenue South
Minneapolis, Minnesota 55438
www.bethanyhouse.com

Printed in the United States of America by
Bethany Press International, Minneapolis, Minnesota 55438

**Library of Congress Cataloging-in-Publication Data**

Gunn, Robin Jones, 1955–
    Seventeen wishes / Robin Jones Gunn
       p.    cm. — (The Christy Miller Series ; 9)
    Summary: Sixteen-year-old Christy goes to summer camp
determined to pack her time with romantic memories.
    ISBN 1–56179–730–8
    [1. Camps—Fiction. 2. Christian life—Fiction.] I. Title.
II. Title: Seventeen wishes. III. Series: Gunn, Robin Jones, 1955–
Christy Miller Series ; 9.
PZ7.G972Se     1993
[Fic]—dc20                           93–11278
                                            CIP
                                            AC

99 00 01 02 03 04 05 / 15 14 13 12 11 10 9 8 7 6 5 4 3 2

*To Ethel Herr,*
*who taught me with her life*
*that I can never love too much.*

*And to The Parts of Speech Critique Group,*
*with wonderful memories of all the years*
*we sat together with our feet beneath Ethel's table.*
*I thought we were learning to write.*
*Now I know we were learning what love looks like*
*when it's dressed in grace.*

# Contents

CHAPTER ONE

# *Act Natural*

"Are you sure you told the guys we were coming this afternoon?" red-headed Katie Weldon asked her best friend, Christy Miller, as they ascended the outdoor steps of the apartment building.

"Of course. I told Todd yesterday we would leave right after church. He said it would take about an hour to drive down here," Christy answered, her long legs taking the stairs two at a time. "The directions were really clear. I'm sure this is the place."

"Number twelve is at the end there," Katie pointed out. Then striking her usual athletic stance, she knocked on the door. No one answered. Katie looked into Christy's distinctive blue-green eyes with an unspoken, "Well? What do we do now?"

Christy bit her lower lip and scanned the piece of paper in her hand. "I know this is right. Knock again. Louder."

Katie pounded her fist on the door and called out, "Hey, Rick, Doug, Todd. We're here!"

Still no answer.

Christy brushed her nutmeg brown hair off her forehead and cautiously peered in a window. From what she could see, no one was inside. "What should we do, Katie?"

"They're probably playing a joke on us. They know what a big deal it was for you to talk your parents into letting you come to San Diego. They're probably trying to freak us out. You know, the 'big college guys teasing the little high school girls' trick."

Katie sounded so confident of her answer that Christy almost believed her. But then Katie usually sounded confident.

"Should we find a phone and try to call them?" Christy suggested.

"Lower your voice," Katie warned. "If they're in there, they can hear what you're saying."

"I don't think they're here. Maybe they ran to the store or something," Christy said, looking around.

Below them she noticed a cement courtyard with a swimming pool surrounded by lounge chairs. "Why don't we go down by the pool and wait for them?"

Katie surveyed the situation, her bright green eyes scanning the apartment complex for any sign of life. "Doesn't it seem weird to you," she whispered, "that for a place that's supposed to be crawling with college students, nobody's around?"

Christy was starting to get the heebie-jeebies. "Come on. Let's go down by the pool. At least we won't look so obviously lost, standing by their door with our luggage."

"Oh yeah, we'll look real natural lounging around the pool wearing jeans and clutching our luggage. If anyone from these other apartments sees us, they'll probably think we're homeless and call the police," Katie sputtered as she followed Christy down the stairs to the pool.

"Then let's put our stuff back in the car."

"Good idea. I'm starting to feel like an orphan. Why would they ditch us like this? You would think one of them could manage to leave a note or something."

The two girls stood at the trunk of Katie's car while she fished for her keys. "Did I give you my keys?"

"Very funny," Christy said. "Of course I don't have your keys. Stop goofing around and open the trunk."

"I can't find them."

Christy let out a sigh. "Did you leave them in the car?"

They both peered in the front window and at the same time noticed the keys dangling from the ignition. Of course, all the doors were locked.

"Good, Katie. Real swift! Now what are we supposed to do?" Christy snapped.

"Hey, relax, will you? I've done this before. All I need is a coat hanger."

"And where are we supposed to find a coat hanger?"

"Let's try the dumpster over there," Katie suggested.

She opened the gates to the garbage area and began to rummage through trash bags.

Christy stood nervously beside the car, guarding their gear. Now they really looked like a couple of bums with Katie sifting through the trash.

*This was supposed to be a nice, simple, Memorial weekend in San Diego to visit the guys' God-Lovers Bible study and to have a fun trip to the zoo. It's turning into a disaster!*

"Found one!" Katie called out, lifting her prized coat hanger into the air. A rotten banana peel clung to her arm.

"Nice work," Christy said. "Now why don't you try to leave the rest of the garbage in the dumpster?"

Katie beamed a victory smile as she shook off the banana peel and straightened out the hanger. She cheerfully gave Christy a rundown of the last time she had locked her keys in the car.

"I was at work, and I had to go in the mall to find a clothing store that would give me a hanger. I figured out that time how to make the loop on the end just right so it'll catch on the knob there. Good thing my car is so old. Your car doesn't have locks like this. We'd be stuck if it were your car."

Christy kept glancing around, aware that now they looked like homeless, garbage-digging hoboes and car thieves.

"Can you hurry it up, Katie?"

"I almost have it," she said, gingerly wedging the hanger between the window and door frame and maneuvering the loop over the lock button. Her tongue stuck out slightly, and she squinted her eyes.

Christy thought Katie looked as if she were playing one of those games at the video arcade in which the player has to manipulate a metal claw inside a glass cage to pick up a small stuffed animal. Christy could never win that game. She had ceased wasting her quarters on it long ago.

Not Katie. Katie was always up for a challenge. Anytime, anywhere.

"Almost," Katie breathed between clenched teeth as the two girls pressed their faces against the car window, pleading with the loop to connect with the black peg.

"Hey!" a loud voice called out behind them.

They jumped and spun around. They were surprised to see that the big voice belonged to a petite Asian girl.

"Are you Todd's friends?" she asked.

She had a bag of groceries in her arms and apparently had arrived on foot, which explained why they hadn't heard her approach. Her long, silky black hair hung over her shoulders, and she peered at them with a delicate smile.

"Yes!" Christy said eagerly. Then feeling obligated to explain what they were doing, she quickly added, "We locked the keys in the car, and we're trying to get them out."

Katie continued recounting their adventure. "We went to the guys' apartment, but no one was there. We thought maybe they were playing a trick on us, which would be typical of those guys, but they never jumped out and said 'Boo,' so we thought we would put our stuff back in the car."

The girl listened as they rattled on with their nervous explanations.

"That's when we found out the keys were locked in the car," Christy said.

Then becoming aware of how silly they must sound, like two inexperienced high school girls babbling on to this independent college woman, she lowered the pitch of her voice and tried to sound calm. "So do you know where the guys are?"

"At the hospital."

Christy felt as if a huge fist had just reached into her chest and squeezed the air out of her lungs. She found just enough breath to ask, "Is it Todd? Is he okay?"

"It was Rick," the girl replied.

The fist released her lungs, and she let out a wobbly sigh.

"Rick?" Katie said, looking like the invisible fist had just grabbed her by the heart. "Is he okay? What happened?"

"I'm sure he'll be fine. He hurt his arm when the guys were in the pool this afternoon. They were doing handsprings off the diving board, and Rick had some kind of competition going. He twisted his arm the wrong way."

"Sounds like Rick," Christy said under her breath.

"We'd better go to the hospital," Katie said, urgently returning to her mission of retrieving the car keys. "Do you know how to get there?"

"I don't think it would help much for you to go. Todd and

Doug took him more than an hour ago. I imagine they'll be back before you could get to the hospital."

"Got it!" Katie said, popping the door open and reaching for the keys. "Are you sure we shouldn't go?"

"I guess you could, if you wanted. I think they'll be back any minute, though. Or you could stay here and help me with dinner. I told the guys I'd have a spaghetti feast for them when they came back."

Christy turned to Katie, who still looked worried, and said, "The way this afternoon has been, I don't think you and I should be driving around San Diego trying to find the hospital. It seems to me we should stay here and help . . . ," she paused, realizing she didn't know the girl's name.

"I'm Stephanie," the girl filled in the blank for her. "And you must be Christy. I've heard a lot about you."

Christy felt her cheeks warming. "And this is Katie," she said.

"Did you happen to hear anything about me, say, from Rick maybe?" Katie asked.

Stephanie smiled a delicate, mysterious smile. Her face reminded Christy of a soft, pink apple blossom.

"Rick has lots to say about a lot of things. Perhaps he has mentioned you."

Christy glanced at Katie, concerned about the way her friend might take such an answer. A bit of a relationship had sprouted between Rick and Katie at the Rose Parade on New Year's Day, but that was five months ago. Katie had tried to further the relationship since then, but nothing had brought Rick back into her life. This weekend was designed to be the test. Christy could tell it hurt Katie that Rick hadn't spoken of her the way Todd had talked about Christy. But then Christy and Todd had almost two years of relational history to draw from.

"I guess we'll stay then," Katie decided, locking the door again, this time with the keys in her hand.

"Bring up your suitcases," Stephanie said. "You're both staying with me tonight. I'm in number ten. Two doors down from the nut house."

"Thanks for letting us sleep at your place," Christy said. "Todd told me he would make arrangements with one of the girls in the complex. I'm just glad you're the first one we ran into!"

"It's pretty quiet around here," Stephanie explained as they headed for her place. "School was out more than a week ago, and almost everyone has gone home for the summer. I work at the same restaurant as the guys. The Blue Parachute. Did they tell you about it?"

Christy nodded. Katie looked a little left out.

Stephanie unlocked her apartment door. "We all agreed when we took the jobs to stay until June so the restaurant could switch over to its summer help. Here we are," she announced, opening the door and revealing a tidy, nicely decorated apartment.

"Welcome to my humble home. Please make yourselves comfortable. My roommate left yesterday, so the empty room is all yours."

Christy and Katie lugged their bags into the bedroom on the right. The only thing in the room was a standing lamp in the corner.

"Todd didn't tell me we were supposed to bring sleeping bags," Christy whispered.

"I'll ask Rick if I can borrow his," Katie said. "Maybe Stephanie has one too."

Soft, classical music floated into their room, and the girls followed its sound back to the living room where Stephanie had turned on the stereo.

"This is a really cute apartment," Christy said, surveying the blue and white striped futon couch, the hanging lamps covered with blue and peach flowered fabric, and the variety of intriguing pictures on the walls.

One of the larger pictures caught Christy's eye. A young woman was wearing a long, pink, lacy dress, with her hair puffed on top of her head like a cloud. From the surrounding garden scenery, it looked like summer, and the woman was seated on a bench, wishfully looking out to the ocean.

"I love this picture!" Christy said.

The scene stirred something inside her. It was the hint of another time and place. A time when women were praised for looking feminine and being dreamers. A place for tea parties and parasols and wearing long, white, lacy gloves for a stroll in the garden.

*I think I was born a hundred years too late.*

"Thanks," Stephanie called out from the kitchen, where she was unloading her groceries. "Would you two like something to drink? Have you ever had iced ginseng tea?"

The two girls made a face at each other and cautiously approached the kitchen.

"Whatever you have is fine," Christy said graciously.

"Do you happen to have any Coke? Pepsi?" Katie ventured.

"I don't," Stephanie said. "But I'm sure the guys do. I have a key to their place. Do you want to go over and get some?"

"Are you sure it's okay?" Katie asked.

"I'm sure they won't mind. They gave me the key because they kept locking themselves out. Sometimes those guys seem like Peter Pan and the Lost Boys, and they think I'm their Wendy."

Christy liked Stephanie. She seemed awfully sweet. There was an international flair about her, and she was intriguing.

"Come on," Katie said. "Let's go raid the guys' refrigerator. This ought to be fun."

Stephanie handed them the key. As Christy turned it in the guys' door, she looked over her shoulder to make sure they hadn't returned.

"Doesn't this feel sneaky to you?" she asked Katie.

"Yeah, it's fun! Let's freeze their underwear or something."

"Katie!"

"What? It was only a suggestion."

"Where do you come up with these things?" Christy asked as the door opened, and the two of them glanced around the room. "What a mess!" Christy said under her breath.

The two spies entered slowly and took in the full spectrum. To their right, in the kitchen area, were folding chairs at a card table with a box of sugary cereal in the middle. Surrounding the box were three bowls with puddles of pink, soured milk from the dissolved cereal. A half-full liter bottle of generic cola stood next to the cereal box.

"I feel like Goldilocks," Christy whispered.

"Me too," Katie said with a giggle. "Let's see where the three bears sleep."

"Katie!"

"I'm not going to steal their underwear, I promise. I was only kidding. Come on. I'm curious."

They stuck close together as they made their way through the living room, which hosted a long brown couch, an overstuffed plaid chair, a small TV balanced precariously on a cement block bookcase, and an old trunk covered with surfing magazines, which served as a coffee table in the center of the room.

"Very stylish," Katie quipped. "It's the ever popular 'early-slob' decor."

Christy noticed Todd's orange surfboard in the corner, serving as a coat rack at the moment.

"This must be Rick and Doug's room," Katie said, peeking around the half-opened door on the right.

Two unmade beds hugged the walls. The floor between the beds was covered with clothes, books, empty potato chips bags, and a neon yellow Frisbee. A bike was tucked behind the door, and a guitar was propped up in the corner with a Padres baseball cap balanced on top.

"How can you tell?" Christy asked.

"Easy. The guitar is Doug's, and the bike is Rick's."

"Todd plays the guitar too," Christy said.

"This doesn't look like Todd. Come on. Let's see what the room of a surf rat looks like."

Christy felt hesitant to follow Katie. Doug and Rick were two of the neatest dressers she knew. If they could live in such a messy room and appear so tidy in public, then what would "Mr. Casual's" room look like?

"Christy," Katie called from the bedroom on the right, "you have to see this!"

Christy looked into Todd's room but couldn't believe what she saw.

The room was immaculate.

"Do you really think this is Todd's room?" she whispered.

"What's that?" Katie asked, pointing to a peculiar box in the center of the room. Standing only a few inches up from the floor, the large, wooden-framed box was covered with a rippled sheet and had a neatly folded blanket at one end.

"It's too small to be a waterbed."

Katie poked it, and the substance under the sheet gave way. "It feels like . . ." She pulled back the corner of the sheet and announced, "It is; it's sand. I don't believe it!"

Christy joined in the examination and felt Todd's unique sand mattress.

Katie started to laugh. "Only Todd would sleep in a giant kitty litter box!"

"I'll bet it's really comfortable," Christy said, quickly coming to his defense. "After sleeping out on the Hawaiian beach while he was in the surfing competition, he's probably more comfortable in the sand than on a mattress."

Katie turned to Christy and smiled, her bright green eyes doing a merry dance. "Like I said, only Todd."

Christy noticed a grouping of pictures and posters on the wall behind the bed. In the center was a poster of a waterfall on Maui where Todd, Christy, her friend Paula, and her little brother David had spent a day last summer. The three other posters were surfing shots. A half-dozen photographs surrounded the posters, all stuck to the wall with thumb tacks.

"They're all of you," Katie said. "Look at that. All these pictures are of you."

Christy was amazed. Over the years she had sent Todd a picture here or there, but she never would have guessed he would save them or would create a place of honor for them.

"Isn't that your picture from the eighth grade?" Katie asked, pointing to a wallet-size picture at the top.

"Oh, no, look at that! It's from ninth grade. That is such a pathetic picture. I must have sent that to him right after we met. That's about the time he left Newport Beach and went to live with his mom in Florida."

Katie took a close look at the small photo and then looked at

Christy. "May I just say you've improved over the years?"

Christy laughed at the little-girl expression on her face in the picture. Her hair was long then, almost to her waist, and hung straight down in an uncomplimentary fashion.

"This one must be tenth grade," Katie said. "That's when I met you, when you moved to Escondido. Look how different you looked with short hair! It was too short then, if you ask me. I like the way you wear your hair now."

Christy had been growing her hair out ever since she had let her aunt talk her into whacking it all off the summer before her sophomore year. Now, at the end of her junior year, it was past her shoulders.

"I can't believe Todd has all these pictures. I don't even remember sending some of them to him," Christy said. "I do remember this one, though," she said, pointing to a snapshot of the two of them at the Hawaiian waterfall in the poster.

"Listen," Katie said. "Is that them coming?"

Christy heard the thump of heavy footsteps coming down the corridor outside the apartment. They both heard loud, male voices approaching.

"Do you think they'll go to Stephanie's first?" Christy asked.

"Why? They don't know we're here. It sounds like they're coming inside. Quick, hide!" Katie dove for Todd's closet. The minute she opened it, a mound of clothes and junk tumbled out, showering her with damp swimming trunks and a sprinkling of sand.

"Ewww!"

"Shhh," Christy said. "They're coming in!"

Katie quickly stuffed the clothes back into the closet and whispered, "What should we do?"

"Act natural!" Christy said, standing perfectly still in the middle of Todd's room, her hands behind her back and a nervous grin pasted on her face.

They could hear the front door of the apartment open. One of the guys said, "Hey, it was unlocked. Is somebody here?"

"What should we say?" Katie asked under her breath. She took her place by Christy's side, looking like her mirror image, with hands behind her back and a goofy grin frozen on her face.

Christy could tell by the pounding footsteps that the three bears were about to discover them. There was no way to look anything other than stupid.

"Katie, think of something, quick!"

# CHAPTER TWO

# Mr. Gizmo

As Christy and Katie heard the guys coming down the hallway toward Todd's bedroom, Katie, quick thinker that she was, shouted, "Surprise!"

Christy quickly joined in. "Surprise!"

She spotted Todd's screaming, silver-blue eyes opened wide in surprise. He started to laugh, and in two giant steps, he had his arms around Christy. She hugged him back, her ear pressed against his chest where his deep laugh rumbled. She wondered if he could feel her heart about to pound out of her chest.

"You sure surprised us!" Todd said, giving Katie a quick hug. He ran his fingers through his bleached blond hair.

Doug and Rick followed with hugs for both the girls. There were lots of explanations and laughter and lots of sympathy, especially on Katie's part, when they saw the bandage around Rick's sprained wrist.

"So Stephanie knows you're here?" Doug asked. He stood a little taller than Todd, but not as tall as Rick.

Seeing the three of them all lined up, Christy realized Rick was the most striking of the three. His dark, wavy hair, deep brown eyes, and athletic build had been the obsession of many girls at her high school last year, including her. No wonder Katie couldn't get Rick out of her mind. In any room, any situation, his looks commanded full attention.

If Christy hadn't dated Rick for a short time and experienced some of the not-so-pleasant sides of his personality, she too might have been staring at him now the way Katie was.

As far as Christy was concerned, she would choose Todd or Doug over Rick any day. Katie, she knew, would have to come to her own conclusion on that, just as Christy had.

"We were supposed to be raiding your refrigerator for soda," Katie explained, her blunt-cut copper hair swishing dramatically as she looked to Christy for support and then back at the guys. "Only we thought we would do a little room inspection first. We were pleased to find your 'kitty litter' box so nice and clean. Only one question, though. Where's the cat?"

Doug started to laugh at Katie, who was pointing to Todd's bed as though she were a game-show model showing off the show-case of prizes.

Doug had a clean-cut appearance, with his sandy blond hair that always looked as though he had just had it cut. He was good-looking in a boyish way and appeared younger than his twenty years. The most outgoing of the three guys, Doug was known for his hugs, which he gave out generously.

"Try it," Todd challenged Katie. "Lie on it and see how it feels."

Katie, ever the good sport, lay down on the sand bed as they all watched. She wiggled her back until she had formed the perfect support.

Folding her hands over her stomach, she said, "Okay, I'm convinced. This is the perfect bed. Did you invent this, Todd?"

"Not much to invent," he said. "A couple of boards, a couple of sand bags, and a blanket. I don't think the patent office would recognize it as a true invention."

"You didn't go in our room, did you?" Doug asked.

Katie and Christy exchanged glances.

Christy said, "We'll never tell!"

"I told you we should have picked up," Doug said to Rick out of the side of his mouth. "Todd had the right idea."

"What do you mean?" Rick said. "Todd just threw everything in his closet."

"We could have done that too," Doug said with a smile. "Might have impressed them."

"If I'm going to impress anyone," Rick said confidently, "it's going to be with my other attributes. Not with my housekeeping skills."

"Obviously," Katie said under her breath.

"I heard that," Rick said.

Christy watched carefully to see if anything might be starting up between the two of them.

"And which of your fine attributes are you going to start with?" Katie teased, getting up from the sand bed. "Perhaps your wonderfully coordinated skills on the diving board?"

"No," Rick countered quickly, "my skill at keeping girls off balance." As he said it, he gently pushed Katie with his good hand so that she toppled back into the sand pit.

Katie gave Rick a firm look of indignation, but Christy could tell Katie was feeling honored to have been the object of Rick's teasing.

"Todd," Katie asked from where her bottom was planted in the sand, "may I show your roommate a handful of your bed? In his face?"

"It's up to you," Todd said. "I'm going to see if Stephanie

needs any help with that spaghetti."

"I'll join you," Christy said.

"I'm right behind you," Doug echoed. "What did you need from our fridge? Drinks and what else?"

Christy and Doug followed Todd to the kitchen, leaving Katie and Rick alone. She could hear Katie's muffled voice teasing Rick and then laughter. So far, so good.

Doug opened the old, gold-colored refrigerator and pulled out a couple liter bottles of soda. The rest of the refrigerator's contents looked as if they might fit nicely into the penicillin family of molds.

"Do you guys ever clean out this thing?" Christy ventured.

"Todd did once, didn't you, Todd? Couple of weeks ago, I think," Doug said. "We're all moving out next week. We'll dump everything then."

Todd was standing by the card table, shaking the box of cereal and looking inside. "Did you guys find the toy yet?"

"Don't think so," Doug said. "What is it this time?"

"Some kind of plastic gizmo that walks down windows," Todd said, his face brightening as he stuck his hand inside.

Christy could tell by the way his one dimple appeared on his right cheek that he had found the treasure and was pretty pleased with himself.

"Check it out," Todd said, tearing the clear wrapper from the gizmo with his teeth and tossing the critter against the window. "It's Mr. Gizmo!"

Sure enough, Mr. Gizmo walked. The first row of tiny suction cups on its feet stuck to the smooth window for a moment and then released as the next row hung tight. It gave the appearance of "walking" down the glass.

"Cool," Todd said, sticking the treasure in the pocket of his shorts. "You two ready to go?"

"We're ready," Rick answered, appearing in the living room with Katie in a headlock with his good arm. With his bandaged hand he pinched her cheek.

Christy would have been furious if Rick had ever treated her like that. Katie gave every indication she was in heaven. *Maybe they are good for each other*.

The group filed out the door, and Christy noticed a large mayonnaise jar half-filled with coins on a shelf. Doug had told her about that jar. The guys used it to collect money for a young boy they supported in Kenya. Christy had seen a letter that ten-year-old Joab had written to Doug and the guys. She also knew Doug carried a picture of Joab in his wallet and showed it around as if he were the proud big brother.

"Guess what, Doug?" Christy said as Todd locked the door and they followed Rick and his crutch, Katie, down the corridor. "I wrote to the organization that set you up as a sponsor for Joab. My family and I adopted a four-year-old girl from Brazil. Her name is Anna Maria. I never thanked you for giving me the information. So thanks."

"Awesome!" Doug said, slipping his arm around Christy and giving her a quick Doug-hug. "Isn't it amazing how little it takes to feed and clothe those kids?"

"Steph," Rick called out at the door of apartment number ten, "open up! It's the Rickster. I've come to collect your sympathy."

"Yeah, right," Stephanie said, opening the door and giving Rick a playfully disgusted look. "Like I'd ever give you anything, least of all sympathy."

Rick let go of Katie and stepped into the apartment, continuing his lively flirtation with Stephanie as if Katie didn't exist.

"Aren't you going to kiss it and make it better?" Rick asked, holding out his sore paw to her with a pout on his handsome face.

"When pigs fly!" Stephanie tossed back at him.

Rick then wrapped his good arm around Stephanie's shoulders and walked into the living room, still pleading for her sympathy.

*Oh, no, look out, Katie! When you put your heart out there on the edge of the wall, it doesn't take much for it to do the ol' Humpty-Dumpty crash.*

Katie seemed fine. She went in the kitchen and stirred the pot of spaghetti sauce as if she had been asked to do so. Christy had never admired her resiliency more than she did at that moment.

"We brought some sodas," Doug said, offering the two bottles for Stephanie to see before he placed them on the counter.

"Want me to finish making this garlic bread?" Todd asked, picking up a knife and slicing the loaf of French bread where Stephanie had left off.

"Sure," Stephanie said, turning her back to Rick and joining them in the kitchen. "Christy, could you help me get a salad going?"

Todd, Stephanie, Christy, and Katie all worked together in the narrow kitchen while Doug and Rick planted themselves on the sofa and turned on the TV.

"Their home away from home—in front of my TV," Stephanie said to Christy, motioning to Rick and Doug over her shoulder. "If you ever want to make sure you have lots of attention from guys in your apartment complex, all you have to do is be the only who subscribes to cable."

"I'll remember that," Katie said, helping Todd wrap the pungent garlic bread in foil. Katie waved her hand above the bread to clear the strong aroma and asked sarcastically, "Are you sure you used enough garlic, Todd?"

"It's good that way. You'll see. It's my secret recipe. Butter, mayonnaise, and lots of garlic."

"And only three thousand calories a slice," Stephanie said with a wink as she turned on the oven and handed Katie a cookie sheet for the bread. "It's good. Trust me. Todd's made it before. That's why the kitchen wallpaper is starting to peel."

Even though she knew Stephanie was kidding, Christy glanced at the wallpaper. There was nothing wrong with it. Every little peach heart stood in place.

Christy liked the way Stephanie used lots of hearts in decorating the kitchen. She especially liked the heart-shaped basket hanging on a nail above the sink. Peach ribbons were strung through the sides with a bunch of silk flowers attached at the bottom.

Christy liked colorful decor like that and thought how fun it would be to decorate her own apartment some day.

When they all sat down to eat a little while later, she decided one day she would have straight-back wooden chairs with padded cushions at her kitchen table, just like Stephanie's. And she would serve her guests on blue and white dishes, just like Stephanie.

Todd was right. The bread was delicious, as was the spaghetti and everything else. The conversation around the tightly packed table remained lively. Everything about this gathering made Christy feel grown-up and included in her circle of college friends. It felt completely different from being a sixteen-year-old living at home with her parents and eleven-year-old brother.

*Oh, no,* Christy suddenly remembered, *I promised I would call home as soon as we arrived!*

"May I use your phone?" she quietly asked Stephanie.

"Sure. There's one in my bedroom."

Christy slipped into Stephanie's room and closed the door. She felt awful for being so forgetful.

Mom answered, and Christy quickly explained about the guys not being there, the keys being locked in the car, meeting Stephanie, and Rick's sprained wrist. When she finished, there was an uncomfortable pause on the other end.

"Honest, Mom, that's what happened, and that's why I didn't think to call."

"Oh, I believe you," Christy's mother answered. "It's just that with all that has gone on during the last few hours, I'm not sure I'm ready for all the adventures you may face between now and when you come home tomorrow night."

"Mom," Christy said, trying her best to sound mature and responsible, "there's nothing to worry about. I'm really sorry I didn't call sooner. Everything is fine, and I'm sure the rest of our visit will be uneventful. I'll call you tomorrow before we leave to drive home. I really appreciate you and Dad letting me spend time with my friends like this."

"Well, have a good time and remember all the things we talked about."

"I will, Mom. Don't worry. I'll be fine."

Christy sat for a moment on the edge of Stephanie's bed after she hung up. She couldn't help feeling a little like a baby in this group where all of them were living on their own except Katie and her. Katie's parents not only let her go on this trip but they also gave her the car with a full tank of gas and told her to have fun. Katie didn't have to check in with them.

Christy felt fully aware of that ever-present, invisible rope that connected her to her parents. The older she became, the more rope they let out and the more they encouraged her to go exploring on independent experiences like this overnight trip to San Diego. Still, that invisible rope kept her anchored to them. In situations like this, when she had to check in, the rope seemed to pull awfully tight, right around her stomach.

Then she had a thought that was even more sobering. *Really soon I'm going to be eighteen. I'll be in college and living on my own like Stephanie. What will it feel like for that rope to be cut?*

Christy decided to be grateful for the linkage while she had it. She felt secure, knowing the invisible rope to her parents was intact and taut. It would be gone soon enough.

*Katie doesn't seem to have any ropes attached to her,* Christy thought. *That must feel scary. As if you didn't know for sure if someone is going to be there to pull you in if you go too far.*

Joining the others, Christy pitched in and helped to clear the table and dry the dishes. Doug washed and Todd put them away.

"Look how lovely my hands are after using this new dish soap!" Doug said in a high-pitched voice, holding up his bubble-covered hands.

"How's this for squeaky clean?" Doug rubbed his finger over the back of one of his plates, continuing to act out his commercial.

"Wait, I have an idea," Todd said, snatching the plate Christy was drying. He pulled Mr. Gizmo from his pocket and threw it on the back of the plate. Mr. Gizmo started to walk down the plate.

Doug whistled his applause. "Good show, good show! Now try it on the refrigerator."

Todd did, and it worked again.

More cheers and whistles came from Doug, and Christy joined him with eager applause.

"The oven door," Doug challenged.

Mr. Gizmo met the challenge.

"Now the true test—can he walk on the ceiling?"

Todd tossed Mr. Gizmo onto the ceiling.

Fwaaap! He stuck perfectly, but he didn't walk. He didn't move at all.

"Boo! Hiss!" Doug appraised the immobile Mr. Gizmo.

"What are you guys doing in there?" Stephanie called from the living room.

"It's the Mr. Gizmo Olympics," Doug said. "And our favorite contender just experienced a major setback."

"I'll get it down," Todd offered, pulling over one of Stephanie's chairs with the flowered cushions.

"Don't stand on that," Christy scolded. "It's too nice to stand on."

"What do you suggest," Doug asked, "waiting for gravity to keep its law?"

Christy had an idea. She twirled the dish towel in her hand and snapped it toward the ceiling, just missing Mr. Gizmo. But the towel gave off a loud, cracking sound.

"Good thinking," Doug said, snatching another towel from the handle of the refrigerator and snapping it in the air. "Take *that*, you Mr. Gizmo, you!"

"You missed," Todd told him, reaching for a towel and giving it a try.

Before Christy knew what was happening, she was stuck in the middle of a towel-snapping war between Doug and Todd.

"Whoa! Wait a minute! How did I get between you guys?" she cried out, trying to break loose from the circle. It was no use. They had her surrounded.

Christy began to snap them back, but they were faster and more experienced at this. On impulse, she scooped both her hands into the bountiful soap bubbles in the sink. With a mound of the white fluff, she glanced at Doug and then at Todd.

"Okay, who's going to get it first?"

Before she could decide which one to "suds," Doug slid his hand under hers and pushed the whole mound into her face. Some of it went up her nose.

Christy let out a squeal and wiped the suds from her eyes in time to see Doug and Todd giving each other a snap of their towels over her head. Just as their towels came down, so did Mr. Gizmo—right on the top of Christy's head.

They all started laughing and Todd grabbed the toy out of her hair.

Just then someone knocked on the door. As Christy blew bubbles out of her nose, seven college students entered the apartment and greeted everyone. Christy reached for the towel in Doug's hand and finished mopping up, feeling embarrassed.

"You okay?" Doug asked, pulling her over to the corner of the kitchen.

"I think so," Christy said, looking up at him. "Did I get it all?"

"Here," Doug said, taking the towel and gently wiping under the corner of her right eye. He then smoothed down the top of her hair where Mr. Gizmo had landed.

"Good as new," he announced. Taking her by the hand, he said, "Don't be shy. Come meet the rest of the God-Lovers."

Christy smiled and greeted the three girls and four guys who had just arrived. She tried to think of a way to remember all their names.

There was another knock on the door, and two more girls entered. One of them was really outgoing as well as gorgeous. She went right to Rick and asked about his bandaged wrist. She soon made up for the lack of sympathy Rick had received from the rest of them.

Everyone found a seat on the floor or by pulling over one of the kitchen chairs. No one said it was time to start. They all sort of fell into place as if this was a familiar habit for all of them. Christy noticed that Todd had disappeared, and she wasn't sure where to sit. Katie was right next to Rick on the couch with the blond on his other side and her friend next to her. Doug seemed to be in charge. Stephanie was on the floor talking with one of the guys.

Christy slipped into an open spot by the wall near the front. A lifetime of familiar "left-out" feelings joined her in the corner and kept her company. As long as she was wrapped up in those feelings, she couldn't make the effort to start chatting with anyone. She was the visitor. They should greet her. No one did.

Todd came back in with his guitar and Doug's. The two of them sat on chairs in front of the TV and took a few minutes to tune their instruments.

Three more girls showed up, and one of them wedged in next to Christy.

"Hi, I'm Beth," she said.

"I'm Christy."

"Nice to meet you. Are you visiting?"

"Yes," was all Christy could explain before Doug spoke up.

"I'm glad you guys are all here tonight," he said. "As you know, most of the God-Lovers have taken off for the summer. This is our last time together until next fall. I thought it would be good if we spent some time thanking God for the awesome stuff He's done in our lives this past year."

Todd started to play his guitar, and Doug joined him in strumming Rich Mullins' song, "Our God Is an Awesome God." Somehow Christy knew that would be Doug's favorite song since "awesome" was his favorite word.

She knew the song and sang along with the others, feeling a little amazed that so many college students were sitting there, openly singing their hearts out to God. One guy toward the front had his eyes closed and both arms slightly lifted up in a gesture of praise to God.

Christy couldn't explain it, but somehow after that first song and then listening to Todd open in prayer, she felt all her defenses dissolve. The people in this room were Christians. All of them seemed to be there to worship God. These college students were some of her brothers and sisters in Christ. Even if she never saw them again, she would spend eternity with them in heaven. She felt included in God's family.

Doug started to strum the next song, which Christy didn't know. Instead of feeling left out, she quietly closed her eyes and bowed her head to listen while everyone else sang.

> *Eyes have not seen. Ears have not heard.*
> *Neither has it entered into the heart of man*
> *The things God has planned*
> *For those who love Him.*

For two hours they sang and prayed and talked about what was going on in their lives. Then Doug read some Bible verses and talked about waiting on God and trusting Him for the future. Everyone seemed to get into what he had to say, especially since most of them were taking off in different directions the next week. Not many of them knew what the future held.

After Todd closed in prayer, everyone started to visit with each other. Christy, feeling warmed by the sweet spirit of the group, walked around and met everyone she hadn't been introduced to before. She had never been this outgoing, and to her surprise, it wasn't that hard.

"Do you want to come out to coffee with us?" Beth asked. "A bunch of us are going. Your friend Katie said she would come, and I'm sure Stephanie is coming."

All Christy's warm feelings disappeared. One of her agreements with her parents for this trip was that she wouldn't go out after dark. It seemed like such a silly rule now. If her parents had been there, they would have seen how responsible all these people were.

Still, if she went without asking, she would be breaking her agreement. Maybe she could call and explain the situation, and they would understand and give her permission to go.

Christy glanced at the clock on the kitchen wall: 9:45. She knew her parents were probably in bed. Her dad worked at a dairy and had to be up early every morning. He usually went to bed before she did. It would *not* be good to call and wake him to ask a favor like this. Still, if she didn't ask . . .

"Come on, Christy. We're going to The Blue Parachute," Katie said enthusiastically. "Grab your purse and let's go."

Todd was talking to some people in the kitchen. It would help if she knew whether or not he was going.

"Ready?" Doug asked, coming alongside her. "We're all going. You want to ride with Todd or me?"

"I . . . I'm not sure," Christy said. She hated having to make decisions like this. Especially when she knew that either way she would come up the loser. Which was the worst to lose? Her friends' approval or her parents' trust?

CHAPTER THREE

# *Elephants, Monkeys, and Snakes*

"Okay, I'll go," Christy said, regretting her impulsive words the minute she said them.

*My parents will never know. I won't tell them. We're only going to a restaurant. What could happen? They would understand if they met these guys.*

"I have room," Todd called out to Doug and Christy, "if you both want to ride with me. Stephanie is going with me."

Christy numbly followed the rest of the group down to the parking lot and watched Katie laugh and joke with Rick on their way to his classic red Mustang. She was one of three girls riding with Rick.

Todd opened the side door of his old Volkswagen bus called "Gus." Glancing at Christy, he asked, "Are you okay?"

"Sure," she answered quickly, certain her guilt showed all over her face. She never had been good at sneaking around. She was especially bad at lying.

Doug moved in for a closer look into Christy's eyes. "No, you're not," he said. "Something's wrong. What is it, Christy?"

"It's just that I had an agreement with my parents that I wouldn't go out after dark once Katie and I got here. I know if they were here, it would be different. They would let me go."

"But they're not here," Todd said, sliding shut the van's door.

"We'll stay too," Doug said.

"I have stuff to make banana splits," Stephanie said. "Not enough for the whole group, but it should be enough for the four of us."

"You guys don't have to stay," Christy said. "I'll stay, and you guys go."

"Why would we?" Todd asked.

"Don't worry about it, Christy," Stephanie said. "These guys don't care where they go as long as food is involved. It'll give us a chance to talk, and that will be nice."

Todd flagged down Rick, who was about to peel out of the parking lot. He jogged over to Rick's window and, bending down, explained the situation to Rick. Christy could feel Rick's gaze as he looked past Todd at her.

She was sure he was remembering all the rules her parents had laid down for her when they were dating.

*That's right, everyone gawk at me*, she thought. *Here I am: Christy Miller, the biggest baby in the world!*

Katie's lighthearted laughter rippled into the air. Todd patted the side of the car three times, the way a cowboy pats his horse's side. With a squeal of tires, Rick peeled out, hurrying to catch up with the other cars that had already left.

As the four of them headed back for Stephanie's apartment, Christy felt an overwhelming urge to keep apologizing. "I'm really sorry, you guys. Thanks for doing this for me."

Doug slipped his arm around Christy and said, "What kind of God-Lovers would we be if we didn't support you when you have an opportunity to honor your parents?"

"I still feel bad for holding you guys back. Really, if you want to go, that's fine. I could stay here by myself."

"Christy," Todd said, "shake it off." He shook both his hands in front of her for emphasis. "You're the only one making a big deal of this."

She might have felt reprimanded or embarrassed by such a comment from someone else. Not from Todd. She could take it from him, and when she did, something inside her calmed down.

Stephanie welcomed them all back into her kitchen, where they set to work creating masterpiece banana splits, topped off with a whipped-cream fight.

Stephanie started to talk about how she was going back to San Francisco next week to spend the summer working at her father's computer store.

"Her parents came over from China," Doug explained to Christy. "It's an awesome story. Her dad was handed a Chinese Bible by some guy who smuggled it into the country. It was the first time he had ever heard of the Bible. He read it and gave his heart to the Lord and then found some other Christians who were meeting in an underground church. That's where he met Stephanie's mom."

Stephanie jumped in. "Actually, they had met at the university, but neither of them knew the other was a believer."

"That's amazing," Christy said, licking the chocolate sauce off the back of her spoon. "How did they end up in San Francisco?"

Stephanie launched into the story of all the hardships her parents endured in trying to get out of China. "They were extra motivated when my mom was pregnant with me. They had to leave before the pregnancy became obvious."

Todd leaned over and explained to Christy, "Mandatory abortion. It's China's way of population control. They already had one kid, and that's the allotment per family."

Christy's eyes grew wide. "You mean you would have been aborted if your parents had stayed there?"

Stephanie nodded.

Christy had heard vague stories before of how hard life was in other countries, but she had never met anyone who had "escaped" and come to America.

"So obviously your parents made it out of the country," Christy said.

"I was born four months after they arrived at my uncle's in San Francisco, so all I know are the dramatic stories. The hard part now is that here we are in a country where we're free to worship God, and one of my younger brothers wants nothing to do with Christianity. I think that's been harder on my parents than anything else they've been through."

Christy thought about Stephanie's words later that night as she lay on the floor in her sleeping bag. Katie and the others hadn't returned yet, and Christy couldn't sleep. She felt as if she had grown up more that night than she had during her entire junior year of high school. The conversation with Stephanie had sobered her and caused her to realize how easy it was for her to be a Christian. She had never been challenged to do anything dangerous because of her faith.

Another part of the grown-up feeling came from being on her own, around college students. It made her feel independent, even though she hadn't been free to go out with everyone. Still, she was away from home, making new friends, and making good decisions. This was one night when growing up seemed like an honorable, wonderful experience.

Just then the front door to Stephanie's apartment opened. Through the half-open bedroom door, Christy could see Katie's silhouette standing there, whispering to Rick.

As Christy watched, Rick braced his good arm against the door frame and bent his head to be eye-level with Katie. Christy knew the move well. He had assumed the same stance with her more than once, right before he had kissed her. His hovering position had the effect of making the girl feel sheltered and yet vulnerable at the same time. She wasn't sure she could watch what would happen next.

But she did.

Rick kissed Katie. Instead of just receiving it, Katie looped her arms around Rick's neck and kissed him back. He pulled away slightly, and Katie removed her arms. Christy could hear muffled whispers, and then she saw Rick back up and wave good-bye.

"See you in the morning," Katie said softly.

She closed the door, and Christy could hear her humming.

*Oh, Katie, I don't want Rick to break your heart!*

Christy pretended to be asleep when Katie stepped into the room. She was sure it was well after midnight, and this would not be the time to have a heart-to-heart talk with her best friend.

*I'll wait to see how things go between them tomorrow at the zoo. I haven't said one discouraging word to her about him yet. But if he treats her badly tomorrow, that's it. I'll do everything I can to break them up!*

The next day, it took Christy more than an hour of walking around the zoo before she began to relax and quit working so hard at being super-sleuth.

Relaxing was difficult for several reasons. Rick appeared to be ignoring Katie, or at best, treating her as though she were an annoying little kid. Katie didn't seem to notice. She came on exceptionally loud and flirty. Twice Christy noticed Katie linking her arm with Rick's, but he didn't allow the connection to remain for long.

Plus Christy felt strained because there were five of them. Stephanie had to work, so Christy, Katie, Rick, Doug, and Todd went on the zoo adventure. A group of five was a lot harder to maneuver than four or even six.

By the flamingo lagoon at the main entrance, the group decided to ride the tram. Katie slid in next to Rick, Christy sat across from them, and Doug scooted in next to her. With no room for Todd, he had to sit on another seat next to some tourists who spoke only Japanese.

They disembarked and headed for the giraffe exhibit, the five of them mixed in with all the other tourists. It didn't feel as though they were their own group at all.

Katie reached the exhibit first and said, "Look at the baby giraffe! Isn't he cute?"

Doug stepped next to Christy, slipped his arm around her, and pointed to the grove of tall eucalyptus trees. "Look at that one giraffe twisting his neck around the tree. Doesn't he look like he's trying to play hide-and-seek, but the tree isn't quite thick enough?"

Christy laughed with Doug, but at the same time she was aware that Todd was walking off to the side by himself. Katie had again grasped Rick's arm and was stretching her neck, trying to entertain Rick with her giraffe impression.

Rick didn't look impressed.

Christy felt uneasy, as though it were up to her to make sure everyone was getting along and having a good time.

*Stop it*, she finally scolded herself in front of the koala exhibit as she watched a baby koala clinging to its mother. *You're not everyone's mother here, Christy. Relax and enjoy the day.*

"I want to see the elephants," Todd said. "Anybody have an idea which way we go?"

Doug pulled a folded zoo map from his back pocket and began to give directions. Rick pulled away from Katie and joined Doug, bending over the map.

"Do they still have the sea lion show?" Rick asked. "That was my favorite when I was a kid."

The three guys huddled around the map, and Christy cautiously sided up next to Katie. "I didn't get to ask you how everything went last night," she said in her best lighthearted voice. "Did you and Rick have a good time?"

Katie looked cross, but she answered calmly, "Yeah, it was great. We all had a good time."

Christy decided to venture a more direct statement. "You and Rick seem to be getting along okay."

Katie grabbed Christy by the arm and jerked her several yards away from the guys. She had tears in her eyes. "He doesn't like me, does he? Last night I thought something might be starting up between us, but all morning he's been pulling away from me and looking at me like I'm an idiot."

"You're not an idiot, Katie," Christy said.

"I feel like one. Why did I ever want to start up a relationship with him? Why is it so important for me to get him to like me?" Now she was crying.

Christy stood close to Katie so the guys couldn't see her crying. "It's okay, Katie. Really. You don't have to get Rick's approval. You don't have to try to make him like you. Just be yourself. You're wonderful just the way you are. If Rick recognizes that, great. If not, it's his loss."

Katie sniffed and wiped her damp cheeks with the back of her hand. Her bright green eyes looked like two emeralds at the bottom of a deep pool.

"Will you make me a promise?" Christy asked.

Katie nodded.

"Promise me you won't let Rick use you. He does that to girls, and you know it. I don't think he does it on purpose. He can't pass up a challenge, and sometimes I think once the challenge is gone, so is his attention. Do you know what I mean?"

"I know, I know. And you have every right to tell me these things, Christy. These are the same things I told you when you were dating him last year."

"Yes, I know," Christy said. "I didn't listen to you very well then, and I wouldn't blame you if you didn't listen to me now. But I still want you to promise me that you won't let Rick use you. You don't deserve to be treated badly by any guy."

Katie wiped away the last tear and peeked over Christy's shoulder at the guys. A smile returned to her face. "Look at those three," she said. "You'd think we were one of the zoo's attractions the way they're standing there cautiously observing us. If we stay here long enough they might throw peanuts!"

Christy looked at them and laughed with Katie. "Come on," she said. "Let's both try starting this adventure all over, okay?"

"Did you ever notice," Katie said, still eyeing the guys, who looked as though they didn't know how to approach this rare, female species, "how many things come in three's?"

"Like the three bears?" Christy asked.

"And three musketeers and three blind mice and," Katie added with a burst of laughter, "the three stooges!"

Christy motioned with a nod of her head as they started to walk back to the guys. "Which one do you want? Larry, Moe, or Curly?"

"You girls all right?" Doug asked, leaving the pack and approaching them.

"Sure," Katie said. "We were just discussing movie stars."

Christy tried to suppress her giggles and smiled at Todd, who shot back one of his warm, understanding smiles.

"How about visiting a famous star?" Doug asked. "It says a dancing elephant is here. Want to go visit him?"

"Sounds good," Katie said, ignoring Rick and smiling brightly at Doug. "Lead on into the jungle, O great trail master."

Doug and Katie led the way, and Christy followed, sand-wiched in between Rick and Todd. The awkward fivesome dynamics returned.

"Why does he do that?" Katie asked a few minutes later when they stood watching the dancing elephant sway back and forth with his ankle chained to the ground. "Does that thing hurt him?"

"It doesn't seem to," Todd said. "I think he hears his own music and goes with it. Pretty cool, huh?"

Christy knew that when it came to someone hearing his own music and "going with it," Todd was king. He and the dancing elephant seemed to have a lot in common.

"How about some real animals," Rick said. "Where are all the lions and tigers? Don't they have any snakes here?"

"We already passed the lion, remember? He was snoozing. The monkeys are over this way," Doug said. "Let's check them out first."

Katie whispered to Christy, "Notice how each guy wants to see the animal he's most similar to?"

Christy nodded and smiled back.

"And did you notice how Rick wants to see some snakes?"

"I know! Remember how Jon, my boss at the pet store, used to compare Rick to a snake?"

"Well, I'm glad I came to my senses before he wrapped his coils around me!" Katie said a little louder.

Christy put her finger up to her lips and whispered, "Shhhhh!"

" 'Sssss' is more like it," Katie whispered back.

"What's with all the secrets, you two?" Doug asked.

Todd answered before Christy or Katie had a chance. "It's a girl thing. Makes them feel in control when they have secrets. You know they're whispering about us."

"You don't know that," Katie said, challenging Todd's philosophy. "We could be talking about something else."

"Like what?" Todd asked.

"Like, well . . . like anything," Katie answered with her hand on her hip. "Besides, you wouldn't know because, like you said, it's a girl thing."

Christy was glad they had stepped in front of the gorilla exhibit so the subject could change. A great, gray-black lowland gorilla sat on his haunches on a rock before them. His hands were folded under his chin, and he appeared to stare at all the zoo visitors.

"Look at that guy," Doug said. "You'd think he got up today just so he could sit there and watch the tourists walk by."

"He's not moving an inch," Todd said.

"I'll make him move," Rick said, picking up a peanut off the ground and tossing it at him.

"Don't throw things," Christy said. "Can't you read all the signs around here?"

"Look," Doug said, "he didn't flinch. The guy is a rock."

"The guy is smelly," Katie said, plugging her nose. "Can't you smell him?"

"I thought it was Doug," Rick teased.

"Ho, ho, very funny, Mr. Stuff-All-Your-Gym-Socks-Under-My-Bed."

Rick laughed. "I wondered what happened to all my socks."

"You guys," Todd said, reading the information sign in front of the gorilla, "it says here they have a 'distinct body odor that is unmistakable and quite offensive to humans.' "

"And then it has Doug's name at the bottom, right?" Rick said.

Doug slugged Rick on his unbandaged arm.

"Actually, it says, 'The odor does not stem from lack of cleanliness. In the wilds, the odor helps gorillas locate each other.' "

The guys all started to laugh as if it were the funniest thing they had ever heard.

"Must be a guy thing," Katie whispered to Christy.

"They are so weird! They'll laugh at anything," Christy whispered back.

"Come on," Rick said. "I want to see the snakes."

Christy and Katie broke into their own bout of laughter.

"Don't even try to understand them," Todd said, leading them on to the next exhibit. "It's a girl thing."

CHAPTER FOUR

# *Katie's Idea of a Good Time*

Two weeks later, as Christy and Katie were driving home after their school yearbook-signing party, Katie asked, "What was with Fred? He made such a big deal about signing your yearbook. What did he write?"

"I don't know," Christy said, shaking her head and then motioning to her book in the back seat, "something like 'keep smiling and see you next year on the yearbook staff.' "

"Are you going to join the staff next year for sure?" Katie reached for the yearbook.

"I signed up, but I still don't know if I want to. I could, because I have that really good camera my uncle bought me for Christmas."

"I'm sure you could take better pictures than the ones Fred took this year," Katie said.

"Do you really think so?"

"Oh, I don't know," Katie said, opening her yearbook to the winter-break section and holding it up so Christy could see the center photo. "Let's see. There might be a little more stiff competition here than I realized. Fred did have a real talent for getting those candid shots."

"Get that picture out of my face," Christy said, refusing to look. Fred had taken a photo at a pizza place over Christmas break. It was enlarged as the center of the photo collage. The picture was of Christy sitting on the end of a booth, and Rick sitting halfway on her lap with his arm wrapped around her. Rick looked like a model, of course. Christy looked like someone who just had ice cubes slipped down her back.

Next to that picture was a small one of Katie goofing off that same night in the pizza place. She had Styrofoam cups on her ears and was pretending to be an elf. It was a much funnier photo than the one of Rick and Christy, and Christy wished the yearbook staff had used that one instead of hers to highlight the junior class collage.

"I guess if I join the yearbook staff I can at least have something to say about the pictures they use," Christy said.

"Might not be a bad idea after this picture." Katie flipped to the ski club page and pointed to the photo of Christy ramming into the ski instructor. Her skis had veered between his legs, and her face was buried in his chest.

"Why did they put my name under the picture?" Christy said with a moan. "No one would have known it was me if they hadn't done that."

"Don't complain. You have more pictures in here than I do."

"And that's a good thing?"

"Sure it is," Katie said. "You're becoming popular. I think it started when you turned down the cheerleader position last year and the whole school knew you did it just so Teri Moreno could take your place. Did you even want to try out again this year?"

"Not at all," Christy said. "Isn't that strange? Last year all I could think about was cheerleading, and now it's the last thing I'd want to do."

Christy pulled into the driveway of her house. "You want to come in for a while?"

"Sure. So what do you want to do?"

"What?" Christy asked as they walked up the steps to her front porch. The jasmine on the trellis was in bloom, and its sweet fragrance filled the air with memories.

"What do you want to do?" Katie repeated. "You don't want to go out for cheerleading, you might go on yearbook staff in the fall, but what do you want to do this summer?"

"Work, I guess. And go to the beach and spend time with you and Todd and everyone."

Christy opened the front door and greeted her mom, who was sitting on the couch watching TV and mending clothes.

"Hi, Christy. Hi, Katie." Mom spoke in a soft whisper.

The light from the floor lamp hit her dark, curly hair in such a way it made the gray strands shine like silver threads woven into a black woolen cap. "Dad's already asleep, and David should be."

"We'll be quiet," Christy promised.

It was difficult since their house was so small, and the three bedrooms all connected to the same hallway.

Once inside Christy's room with the door closed, Katie asked again what Christy planned to do during the summer. Christy scrutinized her friend's face before answering.

"Would I be correct in guessing you already have an idea of what we should do this summer?"

"How did you guess?"

"I can read you like a book, Katie Weldon. If I'm correct, right now you're thinking of something courageous, adventurous, daring, and slightly wacky."

"Who, me?"

Christy positioned her pillow against her headboard and

leaned back. "The last time you had that look on your face, you talked me into joining the ski club and going to Lake Tahoe."

"I'm not talking about skiing this time. I'm talking about summer camp."

Christy hadn't been to summer camp since she was in junior high. She liked the idea the minute Katie said it. "Where? When? With the youth group at church?"

"Yep. I signed us up last Sunday after you left. I wasn't sure you would like the idea, because I thought you might be planning on spending as much time with Todd as you could."

Christy let out a sigh. "You know, Katie, things never change with him. I feel like our relationship has hardly moved forward an inch since he came back from Hawaii. That was more than five months ago. Things seem the same as they were last year."

"At least he's consistent."

"Consistent? Boring is more like it."

"I wouldn't complain if I were you," Katie said. "Todd is there for you. He's always there for you. Shall we compare my last year of relationships?"

Katie lay on her back on the floor, counting on her fingers. "Let's see. There was Glen, the missionary kid from Ecuador who liked to talk on the phone, hugged me twice, and promised to write when he left for Quito two months ago. Of course, I haven't received a single word from him, and he must think I have no social life since I've written him four times."

"That's okay," Christy said. "I'm sure he'll write. Mail from South America probably takes a long time."

"Then there's the Rick experience. Kick me in the head if I ever start to like him again! Aside from one New Year's Eve kiss and one and a half kisses at Stephanie's apartment in San Diego, all I ever got from Rick was a severe blow to my self-esteem. I'm sure he thought it was better mine than his.

"There you have it," Katie concluded. "My sizzling love life! At least you have Todd. Nice, consistent, friend forever, won't mess with your mind, guards your heart, Todd."

"I guess," Christy reluctantly agreed.

Katie sat up and gave a tug on Christy's bedspread. "Stop your whining, girl! Can we have a reality check here? You have it great and don't know it."

Christy didn't try to explain her feelings to Katie. They were hers alone. Feelings of wanting to be romanced. When she had dated Rick, he had brought roses and said incredibly tender things. Todd never said mushy stuff or touched her hair and gazed in her eyes the way Rick had. But with Rick, it felt like a game, and she was the prize.

If Todd would only throw a little tender romance into their close, honest, consistent relationship, it would be perfect. He seemed to be holding back, and so of course, she held back too.

"Hello?" Katie said, waving her hand in the air to get Christy's attention. "Anybody home?"

"I'm sorry. What were you saying?"

"Summer camp. I think we should go to summer camp."

A warm sensation washed over Christy. A feeling of sitting around a campfire at night, of picking wildflowers, and of splashing into a sun-toasted lake. A feeling of mysteriously meeting someone in the woods. Someone new. Someone handsome and tender who would write her long, romantic letters and hold her hand in the moonlight.

"Excuse me," Katie said. "Am I, like, having a one-sided conversation here?"

"No, I'm listening. Summer camp. We're going to summer

camp. We're going to have a fantastic time at summer camp. I'm ready. Let's go!"

Katie's mouth turned up into a smile. "I don't know about you, Christy. I think you're asleep with your eyes open. Perhaps I'd better leave you alone to finish your dream without interruption."

Katie rose to her feet and said, "July fifth to the eleventh. Call Luke this week at church and tell him you agreed to go. He'll be glad. I'll see you later. Sweet dreams!"

Letting herself out, Katie left Christy with a swirl of exciting summer camp thoughts. She would have to ask her parents, request time off from work, and make sure she had enough clothes for the entire week. Maybe this summer would hold some adventure after all.

The next Sunday, Christy talked to Luke, their youth pastor, and asked some questions about the camp.

"It's called Camp Wildwood, and it's about two hours from here," the big, bearded, lovable youth pastor answered. "You'll have eleven girls in your cabin. Your tuition is paid, but I'm afraid I'll have to ask you to come up with twenty dollars for the transportation."

"That's no problem. And I already have the week off from work, so I'm all set."

Luke gave her an appreciative smile and said, "You know, Christy, I really am glad you're willing to do this."

"Willing? Are you kidding? I can't wait! I love going to camp."

"I'm glad. I think it'll be a good week. I want you to know how much I appreciate you and Katie for signing up. Not many of the other students are willing to give up a week of their summer."

"Well, they don't know what they're missing," Christy said. She thought it was great that the church was sponsoring the teens who wanted to go by paying for their tuition.

That afternoon, Todd came over, and they went to the beach. Even though summer was supposed to have arrived, it was chilly, and a thin mist of ocean fog hovered above the sand.

"Carlsbad is such a different beach from Newport," Todd commented as they sat together on a blanket and looked out at the waves. "It's hard to believe it's only sixty miles down the same Pacific coast from Newport. It feels as though I'm on the Atlantic."

"Why?" Christy asked, slipping on her sweatshirt and wrapping the end of the blanket around her bare feet. "Because it's so cold today?"

"No, it's the way the waves break. They seem to come in at a different angle here. I don't know. Could be the weather too. Although it's not unusual for it to be like this in June."

At Christy's home in Escondido, about a half-hour drive from Carlsbad, it had been warm and sunny when they had left. She had put on shorts and a T-shirt over her bathing suit. Her wise mother had tossed her a sweatshirt on her way out the door.

The wind whipped the sleeves of Todd's T-shirt. He seemed comfortable enough. Christy had never really noticed before, but the hair on Todd's legs looked white-blond and was super curly. He didn't even have goose bumps.

"I'm cold," Christy said.

Todd took his gaze off the ocean and looked at her in surprise. "You are?"

Christy smiled at his amazed expression and rubbed the goose bumps on her bare legs. "Yes, I am. I don't come with a built-in fur coat like you do to keep me warm." She playfully reached over and pulled one of the hairs on his leg.

"Ouch!" he said. Then noticing her smooth legs, he asked, "Why do girls do that, anyway? Shave their legs, I mean."

"So they'll look nice. You know, smooth and feminine."

"But then you get cold."

"Never mind," Christy said. Then she added, "Actually, we do it so that guys will feel sorry for us when we say we're cold, and they'll put their arms around us and warm us up."

"I have a better idea," Todd said, standing up and offering Christy his hand. "Let's walk."

Todd's hand felt strong and secure as they strolled down the beach together. Her legs were still cold, but inside she felt warm and content. That's how things had been between her and Todd for the last few months. More than brother and sister, not quite boyfriend and girlfriend.

She felt Todd's thumb rubbing the chain on the gold ID bracelet she wore on her right wrist. He had given it to her a year and a half ago with the word "Forever" engraved on it. It was Todd's promise that they would be friends forever. As it was, their relationship had gone through many ups and downs since they first met two summers ago. But Todd's promise had remained. He always treated her like a close friend. It was just that sometimes, like now, Christy wanted more.

"What are you thinking about?" she asked him.

"About Papua New Guinea," Todd answered. "I was wondering what angle the waves come in there."

*What did I expect? Ever since I first met Todd, he's been dreaming of being a missionary to an island full of unreached natives. He's such a surfer boy, I bet if I cut him, he would bleed saltwater. Why did I think he would be thinking of me?*

"What were you thinking?" he asked.

The question surprised her. Although she asked him for his thoughts often, he rarely asked her. Maybe Todd was becoming a little more like Christy as they spent more time together. She knew she was becoming a little more like him.

"I was thinking about us and wondering what the future held." One thing Christy had learned was to be honest with Todd.

There was a pause. Then Todd squeezed her hand and said, "Me too."

Christy felt her heart beat a little faster.

Todd stopped walking and turned to face her. The filtered sunlight shone on his face, illuminating his clear silver-blue eyes and highlighting his square jaw. His expression remained sober, and no dimple appeared on his right cheek.

"But you know what, Kilikina?"

Christy always melted when he called her by her Hawaiian name.

"If we spend all of today thinking about tomorrow, today will be gone, and we will have missed it."

Christy knew he was right. As much as she wished he would wrap his arms around her, hold her tight, kiss her hair, and tell her that all his future plans included her, she knew he wouldn't. Todd was reserved when it came to physical expression. It was part of his honesty. He once told her he would never purposefully "defraud" her.

When she asked what he meant, Todd said, "I won't deliberately arouse a desire in you that I can't follow through on honestly, before God."

She knew that if their relationship had been full of hugs and kisses and whispered secrets about their future, her desires for him would have been aroused past the point of no return.

As it was now, they could walk away from their relationship

today and, besides missing each other's close friendship, they would have no regrets about making promises they weren't able to keep or painful memories from having become too intimate.

"Then let's enjoy today," Christy said, her eyes smiling at Todd. "I'm glad we can be together. We'd better keep walking, though. I'm starting to get cold again."

Todd squeezed her hand and started down the beach. They spent the next two hours collecting shells, digging for sand crabs, and playing foot tag with the waves. It really was a wonderful afternoon.

When they arrived at home, Mom had tacos waiting for them and a message that Katie had called.

Christy didn't call Katie back until the next morning. The conversation was short, and Katie's news sent Christy back to bed on her first Monday of summer vacation.

"Christy," Mom called, tapping on her bedroom door, "are you okay?"

"Come on in, Mom. I'm bummed. Katie can't go to camp. Her parents won't let her because it's a church activity. Isn't that crazy? They let her take off and do all kinds of stuff you guys would never let me do, but they won't let her become too involved in church. It has to be hard for her, being the only Christian in her family."

"Do you still want to go?" Mom asked.

"Sort of. Not as much as before."

"Maybe we can call Luke and see if some other girls that you know are going," Mom suggested.

"Okay," Christy sighed. "But it won't be as much fun without Katie."

Christy didn't get around to calling Luke. When she saw him Sunday at church, she asked him who else was going to camp.

"You and Katie were the only two girls from the youth group."

Christy couldn't believe it. Their high school group had 250 people in it.

"I'm sorry Katie isn't going. We really need counselors. That's why I appreciated you both signing up."

"Counselors?" Christy squeaked. "Katie signed us up to be counselors?"

"For junior camp," Luke explained. "We need counselors for the fifth-grade girls. You thought Katie signed you up for high school camp? That isn't until the last week of August. Does this mean you want to drop out too?"

Something about the way Luke worded it made Christy feel as though she would be the flake of the year if she withdrew only a week before camp. Especially since Katie had backed out.

"No, I'll go," Christy said, trying to sound as though it didn't make much difference to her. "I have the time off from work, you need counselors. I'll go."

A huge grin spread over Luke's face. "Thanks, Christy. I knew I could count on you! It'll be a real stretching experience, you'll see."

"That's what I'm afraid of," Christy muttered.

The next Sunday, when she arrived in the church parking lot with her luggage and sleeping bag, she knew she wasn't up for this stretching experience. A sea of fourth- and fifth-grade kids ran through the mounds of luggage, yelling, hitting, tattling, and clearly presenting Christy with a glimpse into her next week.

It took more than an hour to organize the troops, load their luggage, and get everyone on the bus at one time. Christy sat in the seat right behind the driver, hoping to ignore most of the spit wads, smacking gum, and rude little boys. She realized her main goal this week would be to avoid getting gum in her hair.

*Katie, I'm going to get you for this one!*

The crazy part was this was Katie's type of activity. She loved being the center of attention with a bunch of kids and had a way of getting them to follow her easily. Those were Katie's special gifts, not Christy's.

A young girl ran screaming from the back of the bus and dove into the empty seat next to Christy as if her life depended on being protected from whatever was chasing her. Christy readjusted her legs to accommodate the flying banshee and asked in her sternest voice, "What is going on here?"

"Eeeeeeek!" the girl squealed, ducking and covering her head with her arms.

A cute kid with bright eyes and dark blond hair skidded down the aisle and slugged the girl in the back.

"Stop that right now!" Christy demanded.

"She took my candy," the boy hollered.

"Is that true?" Christy asked the girl, who was still bent over at the waist. Her matted hair hung over her face. The girl only giggled.

Christy asked again, "Did you take his candy?"

The girl kept giggling as Christy grabbed her by the shoulders and pulled her upright, revealing the stolen candy in her lap.

"Give it back," the boy spouted, grabbing the stash of candy bars and marching to his seat at the back of the bus.

As instantly as the seat beside Christy had filled, it now emptied. Giggling, the candy robber hopped up and returned to where her friends sat.

Christy felt a rush of relief when two college-age guys boarded the bus. With booming voices, they got the kids' attention and commanded them to settle down. To Christy's amazement, they did.

One of the guys announced the rules for the bus ride to camp. The other one asked them to bow their heads and close their eyes because he was going to pray for their trip to camp.

Christy added her own prayer at the end, *Lord, could you assign me a couple of extra guardian angels this week? I think I'm going to need them.*

CHAPTER FIVE

# Camp Wildwood

Two hours later, when the bus rolled under a rustic wooden sign that read "Camp Wildwood," Christy felt an urge to jump bus and run for home. The word "rustic" would be a polite way to describe the camp. Christy's cabin was at the end of an uphill trail that made luggage-hauling miserable. Her fledglings followed her up the narrow, dusty trail, squealing and sobbing and making enough noise to scare off any wildlife for miles.

Somehow Christy knew the only wildlife she would experience this week would be in the form of pillow fights at three in the morning, frogs in her sleeping bag, and raids from the boys' cabins across the creek.

"Okay, girls," she called out as they stepped into their home sweet home. "I'm taking the bunk on the bottom here by the door. Everyone find a bunk. If you fight over who's on top, we'll swap positions halfway through the week."

The girls took to their nesting with lots of noise. Christy tried to let them solve their own problems while she smoothed out her sleeping bag. She found a note from her mom tucked inside.

*May you have sweet dreams every night. Love, Mom.*

Christy smiled and tucked it in her backpack. She pulled out her notebook just as two of the girls were about to exit.

"Whoa! Where are you going?" Christy said, stopping them. Suddenly she understood why, at the camp counselors meeting last night, they had made such a big deal about the counselors taking the bottom bunk by the door. It was the best spot to serve as a door guard.

"Out," the blond one answered.

"Not yet," Christy told her. "We have to have a cabin meeting first."

The girls acted as if she had just ordered them to eat raw Brussels sprouts and marched off to their bunks, pouting.

"Okay, everyone come sit on the floor. We're going to have a quick cabin meeting, and then you have free time until dinner."

"Can't we sit on our bunks?" asked a girl with ebony skin and big black eyes.

"Well, all right. As long as I can see all of you. Wait, I have an idea. Everyone sit on the top bunk. That way we can all see each other."

"I just made my bed," the girl across from Christy complained.

"I'd rather sit on the floor," another said.

"Can we eat in the cabin?" The request came from a plump blond who, from the chocolate smears around her lips, looked as though she had been eating ever since they left the church.

"No, it's one of the rules. The food attracts ants and other critters we don't want to invite into our cabin. Come on," Christy said, hoisting herself onto the empty top bunk above hers.

She realized if one of the bunks was empty that meant one of the girls hadn't made it to the cabin. Rather than leaving to find the lost sheep, she thought she had better go through her meeting as planned. Her list of campers would reveal who was missing, and then she could go after that person and at least know whom she was looking for.

"Quiet down, girls. You two in the back on the bottom bunk, could you join us please?"

It was the blond and her friend who had tried to escape earlier.

Christy looked over her list of names and said, "This will be a short meeting. I need to find out who's who. When I call out your name, please raise your hand."

"We're not back in school," the plump one said.

"What's your name?" the girl across from Christy asked.

"I'm Christy. Christy Miller."

"Do you have a boyfriend?" the blond in the back wanted to know.

"Well, actually," Christy hesitated, "let's talk about all that stuff later. First I need to find out your names." She started down the list. "Amy?"

"Present, Teach," mocked a girl across the room. She wore dangling earrings that looked a little too large for her small ears. Her coffee-colored hair was pulled up in a high ponytail, spilling over her head like a water fountain. With every movement, her hair and her earrings jiggled. She reminded Christy of a wild tropical bird. Even her "Present, Teach" sounded as though a "gawk" should be attached to the end.

"Jocelyn?"

The black girl raised her hand. "That's me." She looked as though she would be gorgeous once she grew into her strong features, like her eyes.

*No eleven-year-old should be allowed to have eyelashes that long. She'll never have to spend a penny on mascara.*

"Sara?"

"What?" the petite blond answered. She looked like a Skipper doll. Her wavy blond hair ran free all over her head, and her ginger eyes seemed to take in everything with a glance. Sara's T-shirt had the word "So?" printed on the front.

"Ruth," Christy called out.

"I like Ruthie better," the girl on the bunk across from her answered. "I hate my name. It sounds so blah."

"I like your name," Christy said. "It's the same as my grand-mother's."

Some of the girls started to giggle, but tears welled up in Ruthie's eyes. "See what I mean? Your grandmother! Nobody my age is named Ruth."

She had a plain face, a long flat nose, and braces. Her skin was perfect, smooth, and without a freckle. Her light brown hair hung straight to the tip of her shoulders and was tucked behind her ear on the left side.

"Well, I like your name," Christy said, hoping to repair any damage she had done in the first fifteen minutes of their week together.

Christy called out the rest of the names. The only one who didn't answer was Jeanine Brown. She ran through the rules about camp boundaries, staying away from the guys' cabins, and not raiding cabins. Her confidence wasn't too high that any of the rules would be followed.

"Any questions?"

"Yeah," said Sara. "Do you have a boyfriend?"

"Sort of," Christy said. "And that's the best answer you're going to get from me. Now go enjoy your free time until dinner, and I'll look for all of you at the dining hall."

"Dining hall?" Jocelyn laughed. "Here it's a mess hall."

"Okay, fine. The mess hall. When the bell rings, go right to the mess hall. And wash your hands before you come in, okay?"

The girls were already elbowing their way out the door. Amy, the bird, called over her shoulder, "Yes, Teach."

Hopping down and tucking away her notebook, Christy kicked her big green duffel bag under her bed and headed out to find the missing Jeanine Brown. Halfway down the trail she heard the familiar squeal of the perky little thief who had collided with her on the bus on the way up. Christy went off the main trail and soon spotted the girl dashing from her hiding place behind a tree and running straight for Christy.

"Hide me!" she shrieked, grabbing Christy by the waist and using her as a shield.

"Give it back," hollered the boy whom the girl had harassed on the bus. He was galloping through the woods toward them.

"Never!" the girl shouted, giggling and pinching Christy's middle as she ducked behind her.

"She took my pocket knife," the exasperated boy said.

Christy jerked free of the girl's clutches, spun around, and in her firmest voice said, "Hand me the knife right now."

The girl sobered, pulled the deluxe Swiss army knife from the pocket of her jeans, and handed it to Christy with a repentant expression.

"What is your name, and who is your counselor?" Christy asked the boy.

"Nicholas. Jaeson is my counselor."

"Fine. At the counselors meeting tonight I'll give this to Jaeson, and he can give it back to you if he thinks you need it this week. As for you, who is your counselor?" she asked the sober-faced girl.

"I don't know."

"What cabin are you in?"

"I don't know."

"Where did you put your sleeping bag and luggage?"

"Down there, by the bus. I didn't know where to go."

"What's your name?" Christy asked, closing her eyes as she waited for the answer. She already knew what it would be.

"Jeanine Brown."

Nicholas took off into the woods, and Christy let out a sigh. "Come with me, Jeanine. I'm Christy Miller. I'm your counselor. Our cabin is at the top of the hill. Let's pick up your stuff."

"Oh, good!" Jeanine said joyfully. "I was hoping you would be my counselor."

Christy didn't feel she could return the compliment to her soon-to-be bunkmate. "Good," was all she managed to say. "Let's get going; it's almost dinnertime."

At least at dinner all her girls showed up. Amy wanted to sit by Christy at the large, round table, and Sara squabbled with Jocelyn over who would sit on the other side. It was nice, in a way, to be fought over. Then Christy reminded herself this was the first night and the first of many meals they would share. She hoped not every meal would be accompanied by so much hassle.

The food was good, better than she had expected. Amy dropped one of her dangling earrings in the bowl of applesauce as it was passed around, and Christy had to fish it out with the serving spoon. Before she could stop Amy, she had licked off the earring and poked it back in her ear.

"Do we have free time after dinner?" Jocelyn asked.

"Yes, but remember you have to stay in the camp boundaries. I'll be in a counselors meeting, so if you have any problems, wait for me outside the door of the lodge. We should be done in about an hour."

"Yes, Teach," Amy replied solemnly, her hair falling down on her face and touching the ends of her eyelashes.

The first question the camp dean, Bob Ferrill, asked in the counselors meeting was if their campers knew the counselors' names.

"Yes," Christy volunteered in the room of five of her peers. "Except one of them keeps calling me 'Teach.'"

"Don't worry," the dean said. "We've heard worse around here. Now we want all of you to meet each other. I prefer you call me Dean Ferrill rather than Bob or Mr. Ferrill."

The girl next to Christy was Jessica, and the other girl counselor was Diane. The guy counselors were Mike, Bob, and Jaeson. They each told where they lived and a little bit about themselves. Mike and Bob were two college guys from Christy's church. Jaeson was from the same church as Jessica and Diane.

Dean Ferrill explained that several of the campers were what he called "potentially high maintenance" because they were from difficult home situations. He explained that some of them would be acting as if they were younger than their age because of their emotional challenges.

"We're not going to label these kids because we want all of them to be treated equally, but we want you to know that you may have expectations of your campers that are higher than what some of them are capable of handling. Be patient. Love them all the same."

He went over the schedule for the evening, stressed the camp rules again, and then prayed. Christy thought his prayer was touching, especially when he prayed for each of the counselors and for the campers as if the salvation of each kid was the most important thing in his life. Christy knew she could survive the week with him on her side.

As the meeting broke up, Christy approached Jaeson. "Hi, I have something to give you. I forgot it back at my cabin. It's a pretty sophisticated pocket knife I confiscated from one of your boys. His name is Nicholas."

"Yeah, Nick said one of the girls wouldn't leave him alone."

Jaeson looked as though he was born to be a camp counselor. He had an athletic build and short black hair, with facial features that seemed chiseled out of stone. His sunglasses hung around his neck on a black foam strap, and on his wrist were half a dozen leather "friendship bracelets" the campers had learned to braid at craft time.

"Why don't you bring it to the meeting tonight? I'll keep it for him."

"Thanks," Christy said.

She hurried up the trail to her cabin to grab her sweatshirt and the knife before the meeting started. When she opened the cabin door, three of the girls scampered like frightened mice.

"What are you guys doing?" Christy asked, scanning the room for a clue. She spotted her make-up bag open on Amy's bed.

"Hey, what are you doing in my things?" She looked at her bunk and saw her duffel bag was open with some of her clothes pulled halfway out.

The three culprits, Sara, Amy, and Jocelyn, stood frozen.

Sara spoke up. "You said you were going to be in that meeting for about an hour. You weren't gone that long."

"Wait a minute," Christy said firmly, feeling her temperature rising. "The meeting has nothing to do with this. You got into my things without permission." She noticed that Amy appeared to have awfully pink cheeks and black smears around her eyes.

"Were you in my make-up, Amy?"

"Yes, Teach. But I was going to put it back."

"That doesn't matter," Christy spouted, looking at the three of them sternly. "You *do not* get into other people's things! Do you understand me?"

The three solemnly nodded.

"Amy, go wash your face. Sara and Jocelyn, put my things back the way you found them. *Now!*"

The girls fled to obey the orders. Sara knelt to repack Christy's bag and started to sniffle.

"You're mean," Sara said under her breath. "I wish you weren't our counselor!"

Christy felt like saying the feeling was mutual when she noticed what Sara was wearing. "Is that my sweatshirt, by any chance?"

Sara pulled the sweatshirt off and threw it on the cabin floor. "I was only trying it on. I wasn't going to really wear it!"

Snatching it up, Christy shook it out and put it on. Then grabbing her backpack, she felt inside for the pocket knife, which was still there. The girls finished zipping up the bag full of now-crumpled clothes and rose to their feet. Sara was still crying, and Jocelyn's lip was lowered in a pout.

"We're sorry," Jocelyn said. "We won't do it again."

Something inside Christy told her to take both girls in her arms and hug them. Maybe these three were some of the ones who had special needs. But she was too upset at the moment. Instead Christy took two steps backward and ordered them to get their jackets and come to the evening meeting with her. Maybe the evening's message would straighten them out.

The girls obeyed, still sniffling. Amy met them at the door, her face scrubbed and her expression almost frightened.

"Get your jacket and come with us," Christy said firmly.

She marched them down the hill to the meeting, making them sit with her instead of with their friends. The singing was lively and fun, but Christy's three prisoners didn't join in. They sat quietly through the speaker's message.

Christy began to feel bad for coming down so hard on them. She knew they were still thinking about what had happened in the cabin and not paying attention to the message. As soon as the meeting was over, she told them they were free to go to the mess hall for the evening snack.

Just before the girls left the building, Jaeson came up to Christy and asked about the knife. She took her backpack off her shoulder to retrieve the knife and accidentally swung it too far, hitting Jaeson in the chest.

"Oh, I'm sorry! I didn't realize how heavy it was."

Jaeson appeared unaffected. He reached over and gently squeezed Christy's shoulder. "You're going to get a muscle spasm before the week is over if you keep carrying that around."

"I'll lighten the load tonight," she promised, noticing that the three girls had reappeared by her side. They were apparently curious as to what was going on between their counselor and this buff guy, who was touching her in public.

Christy handed Jaeson the pocket knife and said, "I told Nick you would decide whether to give it back to him."

"No problem," Jaeson said. "Thanks for catching it for me."

"Can I try on your sunglasses?" Sara asked, looking up at Jaeson, her ginger eyes bright with admiration.

"Maybe tomorrow," he said kindly. "You'd better run over to the mess hall if you want to get any cookies before the guys scarf them all."

"Are you coming?" Sara asked.

"Sure, we'll go with you," Jaeson said. "Come on, Christy. They always have peanut butter cookies on Sunday nights. They're the best."

"You've done this before, I take it," Christy said as they were escorted across camp by three sets of big ears.

"This is my third year. I started last week, and I'm staying until the end of July. How about you?"

"This is my first time as a counselor. I'm not sure I'm going to be very good at this," she admitted, still feeling bad for the way she had treated the girls.

"Oh, you're the best counselor we've ever had, isn't she?" Sara asked the other two girls. "And she's pretty too, isn't she, Jaeson?"

Christy felt her cheeks warming. How could these little girls change their opinion of her so instantly?

Before Jaeson could answer, Amy popped in with, "And if there's anything she needs to learn about camp, you can teach her. 'Cuz she's our Teach, so you can teach her. Get it?"

By then, thankfully, they had arrived at the mess hall, and Jaeson graciously said, "If I can help you out in any way, let me know. I'm sure you'll have a great week."

"Oh, she will, won't you, Teach?" Amy answered enthusiastically before running off with the other girls in a fit of giggles.

That night it took two hours for the girls to settle down. Even then, Christy worried that one of them might fake being asleep and would sneak out the minute she dozed off. She lay half awake, half asleep, listening for rustling in the silence.

After some time, she checked her alarm clock with her flashlight: 1:25.

*I'm never going to wake up at six! And this is only the first night.*

The second night didn't go much better. The day was packed with activities for the campers. Christy thought for sure with all the swimming, horseback riding, and archery, combined with last night's late hours, the girls would willingly tumble into bed.

No, they wanted to talk. About boys.

"You girls are only going into the fifth grade. You're too young to be so interested in boys," Christy said from her bunk once she had gotten them all in bed and the lights out.

"People mature faster now," Sara informed her. "We're much more grown-up than we were last year. When did you first start to like guys?"

Christy had to think back. She remembered going to summer camp with her best friend, Paula, right before they went into seventh grade. When she thought about it, she and Paula did spend most of that week trying to get the boys' attention.

"It doesn't matter," Christy said. "The point is, there's lots more to do at camp than occupy yourselves with guys. Besides, none of them seems to be very interested in you girls yet. You see, girls mature more quickly than boys."

"We know all that, Teach," Amy said from her bunk across the dark cabin. "Tell us stuff we don't know."

"Stuff you don't know?" Christy asked.

"Yeah, like what it's like to be kissed by your boyfriend," Sara said.

"She said she only 'sort of' had a boyfriend," Amy interjected. "I think Jaeson wants to be your boyfriend."

All the girls joined in a noisy chorus of agreement and approval.

"Hush," Christy said. "We have to be quiet or Dean Ferrill will come up like he did last night and tell us to settle down. I don't want to get in trouble again."

"Don't you think he's cute?" Jocelyn said in a loud whisper.

"Who?" Christy said, playing it cool, "Dean Ferrill? Sure, I suppose he's cute, for a man who's old enough to be my father."

"No, not him, Jaeson."

"You know what, girls?" Christy said sternly. "It's too late to have a discussion like this. I want you all to quiet down and go to sleep."

A round of complaints followed.

"I mean it!" Christy said gruffly. "All of you settle down right now."

Just then there was a loud knock on their cabin door. Dean Ferrill's voice boomed out. "Is everything okay, Christy?"

"Yes," Christy answered. "The girls were just going to sleep, weren't you girls?"

Someone faked loud snoring, and another girl said, "Hey, stop knocking on our door! We're trying to sleep in here."

"Good night, ladies," the dean said firmly. "I don't want to have to come back up here to check on you again."

"You won't have to," Christy promised. "We're going to sleep now."

The girls remained quiet as they listened to Dean Ferrill walk away from their cabin.

All of a sudden, into the stillness, Sara called out, "Hey, Dean Ferrill, Christy thinks you're cute, for an old guy!"

# CHAPTER SIX

# What You Can Never Do

"How are you doing, Christy?" Dean Ferrill asked the next morning at the counselors meeting.

"Pretty good. I apologize for Sara's comment last night."

"Don't worry about it. How do the girls seem to be responding spiritually?"

"Not much, I'd say. I could use some pointers on what I should be doing."

"What are your plans for cabin devos?" Jessica asked. She carried herself like a model, with straight posture and gentle movements. She had excelled during the swimming competition the day before.

Her caramel-colored hair was back in a ponytail today, and her delicate face looked as though she followed a strict skin-care program. Without a touch of make-up she looked beautiful.

"Cabin devos?" Christy asked.

"Devotions. What are you doing with the girls at night before you go to bed?"

"Yelling at them," Christy answered, half joking, half serious.

"Devotions really help to calm them down, and I think you'll get the most open responses from them then," Jessica said.

"Would you like to get together during free time this afternoon? I could give you some ideas."

"Great! I'd appreciate that."

Christy thought she noticed Jaeson smiling at her. She wondered if it was because he was thinking she was inexperienced or if he was being nice. The meeting again ended with a wonderful prayer time for the campers. Christy felt certain something of eternal value would have to break through with her girls soon, the way everyone was praying.

That morning at recreation, Christy's girls went up against Jaeson's boys at archery. Christy didn't look forward to the competition. She hadn't shot a bow and arrow since she was in junior high. Thankfully her girls had come to expect her to be the expert in everything, and right now she appreciated all the votes of confidence she could get from them.

The girls all lined up, facing the stacks of hay with the target tacked to the center. Christy picked up a bow and showed her girls how to hold it and aim for the target. She let the arrow fly. It whooshed a grand total of about three feet and landed uncomfortably close to Jaeson's foot.

The campers broke into laughter as the red-faced Christy made her way to the boys' side to retrieve her wayward arrow.

"Sorry," she muttered to Jaeson. "I don't know what went wrong."

"You had your elbow down. Hold it up flat like this," Jaeson said, demonstrating with the bow in his hand.

Christy tried to imitate his stance and elbow position. It didn't feel right. "Like this? Or higher?" she asked.

"May I?" Jaeson asked, putting down his bow and stepping over next to Christy. He put his muscular arm around her shoulders and placed his hand on top of hers. "Pull back like this," he instructed. "Keep your elbow up. Do you feel that?"

Christy was starting to feel something, all right. She felt the eyes of her campers drinking in the scene before them. She knew she would never convince them that he was only helping her.

"Now try," Jaeson said, stepping back.

Christy let go of the taut string, and the arrow zinged through the air, hitting the white part of the circle.

"All right! Good job!" Jaeson praised. "You guys all see that?"

A couple of the older boys said, "Yeah, we saw it, Jaeson. You sure you don't want us to leave so you two can be alone?"

Jaeson ignored the comment. He put his arm around the shoulders of the first boy in line and demonstrated the correct position the same way he had with Christy.

She approached her flock of twittering birdies with a serious expression. "Who's first?"

The girls had giddy expressions in their eyes as they whispered among themselves.

"Sara," Christy called, "you try it first."

Christy wrapped her arm around Sara and imitated Jaeson's correct archery stance. She hoped the girls would think this was the way everyone was taught how to shoot an arrow, with your arm around them.

Ignoring all the "Cupid" comments, Christy patiently showed each girl how to shoot. She was amazed at how readily the girls responded as she put her arm around them. They seemed eager to please her, and she began to see them in a different light. Not as brats, but as babies away from home and needing a big hug.

When their time was almost up, Christy glanced over at the boys and saw Jaeson watching her. He smiled and gave her a thumbs-up sign.

She felt as if, during the last few days, she had been building up a reservoir of wonder about Jaeson. She wondered if he liked her. She wondered if he were looking at her across the mess hall. She wondered if he were going to be at the pool during free time.

With Jaeson's thumbs-up, the reservoir of wonder overflowed, flooding her with thoughts of Jaeson, Jaeson, Jaeson.

At lunch she looked for where he was sitting before she chose her table. The rule was only one counselor at each table. She thought if she spotted him right away, she could sit at the table next to his so their chairs would be back to back. Her plan worked. There was an empty table next to his and an empty chair behind him. She slid in quietly, as if she didn't notice he was there.

"Hi," Jaeson said. "Did you see the final score on the archery practice?"

"No, I didn't. How did we do?"

"Your girls beat my guys by ten points."

"You're kidding! I never would have guessed it," Christy said, smiling. "Thanks for all your help."

"Anytime," Jaeson said, smiling back.

Just then the mess hall doors opened, and the campers were let in. They ran like escaping guinea pigs, not sure where they were going but feverish about being the first one to get there. Christy's girls filled in at her table in record time and took turns poking each other with their elbows.

Jessica came over to Christy's table with two adoring campers holding on to each arm. "Where do you want to meet after lunch?" Jessica asked above the roar.

Christy shrugged, looking to Jessica for a suggestion.

"How about the lodge?"

Christy nodded, and Jessica surrendered to the persuasion of her two-arm fan club.

When Christy went to meet Jessica in the lodge as arranged, she kept checking over her shoulder to see if Jaeson were following her. He seemed to be headed in the direction of the craft barn. Maybe she should go over after her meeting with Jessica—to check on any of her girls that might be there, of course.

"First," Jessica said when they had seated themselves on the old couch, "I'm not trying to tell you how to relate to your girls. I know you're doing a great job. I didn't want you to think I was trying to step in this morning and tell you what to do."

"I didn't think that at all. I need all the help I can get!"

For half an hour Jessica made some good suggestions about how to put a devotion together and what worked best for her last year when she was a counselor for the first time.

"It's actually easier this year with the group I have. They're the youngest batch, the ones just going into fourth grade. Some of them are having a hard time because this is the first time they've been away from home on their own. And they're not real good about their hygiene without being reminded. But they're not real boy-crazy yet. At least not all of them."

"They sure like you," Christy said.

"Well, I think I'm learning from some of the mistakes I made last summer. I didn't realize until after camp what I did wrong, and I'm trying to do it differently this year."

"Can I ask what it was?" Christy asked cautiously. Jessica seemed so approachable, she thought it would be okay to ask such a personal question.

"Christy, I'll tell you, there is one thing you can never do."

Just then Christy's little boy-chaser, Jeanine, burst through the lodge's door, clutching a baseball cap in her fist. With ear-shattering squeals, she ran behind the couch and pleaded, "Don't let him get me!"

Outside the door, Nick obeyed the "No Campers" sign and stayed outside, peering in for a glimpse of Jeanine.

"That's it!" Christy shouted, jumping up and demanding the cap from Jeanine. "This has gone on too long. Give me the cap. Now leave the poor kid alone and don't take anything else of his. Do you understand me?"

Jeanine handed over the cap with the look of a scolded puppy. "I'm sorry," she said in a small voice.

Christy stomped over to the door and delivered the cap to Nick, who looked slightly annoyed. Two of his friends joined him and stood on either side for moral support.

"Will you tell her to stop it?" Nick asked Christy.

"You know what, Nicholas, it's only a game if both of you play. If you stop playing, it won't be fun to her anymore, and I guarantee she'll stop."

"Not likely," one of Nick's bodyguards mumbled.

Nick slipped the cap back on his head, and the three of them trudged off to the baseball field. Christy watched them go and almost laughed aloud. They were miniature versions of Todd, Doug, and Rick.

*Elephants, monkeys, and snakes. Oh, my.*

When Christy turned around, she discovered Jeanine had taken her place next to Jessica on the couch. Jessica, the experienced counselor, was stroking the young girl's hair out of her face and speaking to her softly. Jeanine drank in every word.

"Okay, I'll try it," Jeanine said, hopping up and giving Jessica a look she never would have given to Christy. A look of true admiration and appreciation. Then she rushed out of the lodge.

"What did you tell her?" Christy asked, retrieving her seat on the couch.

"I told her that instead of taking things away from Nick,

maybe she should try giving something to him to get his attention. She's off to make a friendship bracelet at the craft center."

"That was brilliant. How did you think of that?"

"It's what I was about to tell you before she burst in here. The one thing you can never do is love too much."

"Never love too much?" Christy repeated.

"When I left camp last year, I realized I had done a lot of the 'right' things as a counselor, but I hadn't loved the girls in my cabin as much as I could have. Do you know what I mean?"

Christy flashed back to when she had caught the girls going through her clothes. Yes, she did know what Jessica meant.

"You see," Jessica said, "you can't argue with love. When this week is over, what will the girls remember? The squabbles? The team races on the last day? What the speaker said?"

"I'm sure they'll remember some of that," Christy said. "I remember some of that from my days as a camper."

"But what do you remember the most?" Jessica asked. "Not just about camp, but about your whole life? I think we remember the people who loved us."

Christy took Jessica's advice to heart. She knew her new friend was right. Eagerly making her way to the craft barn after their meeting, Christy wondered how that advice might apply to Jaeson. What would he remember about her when camp was over?

More and more thoughts collided in her head as if all her emotions had gathered and were holding court in her brain. She was the one on trial. The prosecuting attorney's voice said she was silly and immature to chase after a guy at summer camp when she had Todd waiting for her at home. Another emotion stepped up as her defense witness and claimed she had the right to build relationships with any guy she wanted to, and this was all part of camp.

Just as she was about to enter the craft barn, Christy imagined all the girls in her cabin as the jury. Their squeaky voices were raised in a loud "Not guilty" inside her head. She felt free to take that step into the craft barn and see what happened next.

She noticed Jaeson right away. He looked up and saw her at the same time.

"Christy," he greeted her, "just the person I wanted to see. Can you help these girls with their bracelets? I'm supposed to meet my guys at the pool in five minutes."

Sara, Amy, and Jocelyn beamed their approval at her and started to talk all at once. Christy stepped over to the side of the table where the three of them were nearly finished braiding their friendship bracelets.

"Can you tie mine?" Sara asked. "I'm all done. Do you like it? Does it look right?"

"Yes, it's very nice," Christy said, tying the two leather straps around Sara's thin wrist. "You did a nice job."

Jaeson squeezed Christy's shoulder and said, "Thanks a million for helping me out here. I'll see you later. At the pool, maybe?"

"Sure, we'll come to the pool," Amy answered for her. "Won't we, Teach? We're really done, aren't we, you guys?"

"I'll see you," Jaeson called over his shoulder as he took off for the pool.

The minute Jaeson was out the door, Sara smiled at Christy and said, "Jaeson asked if you had a boyfriend, and we told him 'no' because you never told us if you really had one or not. We told him you liked him, and he said he liked you."

The three girls gathered around Christy with their eyes twinkling.

"So? Do you like him?" Amy asked.

Christy wasn't sure how much of all this she should believe. She decided a strong, direct answer might work best. "I think Jaeson is a really nice guy. He's a strong Christian, and that's a very important quality to look for in a guy."

"We knew it!" Sara squealed. "We knew you liked him! Come on. Let's go to the pool."

Jocelyn and Amy held out their arms for Christy to tie their bracelets and then joined Sara, racing up the hill to their cabin to put on their bathing suits.

Christy realized Jeanine must have gotten sidetracked because she wasn't busily making her bracelet for Nick. Either that or she had been so enthusiastic she had already finished it and rushed off to present it to her "boyfriend."

Taking a few minutes to close up the craft barn, Christy headed up the hill. The girls met her halfway, already suited and with towels under their arms.

"We'll see you there!" they shouted and scampered on down the hill to the pool.

When Christy met them a short time later, they were having a water war with Jaeson and his guys. She wasn't sure she wanted to step into the middle of their combat. To her relief, the lifeguard blew his whistle and said they were getting too rowdy and had to get out of the pool. She put down her towel on the warm cement.

Her three little drowned rats were the first ones out, complaining and arguing about how the boys weren't playing fair. They wrapped themselves in their towels and sat down right next to Christy, hurling rude comments at the boys.

Jaeson planted himself in the middle of his guys and tried to calm them down. He glanced over at Christy, smiled, and shrugged as if to say, "What am I supposed to do with these clowns?"

Christy smiled back.

"He likes you," Sara said, lifting Christy's left hand and pressing down on Christy's fingernails. "Are these real? I mean, are they yours?"

"Yes, they're mine and they're real."

"They're so long!" Sara exclaimed as Amy and Jocelyn crowded in to feel Christy's nails.

"Not really," Christy said.

"They're longer than mine," Amy said. "How do you make them grow?"

"First of all, try to stop biting them," Christy suggested.

"I bite mine all the time," Jocelyn confessed.

The girls continued to compare their nails with Christy's and each other's. Christy peered over their heads and noticed Jaeson talking with the lifeguard. The lifeguard blew his whistle, signaling for everyone in the pool to stop where they were.

"We're going to put up the volleyball net in the shallow end," the lifeguard announced. "Everyone who wants to play volleyball go in the shallow end. Everyone else stay in the deep end."

Apparently volleyball was Jaeson's idea, because he had already pulled the net from the storage cupboard, and his boys were helping him to set it up.

"I don't want to play with them," Amy said. "They always cheat. We'll stay here with you."

Christy's fan club positioned their towels closer to her, overlapping her towel and dripping all over her.

"You want to play?" Jaeson called out to Christy from the shallow end as soon as he had the net in place.

"No!" Sara answered, grabbing Christy by the arm.

The other girls followed her lead. "She's staying here with us."

Christy felt a strong urge to break free from these wet, clinging urchins, but Jessica's advice prompted her to stay. This was a chance for her to show these girls she loved them. Besides, she wasn't much of a volleyball player on land. She had a feeling the water wouldn't improve her skills.

Now it was Christy's turn to smile and shrug back at Jaeson. He gave her one of his thumbs-up signs and tossed the ball into the water. For the rest of free time, Christy hung around the pool, watching Jaeson, talking to her girls, and wondering if Jaeson would come over and talk to her. He never did, but he looked at her a lot.

At dinner, Christy arrived in the mess hall before Jaeson and took a seat at an empty table, watching the door. He soon came in and headed right for Christy.

"There you are," he said, taking the seat that backed up to hers at the next table. "Your girls told me you didn't have one of these yet."

Jaeson used his teeth to remove one of the leather friendship bracelets from his wrist and offered it to Christy. "You're not an official Camp Wildwood counselor unless you have one of these."

"Thanks," Christy said, holding out her left wrist for Jaeson to tie on the bracelet. Her "Forever" ID bracelet circled her right wrist, and she didn't think the two bracelets mixed.

While Jaeson tied the thin leather straps, the doors opened and the campers ran in. Christy's girls flocked to her table in time to see him finish tying on the bracelet and give Christy a big smile, which she returned. That's all it took for them to all start whispering about how Jaeson and Christy were now going to-gether.

The eager group of matchmakers made sure that Christy sat near Jaeson in the evening meeting and that they walked to the mess hall together for evening snack.

Christy had to admit it was fun playing the role of heroine. Six of her girls had now permanently attached themselves to her and led her by the arms wherever they wanted her to go, telling her how pretty she looked or how much Jaeson liked her.

Jaeson seemed to enjoy being a hero too. Christy could tell he had been through this kind of treatment many times before be-cause of all his years as a counselor. She knew it must be like this for him every week of camp. She also figured she was one in a long line of girl counselors who were destined to be Jaeson's girl-friend for the week.

It didn't matter. Christy was having too much fun to think of why this game should end.

The next morning she found it hard to wake up. It was Wednesday, halfway through the week. They had been warned in a counselors meeting that this was when it would all begin to catch up with them.

The girls seemed to have no problem bouncing out of bed, though. Christy pulled her sleeping bag over her head and tried to catch a few more Z's.

"Aren't you going to take a shower?" Sara asked, rocking Christy by the shoulder. "You always get up and take a shower."

"Just let me sleep five more minutes," Christy pleaded. "Five more minutes."

"But it's almost 6:30," one of the girls said. "You have to get to the mess hall before seven so you can get a table next to Jae-son's."

"Oh, I do, do I?" Christy asked, throwing back the sleeping bag and facing seven curious faces peering at her.

"Yes," they all agreed. "He really likes you, and he would be mad at you if you didn't get there in time."

"Oh, he would, would he?" Christy pulled her legs from her snug cocoon and forced them into the cool morning air and onto the cluttered wood floor.

"You guys, this place is a mess," Christy scolded. "We only received five points yesterday for cabin cleanup. Today I want us to get all ten points. That means everyone has to pick up her junk and put it away."

"Here, wear this," Amy said, pulling a T-shirt from Christy's bag, laying it on her sleeping bag, and smoothing out the wrinkles with her hand.

"And your jeans shorts," Jocelyn advised.

"Okay, okay! You girls get yourselves dressed. And don't forget to pick up all your junk." Christy was beginning to dislike this part of the day when she couldn't go to the bathroom or wash her face without bracing herself against the morning chill on the hike to the rest rooms. Throwing on her clothes and grabbing her towel and make-up bag, she headed out the door.

"We'll go with you," four of the girls echoed. "Wait for us."

Christy stood outside the cabin door, shivering and waiting for her entourage to get its act together. The girls joined her, all chattering brightly as they trudged through the dirt.

When Christy arrived in the bathroom, Jessica was already there with her fan club. She looked fresh and pretty and ready to start the day.

"How do you do that?"

"What?"

"How do you manage to look so awake? I'm exhausted."

"We got to bed on time last night, finally," Jessica said. "I cut my devos short. How did yours work out last night?"

Christy plunged her washcloth into the cold water and washed her face as quickly as she could. "Brrr!" she said, patting dry with her musty-smelling towel. "Devos went well, I think."

The campers were all scurrying around the bathroom. A few huddled around the sink next to Jessica and Christy and imitated the older girls' wake-up routine by splashing cold water on their faces and responding with the same "Brrr!"

"They were great!" Jocelyn answered for Christy. "We talked all night."

"I tried your idea of getting acquainted by each girl telling about her family. We went too long, but they all had lots to say. I think I know them a lot better now."

"And she likes us more, too," Amy added. "Don't you, Teach?"

Jessica and Christy exchanged smiles.

"You can never love too much," Jessica whispered in Christy's ear. Then gathering her things, she said, "You're doing a great job, Christy. I'll see you at breakfast."

Christy felt warmed inside and encouraged. Maybe she was going to make it through this week after all.

CHAPTER SEVEN

# *Tippy Canoe*

Wednesday zoomed by with the usual routine of counselors meeting, morning Bible study, and the whole afternoon free. Christy planned to spend the afternoon at the pool with her girls since Jaeson said he was going to be there. But when she went up to the cabin to put on her bathing suit, she found Ruthie on her bunk bed, crying.

Christy sat on the edge of Ruthie's bed, ducking her head to fit under the top bunk. She placed her hand on Ruthie's back and slowly rubbed it. "Are you okay?"

Ruthie's sobbing slowed to a sniffle. "Nobody here likes me."

"Yes, they do. Everyone likes you. I like you very much," Christy said.

"Everybody has her own friends here. I don't have anybody. Nobody asked me to go with them. They all took off without me."

Christy kept rubbing Ruthie's back and stroked her light brown hair back from her peaches-and-cream face. "I'm sorry," was all Christy said.

She thought of plenty of advice to give Ruthie about how she should be the friendly one who pursues the other girls and how it wouldn't do any good to lie here feeling sorry for herself when there was so much outside for her to do. But Christy remembered the times she had felt left out, lonely, and sad. It had always helped to throw herself on her bed and have a good cry.

What she didn't like was when her mom had come in and told her how she should act or what she should be feeling. Christy always wished her mother would just let her cry and feel sad with her for a few minutes.

Christy sat silently rubbing Ruthie's back as she finished getting out all her tears. Eventually the only sound was a few sniffs from Ruthie into her damp pillow.

"Here," Christy said, reaching over to her backpack on the floor and pulling out a packet of tissues. "Try one of these instead of your pillowcase. You're going to have to sleep on that thing tonight, you know."

Ruthie accepted the tissue and blew her nose. "You probably think I'm acting like a baby."

"Not at all," Christy said, handing her another tissue. "I think you're a lovely young girl turning into a beautiful young woman."

The girl honked her nose loudly as she blew. "Sorry," she said, repressing a giggle at how loud her nose sounded.

"That's okay," Christy said. "You feel better?"

Ruthie nodded and offered a smile.

"Good. Now what do you want to do this afternoon? You and I can do it together."

"I wanted to go out in a canoe, but nobody else wanted to go with me."

"I'll go with you," Christy said.

"Are you sure?" Ruthie asked. "Wouldn't you rather be with Jaeson?"

"No, I'd rather be with you."

Ruthie sprang from the bed, her hope renewed, and led the way to the door. Christy followed, feeling pleased with Ruthie's comeback. On the trail to the lake, Ruthie slipped her hand into Christy's and gave it a squeeze. Christy squeezed back.

"How did you get so good at knowing what to do when a girl is crying?"

"I happen to be the pity-party expert," Christy said. "When I was your age I used to cry about stuff all the time."

"And you don't cry anymore?"

"Sure, I still cry, but not as much. I still have some of the same feelings that used to send me to my pillow when I was younger, but they don't make me cry as much anymore."

Ruthie let go of Christy's hand and skittered a few feet into the woods, where she picked a small yellow wildflower and brought it back to Christy.

"Thank you, Ruthie," Christy said, slipping the flower behind her right ear. "And I really do like your name. There was a Ruth in the Bible, you know. There's a whole book written about her because she was such a loyal friend. That's how I'll always re-member you: as Ruthie, my loyal friend."

Ruthie flashed a rare, full smile, revealing her mouthful of sil-ver braces. She looked like a different girl from the sullen one who had told Christy she hated the name Ruth.

They walked through the clearing onto the gravel beach by the lake. Ruthie was the first to notice that two of the other girls from their cabin, Sara and Jeanine, were there.

Christy knew if Jeanine was here Nick probably was not far away. Sure enough, Christy spotted Nick and his two friends at the boat shack, apparently getting a canoe.

"Why don't you ask those two girls if they'd like to join us on our canoe ride?'' Christy suggested to Ruthie. "I have a strong feeling at least one of them would like to."

Ruthie ran off to invite Jeanine and Sara while Christy headed for the boat shack. Not until she was in front of the shack did she notice Jaeson was the one behind the window passing out life vests.

"Christy, just the person I wanted to see. How do you feel about taking these guys for a canoe ride? I told Mike I'd fill in for him here until four."

"She's taking us out," Jeanine answered, stepping up to the window with Ruthie and Sara.

"We could take one of the guys," Jeanine added, flashing a grin at Nick.

"Nope," Jaeson said. "Only four to a canoe."

Jaeson looked at his watch and then back at Nick and his two friends. "I probably shouldn't do this," he said, "but you guys have gone out before, and you pretty much know what you're doing. I'll let you three go by yourselves. Christy, can you keep an eye on them and try to stay close to them out on the lake in case of any accidents?"

"Sure, that's fine," Christy said.

"And I'll be right here watching you guys," Jaeson added, handing out the life preservers. He caught Christy's wrist when she reached for her preserver and gave it a squeeze. "Thanks. You're a honey."

Christy's campers heard him say it, and they huddled close to her as they walked over to the canoes.

"He likes you!" Jeanine declared nice and loud.

"Shhhh," Christy said. Then bending close to Jeanine, she asked, "How's it going with you and Nick?"

"Okay, I think. He hasn't hit me yet today."

"And you haven't taken any more of his things, have you?"

"No. I gave him a bracelet like Jessica said, but he's not wear-ing it."

"That's okay." Christy gave her a little squeeze around her plump orange life vest. "I'm proud of the way you're acting."

Jeanine beamed.

It took Christy's troop longer to launch their boat than the boys. They suddenly had four captains and no mates. Jaeson came over and helped by giving their canoe a good swift push. Christy sat at the front with a paddle in her hand, Ruthie took the middle bench, and Jeanine and Sara insisted on sharing the back seat, each with a paddle in the water.

"Make sure you paddle in the same direction," Jaeson called out as they began to bob on the calm lake.

"Farewell!" Sara cried out dramatically, standing up and turn-ing to wave good-bye to Jaeson.

"Sit down!" they all yelled at her as the canoe began to tip.

"Okay, listen," Christy called over her shoulder. "All of you follow my lead. If my paddle is in the water on this side, then you put your paddle in on this side. And the same over here." She demonstrated for them, hoping none of them would guess that she hadn't been in a canoe since she was their age. Even then, it was with her Uncle Tom in Minnesota, and he had done all the paddling.

The crew followed orders, and everything seemed smooth. No problem.

"Let's catch up with the boys," Jeanine said, eagerly paddling on her side. The canoe swerved to the left toward the shore.

"We have to paddle all together," Christy said. "Remember what I said? Follow my lead."

She dug her paddle into the water for three strong strokes on the left side of the canoe to straighten them out and at least point them in the boys' direction. Christy switched her paddle to the right side, but apparently the girls weren't watching. Sara and Ruthie kept paddling on the left. It seemed they were getting nowhere.

Christy barked out more instructions. The canoe gently drifted toward the middle of the lake, no thanks to their efforts.

"Look at the ducks!" Sara said. "They're coming right up to the canoe. Let's sit here and watch them."

"No, we need to catch up with the boys," Jeanine objected. "Remember what Jaeson said. We have to stay with them, and they're headed for the other side of the lake."

"What's over there?" Christy asked.

"That's where they have the counselor hunt on the last full day," Sara explained. "All the counselors row over in canoes and hide, and then we run around the edge of the lake to find them. Whoever finds their counselor first has to get their counselor's sash and run all the way back to the boat shack."

"But the counselors get to try to beat them," Jeanine added. "They come back in their canoes and have to plant their flags by the boat house."

"Sounds like a lot of fun," Christy said.

"Whoever loses has to serve the food at the banquet on the last night. We have team captains, and if the campers lose, they serve the counselors, who all sit together at one table."

"And if the counselors lose?" Christy asked.

"Then they have to serve all the tables."

"Well, I hope we win. I wouldn't mind having dinner served to me," Christy said. "Paddle on the right, girls. We're starting to drift too far."

They worked their way across the lake, improving as they

went, until they almost caught up with the boys. Christy could feel strange muscle twinges in her upper arms. She never would have guessed paddling was such hard work or that this small lake was so far across.

"How are you guys doing?" Christy called out when they were within a few yards of the guys' canoe.

"We're fishing," Nick said. He pulled his stick out of the water and revealed a brown string attached to it with a wiggly worm at the end. Christy thought their Tom Sawyer fishing pole looked quite clever.

"Ewww!" Sara said. "That's a worm."

"Duh," said one of the boys.

"I hate worms," Sara said.

Nick dangled the fishing pole over toward the girls' canoe so Sara could look at the worm close up. It came within a few feet of her face, and she screamed.

"Hey," Jeanine yelled when she looked closely at the brown string attached to the stick, "that's the friendship bracelet I made for you!"

"Turned out to be good for something," Nick said, laughing.

"I want it back!" Jeanine yelled. "I worked hard on that. You're not supposed to use it for a fishing line!"

Jeanine stood up and lunged for the line, which Nick jerked away. Before Christy knew what was happening, Jeanine toppled from the canoe and into the lake.

"Jeanine!" Christy screamed, turning around and trying to steady the topsy-turvy canoe. Sara stood and tried to reach for the soaked Jeanine.

Ruthie leaned back to compensate for Sara's weight being thrown to one side, but it was too much of a compensation. The canoe tottered to the left, dumping Ruthie into the lake and then to the right, dumping Sara in after Jeanine.

"Girls!" Christy called out futilely. The canoe rocked back and forth, and Christy tried to steady it as the three drowned rats, buoyed up by their life vests, each tried to pull themselves into the canoe on opposite sides. The girls were laughing and didn't seem to mind the dunking a bit.

"Wait!" Christy cried. "Stop! This isn't working. We're so close to shore, why don't you swim in, and I'll pick you up there?"

The girls, still laughing, willingly dog-paddled the short distance to shore and waited there for Christy, dripping wet and shivering.

The boys were laughing so hard they didn't hear Christy tell them to stay put while she went for the girls. They must have decided their best course of action was to get as far away from the girls as they could, since they knew retaliation would be on the girls' minds. The boys took off, paddling full speed back to the boat shack, leaving Christy to manage the rescue landing by herself.

The girls helped pull their canoe into shore and stiffly tried to get in. That's when the laughing stopped and the complaining began.

"They made us fall in," Jeanine sobbed. "I'm going to get back at them."

"I'm cold," Sara complained. "Didn't you bring a towel?"

"It's back on the other side," Christy said. "Once we get over there you can use it."

"But it's so far," Ruthie moaned. "We're going to freeze to death."

"It's not that cold," Christy said. "Try sitting in the bottom of the canoe. You'll keep out of the wind better that way."

"But there's water in the bottom," Sara said.

"That's okay," Christy coaxed them. "You're already wet. It won't hurt you."

The girls wedged themselves into the hull of the canoe and crossed their arms in front of them around their bloated vests, trying to keep warm. Christy, at the helm, tried her best to maneuver the canoe across the lake. It seemed impossible to move the canoe in the direction she wanted it to go. Without anyone paddling at the rear, the canoe floundered through the water, more motivated by the wind and waves than by Christy's determined efforts with the paddle. She was definitely doing this the hard way.

Her complaining crew kept giving her advice about which side she should be paddling on and why she was doing it all wrong. Christy endured the remarks for ten minutes and then lost it. "Would one of you like to try this?" she barked. "It's not exactly easy."

"I'll help you," Ruthie offered. She rose to sit on the middle seat and stuck a paddle into the water on the same side as Christy's. Together they plunged the canoe through the water and made some headway.

Ten minutes later they reached the shore. By then the girls were mostly dried out. The boys had landed a good fifteen minutes earlier and had long since disappeared.

Jaeson met them at the shore, wading waist deep in the water to help bring in their canoe. He lifted each of the girls from their floating prison and offered his hand to Christy so she could step out onto the gravel. She felt like an incompetent counselor, having dumped her girls and having lost track of the boys. If she had fallen in herself, she might have felt better at this moment. At least she could have been another victim and not the responsible person.

Jaeson held onto her hand and drew her close. In a low voice he said, "Would you be interested in a free canoe lesson?"

A smile returned to Christy's face. "Why?" she teased. "You think I need one?"

"It's up to you," Jaeson said. "I thought you might want a little edge on the campers for the counselor hunt on Friday."

"Okay, you talked me into it," Christy said. "You say when, and I'll be there."

"I'll let you know tonight at dinner," Jaeson said, giving her hand a squeeze before letting it go.

At dinner, Jaeson and Christy sat back to back in what had become their usual spots at the tables. During the meal Jaeson leaned back four times to make comments in Christy's ear. It was hard to hear him above the roar of the campers. But it didn't really matter what he said. Just the attention was fun.

She did notice when dinner was over that he hadn't mentioned a time for the promised canoe lesson. Maybe he had forgotten. Christy tried not to feel discouraged. After all, this was only Wednesday, and they had the whole next day to practice, since the race was on Friday.

"Come play softball with us," her girls urged, pulling her by the arms from the mess hall. "We have to hurry! We only have a half-hour free before the evening meeting starts."

Christy let the girls lead her out to the baseball field where some of the campers had already started up a game. When they saw her coming, they all insisted she be the pitcher. She was good at hitting the ball, but she wasn't too confident her pitching would win any awards.

Taking her place on the mound and winding up, she let the softball fly over home plate. Thump! One of the girls from Jessica's cabin hit the ball, and it sailed to center field. Her teammates cheered, and the girl took a playful bow when she made it safely to first base.

Another wind up, and the next girl made contact with the first ball Christy pitched. Same with the next hitter; the bases were loaded. A timid, skinny fifth-grader stepped up to the plate next, and Christy threw three of the gentlest, slowest balls she could throw. The girl swung at all three and missed.

"One more pitch," a deep voice called out from the side of the field. It was Jaeson. He stepped up behind the discouraged little hitter, wrapped his arms around her, and showed her how to hold the bat the right way.

"Okay, Christy," Jaeson called out, his arms still around the batter. "Give us your best shot."

Christy pretended to be spitting on her hands and sending signals to the catcher.

"Come on, pitcher," Jaeson yelled, "let us have it!"

With a dramatic windup, Christy let the ball go. It was a ridiculous pitch that landed almost four feet away from the plate on the left side. Everyone laughed, including Christy.

"If that's your best," Jaeson heckled, "we don't want to see your worst."

"I was just testing you," Christy called back. "Wanted to see if you would swing at anything. Here comes a good one."

Christy pitched a nice, slow ball straight over home plate. With Jaeson's help, the girl smacked the ball almost all the way to the woods. Everyone cheered as she ran the bases with Jaeson by her side. The other three runners came home with hoots and hollers.

A fielder threw the ball to second base just as Jaeson and the girl touched third. Now it was a battle to see if they could make it home. Jaeson picked up the girl, carrying her under his arm like a football, as he charged home. They made it a few seconds before the ball did, and Jaeson put the girl down firmly on home plate, like an explorer planting a flag and claiming the land.

A small crowd of campers had gathered, and everyone was still cheering when the next girl stepped up to bat. "I want Jaeson to help me too," she said.

"Naw, you can do it yourself. Go ahead and try," Jaeson coached from the sidelines.

With the first pitch, the girl looked as though she deliberately swung and missed. Perhaps she hoped her lack of coordination would bring Jaeson to her side.

"Come on," he called out. "I know you can do better than that."

She positioned the bat over her shoulder and turned to Christy with a fierce look on her face. Christy wanted to laugh. This girl was taking the game more seriously than it was intended. Christy gave her an easy, low ball, and the girl hit a grounder that dribbled right back to Christy. Watching the girl run to first base out of the corner of her eye, Christy made sure she was almost there before snatching up the grounder and tossing it to first base. The girl was safe. By the look on her face, she was quite proud of herself.

In the distance, they heard the camp bell ringing, which was their signal to go to the evening meeting. Everyone groaned. Christy's girls complained they didn't have a chance to bat.

"Can we finished our game tomorrow?" they asked.

"Sure," Christy agreed. "How about tomorrow right after lunch?"

"You were too nice to them," Sara said. "You were trying to make them win."

"She would pitch the same way if you were up to bat," Jaeson said, coming to Christy's defense and joining them as they headed back to main camp. "That's what counselors are supposed to do, be fair to everybody."

The girl Jaeson had helped around the bases now had a hold of his arm and looked as though she intended to remain attached permanently to him. Sara grabbed Jaeson's other arm.

Looking up at him with her ginger eyes, she pleaded, "Will you play with us tomorrow afternoon? Pleeeease?"

"Sure," Jaeson said, catching Christy's eye and giving her a big smile. "Christy and I make a good team, don't you think?"

That comment prompted a round of agreement from the girls, including Jocelyn's bright statement, "Why don't you two get married? Then you could do this every day for the rest of your lives."

"Hey, yeah!" Jeanine agreed. "You could build a little cabin over there in the woods, and we'd all come and stay with you. You could take us canoeing and play baseball everyday."

Christy was too embarrassed to look at Jaeson, but she could feel his amused glance. Fortunately they were back at camp and could file into the meeting hall with the rest of the campers. The singing started a few minutes after they walked in. Christy's girls, full of energy, sang loudly, nudging each other and making up their own hand motions to go along with the motions they had already learned. Christy looked across the room and noticed Jaeson sitting with his boys. He turned and gazed back at her, giving one of his thumbs-up signs. She smiled back, hoping her girls hadn't noticed.

Then Christy spotted a film projector set up in the back. She remembered Dean Ferrill telling them at the counselors meeting they had a movie for the kids tonight that should get them thinking. At devos that night the counselors were supposed to take advantage of the film's message to see if any of their campers wanted to make a commitment to Christ.

The lights were out, and the movie started. Christy felt a firm hand on her shoulder. Jaeson whispered in her ear, "Come with me."

Christy slipped out without her girls noticing and followed Jaeson. As soon as the door to the meeting hall closed behind them, he took Christy's hand and said, "Time for your canoe lesson."

"Now?"

Jaeson, still holding her hand, pulled her along with him as he jogged toward the lake. "Now's the best time. Right after sunset. The water is smooth, and it's nice and quiet."

"But are you sure this is okay?" Christy puffed. She couldn't help but feel they were sneaking off, leaving their campers behind. They would get in trouble for this, she just knew it.

"We'll be back before the movie is over. It won't be a problem. Trust me."

Jaeson kept a firm hold on her hand as they wound through the woods. They arrived at the boat shack winded. He had the wild look of an adventurer in his eyes when he handed Christy her life jacket and paddle. She still felt they were doing something wrong and would get caught.

"Are you sure this is okay, Jaeson?"

"You want to learn to canoe, don't you? Now's your golden opportunity. Just look at the lake. Isn't it beautiful?"

She had to admit Jaeson was right. The lake looked like the polished floor of a ballet studio, with the fading golden lights of the summer evening dancing across it.

"Get in," Jaeson ordered when he had positioned the canoe halfway into the water.

Christy carefully balanced her way to the front bench and held on, trying to keep the canoe steady. Jaeson dropped his full weight on the back bench and used his paddle to push off from shore.

Suddenly it was quiet. The only sounds were the calm water rippling up against the canoe's side and the evening chorus of bullfrogs and crickets along the shore.

"Jaeson," Christy whispered, "are you sure we should be out here?"

"Relax, will you? I've done this a bunch of times." Then Jaeson's voice became softer and he said, "Isn't it beautiful out here? I love this. Come on, relax, Christy. I promise tonight will be the highlight of your whole week."

Christy's fingers clutched the paddle in her lap. Her eyes darted back and forth across the darkening waters as they headed for the middle of the lake.

*Relax, huh?*

CHAPTER EIGHT

# *Moonlight Picnic*

When they reached the middle of the lake, Jaeson said, "Now, the first thing you need to know is how to hold the paddle. I noticed you were holding it like this today."

He showed Christy in the dim light that he had both hands on the neck of the paddle. "You need to put one hand on the top like this and the other right about here."

Christy held up her paddle and followed his instructions.

"Good. I knew you would be a fast learner. When you're in the canoe alone, you have to paddle from the back if you want to control which way it goes. You were trying to steer it from the front this afternoon. Watch."

Jaeson dipped his paddle in the water on the right side, and as he gave a mighty stroke, the canoe lunged forward. Another stroke on the left side, and the canoe charged again. Jaeson kept the canoe going straight from his control point at the back.

"You try it," Jaeson said. "Turn around and face me, and your end will become the back of the canoe."

Christy lifted one long leg and tried to swing it over to the other side without tipping the canoe. It felt terribly awkward. She managed to get both legs over and sat facing Jaeson. It was too

99

dark to see his expression clearly, but she thought he was smiling at her.

*Does he think I'm a klutz or what? I can't tell if he's smiling at me or laughing at me.*

"Are you right-handed?" Jaeson asked.

"Yes, why?"

"I have a theory that you'll have more strength paddling on your left side, because your right hand will be on top of the paddle and that's your strongest. So start your paddle on the left side. Remember to put your hand on top."

Christy followed his instructions.

"Good. Always start with a strong stroke and then switch to the other side and give it another strong stroke."

Christy did, and Jaeson praised her. "See how different it feels when you're at the back of the canoe? You have much more control."

"You're right," Christy said. "Thanks for the lesson."

Jaeson started to scan the treetops on the other side of the lake. "It won't be here for another ten minutes," he said. "Good thing I brought provisions for us."

"What won't be here?"

"You'll see. Thirsty?" Jaeson reached for a bundle on the floor in the center of the canoe.

Christy had noticed it when she had climbed in but thought it was just a blanket. He undid the bundle and revealed a variety of "provisions."

"What's that?" Christy asked.

"Our moonlight picnic," he said, placing a lantern onto the center seat. He lit the wick inside. Jaeson pulled out a glass and scooped up some lake water and placed it next to the lantern. He picked up a dozen squashed wildflowers from the bundle and dunked them in the vase.

Christy laughed at his creativity. "This is charming, Jaeson."

"Charming?" he repeated. "It's been called many things, but I think I like charming the best so far."

Christy took it from his comment that during his years as a camp counselor, he had taken more than one girl out for a moonlight picnic. She wondered if tonight was any different for him. Was she special to him? Or was she just another girl counselor he could flirt with for the week? She wanted to be his favorite, the only girl he had ever done this with. She wanted it to be romantic and as wonderful for him as it was for her.

Jaeson handed Christy an opened bottle of mineral water and a napkin.

"Thank you, kind sir," she said, playing along with the fun.

"And now for the best part," Jaeson announced. "Peanut butter cookies saved from Sunday night!"

He handed Christy a cookie that was about seventy-five percent there.

"That's the biggest one," he said. "They get a little crumbly after the second day."

Christy laughed. "This is great, Jaeson! How fun. Thanks for bringing me out here."

She bit into the cookie and listened to the sound of the lake gently lapping at the side of the canoe.

"Oh, I almost forgot." Jaeson rummaged through the bundle and came up with a Walkman. He popped in a tape, cranked the volume all the way up, and balanced it on the middle seat with the earphones pointed in Christy's direction. The music came out soft and just loud enough.

"A little music," he said.

Christy felt like giggling; this was all so fun. A breeze blew over them, bringing with it the cool, pungent smell of the moss with just a hint of coconut tanning lotion.

"So," Jaeson said, leaning back slightly and taking a bite out of his cookie, "tell me your dreams."

"What?"

"What do you wish? What are your dreams for the future?"

Christy was caught off-guard. Whenever she dreamed of the future, the dreams included Todd. She couldn't tell that to Jaeson. Not here with the music and lantern light and everything.

"I don't know if I really have any dreams or wishes for the future," she answered.

"Sure you do. You have to. Everyone has to have a dream. Do you want to hear mine?"

"Sure," Christy said.

"I want to be a pilot. I want to fly my own plane. Not those big commercial airplanes or military jets. I want a little plane. I'd even be happy as a crop duster. That's my wish."

"Have you taken any flying lessons?" Christy asked.

"No, but I have some information on them. I'm saving up my money, because they're not cheap. Maybe by this fall I'll start lessons."

"That's a good dream," Christy said, taking a sip from her bottle. "I bet you'll make a great pilot."

"Your turn," Jaeson said. "What's your dream?"

"Well, I only thought of one thing. I've never told anyone this before, I don't think."

"You can tell me. All secrets shared on moonlight picnics are safe with me." Jaeson reached for another cookie and listened intently, waiting for her answer.

"I'd like to go to England. To Europe, actually. I've always wanted to visit a real castle and go for a ride in a gondola in Venice. That's my dream," Christy said, feeling brave.

"That's a jolly good dream," Jaeson said with a British accent. "You do have a bit of a Mary Poppins look about you. I'm sure your wish will come true."

Just then he spotted something over the top of Christy's head. It was easier to see his expression now, and Christy noticed his face lighting up with delight.

"Here he comes," Jaeson said. "Look!"

Christy turned around and saw what Jaeson was so excited about. The moon, a big, fat, buttery ball, had just popped over the treetops and was dripping its golden light onto the lake.

"Right on time," Jaeson said, gently paddling the canoe around so Christy wouldn't have to look over her shoulder.

"It's so beautiful!" Christy whispered as they watched the moon rise over the lake and shine on them like a searchlight. Everything around them took on a hazy, amber glow, and for some reason it felt warmer.

They sat in silence, enjoying the night show and listening to the muted melodies floating from the Walkman. Christy knew Jaeson had been right when he said this would be the highlight of her week. Still, as wonderful and romantic and peaceful as everything was, thoughts of Todd crept into the fantasy evening.

*There's nothing wrong with me being here with Jaeson and enjoying this romantic moment with him. It doesn't change anything between Todd and me.*

Just then Jaeson leaned toward Christy, his hand reaching for her face.

*Is he going to kiss me? What should I do?*

Jaeson's hand brushed against her cheek. "There. You had some cookie crumbs on your cheek."

"Oh," Christy's hand flew to her cheek and brushed away a few tiny crumbs Jaeson's hand had missed. Her skin felt hot to her touch, and she hoped Jaeson couldn't see her blushing in the moonlight.

"When do we need to leave to get back before we're missed?" she asked, trying not to sound as nervous as she felt.

"Oh, about now. Are you sure you want to go? This is the most peace and quiet you'll have for the rest of the week."

Christy wanted to stay. She wanted to float on the quiet lake for hours and stare at the moon and share her secret dreams with Jaeson. She wanted the fantasy to go on and on. But inwardly the struggle was growing. Should she be here, alone with Jaeson? Would they get in trouble for leaving the meeting? Would she do or say anything with Jaeson that she would later regret?

"I guess we should go back," Christy said with a sigh. "This has been wonderful, Jaeson. The music, the flowers, the moonlight. I love it. I loved being here with you."

"Thanks. I'm glad you liked it." He extinguished the lantern light. "I'll take you back. Remember, though, it was your choice, not mine."

He lifted the bunch of flowers from the vase and handed them to Christy. "To remember me by."

She took them and said, "I'll keep them, Jaeson, and I know I'll never forget you or tonight."

She could see his smile in the moonlight and felt content and a little relieved things had gone just as far as they had and no farther.

Dipping her paddle into the water, she asked, "You want me to practice paddling us back to shore?"

"Good idea. Remember to start on your left side."

Christy tried to remember all Jaeson's pointers as she plunged the paddle deep into the water and headed them for shore. It was a lot easier than her afternoon experience had been, and in no time, Jaeson's end of the canoe scraped up onto the gravel.

"Excellent," Jaeson said, hopping out and pulling them up on shore. "I'll put the gear away if you want to head on back. Or you can wait for me if you want."

The thought of wandering through the dark woods by herself didn't thrill Christy, so she helped Jaeson put the stuff back where it belonged. He stuffed the picnic bundle into a corner in the boat shack. Christy couldn't help but wonder if it would sit there until next week when Jaeson would take another girl counselor out on the lake.

He took her by the hand again, and they hurried back to the meeting hall where the campers were just beginning to stream out the open doors and run for their snacks.

"See?" Jaeson said, letting go of her hand and joining the throng headed for the mess hall. "No problem."

Christy almost believed everything was okay until devotions in her cabin that night when she was supposed to discuss the movie with her girls. As they all started to jabber about it, Christy had no idea what they were talking about. Quickly taking another direction, she asked the girls to be quiet and listen so she could tell them her testimony.

"Why do they call it a testimony, Teach?" Amy asked.

"Well, I guess because you're telling something that happened to you and you're letting people know that what you're saying is true," Christy explained. Then she went on to tell the girls how she had grown up in a Christian home.

"How can a house be a Christian?" Sara popped off.

The other girls laughed, and Christy calmed them down, saying, "Of course a house can't be a Christian. What I meant is both of my parents are Christians, so I grew up going to church."

"Me too," Ruthie said, and several other girls chimed in that their parents were Christians too.

"It wasn't enough for me to just know about God," Christy said. "I had to invite Him into my life. I did that when I was fifteen. I prayed and asked God to forgive all my sins and to come into my life. He did, and since that time I've slowly been changing and becoming more the person God wants me to be."

"How can there be a Christian school?" Sara asked. "The people who go there could be Christians, but the school can't become a Christian."

The other girls joined in with their opinions on the difference between a school of Christians and a Christian school. Christy felt certain none of them had heard her testimony, and even if some of them had, it didn't seem to matter much to them.

"Okay, girls. That's enough. I'm going to turn out the lights, and everyone needs to be in her sleeping bag." She snapped off the light and climbed into bed.

"Now I'm going to pray, and if any of you wants to pray, you can. We'll all be silent for a little bit so anyone who wants to can pray, and then after a while I'll close, okay? Let's pray."

It was silent for about two seconds, and then one of the girls gave a loud snort, which prompted lots of muffled giggles. Then someone else did her best to manufacture a belch. Jocelyn whispered, "Stop kicking my bed, Sara."

"Girls," Christy said firmly, "we are praying."

It became silent. Completely silent. None of the girls prayed, so Christy jumped in after two minutes of silence. She prayed specifically for each of the girls, the way they did in the counselors meetings. Then she prayed for the other campers, the counselors, the camp staff, and the campers who would be coming next week.

Her prayer lasted more than five minutes, and when she finished, not one girl was still awake.

*Well*, she thought, *that's one way to get them to sleep at night!*

Christy fell asleep immediately and had wonderful dreams about being in a row boat on a placid lake with swans swimming around her. Behind her was a huge, storybook castle. She held a lacy parasol and twirled it with her white-gloved fingers. Across from her sat a man dressed in a tuxedo who was pouring tea into a china cup. When he asked if she would like one lump of sugar or two, he looked up, and she saw that it was Todd.

When she woke up with the alarm at 6:00 the next morning, she felt rested. Bouncing out of bed, she headed to the rest room for a brisk morning shower. Jessica was already there, and Christy told her about her new devotional tactic for praying the girls to sleep.

"The only bad part was they didn't pay attention when I gave my testimony, and none of them prayed. I don't think any of my girls are interested in spiritual things."

Jessica wrapped a towel around her wet hair, and pouring some astringent on a cotton ball, she began her facial-cleansing routine. "I think the next step is for you to spend time with each of them one-on-one and find out where they are."

"How can I do that? It's Thursday already. That's not much time. Besides, what do I say? 'Let's have some quality time. We've got three minutes. So tell me if you're saved or not, and if you want to be or not.' "

Jessica laughed. "Not like that, Christy. Just sit down with each of them individually, tell them you care about them, and ask if there's anything they want to talk about. We don't know which ones are ready to give their hearts to the Lord and which ones aren't. God knows. All we need to do is give them an opportunity to talk about it and offer to answer their questions."

Christy combed through her wet hair. "You're right. I'll figure out a way to get together with each of them. I hope you know that if you weren't here giving me all this good advice, I'd be completely lost."

"I'm sure you would do fine," Jessica said. "I'm glad we're here together, though. I want to be sure to get your address so we can stay in contact after camp."

"Me too," Christy agreed. "My friend Katie is never going to believe I said this, but I'm glad I came. It's been a great week."

"It's not over yet! We still have to live through the counselor hunt tomorrow."

The hunt was the first thing they discussed at the meeting that morning.

"I suggest," Dean Ferrill said, "that you each take a hike over to the other side of the lake sometime today and scope out a hiding place. This will help save a lot of time tomorrow when you get over there."

Since Christy had promised the girls she would pitch at their softball game after lunch, she wasn't sure when she would have a chance to hunt for a spot. Fortunately it was hotter than usual that afternoon, and after three innings, both teams were ready to quit and find a cooler sport. The minute one of them suggested volleyball in the pool, they all disappeared, leaving Jaeson and Christy alone to put away the equipment.

"You coming over to the pool?" Jaeson asked.

"Actually, I thought I'd better find myself a good hiding place across the lake."

"Good idea. I'll go with you. I can show you some places I've used before."

They walked around the lake rather than taking a canoe. At

one spot where the trail became narrow, Jaeson reached his hand behind him, offering it to Christy. She felt comfortable holding Jaeson's hand.

"Here's one spot I used last year," Jaeson said, stopping and pointing straight up.

"Where?" Christy asked.

"Up there. This is an easy tree to climb. It was a lot of fun, because the kids never thought to look up even though I showered them with pine needles."

"I'm not much of a tree climber," Christy said hesitantly. "Do you have any other suggestions?"

"Sure. Follow me."

Jaeson led her through the woods, pointing out five possible hiding spots. She liked the last one best and decided that was the one for her. It was a hollowed-out tree trunk behind a huge tree that grew close to the trail. The campers would have to go off the trail and around the tree to find her. She thought it would be good to bring a towel along so she wouldn't have to sit on the moldy bark inside the tree.

Jaeson took her hand again and began to lead her back. He stopped at the good climbing tree and said, "I think I'll try going up again this year. Worked great last year."

He then coached Christy on canoe strategy. She loved this feeling. The birds were singing above them, the shimmering lake was peeking at them from behind the trees, and she was on an afternoon walk hand-in-hand with the cutest counselor at camp. This is what Christy dreamed camp would be like. Nothing of her previous life seemed to matter now. She had two more days at Camp Wildwood, and she intended to enjoy every minute of them.

# CHAPTER NINE

# *View From a Hollow Tree*

At dinner that night Jocelyn wasn't eating. Christy asked her if she felt okay.

"My stomach hurts," she said.

Christy felt her forehead and said, "You feel pretty warm. Let's get you over to the nurse's office."

Turning to Jaeson, who sat behind her as usual, Christy asked, "Can you keep an eye on my girls? This one needs to see the nurse."

With her arm around Jocelyn, Christy escorted her from the noisy mess hall and across the grounds to the nurse's small white building.

When they were only a few yards away, Jocelyn said, "I think I have to throw up."

"Can you make it to those bushes?" Christy asked, helping Jocelyn walk a little faster.

They made it just in time for Jocelyn to be sick. Christy turned away and held her breath. This was a part of camp counseling she hadn't planned on. Rummaging through her pockets, she found a tissue. Still holding her breath, she held it out to Jocelyn and said, "Here."

Jocelyn groaned and started to cry as she wiped off her mouth. "I feel awful!"

"We're almost there, honey," Christy said, wrapping her arm back around Jocelyn and coaxing the sobbing girl along.

Fortunately the nurse must have heard them coming because she opened the door and helped Jocelyn to a clean cot.

"Her stomach hurts," Christy explained. "She threw up out there in the bushes."

"You poor little thing," the nurse said, placing her hand on Jocelyn's forehead. "What did you eat today?"

"She didn't eat any dinner," Christy said.

"What about during free time? Did you have any snacks?"

Jocelyn slowly nodded her head and listed half a dozen snack foods and types of candy bars she'd eaten.

The nurse placed a cool washcloth on Jocelyn's forehead and whispered to Christy, "Sounds like a case of junk food overload. I'll give her something to settle her stomach, and she'll be fine."

Christy patted Jocelyn on the arm and said, "You do what the nurse says, and I'll check on you later, okay?"

She was about to slip out when the nurse said, "Could you do me a favor? Would you fill up the bucket on the side of the building and then wash down the site where she vomited?"

Christy shuddered as she doused the spot with a bucket of water. This was definitely the part of being a counselor that she could do without. For good measure, she filled a second bucket and poured it over the area so no signs of the accident remained.

*I'm glad I got her out of the mess hall when I did!*

The doors to the mess hall opened, and the Camp Wildwood wild campers scattered to make use of their short free time before the evening meeting.

*Oh, great, dinner's over, and I didn't finish eating. Actually, I don't feel like eating anymore.*

Christy had planned to spend time with her girls individually today, but with the baseball game and the walk with Jaeson, the afternoon had flown. Jeanine was the first of her girls she spotted exiting the dining hall. She caught up with her and asked, "Do you want to do something?"

Jeanine looked at her funny. "Like what?"

"I don't know. Go for a walk, sit by the lake, and talk."

"Why?"

"Well, just so we can have some time together," Christy said, scrambling for a better approach.

"We've been together all week," Jeanine said. "We're bunk-mates even."

"I know, I just thought maybe, well . . . never mind."

"No," Jeanine said, clutching Christy's arm. "We can do something if you want."

Now Christy wasn't sure who was the leader and who was the follower. "Why don't we just go out in the woods and talk. I know where there's a bench not far from here."

"Okay," Jeanine said cheerfully. "If that'll make you feel better."

Christy led Jeanine to the bench. She had planned her opening line during their walk and sprang it on Jeanine. "I want you to know that I think you're wonderful, I care about you, and I want to know if you have any questions about God."

Jeanine looked at her a moment before answering. "Nope."

"Okay, that's fine." Christy had no idea where to go next with her big witnessing opportunity. "So you feel as though everything between you and God is fine?"

"Yep. My parents prayed with me when I was little, Jesus lives in my heart, and I know I'm going to heaven. Do you think you could braid my hair like that other counselor Jessica braids her girls' hair?"

"I could try," Christy floundered.

*Why don't any of these girls want to talk about spiritual things?*

"Good," Jeanine said, turning her back to Christy and scrounging in her pocket. "I have a rubber band here." She proceeded to extract at least two dozen rubber bands from her pocket.

"What are all these for?" Christy asked, trying to smooth Jeanine's matted mane with her fingernails before she pulled all the pieces together in a French braid.

"Jessica told me to try giving something to Nick instead of taking stuff from him, you know? I tried it with the leather bracelet, but you know how that turned out. So now I'm giving him something else. A rubber band in the back of the head whenever he's not looking. He still doesn't know it's me."

Christy was glad Jeanine couldn't see her face. She couldn't repress her smile.

"How come guys don't start to like girls at the same age as girls start to like boys?" Jeanine asked, patiently holding her head still.

"I don't know. Maybe God is giving the girls an extra year or two to polish up on their manners. That way, when the guys are old enough to be interested in them, they'll be the kind of girls worth being interested in."

"I never thought of it that way," Jeanine said, genuinely persuaded. "Will you teach me how to have better manners?"

"Sure, if you'd like. Hand me a rubber band." Christy tied off the end of Jeanine's braid.

Then Jeanine turned eagerly to face Christy. With her hair off her face, Jeanine was a pretty little girl.

"First, I'd say lose the rubber bands. I don't think that's going to help with Nick at all. Next, try to eat with your mouth closed and not to talk when you have food in your mouth."

"What else?" Jeanine asked.

"Well, sitting up straight always helps."

Jeanine immediately straightened her back and held her head up high. "Like this?"

"Yes, that's very good. I might mention screaming next. There's a place for screaming. Like in the pool or on a roller coaster. But for the most part you don't need to scream a lot during the day just for the sake of screaming."

Jeanine nodded solemnly. "What else?"

"That's a good start. Always try to say kind things and be considerate of others."

Jeanine beamed, looking anxious to take off and try some of her new charm techniques on Nick. Just as she was about to hop up, Christy touched her arm and asked, "May I bless you, Jeanine?"

"Bless me? But I didn't sneeze."

Months ago, one chilly morning on the beach, Todd had placed his hand on Christy's forehead and blessed her. At the time she didn't want the blessing and didn't receive it well. But his act had stayed with her all this time. For some reason Christy felt the urge to bless this girl, who was blossoming into a young lady right before her eyes.

"Just close your eyes," Christy instructed. She then placed her hand across Jeanine's forehead and said, "Jeanine, the Lord bless you and keep you. The Lord make His face to shine upon you and give you His peace. And may you always love Jesus first, above all else."

Jeanine opened her sparkling eyes. A big smile spread across her face. "That was neat!" she said. "What does the 'love Jesus above all else' mean?"

"It means in every situation you face as you're growing up, may you fall in love with Jesus and love Him more than you love anything else."

"Thanks, Christy," Jeanine said, hopping up and impulsively giving Christy a hug. "You're the best counselor in the whole world!" Then off she ran down the trail.

Christy sat for a moment, thinking about the advice she had just given. She wished she could say she already had that kind of love for Jesus. She did love Him, but she wanted to love Him even more. Todd once said that was good because it meant she was "hungering and thirsting after righteousness."

Even though her talk with Jeanine hadn't gone the way she had planned, she felt good. She had given Jeanine what she needed, and maybe the blessing would help Jeanine feel loved.

Christy sat with Amy, Sara, and Ruthie at the evening meeting. She was glad Amy and Sara had included Ruthie into their little group. Christy quietly told Amy and Sara in the cabin that night that she liked the way they were being good friends with each other and with other girls in their cabin. Both girls looked pleased and proud.

For devotions, Christy read them her favorite psalm, Psalm 139. Then she talked for a few minutes about how much God loved each of them and how much He wanted them to promise their hearts to Him.

Christy felt as though her "message" had gone well and anticipated lots of discussion afterwards—and hopefully a conversion or two. She gave her closing line and waited for their responses.

All of them had fallen asleep except Sara.

Christy tried to hide her disappointment as she asked Sara, "Do you have any questions?"

"Yes," Sara said, "has Jaeson kissed you yet?"

"No, of course not."

"Why not? You like him and he likes you."

"Sara, that's not enough of a reason to kiss a guy. When you give away kisses, you're giving a little part of your heart that you can never take back. You have to be careful that you don't give away too many pieces too soon or to the wrong person."

"You *have* been kissed before, haven't you? What was it like? Did you close your eyes?"

"Sara, let's talk about this later. I think we both need some sleep, okay?"

Christy pulled up her sleeping bag over her ears and only heard a muffled response from Sara about how nobody ever wanted to talk about it. Promising herself she would talk to Sara tomorrow about kissing, Christy fell asleep.

She floated in and out of a confusing dream in which Jaeson tried to kiss her and she didn't know how to respond.

Friday dawned overcast and chilly. It was the first morning Christy put on jeans instead of shorts. She passed on the chance to have an invigorating shower and pulled her hair back in a ponytail rather than washing it. Her neck was stiff. She felt as if she had been at camp for six months instead of six days.

Everyone at breakfast seemed on edge too. Perhaps it was because this was the last full day of camp or because it was cold and rainy outside. Whatever it was, the mood hung over the camp all morning. At lunch two of her girls argued over the last half of a grilled cheese sandwich until one of them fell backwards with her chair. If Christy hadn't rushed over in time to hold them back, there would have been a major fight.

"Here," Jessica said, offering Christy's table a plate of sandwiches. "My girls aren't very hungry."

Jocelyn grabbed the first sandwich. Ever since her recovery early that morning, she had been eating everything in sight.

Jessica then confided in Christy over the roar of the savage campers, "I don't like it when they get this way before the counselor hunt. You would think they were out for blood!"

"Our blood, I suppose," Christy answered.

Jessica nodded and headed back to her table of sassy whiners, who kept asking when they could leave so they could go to the snack shack and buy candy bars.

The instant they burst out of the dining room, the sun popped through the clouds and looked as though it would stay around all afternoon. Within minutes Christy felt boiling hot in her jeans and sweatshirt and decided to change into shorts before the counselor hunt. She also wanted to take along a towel to sit on inside her tree.

The cabin was a disastrous mess. The girls hadn't worked on it at all during cabin cleanup, and since Christy was in the counselors meeting during that time, she hadn't been there to motivate them. They had lost points for the mess, but her girls didn't seem to care.

Christy hurried down to the lake. Six canoes were lined up on the shore with a bright flag mounted on the stern of each. Christy was assigned the canoe with the orange flag and tied the matching orange strip of cloth to her waist. She was to relinquish this sash to the first camper who found her.

Dean Ferrill gave the rest of the instructions, and Christy mounted her "trusty steed" with a surge of excitement. With paddle in hand, she waited along with the other counselors for the signal.

"On your mark, get set . . . ," Dean Ferrill's shrill whistle blew, and Christy plunged her paddle into the water on the left side, just as Jaeson had told her. She got a good, swift start and was ahead of the other girls by several yards in no time. With each stroke she felt the muscles in her upper arms stretching and letting her know she was giving it all she had.

Christy was glad she had changed into her cut-off jeans and her Camp Wildwood T-shirt when she felt the sun beating down on the tops of her legs. The sun's intensity seemed double because of the reflection off the water.

From the shore behind her, Christy could hear the shouts from the campers. They were to stay put until the first counselor's canoe touched the shore on the opposite side. Then they were released to run around the lake and find the counselors.

Jessica was right. From the way the campers' yells and screams echoed across the lake, they did sound as though they were out for blood.

Near the middle of the lake, the three guys overtook Christy and passed her, the three of them stroking in unison, with their canoes lined up neck and neck.

Then Jessica passed her and called out, "Keep going, Christy. We're almost there."

Christy paddled harder, keeping her canoe straight and aiming for a nice, big open spot on the shore. Jaeson hit the shore first. Then Mike, Jessica, and Bob. Right behind them, Christy's canoe made the welcome sound of hitting mud and gravel. She hopped out, pulled her canoe to shore, and ran with soggy tennis shoes to her hiding spot in the hollowed-out tree.

She found the tree with no problem but realized she had left her towel in the canoe. From the echoing sounds of the wild campers running around the lake, she knew she didn't have enough time to go back to retrieve it.

With her muddy tennis shoe, she tried to scrape out some of the gunk on the floor of her hiding place. It seemed she was leaving more mud inside than she was managing to get moldy bark out. The campers' voices sounded closer.

Christy gave up and wedged herself into the triangular hideout. Drawing her long legs up close to her chest, she wrapped her arms around them and tried to make herself as small as possible. Then she tried to slow her breathing down to a calmer pace.

The inside of the tree was actually kind of interesting. A few inches from her face, the wood appeared to be rippled in several layers around the opening of the trunk. It smelled musty but in an earthy way that didn't bother her.

As a child, Christy had always liked stories about woodland critters who lived in the trees. She pictured one of her storybook elves or dwarfs being delighted to use her hideout as his home.

The first camper's footsteps came pounding down the trail right behind Christy's tree. She held her breath but feared her loudly pounding heart would give her away. Several more ran by, yelling and screaming, and Christy actually felt frightened. Not that they would find her; that was the game. But what if they were so wild this afternoon that they thought it a good idea to tie her up and leave her there?

She wiggled slightly, trying to improve her position. The bark was poking her and she felt tingles up and down her legs, probably from them falling asleep. As her eyes adjusted to the darkness of her cave, Christy realized that the bark in front of her face appeared to be moving. She looked closely and discovered a nonstop string of red ants marching across the entrance, only inches from her face.

With great control she kept herself from screaming or even moving an inch. Another hoard of campers thundered behind her down the trail. She kept silent. Then she felt that tingly sensation from her legs move up her arms and onto her hands. At that moment, she realized she was covered with ants.

"Yiiiiii!" she screeched, ejecting herself from the tree and jumping around in the woods, slapping her arms and legs in a futile effort to get the ants off her.

Two girls from Jessica's cabin found her in the midst of her furious dance and ventured carefully toward her. "Can we have your orange strip?" they asked cautiously.

"Come and get it," Christy said, still shaking and stamping her feet. Dozens of red ants fell to the ground. But it wasn't enough.

One of the girls timidly drew near and snatched the end of the orange cloth. As she pulled it from Christy's waist, another dozen ants emerged and raced down the cloth and up the girl's hand.

Now she too was screaming and shaking, doing the Christy ant-dance.

"What are you two doing?" the other girl asked. "I'm taking this back to the other side!" She grabbed the orange cloth, shook it out, and took off running.

"You're supposed to get in your canoe and beat her back," the girl explained.

"I can't," Christy wailed. "I still have ants in my pants!"

"Maybe if you run to the canoe, they'll fall out, and then if there are any left, you can sit on them and squish them all."

Christy was close to tears. "They sting. My legs feel like they're on fire!"

"Then jump in the water," the girl suggested. "Look, they bit me, too." She held out her hand, revealing a baker's dozen red spots.

"This is awful!" Christy cried. "Are you okay?"

"I'm going to go to the nurse."

"Good idea," Christy said, slapping herself on the legs as she raced to the canoe. Then, because the cool lake water seemed like the only thing that could possibly stop the stinging, she jumped in and came up soaking.

"Christy!" Jaeson called out as he ran up and pushed off the canoe next to hers. "What are you doing? Get in your canoe! Come on! I'll push you off. We can paddle together."

In spite of her misery, she jumped into her canoe and let Jaeson push her off, knowing she had no time to explain. With quivering arms, she numbly followed Jaeson's shouted-out instructions.

"Paddle left. Paddle right. Come on, Christy, faster!"

Her hair was dripping in her face, and her legs were shivering and burning at the same time. She glanced at her arms and saw the red marks beginning to swell.

"Paddle left. Paddle right. Faster!"

"I can't keep up!" she cried out to Jaeson. "You go ahead."

Jaeson pulled out in front of her, and with a quick thumbs-up, his strong arms shot his canoe through the water like a well-aimed arrow. He made it to shore and planted his flag before his runner arrived. Since he was the first counselor back and most of the campers were still on the other side, it seemed a hollow victory with so few to cheer for him.

Christy paddled slowly but steadily, trying with all her might to ignore the increasingly painful stinging in her arms and legs. She still was a ways from shore when her arms gave out. "Come on, Christy," Jaeson called. "You can do it! Paddle left. Paddle right."

She tried, but it seemed pointless. Her chest was heaving from being so winded, and her head began to throb. The breeze nudged her a few feet closer to shore as she tried to catch her breath.

"Come on, Christy," Jaeson called again. "Your runner is almost here! Only a few more paddles."

Christy stroked three times on each side of the canoe and seemed to drift backwards rather than forward. She looked to the shore and saw Jaeson waving his arms and coaching her to give it full steam.

Just then the girl with Christy's orange strip in her hand shot through the woods and crumpled on the gravel as she plunged her strip of fabric into the hole meant for Christy's flag. The score was now counselors One, campers One.

Hanging her head, Christy realized how dizzy she felt. Hearing a splash in the water, she looked up and saw Jaeson swimming out to her canoe. He took hold of the rope in the front and towed her the twenty more feet to shore.

"I'm sorry," Christy apologized, reaching for Jaeson's hand to help her out.

"Christy, what happened? You're covered with red spots!"

"Ants," she breathed out, feeling completely exhausted. Her soggy tennis shoes slipped on the gravel, and Jaeson caught her just before she fell.

"You're going to the nurse," he said. "Put your arm around my shoulder. I'll help you walk to camp."

"Are you okay?" Dean Ferrill asked when he came over and saw Christy's polka-dotted skin.

"I'll take her to the nurse," Jaeson offered. "Cheer the rest of the counselors in for us, okay?"

Limping and leaning against Jaeson for support, Christy felt ridiculous to have been defeated by a bunch of stupid ants. She said nothing all the way to the infirmary. Jaeson talked the whole time about other mishaps he had seen at camp over the years, everything from broken collarbones to split lips. Somehow nothing he said made her feel better.

"Red ants," Jaeson told the nurse when she opened her door. The nurse took a quick look at Christy's arms and said, "Oh, my, this doesn't look good."

"Wait till you see this," Christy said, exposing the back of her raw legs to the nurse.

"Oh, my gracious! What did you do, girl, sit on their convention center?"

"I think so," Christy said, trying hard to smile but not having much success.

"I'll check on you later," Jaeson promised and left Christy in the hands of the sympathetic nurse.

"Let's get you in the tub and make sure all those critters are off you," the nurse said. "I hope you didn't have any special plans for the evening, because I'm afraid you're not going anywhere for a while."

A few minutes later Christy lowered herself into the lukewarm tub, anticipating a soothing sensation. Instead, the water felt like a thousand needles were plunged into her flesh. She itched like crazy.

"Whatever you do," the nurse called to her through the closed door, "don't scratch. I've put something in the water to draw out the poison. If you scratch, you'll only spread it."

The camper from the woods with the ant bites on her hand had arrived, and the nurse was checking her hand as Christy soaked.

"I hope you know," Christy called back, "that this is about the worst torture a person could ever go through."

"I know. I'm sorry. But it *will* help. Trust me."

At that uncomfortable moment, Christy knew she had no other choice.

CHAPTER TEN

# Sara's Promise

After drying off and putting on some clean clothes, Christy lay on her stomach on the infirmary cot so the nurse could smear her spotted legs with a cold, gooey lotion. She wanted to cry. This had to be one of her life's all-time worst experiences.

Covering Christy with a sheet, the nurse instructed, "Don't move. Stay on your stomach and try to get some rest."

*It's funny, but I never thought much about wanting to sleep on my side or my back until she told me I could only lie on my stomach.*

Christy wiggled and clenched her teeth. How could she rest? The lotion stung almost as bad as the ant bites.

"How's the patient?" Dean Ferrill's voice called from the front door.

"Trying to rest. She was attacked pretty severely," the nurse said. "You can go on in and see her if you like."

The dean had to walk all the way around to the front of Christy's cot and squat down on one knee so he could look her in the face.

"You okay?" he asked with such a tender tone that Christy couldn't hold back the tears.

"I'm fine," her voice said, but her tears told him differently.

She blinked, trying to stop from crying. Then she realized she couldn't use her hands to wipe the tears from her face because the pink lotion would get in her eyes.

"Here," Dean Ferrill said, recognizing her dilemma and reaching for a tissue. He wiped her eyes for her. "You're going to be fine in a day or two."

"Who won?" Christy asked.

"The campers won this year. They're pretty happy about it too."

"It's because of me, isn't it?" Christy said.

"No, don't think that. You did a great job. You gave it all you had. I'm proud of you."

Christy rested her pink hands under her chin on the pillow. "At least I don't have to serve tables tonight."

The dean smiled at her joke and said, "So that was your motive for sitting on the world's largest ant farm?"

"There must be easier ways," Christy said, feeling a little better.

"Actually, you've been working hard serving your campers all week, and I think you've done a terrific job. I'd love to have you as a counselor any time."

"I don't feel I accomplished anything spiritually with the girls. I tried talking to them about their relationship with God, and I even sat down with some of them one-on-one. Either they said they were already Christians, or they didn't want to give their hearts to the Lord, or they just didn't get it."

The dean's face took on another one of his understanding expressions. "Christy, you've done your part. You've told them how to receive eternal life. How much they understand is up to God. And how they respond is up to them, not you."

"But none of them responded. At all."

"You don't know what's going on in their hearts. We've planted lots of seeds in these kids this week. Some of them might sprout a week from now, some ten years from now. That's God's business."

"I just wish I could do more," Christy said with a sigh.

"You can. You can pray. Always pray. Actually, it looks to me as though you're in a pretty good position to pray for us during the rest of the evening."

Christy wished she could see her "infirmity" with as much of a spiritual reason as Dean Ferrill did. After he left she thought about how he might be right. She couldn't do anything else to-night. She couldn't serve tables at dinner or practice with the counselors for their closing-night skit. She couldn't even have her final night of devotions with her girls. The camp secretary was going to stay in Christy's cabin that night so she could remain in the infirmary. About the only thing she could do was pray.

Wiggling her still-stinging legs under the rough sheet, Christy tried to find a comfortable spot for her head on the pillow and began by praying for Jaeson and the other counselors. She prayed for her girls, all the other girl campers, and then all the boy camp-ers. She prayed for the kitchen staff, office staff, leaders, and bus drivers. It didn't seem she had left out anyone except maybe her-self.

She wasn't sure what to pray for herself. A quick recovery? For the sting to go away? Death to all red ants on planet Earth?

"Can she have visitors?" Christy heard Jaeson asking the nurse.

"Sure, go on in. She can't move, so why don't you take this stool. You can sit by the head of the cot."

Christy tried to twist her neck around without moving the rest of her body. She saw Jessica holding a plastic cup with wildflowers and Jaeson following her with the nurse's stool. "Hi," she greeted them, trying to sound cheerful, while fully aware of how silly she must look with pink polka dots all over her face and arms.

"You poor thing,' Jessica said, planting herself on the floor cross-legged and holding up the cup of flowers. "I wonder where I can put these so you can see them."

"Right there on the floor would be fine. Thanks, Jessica. They're pretty."

Just then, a chorus of boys' voices started to sing under the slightly opened window. "The ants go marching one by one, hurrah, hurrah. The ants go marching up Christy's legs, hurrah, hurrah."

"Hey!" Jaeson yelled, opening the window all the way and sticking his face out where they could see him. "You guys are in big trouble! I've got all your names. You're going to get it!"

The boys immediately scattered. Jessica pressed her lips together to try to keep from laughing.

Christy broke the silence with a ripple of laughter. "That was pretty clever of them," she said.

Jaeson and Jessica laughed with her.

"Are you feeling any better?" Jessica asked.

"A little, I guess. Sorry I won't be able to help you guys serve tables. And I'm really sorry I made us lose the race."

"Don't worry about it," Jaeson said. "I feel awful since I'm the one who showed you that hiding place. I promise there weren't any ants two years ago when I hid there."

"It's not your fault, Jaeson," Christy said. "I should have looked before I crawled in or at least worn jeans. I was going to take a towel, but I left it in the canoe. I feel bad because I'm letting you down with the dinner and the counselors' skit and everything."

"We were able to rework the skit. It's going to be fine. The main thing is that you get better, Christy."

"I'll try," she said.

"We need to get ready for dinner," Jessica said. "We'll check on you later, okay?"

"Oh, Jessica, if you have time, could you braid Sara's hair? I promised I'd do it for the dinner tonight."

"Sure. Anyone else you want me to check on for you? I think the camp secretary is already up in your cabin."

"No. Just tell them all I said hi, and I'll see them in the morning."

Jessica adjusted the cup of flowers on the floor so they faced Christy. "I think the purple ones are the prettiest," Jessica said. Then kissing the tip of her finger, she touched the "kiss" to the end of Christy's nose.

Christy smiled up at her and said, "That's about the only place on me that didn't get bit!"

Jaeson and Jessica left. She felt awfully alone.

"I'm going to dinner," the nurse announced about fifteen minutes later. "I'll bring something back for you. Are you too warm or too cold?"

"No, I'm fine. I'm getting a little stiff, though. Can I at least turn on my side?"

"It'd be better if you could wait. The majority of your bites are on the back of your legs, and I want them to remain exposed to the air."

"Okay," Christy sighed. "Are you sure you didn't find this remedy in the medieval book of tortures under 'How to Drive a Person Crazy'?"

"At least you still have your sense of humor," the nurse called over her shoulder as she left.

*Yeah, my sense of humor and I are going to have a great time tonight.*

Christy tried to pray again, going through and remembering everyone she could think of at camp. Near the end, right after she prayed for the bus driver, she dozed off and didn't wake up until she heard the door open.

*The nurse must be here with my dinner. I'm not exactly hungry. I sure could use something to drink, though.*

Soft music began to play behind her, and she twisted her head to see Jaeson, dressed in a crisp white shirt with a black bow tie, walking toward her. He had a white towel draped over his arm, and in both hands he balanced a tray decked with his Walkman, a can of 7Up with a straw sticking out of it, and a plate of chicken, mashed potatoes, and green beans.

"Dinner is served," he said in his best British butler voice. "I asked the nurse if I could bring this to you for her."

Christy should have felt delighted and honored by Jaeson's clever display of attention. Instead, she felt helpless, lying there with her painted clown face, not even able to cut her own meat.

"You didn't have to do this," she said.

"Oh, yes I did. It's the camp rules. If one counselor causes another counselor to end up in the infirmary, said counselor must serve the invalid dinner."

"I'm not exactly an invalid," Christy said.

"Oh, really? Then you'll just have to pretend for me. Do you want a drink?" Jaeson sat on the stool, balancing the tray in his lap and cutting up Christy's chicken into little pieces. He seemed perfectly content to continue acting out his part.

That's when it hit Christy that everything with Jaeson that week *had* been pretend. The moonlight picnic, talking about their dreams, all his smiles at her on the archery field and at the pool. They were pretending to be boyfriend and girlfriend for the week.

Tomorrow she would leave, and Jaeson would start the game all over again with some other girl next week.

"Is that what all this is to you?" Christy asked. "One big game of pretend?"

"What do you mean?" Jaeson said, scooting closer to her cot and using his knees as a table for Christy to eat off of. He handed her the fork and smiled.

"I mean, I don't know anything about you, and yet you've treated me all week like I'm you're girlfriend."

Jaeson looked surprised. "Why? Because I taught you how to shoot an arrow and showed you the moon from a canoe?"

"I'm not accusing you of doing anything wrong," Christy said, realizing how unkind her statement must have sounded to a guy who was nice enough to bring her dinner. "I've been playing along the whole time. I've liked doing things with you and holding hands and the moonlight picnic and everything. It's just that tomorrow it's going to be all over, and it'll seem like it was just a dream."

"That's how it is," Jaeson agreed. "You'd better start on the potatoes. They're going to be cold soon."

Christy took a fork full of potatoes and regretted the way she had blurted out her thoughts.

"Dreams aren't bad, are they?" Jaeson said cautiously. "If you both know you're playing the same game, then it's okay, and nobody gets hurt, right?"

Christy thought that somehow it didn't seem right or feel right. She didn't know how to say it in a way that would make sense to Jaeson, so she took a bite of chicken and said, "This is good. Thanks for bringing it to me. I guess I was hungrier than I thought."

"You're very welcome. And if you're upset about anything I

said or did this week, I'm sorry. I wasn't trying to hurt you. I just wanted to enjoy the week with you."

After Jaeson left, Christy lay alone in the quiet room thinking about his words. Why should they bother her? She had played the camp-romance game. She had wanted to. Why did her heart feel achy now?

*It must be that I'm leaving tomorrow, and this whole dream will disappear. What will I have left of my relationship with Jaeson? He hasn't indicated he would ever want to see me again or that he would write or call. Take me out of the week and put in another girl, and I'll bet he would do everything the same with her. Next week he probably will.*

Christy decided she and Jaeson had had a dream relationship. It had started in her head, and she had convinced her heart it was real. Tomorrow it would be gone, evaporated like a morning mist. And she already knew it would not be her head that would be sad, but her heart. This dream relationship would leave her craving more.

She had plenty of time to contemplate all this while she lay on her full stomach, listening to the sounds of the evening meeting floating through her window. From the roar of the campers' laughter, the counselors' skit must have been hilarious. The singing sounded good. Much better than it did when she sat in the middle of her girls and heard their high voices singing as loud as they could. From her position across the camp, the distant music sounded sweet. She hummed along softly when she recognized the songs they were singing and realized for the first time that every song they had learned that week was Scripture put to music.

*What a great idea! Without knowing it, the kids have learned a dozen Bible verses this week.*

The last song they sang was Christy's favorite. She had heard it for the first time more than a month ago at the God-Lovers Bible study. From her cot she softly sang along.

*Eyes have not seen. Ears have not heard.*
*Neither has it entered into the heart of man*
*The things God has planned*
*For those who love Him.*

Christy thought about her dreams, her fantasies, and her wishes. If the words to the song were true, which they had to be because they were from the Bible, then her dreams for her life were nothing compared to God's dreams for her. Her part was to love God. And that was a true dream relationship that started in her heart and went to her head. Why was it she kept having to relearn this same lesson?

Drifting off into a peaceful sleep, Christy dozed for some time before being awakened by the disturbing awareness that someone else was in the room, watching her.

She snapped her head up and squinted, looking around in the dark room. "Who's there?"

"It's me. Sara," the tiny voice came from behind her.

"What's wrong, Sara? Are you okay?" Christy asked, trying to wake herself up and remember why she was here and who Sara was.

Suddenly the light snapped on, and Sara stepped over to the stool and plopped herself down, ready to talk.

"I'm glad you're awake," Sara said. "Everyone else is at the campfire, but I had to talk to you."

Christy slowly opened her eyes, hoping they would adjust soon to the light. "Does anyone know you're here?"

"I asked Jessica, and she said it was okay. She fixed my hair for me tonight for the dinner. Do you like it?"

Christy peered at the pesky little "Skipper" doll. Jessica had made two thin braids on each side of Sara's hair and tied them together in back with a thin, pink ribbon. It looked like a fallen halo, and the rest of Sara's wild, blond hair billowed out beneath it.

"It's darling," Christy said. "What did you want to talk about?"

"Well, you know," Sara said shyly.

Christy remembered her promise from the night before to talk to Sara about what it was like to kiss a boy. She let out a deep breath. To think this little "angel" woke her up to ask about kissing was more than Christy had patience for at the moment.

"Sara, I don't know if this is such a good time."

Sara lowered her brown eyes and looked disappointed.

"I mean, isn't there someone else you could talk to after the campfire? Jessica, maybe?"

"I guess," Sara said slowly. She stood up, shuffling her feet and stalling by the door. "It's just that you said if we ever wanted to talk about giving our hearts to Jesus, that you would be happy to talk to us."

"Sara," Christy cried out, "don't leave! Come back here and sit down."

Sara plopped back down on the stool, looking surprised.

"I'm sorry," Christy said. "Of course I want to talk to you about Jesus. I thought you were here to talk about kissing."

"Oh, no," Sara said, the sparkle returning to her eyes. "I already asked Jeanine. She kissed Nick today in the woods during the counselor hunt, and she said it was kind of yucky. She only kissed him on the cheek when he wasn't looking, but she said it tasted like salty mud." Sara gave a little shiver. "I don't think I want to kiss a boy for a while."

"Good," Christy said, laughing. "It's better to wait until the boy is old enough to see the benefit of bathing more than once a month. It's also a whole lot better when it's the boy's idea too and not just yours. That will take a few years, though. Be patient."

"Don't worry, I will," Sara said.

"You wanted to ask me about how to become a Christian?" Christy prodded.

"Yeah. How do you do it?"

Christy was about to launch into a detailed explanation of how our sin separates us from God, how Christ is the sacrifice that paid our debt, that salvation comes from repenting of our sins and trusting our lives to Christ. But then a little voice in her head reminded her that the campers had been hearing that all week from the speaker. Sara wasn't asking *why* she needed to give her heart to the Lord; she was asking *how*.

"God already knows what you're thinking, Sara. Do you want to ask Jesus to forgive your sins and come into your heart?"

"Yes."

"Then tell Him."

"Isn't there a special prayer, or something I'm supposed to do?" Sara asked.

"No, this is between you and God. You be honest and tell Him you're sorry for all the things you've done that made Him sad. Then tell Him you want Him to rule your life."

"That's it?"

"Yes," Christy said, "because, you see, it isn't your words, it's what's in your heart that God looks at."

Sara started to cry. "That's what I want. I want God in my heart."

"Then let's pray, and you tell Him." Christy reached her stiff arm over to Sara and held her hand.

As she listened, Sara told God she was sorry. She asked Him to forgive her and come into her heart and ended with a hasty "Amen."

Looking up at Christy with tears sparkling in her eyes, Sara said, "I don't feel anything."

"I didn't either when I gave my heart to Jesus. But it's not a feeling. It's a promise. God will keep His part of the promise and forgive you. Now you have lots of years ahead to keep your part of the promise and fall in love with Him."

"I think I do feel different now," Sara said. "I feel good that I finally did it. I've been wanting to ever since that night in the cabin when you talked about this."

Christy looked into Sara's innocent face. She felt a ball of joy catch in her throat as she said, "You know what, Sara? The Bible says that all the angels in heaven are rejoicing right now because you've just joined God's family."

"Really?"

"Really!"

"I didn't know I meant that much to God."

"Oh, Sara," Christy said, feeling a tear of joy escape and skip down her cheek. "If you only knew! If you only knew!"

# CHAPTER ELEVEN

# Seventeen

"So who was the letter from today?" Katie asked Christy as the two of them were driving in Katie's car a few weeks later.

"Sara," Christy answered. "I found a card with the meaning of her name on it and sent it a few days after camp. Sara means 'Princess.' She said in her letter she put the card on the wall above her bed."

Christy glanced at Katie and could tell by the way her jaw was twitching that she was clenching her teeth. Whenever Katie held something inside, her cheek would ripple in tiny spasms.

"Is it still hard on you that I got to go to camp and you didn't?" Christy asked cautiously.

The last time she had brought up the subject, Katie had cried.

"It's getting better. I'm glad all your campers are writing to you. Sounds like they really love you a lot," Katie said. "I hope someday my turn will come to be a camp counselor. I know it sounds crazy, but that's a major goal for me."

"It doesn't sound like a crazy goal, Katie. Maybe next year. I can't help but think God will honor your heart's desire. Especially since you honored Him by abiding by your parents' wishes this year."

Katie shook her head and changed lanes as they neared Newport Beach. "Now Christy, you know God doesn't work in such predictable patterns. But doesn't it seem ridiculous the way my parents see things? I mean, here we are, driving alone in my car an hour and a half to Newport Beach to stay for the weekend, and they didn't even ask where I was staying, for a phone number, or anything. Yet when I wanted to go to camp, they said 'no' simply because it was associated with the church. They said they didn't want me to get too involved with religious people. Why are they like that?"

"Maybe they've seen too many weird things that have been labeled a church-thing even though Christianity had nothing to do with it," Christy suggested. "Think of all the horrible stuff on the news, and then they show some murderer who says God told him to do it. I think a lot of people have the wrong idea of what a true Christian is."

"I guess you're right. Now I understand why Doug said they named their group the 'God-Lovers.'"

"I think you're right," Christy said. "I heard him say once that his main goal in life is to love God. That must be how he came up with the name. By the way, let's be sure to call him right when we get to my aunt and uncle's to tell him we'll be there all weekend. I told Todd we were coming, but I don't know if he told Doug."

"I told Doug," Katie said.

"You did? When?"

"Oh, last week sometime. I just happened to be talking to him. What time is it?"

"You didn't tell me," Christy said, her curiosity aroused. "Did you call him, or did he call you?"

"Does it matter?"

"Maybe."

"Okay, I called him. There's no law against calling a guy, is there? Do you know what time it is?"

Christy checked her watch and smiled at her defensive friend. "It's 1:15, and no, there's not a thing wrong with it. I kind of like the idea of you and Doug together."

"Really?"

"He's a great guy, and I think you two make a cute couple."

"Now that I'm over Rick," Katie added. "Which, I might say, didn't take very long."

A smile crept onto Christy's face. She kept her thoughts to herself, but soon realized her best friend could read her mind anyway.

"I know what you're thinking," Katie said. "And you're right. Rick was one of those phases we all have to go through while we're growing up. Now that I have that out of the way, I'm ready for a real relationship."

"With someone by the name of Doug, perhaps?"

"Perhaps."

"You have my blessing on that one," Christy said. "So our plan is to get there, call Doug and Todd, and set up something for the four of us to do tonight."

Now it was Katie's turn to smile and keep her thoughts to herself. Only this time Christy couldn't read her best friend's mind. Katie kept a shadow of a smile on her face all the way to Uncle Bob and Aunt Marti's. But she began to act jittery when they arrived.

"We'll get our stuff out of the trunk later," Katie stated, looking down the street as they shut the car doors and started up the walk to Bob and Marti's luxurious beachfront house.

"What are you looking for?" Christy asked.

"Who, me? Nothing." Katie laughed when she said it. A nervous laugh that made Christy think maybe Katie was hoping to see Doug's truck already there.

"I'll ring the doorbell," Katie said, skipping a few steps ahead of Christy and pressing the doorbell three times. She looked over her shoulder again and smiled at Christy.

No one came to the door.

"We could just walk in," Christy suggested. "This *is* my aunt and uncle's house, you know. Come on."

"No, wait," Katie said, grabbing her arm. "I'd feel better if we waited for them to answer the door."

Again Katie pressed the buzzer. Ring, ring, ring. It was as if she were trying to signal in some kind of secret code.

Christy heard the rush of feet running up behind her. Before she could turn around, someone covered her head with a pillowcase and grabbed her hands behind her back.

She screamed and kicked her left foot into the blackness. "What's going on, Katie?"

"You're coming with us," a deep, gruff voice behind her said.

She could tell by the grip that a guy held her hands. Her heart was pounding from the surprise of it all, but she wasn't really afraid. This kidnapping had all the marks of something Katie had cooked up.

The guy led her down the front steps and what seemed to be over toward Bob's garage. She heard the garage door open and a truck engine start up. Katie was whispering something about "in the back."

Next thing Christy knew, she was being hoisted into the back of what she imagined to be Doug's truck, with the mysterious guy next to her holding her hands to keep her from removing the pillowcase. The truck backed out of the driveway with a bump and sped down the street at what seemed to be an alarming speed.

"Where are we going?"

"You'll find out," the gruff voice said.

The truck turned a corner so quickly, Christy thought she might fall over. Then came another quick turn and another. She had no idea where they were. Another fast turn caused her to lean against her captor. Before she could balance herself back to a sitting position, they flew over another bump and came to an abrupt halt.

"Get out," the voice ordered.

For the first time, she felt frightened. She had been so sure the kidnapping was something Katie had arranged for her birthday, which was in two days. But she was all turned around and had no idea where she was. She felt panicky.

The guy practically lifted her out of the back of the truck. Christy could feel another hand on her upper arm, helping her down.

"Okay, you guys," she said with a nervous laugh. "This is all real funny." She tried in vain to peer through the weave on the pillowcase.

Her escort led her in a circle on what felt like asphalt beneath her feet. Then he directed her to take one step up, then one step down, then a few steps to the right. Christy could hear the ocean, so she knew they couldn't be far from her aunt and uncle's house. But where? Who was holding her hands and directing her to walk forward with baby steps? It didn't feel like Todd. Doug, maybe? But then who was driving the truck?

They went a few more steps, and Christy thought she smelled her uncle's after-shave. "Uncle Bob, I can smell you," she blurted out.

Christy heard Katie's squelched giggle, but no one else made a sound. At first she thought it was just her guide and Katie. Now it seemed more people were around her, watching her, trying to muffle their footsteps. How many more? And where was she?

"This way," the gruff voice directed, urging her to the right. "Up two steps."

She knew her feet were now on cement. She felt a strong ocean breeze, and she could hear the roar of the waves. Christy was certain more people were around her. She could hear whispers and feet shuffling. Through the dense pillowcase she thought she smelled the scent of matches.

Another step forward, and she felt something light and buoyant brush across the left side of her head. It was a strange sensation. A strong urge came to bat at it, but her hands were still held firmly. Christy managed to catch a peek of gray cement at her feet when she looked down through the opening of the pillowcase.

*Where am I?*

With an unexpected yank, the pillowcase came off her head, her hands were released, and a loud blast of "Surprise!" nearly knocked her off her feet.

A crowd of all her beach friends stood before her on Uncle Bob and Aunt Marti's wildly decorated patio, singing "Happy Birthday" and beaming over their big surprise.

Todd held out a huge birthday cake. It was loaded with pink frosting roses and seventeen lit candles. Todd's silver-blue eyes met hers as the song ended.

With a smile he said, "Go ahead, Kilikina. Make a wish."

Catching her breath, Christy stared at the cake. A tiny little runner in her brain took off sprinting for her "wish" file and pulled out the first thing it found there. Then the runner dashed back from the file to present her with her wish.

*I wish I could go to Europe*, she thought, and she blew out the candles with one big puff.

Everyone clapped. Todd set the cake down on the patio table, where Aunt Marti set to work cutting slices and invited the guests to scoop their choice of ice cream.

Christy laughed with her friends as they chattered about how shocked she looked when they took off the pillowcase.

"I want to know who put that thing on my head," Christy said.

"Me," Doug admitted. "You and Katie came too early, and your aunt told us to think of some way to stall you."

"We had to drive you around the block," Bob added. "Hope you weren't too shaken by the experience."

"I figured it was you guys, of course," Christy said, looking at Doug. "But I couldn't imagine what was going on or where we were."

"Your uncle drove my truck," Doug said. "Can't say he's the smoothest person I've ever met when it comes to shifting gears."

Katie handed Christy a huge piece of cake with a mound of chocolate chip ice cream smashed into the pink rose on top. "Did we surprise you?"

"Slightly! When did you plan all this?"

"Your aunt called me last week, and we put our heads to-gether. That's why I acted so casual when you invited me to come here for the weekend. I kept the secret pretty well, don't you think?"

"No kidding! I had no idea. Thanks, Katie. I was definitely surprised."

"That's for later," Katie said, pointing up.

Christy looked up at the pink pig piñata strung from the slat-ted wood covering over the patio. She noticed the whole patio was laced in crepe-paper streamers and dozens of bright-colored balloons. It kind of looked as though a five-year-old was having a party, but she liked it. She knew her aunt had thrown herself into making the party a success.

All of Christy's beach friends were there: Heather, Tracy, Brian, Leslie, Doug, Todd, and a few others. But Christy glanced around and noticed Rick wasn't anywhere in sight.

"Everyone," Marti called out, waving her hands above her head to get their attention. Being petite was not an advantage to her at this moment. Her best advantage was that she had managed to keep a youthful flair about herself.

"As soon as you're finished with your cake and ice cream, there's a trash can over in the corner. The ice chests in both corners are filled with cold drinks anytime you want one this afternoon. Bob and Todd are going to set up the volleyball net, aren't you, boys?"

Bob gave Marti a playful salute. "One volleyball net coming up."

"We'll open gifts after the barbecue tonight," Marti continued. "And this sliding door will be open all afternoon, if you need to come in to change or anything. Now all of you have fun on the beach and remember to use your sunscreen."

"I'll get our stuff out of the car," Katie told Christy. "Are you still surprised?"

"I think I'll be in shock for the rest of the day!"

Katie smiled and said, "Good." As she turned to go, her copper-colored hair swished like an oriental fan whispering open.

Christy couldn't finish her humongous piece of cake and asked Todd if he wanted the rest of it. He held up his hand and shook his head.

"Try Doug," he suggested. "He has a higher tolerance for

pink sugar roses than I do."

"Todd," Bob called out from the sand a few yards away, "are you going to help me with this?"

"Sure," Todd called back. Then giving Christy a squeeze on the elbow, he said, "See you on the beach."

It took Christy and Katie only ten minutes to change into their bathing suits and cover-ups in the guest room and scamper down the stairs to join the group.

As they stepped out onto the sand, Christy said, "I notice Rick isn't here."

"Is that a problem?" Katie said.

"I don't know, is it?"

Katie stopped, her feet burrowing down in search of cooler sand. "What is that supposed to mean?"

"Did you not invite Rick because of how things turned out between you two? I mean, he's close friends with Doug and Todd. He's going to hear about the party."

"I asked Doug to call him," Katie explained. "I didn't want to talk to him. He told Doug he might show up later in the day. We planned this to be a day-long party, in case you hadn't figured that out. Your aunt is the ultimate party woman. She bought steaks for everyone for the barbecue and stuff for s'mores around the campfire. She rented a stack of movies in case anyone wants to stay up for a marathon movie night. I'm not going to hold my breath, but Rick might show up later. If he does, I promise to be civil to him."

"Okay, that makes me feel better. As long as you invited him, that's the main thing. What he does with the invitation is his choice. I just don't want him to feel shut out."

"Don't worry. I may not cherish the thought that I once was somewhat interested in Rick—," Katie said.

Christy interrupted with a roll of her eyes at Katie's understatement.

"But I have a good teacher showing me how to be friends with a guy after the crush is over."

"Who, me?" Christy said.

"No, the Little Mermaid," Katie teased. "Of course you."

Christy thought back to what a great teacher Jessica had been to her at camp, and she said, "You know, I think once we figure out what real love is, it becomes clear we can never love a person too much."

Katie looked thoughtful. Then tilting her head, she looked at Christy and said, "Is this what happens when you're about to turn seventeen? Your mind fills with deep ponderings, and you can suddenly explain the meaning of life to the rest of the world?"

Before Christy could answer, a bright orange volleyball flew through the air, bopping Katie on the top of her head.

"Hey!" Katie called out, spinning around, scooping up the ball and looking to see who threw it.

"Over here!" Todd called. "You're on our team, Katie. You want to play, Christy?"

She hesitated. Christy had never been good at sports like Katie was. But this was her birthday party. She imagined a person should be able to overcome at least some of her self-consciousness by the time she turned seventeen.

"Sure," she hollered back at Todd. "Which team am I on?"

"I need you over here," Uncle Bob said.

For the next hour, an intense game of volleyball ensued. Christy had a lot of fun, even though she didn't get the ball over the net too many times. Doug, Bob, and two of the other girls on her team made up for Christy's less-than-stellar performance. In the end, Todd and Katie's team won.

Todd somehow came up with the idea that the winning team should throw its opponents into the ocean. Before Christy realized what was happening, Todd single-handedly wrestled her down to the shore with a little-boy grin plastered all over his face.

Christy screamed and wiggled, but Todd held her arm tight. Just when her feet touched the cool, foamy part of the wave at the shoreline, she thought she had a chance to make a break for it. That's when Doug rushed up behind them.

"Yahoo!" Doug screeched, wrapping his gorilla-length arms around both Todd and Christy and taking them with him on his kamikaze plunge into the wave.

The three friends came up for air, laughing, dripping, and splashing each other. Doug dove under the water and grabbed Christy's ankle. She pulled away and surprised Doug with a splash of water in his face when he surfaced. Another wave crashed on them, tumbling them all to the shore.

Christy stood in the wet sand, still laughing and wringing the salt water from her oversized T-shirt, which now clung to her.

"Ready for another dip?" Doug asked.

"Maybe after I get the sand out of my ears," Christy said. "But I noticed Katie looking awfully relaxed over there." She pointed to Katie, who was lying stomach-down on her beach towel.

"Say no more," Doug said.

He and Todd charged through the sand, startling Katie from her rest. Within minutes they had pulled their three-point plunge maneuver into the ocean.

Christy retreated to Katie's now-vacant towel next to Tracy and Heather and tried to dry off.

*I guess some things never change*, she thought, remembering summers past on this same beach when she and these girls had watched Todd and Doug perfect their "throw the screaming girl into the ocean" routine.

Christy stretched out her long legs on the towel and felt the hot July sun drying up all the salty beads on her legs. Planting the palms of her hands behind her in the sand, Christy gazed out at the shimmering blue ocean. Katie's red hair popped up from under a wave. Next came Doug with his contagious laugh dancing toward her on the ocean breeze.

Todd, like a playful dolphin, rode the next wave to the shore. Then emerging from the water, he tilted his head back and shook his sun-bleached blonde hair so that all the droplets raced down his back. Christy had watched Todd shake his hair that way many times, but this was the first time she noticed what a distinct Todd-thing it was.

*I'm glad some things don't change. I wish I could be this age, on the beach, with these friends, for the next fifty years. I don't want things to change. Ever.*

Christy realized she was wishing almost the opposite of everything she had wished before. For years she had wished things would be different, especially that her relationship with Todd would change and move forward. Now she wanted it all to stop and stand still so she could observe and enjoy every little pinch of her life.

She knew the empty feeling when a camp romance ends. She knew the heady pleasure of dating a guy like Rick. And she knew the exquisite treasure of Todd's forever friendship.

Christy tilted her head back and felt the sun kissing her face and neck. She remembered Todd's blessing that she had passed on to Jeanine: "May the Lord make His face to shine upon you and give you His peace."

At this moment, Christy knew His forever peace. She felt His face shining upon her. With her eyes closed and a smile tiptoeing onto her lips, Christy silently made seventeen wishes. And all of them started with Todd.

# Don't Miss These Captivating Stories in
## THE CHRISTY MILLER SERIES

# THE SIERRA JENSEN SERIES

If you've enjoyed reading about Christy Miller,
you'll love reading about Christy's friend Sierra Jensen.

**#1 • Only You, Sierra**
When her family moves to another state, Sierra dreads going to a new high school—until she meets Paul.

**#2 • In Your Dreams**
Just when events in Sierra's life start to look up—she even gets asked out on a date—Sierra runs into Paul.

**#3 • Don't You Wish**
Sierra is excited about visiting Christy Miller in California during Easter break. Unfortunately, her sister, Tawni, decides to go with her.

**#4 • Close Your Eyes**
Sierra experiences a sticky situation when Paul comes over for dinner and Randy shows up at the same time.

**#5 • Without A Doubt**
When handsome Drake reveals his interest in Sierra, life gets complicated.

**#6 • With This Ring**
Sierra couldn't be happier when she goes to Southern California to join Christy Miller and their friends for Doug and Tracy's wedding.

**#7 • Open Your Heart**
When Sierra's friend Christy Miller receives a scholarship from a university in Switzerland, she invites Sierra to go with her and Aunt Marti to visit the school.

**#8 • Time Will Tell**
After an exciting summer in Southern California and Switzerland, Sierra returns home to several unsettled relationships.

**#9 • Now Picture This**
When Sierra and Paul start corresponding, she imagines him as her boyfriend and soon begins neglecting her family and friends.

**#10 • Hold On Tight**
Sierra joins her brother and several friends on a road trip to Southern California to visit potential colleges.

**#11 • Closer Than Ever**
When Paul doesn't show up for her graduation party and news comes that a flight from London has crashed, Sierra frantically worries about the future.

**#12 • Take My Hand**
A costly misunderstanding leaves Sierra anxious as she says goodbye to Portland and heads off to California for her freshman year of college.

# A Time to Cherish

# A Time to Cherish

## ROBIN JONES GUNN

**BETHANY HOUSE PUBLISHERS**
MINNEAPOLIS, MINNESOTA 55438

A Focus on the Family book published by
Bethany House Publishers
A Ministry of Bethany Fellowship International
11400 Hampshire Avenue South
Minneapolis, Minnesota 55438
www.bethanyhouse.com

Printed in the United States of America by
Bethany Press International, Minneapolis, Minnesota 55438

ISBN 1–56179–731–6

99 00 01 02 03 04 05 / 15 14 13 12 11 10 9 8 7 6 5 4 3 2

# Contents

# CHAPTER ONE

# *No Guarantees*

Christy Miller suddenly woke up. She kicked the heavy sleeping bag off her sweaty legs and squinted her eyes in the darkness, trying to remember where she was. Her bed seemed to tilt back and forth with a gentle roll.

Then Christy remembered. She was on a houseboat: Aunt Marti's idea of a Farewell to Summer party over the Labor Day weekend.

She could hear her best friend, Katie, gently snoring across the cabin. Christy pulled on her sweats and placed her bare feet on the cool floor. Padding her way to the boat's front deck, she closed the sliding glass door behind her and drew in a deep breath of fresh morning air.

The sky had not quite awakened but seemed to be slowly rising, rubbing the thin, pink-cloud "sleepers" from its eyes and checking its reflection in the still lake-mirror.

The day promised to be perfect. She could smell it in the sweet breeze rising off the water. Just then something splashed in the water. She quickly figured out it must be either Todd or Doug. The two of them had slept under the stars on the houseboat's roof.

Soon Todd's white-blond head popped up out of the water. He didn't notice Christy watching him and kept swimming with quiet, easy strokes. Turning to float on his back, he spoke into the dawn.

"O Lord, our Lord, how majestic is Your name in all the earth! You have set Your glory above the heavens!"

Christy couldn't help but smile. That was so like Todd.

She moved closer to the railing, wondering if she should interrupt Todd's conversation with God. On her last step, her foot tagged the corner of a folded-up beach chair, causing it to tip over and clatter loudly. Todd spun around in the water and began to swim back toward the houseboat.

Christy quickly smoothed back her nutmeg brown hair and tried to tuck the wild ends into her loose braid. *I probably look awful! Groggy, to say the least.*

Then she realized this was Todd, and he had never been the kind of guy to judge anyone by outward appearances. Hopefully he would keep that in mind when he saw her fresh from her sleeping bag.

Todd grabbed onto one of the ropes hanging from the front of the houseboat and pulled himself up the steps onto the deck.

"Hi," Christy whispered shyly. "How's the water?"

Todd smiled and reached for a beach towel on the railing. His silver-blue eyes met Christy's, and he whispered back, "You want to find out?"

"Not really."

"Not even a little cold shower?" Todd asked, shaking his hair in front of her like a dog.

"Okay, okay," Christy said with a giggle, holding up her hands in defense. "You convinced me; it's cold!"

"Refreshing," Todd corrected her, slipping a navy blue

hooded sweatshirt over his head and sticking his hands in the front pocket. "You the only one up?"

Christy nodded. "I think so."

"It was a long ride here yesterday," Todd reasoned. "They'll probably all sleep in. What got you up this early?"

"I was burning up in my sleeping bag. It must be designed for subzero temperatures."

"I know the perfect way to cool you off. Let's go for a spin around the lake."

"In what?" Christy asked. "If we start up the ski boat, we'll wake everyone."

"Then we'll take the raft," Todd said, pulling the big, yellow inflated monster from the side of the houseboat. He dropped it into the water. "Ladies first."

Christy went through all her mental resistance in record time. Would they get in trouble for going out like this without telling anyone? No, Bob and Marti trusted Todd. What if she got her sweats wet? So what? She could change into something dry when they came back. Unable to think of a reason why she shouldn't go, Christy lowered herself into the wobbly raft.

Todd grabbed two paddles, put up the hood on his sweatshirt, and with the beach towel wrapped around his wet swim trunks, joined Christy. They silently paddled away from the cove and headed for the open part of the lake.

One look at Todd's face and Christy knew he thought this was an adventure. Todd thrived on adventure. His lifelong ambition was to become a missionary and live in the jungle.

Christy liked adventure, too. At least the little bit she had experienced in her seventeen years. But she wasn't sure how she felt about spending the rest of her life in the jungle. Maybe if she had one of those butane curling irons that didn't need to be plugged in.

"Isn't it beautiful?" Todd asked, looking up at the awakening sky. He pointed to a trail of puffy white clouds stomping across the seamless blue. "The clouds are the dust beneath His feet."

Christy smiled at Todd's poetic flair. He looked like a monk with the hood covering his head. "Did you just make that up?" Christy asked.

"No," Todd confessed. "An Old Testament prophet did. Nahum, to be exact. I always think of that verse when I see clouds that look as though God just went for a morning stroll across the face of the earth."

Christy knew the look in Todd's eyes. She had seen it many times during the two years she had known him. Two years filled with more ups and downs than an elevator. Yet one thing had never changed: Todd's love for God. More than once Christy had wished Todd would become even one-tenth as committed to her as he was to God.

It wasn't that she didn't love God, too. She did. She had promised her heart to the Lord more than two years ago and had grown a lot as a Christian since then. But all Todd had ever promised her was that they would be friends forever. What did that mean?

Next week she would begin her senior year in high school, and Todd was now a sophomore in college. How old did a guy have to be before he made a substantial promise to a girl?

"You know what this reminds me of?" Todd asked. "That morning on the beach."

"You mean Christmas morning a couple of years ago when we made breakfast and the sea gulls scarfed it all?" Christy said.

Todd smiled. "I almost forgot about that. No, I mean that

morning last year. Remember? We just happened to meet on the beach in the fog.''

A knot tightened in Christy's stomach. That was not a morning she liked to remember. ''And here we are,'' she said, ignoring the knot, ''out together again at the break of day. Only this time you're not telling me you're going off to Hawaii indefinitely to surf.'' Christy hesitated. ''Or are you?''

''Nope,'' Todd said, putting down his paddle and letting the raft float. He propped his hands behind his head and leaned back against the pudgy side of the raft. ''And you're not trying to give me back your ID bracelet, either.''

Christy glanced down at the gold bracelet on her right wrist. The engraved word ''Forever'' glinted in the rising sun. ''I wanted you to be free to go to Hawaii and not feel obligated to me.''

''And I wanted you to be free to date Rick and not feel like I was holding you back,'' Todd countered.

Christy sighed. ''I wish now that you had held me back. I don't have pleasant memories of dating Rick.''

''Had to be your own choice,'' Todd said. ''No one else could make that decision for you. That would be robbing you of who you are. There's great value in everything that happened. You just have to look for it.''

Christy leaned back and felt the sun warming the left side of her face. She thought hard about Rick and his overpowering ways, wondering what possible great value had come out of their relationship. Maybe going with Rick had taught her more about the kind of guy she *did* want to be with. Now, more than ever, Todd was definitely that guy.

''What would you like from me, Christy?'' Todd suddenly asked, as if he had been reading her thoughts.

''What do you mean?''

"You want more of a commitment than what we have now, don't you?"

Christy felt her cheeks turn red—and not because of the sun. "Why do you say that?"

"Your aunt had a little talk with me on the way up yesterday when you were in the truck with Katie and Doug. She told me that if I didn't stake my claim soon, you'd take off with some other guy. She thinks it's time we officially start going together, let people know we're a couple."

Now Christy felt really embarrassed. Aunt Marti was always speaking her mind, but Todd never seemed to pay much attention to her. Why was he bringing all this up now?

"Todd, you know my aunt. That's her idea, not mine."

"Yeah, I know, that's what she said."

Christy shook her head. "Todd, I apologize—"

"No need. I would have let it go except Doug has been asking me about our relationship. I guess you know he's been wanting to go out with you for a long time."

"Doug?"

Todd nodded. "You mean you didn't know?"

"No. I was hoping he and Katie would get together."

Todd shrugged. For several long minutes it was quiet.

"So," Todd said, leaning forward and looking Christy in the eye, "I guess I'm feeling like we have to start making some decisions about us. What do you really think, Kilikina? Do you want more of a commitment from me?"

Christy always melted inside when Todd called her by her Hawaiian name. For a long time she had wished he would ask her this kind of question. But she hadn't expected it. Not here. Not this morning. If it weren't for her bare feet being nearly numb from the puddle of cool water in the raft, she would have thought she was still asleep, and all this was a romantic dream.

"I don't know," she said, surprised to hear such a wishy-washy answer pop out.

"Then tell me how you feel."

"About you?"

"About me, about us. I need to know what you're thinking and feeling."

"Well, I feel really good when I'm with you," Christy began. "Really comfortable. I miss you when I don't see you. I think about you all the time, and I pray for you every day. You make me feel closer to God, and I never feel pressured to try to be anything other than myself around you. I like you more than any other guy I've ever known."

A slow smile crept onto Todd's face. It was as if Christy's words were warming him from the inside out. She had never been able to tell him so clearly how she felt about him. It felt good to put her heart out there in the open. She had tried doing the same thing a year ago at their early morning encounter on the beach, but it obviously wasn't the right time. Todd wouldn't receive her words last year. This morning they made him glow.

"I feel the same way about you," Todd said. "It's been important to me all along that we take things slowly. I never wanted our relationship to grow too fast."

"Two years is not exactly too fast," Christy said with a teasing smile.

"Just about right, I'd say. That's the way it is with God, you know. He's always on time but rarely early."

Christy couldn't believe how smoothly this conversation was going. She and Todd didn't talk about their feelings very often. A hint of apprehension and excitement started to hedge in.

It was silent again as the morning ripples on the lake gently rocked their raft back and forth. Todd broke the quiet with a nervous chuckle. "I don't know how to say it. What's the term for us? Are we now officially 'going together' or what?"

"I don't know, are we?" Christy asked cautiously.

"That's what you want, isn't it?"

"Yes, I mean, if that's what you want."

"That's what I want," Todd said firmly. "I want to be your boyfriend, even though I hate using that term. You reflect what's in the heart. Something doesn't come from inside you simply because you speak it into being. If it's truly in your heart, it will come out in what you do."

Christy nodded. She knew exactly what Todd meant. Their relationship had always been beyond labels. Todd had consistently been true to his word to be her friend, no matter what happened.

"So now we're officially a couple," Todd said, squaring his broad shoulders and smiling so the dimple showed on his right cheek. "Do you feel any different?"

"No, not exactly."

"Neither do I. Maybe that's good. Maybe everything is still at the same level with us, only now we have an answer to give everyone else. We're going together."

Christy liked the sound of Todd's deep voice saying, "We're going together." She loved the feeling of being more secure in their relationship.

"I'm glad," she told him softly.

"Me too," Todd said, then tenderly added, "You are an incredible person, Kilikina. I hold you in my heart. You are the only girl I've ever kissed. I haven't been the same since that night right after we met and I followed you out to the jetty when you left Shawn's party."

"I felt like such a baby that night," Christy remembered. "Everyone was drinking, and I was so naive!"

"You were innocent, Christy. You have no idea how beautiful that made you."

Christy felt like crying. "Todd, I . . ." She didn't know how to put into words everything she felt right then. "I'm really glad, I mean, this is so . . . I don't know. It's so *right*. I'm really happy we're moving our relationship forward."

Just then the roar from a ski boat engine broke their magical moment. Todd squinted and then started to wave at the boat. "It's Doug and Katie. I bet he's ready to start some serious water skiing!"

Doug cut the engine on the boat and slowly drifted toward the raft. "Ahoy, mates!" he called out. Doug wore a bandana "pirate style" around his short, sandy blond hair. The broad smile that spread across his face showed he was in his typically great mood. "Would ye be needin' a hoist back to the cove before ye find yourselves shipwrecked?"

Todd turned to Christy and said, "That wouldn't be so bad, would it?"

"Which?" Christy asked. "Being hoisted back to shore or being shipwrecked?"

Todd didn't answer, and for a moment the two of them locked gazes, their eyes revealing a thousand secrets of the heart.

"I think we're interrupting something," Katie said, her red hair swishing as she looked at Christy and Todd and then at Doug. She held up an orange flag used to indicate a downed skier in the water. Waving it like a fairy wand, she asked, "Tell us, you two, what did we miss out on this morning? Anything you'd like to share with the rest of us?"

Christy felt herself blushing again and wondered how old she would be before she outgrew this reflex.

"We've been checking out the dust of God's feet," Todd answered. "And making some promises," he added in a whisper loud enough for only Christy to hear.

"So how about us making some of our own wave-dust?" Doug asked. "You ready to break up some of this glass?"

"Wait! We want you to tow us first," Katie yelled. "Let me get in the raft with Christy, and you guys can tow us back to the houseboat."

"As long as you promise to go *slow!*" Christy said.

Doug threw out a long rope for Todd to secure the raft to the back of the boat while Katie made the transfer from boat to raft. Todd climbed up the stepladder by the rudder and tightened the knot on the rope.

"Okay, here are the signals," Todd said. "Thumbs up means go faster. A finger across your throat like this means stop, and a thumb down means slow down."

Christy put her thumb down. "I mean it, you guys, go slow!"

"You'd better find something to hold on to," Todd called from the boat. He tossed two orange life vests into the raft and instructed them to put them on.

Christy fastened the vest over her sweats and grabbed onto a black handle on the side of the raft. "Whose idea was this anyway?"

"Mine," Katie said without regret. Then looking into Christy's blue-green eyes, Katie said, "What?"

"What, what?" Christy repeated back to her.

"What's up with you?"

"What do you mean?"

Katie put her hand on her hip, tilted her head, and examined her best friend's expression. "I was right. There was something going on between you two this morning. You have a secret, Christina Juliet Miller, don't you?"

Christy didn't answer with words, but the smile skipping across her lips gave it all away.

"I knew it!" Katie cried loud enough to awaken any lazy fish who weren't up yet. "Don't tell me; let me guess. You and Todd are finally going together! Am I right?"

Christy looked up into the boat, hoping to see Todd's assuring grin. Instead, she saw Doug's usually smiling face transformed into a grim frown.

Just then Doug started up the boat with a roar. The rope pulled tight, and the raft lurched in the water.

Christy let out a scream and yelled, "Go slow!"

Doug jammed the ski boat into high. Their raft felt as if it suddenly became airborne. The girls held on, screaming and trying to motion the "slow down" and "stop" signals to the guys.

Doug turned to the right, and the raft flew over a wave and skittered outside the wake. Before they could get their balance, another, larger wave rushed up from underneath the raft, flipping the girls into the water.

Their life vests brought them bobbing up to the surface at the same time, and Katie and Christy began to tread water and hurl threats at the guys.

"Doug did that on purpose!" Katie said as the boat slowly motored in a circle to come back and retrieve them. "And I have several ideas of how we can get him back this weekend."

Even across the sparkling water, Christy could recognize the mischievous glint in the eyes of her red-haired friend.

"I leave all the revenge games to you," Christy said, aware of how heavy her soaked sweats had become as she kicked her legs in the water. "I don't want to start anything unless there's a guarantee I won't get hurt in the end.''

Katie tilted back her head and laughed. "It's too late for that!''

Christy was now next to Katie in the water. The guys threw them a rope.

"One dunk in the lake by Doug doesn't mean it's too late,'' Christy said.

"Oh, I didn't mean Doug,'' Katie answered. "I meant with Todd. Something happened with you two this morning. I can tell. And whatever it was, I have a feeling it's too late for any kind of a guarantee you won't get hurt in the end.''

# CHAPTER TWO

# Just Enjoy Today

When the foursome arrived back at the houseboat, Uncle Bob called to them from the window above the kitchen sink, "You're just in time for pancakes. Could you smell them out there on the lake?"

The guys docked the boat, and the soaked girls wrung out the bottoms of their shirts one more time before stepping onto the deck.

"The guys want to go back out skiing while it's still calm," Katie told Bob.

"No problem. Breakfast is served all morning long in my galley." He opened the sliding screen door and, taking a good look at Christy, asked, "Are you planning to enter some kind of contest for drowned rats that I didn't know about?"

"The only drowned rat contest around here," Katie informed him, "is going to involve two certain young pirates."

"Anybody we know?" Bob asked, his merry eyes twinkling. For a man in his fifties who had never had children of his own, Bob always seemed to enjoy Christy and her friends. His easygoing manner made him everyone's favorite adopted uncle. The only one who ever had run-ins with Bob was Aunt Marti, but then, she had tiffs with everyone at one point or another.

"Come on, Katie!" Doug called out from the boat. "We need you to come with us to hold the flag."

"My public beckons me," Katie said, dramatically placing the back of her hand against her forehead. "Oh, the price of popularity!"

Christy giggled at her fun-loving friend. "Go answer your call, Katie. I shall stay behind to put on dry clothes and stuff my face with pancakes. Do you want a dry T-shirt?"

"Not a bad idea. Throw me a towel, too."

As soon as the boat left with Katie vigorously waving the flag in a playful farewell, Christy changed into her bathing suit and a big T-shirt. Undoing her matted braid, she joined Bob in the kitchen and began to brush out her soaked hair. The excess water dripped onto the floor as she flipped her hair down so she could brush it from the underside.

"Gorgeous day," Bob said, scooping another round of sourdough blueberry pancakes onto the already heaping platter. "Couldn't have asked for better weather."

"Good morning, all!" Aunt Marti called out, opening the door to their back bedroom.

Just then Christy flipped her long hair over to hang down her back. Beads of water, launched from the ends of her hair, flew across the small kitchen and, as if they had been directed at Marti, all hit the target.

"Oh, stop that this instant!" Marti said with a squeal.

Christy turned to see her petite aunt adorned in a perky little sailor shirt with sprinkles of water all over it. Even her perfectly styled short, dark hair now had moisture clinging to the bangs. "I'm so sorry, Aunt Marti. I didn't mean to do that."

"It's all right," Bob said, jumping in with a towel for his indignant wife. "Just a little morning wake-up for you, Martha. I hear it works better than a cup of coffee."

"I was already awake, thank you," Marti replied stiffly, snatching the towel from Bob's hands. Scanning the room, she asked, "Where are the boys?"

"Out skiing with Katie," Bob said.

Marti's expression changed. It seemed she wasn't quite as upset once she realized her only audience had been Bob and Christy.

Giving her flawless makeup one more pat with the towel, Marti turned to Christy with a scowl and said, "You might consider doing your hair in the bathroom for the remainder of the trip."

"I will. And I'm sorry. I didn't see you."

Bob handed Marti a mug of coffee and said, "Vanilla hazelnut, your favorite. Are you ready for some breakfast?"

Marti accepted the peace offering and sat down at the table. Christy sat across from her and helped herself to three steaming pancakes.

"These sure smell good," she said, hoping Marti's sour mood would pass quickly, especially before Christy's friends returned. She had seen many of Marti's moods come and go over the years, and she knew a lot of it was just her aunt's personality. Still, Christy couldn't help but feel grinding guilt in the pit of her stomach, as if she were responsible for whether or not Marti was in a good mood.

"It was a beautiful sunrise this morning," Christy said, hoping to get the conversation moving. "Are you going to eat with us, Uncle Bob?"

He looked at the three pancakes browning in the skillet and, turning off the burner, said, "Sure. I suppose we have enough to get us started here." Bob plopped the hotcakes onto his plate and slid into a chair at the head of the table.

"Would you guys mind if we prayed?" Christy asked. She had been through this a number of times, since her aunt and uncle weren't the pray-before-meals kind of people. Christy had decided she wouldn't give up praying around them just because they didn't normally do it.

Bob and Marti exchanged glances before respectfully bowing their heads. Christy prayed aloud, thanking God for their safe trip, for the beautiful day, for the food and then for Katie, the guys, Bob, and Marti. When she looked up after saying "Amen," Marti already had her head up and was glaring at her.

"A person's food could go cold waiting for you to pray your blessings on the world," Marti said.

Obviously she hadn't snapped out of her bad mood yet. Christy decided it would be best not to say anything for a while and set to work cutting her pancakes.

"How you can eat like that and stay slim is beyond my understanding," Marti said, sipping her coffee, which apparently would be her entire breakfast. "I hope you're working on your thighs like I told you. It has always been a problem for the women in our family, and you can see how your mother's thighs have succumbed to heredity. Make sure you don't sit back and let the same thing happen to you."

Christy put a large bite of pancake in her mouth and enjoyed it thoroughly before saying, "Actually, Aunt Marti, I think my mother is just fine the way she is, and I think I'm fine just the way I am. As long as a person is healthy, I don't think it should matter what their body shape is."

"You may not care, but men certainly care. Keep that in mind if you think you're going to attract a young man simply because you're 'healthy.' "

"I don't have to worry about attracting young men," Christy said under her breath. She knew better than to drop hints to her aunt. Especially hints about Todd. Especially if she wanted it to remain a secret. Still, the news that she and Todd were now going together would probably snap Marti out of her critical mood.

"What did you say, Christina? I couldn't hear you."

Christy put down her fork and took a deep breath. "I guess you both would be interested to know that Todd and I had a talk about our relationship this morning, and—"

Marti clasped her hands together and said, "I knew it! I knew he'd take my . . . I mean that Todd would take the initiative to cement your relationship. This is wonderful, Christy!"

"Well, nothing is really different except maybe that we've defined things."

"So now you two are promised to each other. This is wonderful!" Marti's whole countenance had changed from gloom to sunshine.

"We're not 'promised,' " Christy corrected her. "We're 'going together.' That's how Todd phrased it."

"This is absolutely perfect," Marti said triumphantly. "You're going steady! That is the first step, and for you two, it's definitely the next step." She pushed away her coffee cup and leaned across the table to give Christy her insights. "A steady boyfriend your senior year will make things so much easier for you. Football games, Christmas banquets, the prom—you'll never have to worry about having a date. When you graduate, Todd will have two more years of college, and you two should attend the same university during that time. I prefer something close to home. Perhaps Irvine or UCLA. You can get married the summer after your sophomore year since Todd will be graduated. Then, while you finish your last two years, Todd can complete his master's. It's just perfect!"

Christy couldn't help but laugh. "You have it all figured out, don't you? But what if that's not what God wants?"

Marti looked surprised. "Why wouldn't it be? Doesn't God want the best for you? I think even God would have to agree that Todd is the best for you."

Christy laughed again at her aunt's theology. "I think God gives His best to those who leave the choice up to Him."

Marti processed that thought for a minute and was about to counter with a comment when Bob spoke up. "Just enjoy today, Christy. None of us knows what the future holds. You need to live for today and let everything come as it will."

"There's certainly nothing wrong in planning for the future," Marti said. "If Christy doesn't think through these important steps now, she might make some terrible mistakes she'll regret the rest of her life."

"But she doesn't need to make all of those choices today," Bob said softly. Turning back toward Christy, he reached for her hand, gave it a squeeze, and said, "We're real happy for you, Bright Eyes. Todd's a lucky guy to have a young lady like you in his life. I'll make sure he realizes how lucky he is."

"And you make sure you're always worthy of him," Marti advised. "There aren't many like him left in this world."

"I know," Christy said, feeling her heart warming at the thought of Todd.

But in the back corner of Christy's mind, Katie's words of warning hung like a small, gray storm cloud heading her direction. Christy brushed the thought away. What did Katie know about relationships, anyway? She had never even had a boyfriend. Maybe all that would change this weekend, if Doug would only notice what a treasure Katie was.

"More pancakes?" Bob offered.

"Not for me," Christy said. "They were sure good. I imagine the guys will put away what's left."

Christy's prediction was correct. Todd ate at least fourteen pancakes, and she lost count with Doug somewhere after twenty-three. Katie kept up until the guys hit the double digits.

"These are the best pancakes I've ever had," Katie said, wiping her mouth. "They must be loaded with sugar for me to like them so much. Sugar is one of my four basic food groups, you know."

"You kids think you're ready for some more water fun?" Bob asked. "I'm ready to take the boat out for a bit. Anyone want to go with me?"

All four of them eagerly took Bob up on the offer. When Christy climbed into the boat, she sat in the first available seat, which happened to be next to Doug. As soon as she sat down, Doug popped up. Without looking at Christy, he said, "I imagine you'd rather sit by Todd. I'll move."

*What's wrong with him? He wouldn't look at me during breakfast, either. He's acting pretty immature for a college student. Just because Katie announced Todd and I are going together, doesn't mean Doug and I can't still be close friends.*

Todd was the last one to board, and he took the empty seat next to Christy. "You want to get some skiing in first, Bob? Doug or I would be glad to drive if you do."

"You guys go ahead. I'd like to get a feel for the lake first. Who's up? Doug?"

"Sure, I'll go. I'm ready to try one ski this time," Doug said. He buckled up his life vest, and when Bob stopped the boat in the deeper water, Doug jumped into the lake. It took him only a few minutes to secure both feet in the one ski and get into position. "Okay, hit it!" he yelled, and Bob obliged by charging the boat through the blue water. Doug got right up and balanced on the ski as if he had done it a hundred times before.

"Are you sure he's never gone on one ski before?" Katie asked. "Look at him; he looks like a pro!"

Doug appeared to become braver as he slid from side to side behind the boat, each time bouncing over the curling wake. Bob zipped around the lake more aggressively when he saw how well Doug handled each twist and turn.

One sharp turn to the right brought them head-on with the wake of a speed boat that had just passed. The impact of the water caused their boat to rise up and come down hard. For Doug, the crashing waves created behind the boat proved disastrous, and he took a big tumble.

"We should have had that one on camera," Katie exclaimed, lifting the flag high as Bob slowed way down and circled back to pick up Doug. "Wasn't he fantastic?" Then louder, so Doug could hear from his crouched position in the water, "You were fantastic, Doug! Wish I had a picture."

He waved to Katie, and it seemed to Christy that his cheerful disposition was returning. Once he climbed back in the boat, his laughter convinced Christy that whatever was bothering him had somehow been left behind during his successful skim across the lake. Shivering, smiling, and soaking wet, Doug bent over Katie and gave her one of his famous hugs before looking for his towel.

"There," he said, "now you're ready to get the rest of yourself wet and show us how *you* do on one ski."

"You eel!" Katie cried, shaking her arms to remove the wet. "I'll show you! I'll make your run look like a cartoon clip. Stand back, everyone. I'm a woman on a mission." Katie handed the flag to Christy, buckled up her life vest, and jumped into the water. "Throw me that ski, Mr. Big Shot. You're about to be humbled."

Clearly unafraid of anything requiring athletic ability, Katie tried three times to get up. Each time she lost her balance and surfaced to the roar of Doug's heckling. The fourth attempt proved to be the winner, and as soon as she gained her balance, Katie leaned back and confidently let go with one hand to wave to the crew.

"She's going to eat it big time," Doug said, his eyes glued on Katie's overly confident frame as she jumped over the wake and came down hard on the ski. She retained her balance. "I don't believe it! She's a maniac!"

Christy couldn't help but admire Katie. She was really good. Anything she ever attempted in the realm of sports came to her easily. It was the opposite for Christy. The worst part was knowing that some time during this weekend she would have to try water skiing. None of these guys would accept "I don't feel like it."

Her chance came all too soon. Katie showed off for a good ten minutes before she tried one daring stunt too many and crashed into the water. "You're next, Christy" were Katie's first words as she climbed back into the boat. "The water is warm. Really."

"I'll go in with her," Todd volunteered. "It's easier to figure out the right position the first time when you have someone in the water with you."

Now Christy knew she couldn't put off the inevitable. Not when Todd was willing to do all he could to help her. She fastened her life vest and, reaching for Todd's assuring hand, jumped into the water by his side.

"Brrr!" she called out as soon as she surfaced. "What do you mean the water is warm, Katie? It's freezing!"

"No it isn't," Katie called back. "You'll get used to it. Believe me, once your adrenaline kicks in, you won't feel a thing."

"Here you go," Todd said, holding the two skis in place above the water. "Put your arm around my shoulder and start with the right foot."

It was a clumsy sensation for Christy, trying to balance while buoyant and maneuvering a long water ski onto each foot. Todd patiently helped her get both skis on and instructed her to "sit" in the water with the tow rope wedged between the skis. "Keep both skis pointed up," he said. "Try to sort of sit on the back of them, and when the boat pulls you out of the water, lean back. Your natural reflex will be to let go when you feel the tug, but just hang on, point your toes toward the boat, and lean back."

Christy shivered and let out a bewildered sigh. "That's a lot to remember."

"You can do it. Relax. This is fun."

"It is?"

Todd laughed and started to swim back to the boat. Christy waited in the water, feeling uncomfortable with the life vest pushing up to her ears and her ankles bent at a weird angle in the skis.

Todd climbed in the boat and waved to her. "Are you ready?"

"I guess," Christy called out.

"Say 'hit it' when you're ready," Katie informed her.

She didn't feel ready. Still, she truly wanted to do this. She would love to frolic over the waves like Katie had.

With a quick mental review of all she was supposed to do, Christy yelled, "Hit it, but go slow!"

The "go slow" part was lost in the roar of the motor starting up, and as soon as the taut tow rope lurched forward, Christy let

go. Bob turned the boat around, and as they circled, Todd tossed
the tow rope to her.

"Remember? You hold on, point your toes, and lean back."

"Right. I've got it this time," Christy said, lacing the rope between her pointed skis. Before she had time to entertain any
doubts, she yelled, "Go ahead, hit it!"

This time she held on with all her might and kept her skis
pointed straight. Before she knew it, she was up. She was actually
standing on both skis, and the skis were gliding across the water.
There was only one problem—she was still in a sitting position,
bent at the waist, her arms out straight, and her rear end sticking
up in the air.

"Stand up!" she could hear her friends calling from the boat.
"Lean back!"

The pull of the rope was too strong. She couldn't pull herself
to a standing up position, let alone lean back. She continued her
ride across the lake with knees bent, arms out straight, and head
down, feeling as though she were flying with her legs in cement
blocks.

Then, without warning, she lost her balance and dove face
first into the unfriendly water. The skis flew off. She let go of the
rope, and in an attempt to scream, she swallowed enough lake
water to fill a goldfish bowl. Worst of all, half the water had entered through her nose. She felt as though all her eyelashes had
been peeled off in the process.

Bob was the only one not laughing when the boat drew near
to retrieve her. "You want to try again?" he asked calmly, as if she
hadn't just made a major spectacle of herself.

"I don't think so," Christy answered, coughing up big bubbles
of lake water and trying not to cry.

"Grab this rope," Todd said. "Pull yourself to the ladder at the back, but be careful the rope doesn't get tangled.''

It took a lot of effort to climb into the boat because her arms were quivering and her ankles felt as though they were still locked in cement. Todd had jumped into the water and was calmly fitting the skis on for his turn, as if nothing unusual had happened during Christy's attempt.

It was Katie who offered Christy a helping hand to get her back on board. Katie was still laughing, her green cat eyes brimming with tears of hilarity. "I always knew you were athletically impaired, Christy, but that was the funniest thing I have ever seen!"

Christy felt like telling Katie to just shut up, but she swallowed her anger and reached for a towel to bury her face in. It was bad enough to have gone through such a humiliating experience with people she knew watching her; she didn't need Katie's insults as well.

From the water Todd called out, "Hit it," and Bob cranked up the boat. With the greatest of ease, Todd rose to his feet the first time and made his jaunt around the lake. Baby stuff. Anybody could do it. Anybody but Christy.

Katie *was* right. She was athletically impaired. The only sort of athletic thing she had ever done well was trying out for cheerleader. Christy had worked hard for weeks to get the routines down just right. Maybe she could ski too, if she really tried and gave herself time.

Wrapping the towel around herself, Christy decided whether she learned to ski or not didn't matter. What mattered was that she gave it her best try, knowing it would be harder for her than for her friends.

Christy watched Todd riding smoothly behind the boat. She wondered if everything in her life was going to be harder for her than it was for her friends. She hoped she would always have the courage to at least try.

A slow grin forced its way across her lips as she thought of how she must have looked out there, bent at the waist, skimming across the water like some kind of contestant in a contortionist contest. It reminded her of when she and Katie had taken snow skiing lessons, and Christy had slid out of control and crashed into the ski instructor. The two friends had laughed together over that incident for the rest of the day. She realized she needed to lighten up. To laugh at herself. To take her uncle's advice and just enjoy today.

They spent the rest of the morning on the lake and were ready for lunch when they returned to the houseboat sometime in the early afternoon. Marti scolded them for being gone so long and not checking in.

Todd gave her a side hug and said, "You should have known we were okay. It's only when we never come back that you need to worry."

Marti smiled up at her favorite young man. "Now what kind of sense does that make, Todd? In the future you need to give me a better time reference so I won't have to worry."

Todd reached for a tortilla chip from the open bag Katie offered to him and, crunching loudly, said, "Okay, Marti. Just to make you happy we'll set a time. Or better yet, why don't you come out on the boat with us?"

Marti thought it over while Todd stepped to the table and began to make himself a sandwich from the fixings Bob was setting out.

"I suppose I should go out at least once this weekend."

"After lunch, maybe?" Todd challenged.

"Maybe. As long as it's with just you and Christy." Then with a proud look she added, "My favorite new couple."

Doug, who was sitting at the table spreading mayonnaise on his bread, suddenly stood up, pushed his chair back with his heel, and disappeared out the sliding door. No one seemed to notice except Christy. The rest of them dove into their sandwich making, but Christy's heart was beating hard.

She felt responsible for Doug's reactions. Doug had always been like a big brother to her. She couldn't stand to see him acting like this, and she knew she would be miserable the rest of the weekend if she didn't talk to him.

Gathering her courage, Christy drew away from the group and slipped out onto the deck in search of Doug.

# CHAPTER THREE

# *Marooned!*

Christy made her way around the narrow walk on the side of the deck and cautiously approached Doug, who was at the front of the houseboat, shaking out a beach towel.

"Hi," Christy said. "Are you okay?"

"Sure," Doug said, turning to face her. "Why shouldn't I be?"

Christy thought he looked angry. "Are you sure?"

The corners of Doug's mouth turned up into a smile. "Sure as sure can be. I came out for a towel so I wouldn't get the seat wet from my trunks."

"Oh." Christy wasn't sure what else to say. "Good idea."

She thought of their trip up to the lake the day before and how Doug had teased her and given her at least two hugs along the way. Today he hadn't come within ten feet of her. It wasn't her imagination. Something was wrong.

"Doug, somehow I don't believe you. Can't you be honest with me?"

Releasing a sigh, Doug folded his arms across his broad chest and leaned against the railing. "Okay. You want honest? You and Todd getting together has made me feel something."

"What?"

"I don't know. Don't get me wrong, I'm really happy for both of you. I just don't want things to change between us now."

"Nothing is going to change."

"Maybe, maybe not. I've had friends who suddenly became invisible when they started going with a girl. And I have a hard time staying friends with a girl once she's 'taken.' "

"It won't be like that with us," Christy promised. "Todd and I will still both be close friends with you."

"Promise?" Doug asked.

"Yes."

"I confess I'm skeptical, but for now I'll accept that. Let's not talk about this any more and just see how things go. I'm starving! How about you?"

Christy laughed. "How could you be after all those pancakes?"

Doug shrugged and opened the sliding door, motioning for Christy to go first.

After lunch Katie wanted to ski and Christy wanted to lay out on the flat roof of the houseboat. Doug said he was up for more boating, and Todd said he would do "whatever." It seemed like the perfect chance to let Doug and Katie go out on the boat alone. Then Marti stepped in.

"But Todd and Christy haven't taken me out yet in the boat. I suppose I really should go while the weather is nice." Marti reached for her wide-brimmed straw hat. "I only want to go out for a quick motor around the lake."

"Then let's go," Todd said obligingly. "You up for it, Christy?"

"Sure," she said, casting a quick glance at Katie as if to nudge her to spend the time getting closer to Doug. "Let me grab my sunglasses."

Todd helped Marti onto the boat. As soon as her foot touched the deck, a cloud hid the sun. Just as quickly as the cloud blew in, it blew away, and the afternoon sun beat down on Christy's back as she stepped onto the boat.

"I'm going to take the houseboat that direction," Bob told Todd, pointing to the right. "I thought I'd find a new cove for us to park in tonight. It should be easy to locate us when you come back."

Todd nodded and called out, "Later." He started up the engine and slowly headed for the open part of the lake. "You ladies mind putting on life vests? It's boating rules, you know."

"We won't need them," Marti reasoned. "We're only going for a jaunt, and I certainly don't plan on getting wet."

Christy followed Todd's example and slipped on a vest, leaving it unhooked. If nothing else, the vest cut down some of the breeze as they left their protected cover.

For the next fifteen minutes, Marti held on to her hat and directed Todd where to go. He followed her commands and turned into what looked like a long finger of Lake Shasta that was too narrow for houseboats.

Another cloud covered up the sun, and Christy shivered. She wished she had worn more than her damp bathing suit and T-shirt.

Todd steered the boat down the narrowing waterway, pointing out some little hidden coves off to the left.

"Let's go over there," Marti suggested. "Might be a good place for a picnic lunch tomorrow."

Todd expertly pulled the boat into the first hidden cove they came to. Then he jumped into the waist-deep water to secure the boat and called to Marti and Christy to join him in exploring their secret cove.

"How do I get to shore without getting wet?" Marti asked after she watched Christy slide into the water and slosh her way ashore.

"You have to get wet," Todd said. "It's not that deep. Go down the rope ladder on the side."

Christy watched as her aunt hesitated, deliberated, and finally decided to make the sacrifice and join the two of them on the pebbly beach.

"Oh," she screeched when her foot first felt the water, "it's so cold!"

"You're doing great," Todd said, wading out and offering her a hand into shore.

A huge cloud covered the sun. Everything around them seemed unusually quiet and still.

"It feels as if we're a hundred miles from the rest of the world," Christy said, surveying the surroundings. The small beach extended only twenty or so feet behind them before sloping up into a hill. The hillside was sparsely vegetated at its beginning but soon sprouted thick clumps of tall, straight trees that all pointed to the sky like a line of steady, green soldiers. "This is beautiful," Christy said.

"A bit chilly," Marti noticed. "What happened to our sunshine?"

"Let's go exploring," Todd suggested.

"It's too dangerous," Marti said. "We should get going so we can find the houseboat before a storm breaks out. I've heard the weather on a lake can be very unpredictable. Come now. Let's go."

"Shh," Todd whispered. "Did you see that?" He had his back to Marti and was scanning the forest behind them. "Over there, it's a deer! See? Up to the left, behind those two trees."

Christy spotted it and slowly moved closer to Todd. "It's watching us. Isn't it cute? Too bad we don't have some apples to feed it."

"What are you talking about? I don't see anything." Marti marched over toward Todd and Christy, but her sudden movements startled the deer back into the shadows.

"It's gone now," Todd said. "If we come back tomorrow for a picnic, let's be sure to bring some apples."

"Fine," Marti said, sounding irritated. "You can bring it apples tomorrow. Right now, let's get back to the houseboat."

Christy realized how miserable her aunt was, being out of her comfort zone like this. Christy knew the houseboating idea had been Bob's, but he had talked Marti into it by showing her in the brochure that the houseboat contained all the comforts of home. Apparently Marti had experienced enough of the great outdoors by coming to shore and was now ready to go back to her "home" and all those comforts.

The three of them boarded the boat, and Christy had to agree that it felt a little isolated and almost spooky in this silent cove, especially since the sun kept sliding behind the clouds. Todd waited until Christy and Marti were seated and then turned the key in the ignition. Nothing happened. He tried again; a slow, grinding sound emerged. Todd pushed a couple of switches and tried the key again. Nothing.

"What's wrong?" Marti demanded. "What's wrong with the boat?"

Todd tapped his finger on one of the oval gauges and calmly answered, "It appears we're out of gas."

"Out of gas! Didn't you bring an extra can along?"

"No."

"How could you let this happen? After all the skiing you did this morning, didn't you think to check it before we left?"

"No, I didn't."

"We're marooned!" Marti wailed.

Christy felt a little distressed, but nothing close to what her aunt was expressing. As a matter of fact, Marti would have made a great character on the old TV sitcom "Gilligan's Island."

"What are you going to do?" Marti asked. "No one will ever find us in here!"

"I'm going to pray," Todd said matter-of-factly. "Care to join me?"

"I will," Christy offered, getting up from her seat and joining Todd in the front of the boat. The two of them prayed simply and sincerely for God to send help.

Twenty minutes later, Christy pulled the life vest closer around her. It was getting colder, and she wished they had at least brought beach towels along to wrap their legs in.

Todd and Christy were the only ones talking to each other. Marti had covered herself with a life vest and sat huddled on the vinyl seat looking miserable and not saying a word, which Christy had decided was a good thing. Hearing what Marti was thinking right now would not bring much joy to their situation.

Another twenty or thirty minutes passed. The sun continued to play its peek-a-boo game with the clouds, and now no one was saying much of anything. Christy thought how ironic it was that earlier that morning Todd had whispered to her that being ship-wrecked wouldn't be such a bad thing. He must not have factored Aunt Marti into the scenario.

Then, as if the volcano inside Marti could hold back no longer, she let forth a steady flow of fiery accusations. Christy had never seen her aunt this mad.

"That's it!" Marti concluded. "You have to go for help, Todd.

I don't care how you do it. Walk over this hill to the other side
or swim out to the main part of the lake. It will be dark soon, and
I refuse to sit here and wait to be eaten by wild animals!"

Christy knew they had at least three hours of sunlight left,
and the only wildlife they had seen was the timid deer. Still, she
knew better than to challenge her aunt's fears. She wondered if
she should go with Todd or stay with her aunt. She knew what
she would rather do.

"We'll wait here," Todd said calmly yet with settled authority,
as if he had already thought through all the options.

Marti looked furious. Not many people opposed her even in
the best of circumstances. "I suppose you're waiting for God to
send an angel to rescue us."

"Angel, human, either one will do."

"This faith thing of yours has gone too far, Todd. It's fine
when you want to have theological discussions with Bob, but
when people's lives are at stake . . ."

Todd put out a hand to silence her. He seemed to be listening
for something. Christy turned her head and listened, too.

"I'm not finished! You *will* listen to what I have to say, Todd
Spencer, if it's the last thing you do before we perish in this stupid
boat."

Todd stood up and, still listening, made his way past Marti to
the back of the boat.

"Will you at least have the courtesy to look at me when I am
talking to you? You can't keep trusting God to do for you what
you should be doing for yourself! He has too many other things
to attend to, like world peace. I'm sure God does not have time
to answer the pointless prayers of . . ."

Todd put his first two fingers in his mouth and, facing the
opening of the inlet, let loose with a whistle so shrill that Christy

covered her ears. "It's a Wave Rider," he announced. "Help me flag it down, Christy."

Christy stumbled quickly to the back of the boat and slipped off her life vest, ready to wave it in the air.

"You can't be sure they're coming this way," Marti muttered, remaining in her seat but craning her neck.

They could all hear the high-pitched roar of the jet ski now, and it definitely was coming their way. Christy began yelling along with Todd's whistling. The minute the Wave Rider came into view, Christy waved the life vest over her head, and Todd waved his arms.

Just as quickly as the Wave Rider came into view, it shot past the cove and disappeared.

"What did I tell you?" Marti said. "Why don't you ever listen to me?"

"I think it's coming back," Christy said, straining to hear any change in the sound of the Wave Rider's motor.

"You're right," Todd said. "Get ready to wave your vest again." Before he finished speaking, the Wave Rider appeared and made a quick turn into their secret cove. The driver, a girl with long, dark hair, wearing a bright pink life vest, cut the engine and floated over to the boat. She had a dark tan, the color of chocolate cinnamon, and a white smile like a crescent moon.

"Need help?" the girl called out.

"Ran out of gas," Todd answered. "Can you give me a lift to the marina?"

"Sure. Hop on."

"Make sure your aunt stays here," Todd said to Christy. "I'll be right back."

"I heard that!" Marti said. "Of course I'm going to stay here. Where do you think I'd go? Just don't be getting any ideas in your head that this young girl is an answer to your prayers."

"You prayed for help?" the girl asked.

"Yep," Todd said, sliding into the water and swimming over to the Wave Rider.

"Are you by any chance a Christian?" the girl questioned.

"Christy and I both are," Todd said.

"This is so cool!" the girl said excitedly. "I'm Natalie. I'm a Christian, too! And you're not going to believe this, but I actually came down to this part of the lake because something inside kept kind of nudging me to go this way, you know what I mean?"

"Oh, this is ridiculous," Marti spouted, slouching back in her seat.

Christy felt like laughing at her aunt's refusal to believe in answered prayer even when she saw it with her own eyes. She knew it wasn't funny, but why couldn't her aunt see God had responded to their request for help?

Todd positioned himself on the back of the Wave Rider, and he and Natalie waved and took off, leaving Christy alone with her aunt. She waited a few minutes before trying to start a conversation.

"Why is it so hard for you to believe in God, Aunt Marti?"

"I believe in God."

"I mean, to surrender your life to Him and ask Jesus to be your Savior?"

"I refuse to get into a religious discussion with you, Christina. You are far too young to understand such things."

Christy hushed up. All she could think was, *I'm glad Jesus didn't consider me too young when I gave Him my heart.*

Todd and Natalie returned in less than an hour, and the boat started right up. "Thanks!" Todd called out, waving to Natalie as she took off. He slowly directed the boat out of the inlet but cranked it into high gear as soon as he hit the open lake.

"Slow down!" Marti squawked. "It's too cold! You're going to miss the houseboat if you go too fast."

Todd slowed a little and told Christy, "Keep looking for the houseboat. They could be anywhere along this part of the shore."

It really was chilly, with the wind off the lake and the late afternoon sun hanging low in the sky. The sun looked so much different from the one that had greeted Christy and Todd at daybreak. This big, sinking orange ball looked tired and ready for a rest, and so did Christy.

They finally found the houseboat after several trips in and out of a variety of coves along the shoreline. Katie was fishing off the roof, and Bob and Doug sat on the back deck, deliberating over a game of chess.

"They're here," Katie called out. "Finally! Where have you guys been?"

Christy noticed that another houseboat was parked across the cove from them. Katie yelled so loudly Christy felt sure the people in the other houseboat must be ready to come out on their deck to find out what all the commotion was about. Todd docked the boat, but before he or Christy had a chance to explain why they were gone so long, Marti started in.

"It was absolutely horrible," she moaned to Bob, who offered her a hand out of the boat. "We were shipwrecked for hours! I'm frozen to the bone!"

"We ran out of gas," Todd explained to the curious eyes that looked to him for an explanation. "We prayed, and God sent an angel on a Wave Rider."

"Why don't you come on in and take a warm shower," Bob suggested. "Everything is ready for dinner except the steaks, and the coals are perfect, so I'll slap 'em on the grill. You got back just in time."

Christy gladly took Bob's suggestion to hop in the shower. She was surprised at how nice the shower was in the houseboat, and they had plenty of hot water. There was even a place to plug in her hair dryer. She took her time drying and combing out her hair. Better to finish that in the bathroom than to fling her wet hair all over her aunt again.

As it turned out, Christy didn't have much to worry about. Marti didn't emerge from her room for the rest of the night. Bob, the ever-patient and loving husband, prepared her dinner and took it to her.

Christy felt fresh after her shower and only slightly ruffled from the day's adventure. She slipped into a pair of jeans, a favorite cream-colored knit sweater, and a pair of weathered white tennis shoes. The water from the shower made her hair especially soft, not frizzy like the water at home in Escondido. She could feel a little bit of sunburn on her cheeks and thought how rosy and cheerful it made her look.

Quickly dabbing on some mascara and going over her lips a second time with a tube of clear lip gloss, Christy took another look in the mirror. She felt pretty. Pretty in an outdoors, healthy, glowing sort of way. She wondered if Todd would notice.

Just then Katie knocked on the door and said, "Are you coming, Christy? The steaks are almost ready."

Christy opened the door and pulled her friend inside. "Well?" Christy whispered. "How did it go with Doug this afternoon?"

"What do you mean, 'how did it go?' How was it supposed to go?"

"I thought you guys might start to, you know . . . get together, sort of, if you had some time alone."

"Christy, what makes you think Doug is at all interested in me?" Katie's words came out almost sad.

"I think you two would be perfect for each other. He's a great guy. It would help if you would show him a little more attention. Let him know that you like him."

"And what makes you think I like him?" Katie asked.

"Why wouldn't you? He's tall, good-looking, athletic, a super-strong Christian, and a lot of fun to be around. I'm sure he likes you."

"Then he'd be the first guy ever," Katie said dryly.

"And what a great first guy!" Christy tried to cheer her friend on. "Come on, Katie. You've got to emotionally walk away from all those bad memories of Rick, and who was that missionary kid from Ecuador? Glen? It's time to move on."

"You're probably right." Katie glanced in the mirror and noticed that her freckled nose was sunburned. "Oh, no, now I'm going to peel."

Christy looked in the mirror. The contrast between the two girls was evident. Katie's fair skin, green eyes, and copper-colored hair made her look young, almost childish. Christy's tan made her blue-green eyes stand out. Her smooth skin looked flawless next to Katie's freckles, and her clean hair looked silky compared to Katie's unbrushed hair.

"How can I compete with that?" Katie asked, motioning to their reflections and focusing on Christy.

"We're not competing, Katie. This is not some sport. Besides, if it were, you'd whomp me hands down. This is just the guys, and I'm with Todd, so why don't you see what you can do about getting together with Doug?"

It surprised Christy to hear herself talking like that. She had never pushed Katie toward any guy before. She knew her motive was to get Katie and Doug together so she wouldn't have to feel awkward around Doug.

"Ladies," Bob's voice called through the closed bathroom door, "we're about to sit down to dinner, and we have a guest. Care to join us?"

"We'll be right there," Christy called back. "Is there any way I can encourage you by telling you you're wonderful just the way you are, and you're adorable, and any guy would be crazy not to see how terrific you are?"

"Do you really think so?" Katie asked.

"Yes, I really think so. And I think Doug would definitely be interested in you if you showed some interest in him."

"You sure?"

Christy nodded. "Come on, let's go out there and see what happens."

"Okay," Katie said, smoothing back her hair before opening the door. "Here goes nothing."

The two girls walked side by side down the short hallway to the kitchen. What they saw made them suddenly stop and stare.

# CHAPTER FOUR

# *Try, Try Again*

Todd was standing next to the table with his arm around a stunning young girl. She looked as though she couldn't be much older than fourteen, but her figure made her look more mature. Her dark hair was pulled back by her sunglasses and her lips curled in a charming crescent-moon smile, revealing perfect white teeth set off by her deep, chocolate cinnamon skin.

"Christy," Todd said, "guess who's in the houseboat across the cove from us?"

"Natalie," Christy said, forcing a friendly smile, "what a surprise!"

Katie poked Christy in the side as if to silently ask, "And who is Natalie?"

"Katie, this is Natalie. Natalie is the one who rescued us this afternoon."

Todd moved his arm from Natalie's shoulders and was about to say something when Doug came in from the side of the houseboat with a platter of barbecued steaks in his hand. He apparently hadn't seen Natalie arrive.

"Hi!" Doug said brightly, his grin dancing across his face. Doug looked to Todd for an explanation.

"This is Natalie. Our angel on the Wave Rider."

Natalie giggled. It was a cute, innocent giggle. What was it Todd had said about how irresistible innocent girls were?

"Would you like to join us for dinner?" Doug offered. "We have plenty."

"We already ate," Natalie said. "I just happened to notice it was your boat parked over here so I thought I'd come say hi."

"This is awesome," Doug said. "We're going to have a campfire on the beach after dinner; you'll join us, won't you?"

"I guess. Sure. Thanks for asking."

Then, as if someone had said to Katie, "Let the games begin," she jumped into the conversation. Gaining Doug's attention obviously was her goal. "Those steaks look great, Doug. Did you cook them? I bet you guys are hungry. I sure am. We should sit down to dinner, don't you think?"

Bob, who had been observing all this from the kitchen sink where he was pouring a pan of hot peas into a serving bowl, joined Katie's team. "Good idea. Let's sit down."

"I'll let myself out," Natalie said softly. "I guess I'll watch for your campfire later on."

"Don't leave," Doug said, sliding onto the vinyl bench seat and patting the spot next to him. "There's plenty of room, Natalie. Come sit by me."

Katie took the challenge and bolted to the table where she slid in on Doug's other side. "Are you as hungry as I am?" Katie asked Doug, looking for an answer from him.

Christy found herself a chair and pulled it up to the table. She wasn't sure how she felt about what was going on here. In a way she was glad Katie was flirting a little with Doug. Maybe all Katie needed was the competitive factor that Natalie brought into the situation. Still, Natalie had to be several years younger than Katie and Christy. If she were about fourteen, that would make Natalie eight years younger than Doug. Surely he knew that. He wasn't really flirting with her, was he?

Throughout dinner Natalie giggled at all of Doug's comments, and Katie popped off with some of her classic lines at the right moments. Christy wondered if Todd had any clue as to what was going on.

*Do guys ever?* she thought.

After dinner Christy helped Bob with the dishes. Todd and Doug, followed by Katie and Natalie, took off to start the campfire.

"I brought some marshmallows," Bob offered, handing a bag to Christy after the dishes were done. "Some coat hangers are in the hall closet. Why don't you join the others?"

Christy went in search of the coat hangers and glanced toward the shore out the window. The fire was already glowing. In the darkness she could make out Doug's frame with both girls on either side of him, in the exact spots they had occupied at dinner.

Natalie seemed like a sweet girl, and it was fun to meet another Christian and to have been rescued by her. Christy just hoped that, being so young and vulnerable, Natalie wouldn't misinterpret Doug's attention. Even more than that, Christy hoped Katie wouldn't get hurt, especially after Christy's big pep talk with her.

*Did I do the right thing, pushing Katie toward Doug like that?*

Armed with marshmallows and five coat hangers, Christy grabbed a beach towel and headed for the campfire. She spread her towel on the smooth rocks next to Todd and asked, "Anyone ready for a marshmallow?"

Doug didn't hear her. Katie had him tangled up in a thumb wrestling contest.

"I'd like one," Natalie said, leaving her post next to Doug and joining Christy. As she skewered the white puff, Natalie looked past Christy and said to Todd, "I still can't believe you guys are all Christians. That is so cool!"

Todd, Christy, and Natalie chatted, quietly roasting marshmallows while Doug and Katie continued their contest. When they seemed to have had enough thumb wrestling, Doug and Katie joined the other three and started another competition. This time it was to see who could get his or her marshmallow the brownest without burning it.

After three marshmallows, Christy was full of the sticky sugar and placed her coat hanger against one of the large rocks lining the fire pit. As she let go of the hanger, Todd stretched out his hand.

She thought he was reaching for her coat hanger, but instead he grasped her hand and wrapped his thick, warm fingers around hers. She turned to him and smiled. Todd smiled back. They were together, sitting close under a star-filled sky, holding hands. This was what Christy had always dreamed going together would be like. She moved a little closer to Todd so their hands could rest comfortably on his folded leg.

That's when she noticed Natalie looking at them, and Christy realized how awkward Natalie must feel with two college guys paying all their attention to Katie and Christy while Natalie sat alone like a leftover. Christy remembered how explosive her emotions were when she was fourteen, and she tried to draw Natalie into a conversation. Even though Todd and Christy were sitting close and holding hands, Christy thought it didn't have to mean they excluded Natalie.

Doug and Katie continued their marshmallow competition until the entire bag had been devoured. During their contest Natalie and Christy talked about school, family, and church. When the topic of Jet Skiing came up, Doug sat down next to Natalie with a string of questions.

Now it was Katie's turn to look like the leftover. The more Doug and Natalie talked, the more Katie seemed to withdraw. When Natalie asked Doug if he wanted to try out her Wave Rider tomorrow morning, Doug lit up with excitement and gave Natalie one of his hugs.

Christy wondered how Natalie would interpret Doug's affectionate expression. She seemed to glow a little brighter in the dwindling firelight as the two of them made their morning plans. There was no problem trying to guess how Katie took Doug's gesture toward Natalie. Katie excused herself from the group and walked back to the houseboat.

Instinctively Christy wanted to rush to her friend's side and comfort her. Still, she didn't want to leave Todd and the warmth of his hand encircling hers. Even though Christy knew it was probably not the best decision, she let Katie go off by herself.

"You think she's okay?" Todd asked.

"I think so. It's been a long day for everyone," Christy said.

*After all*, Christy told herself, *Katie should be old enough to handle these kinds of disappointments on her own without always having me there to cheer her up. She'll meet a nice guy someday who will appreciate her.*

Christy tried to convince herself it wasn't her fault Doug didn't seem to be as interested in Katie as Christy had hoped he would be. Doug and Katie had been around each other before at get-togethers, but somehow Christy had imagined this would be the trip that would draw the two of them together the way she and Todd were finally together.

*Oh well*, Christy thought with a sigh, *I guess it wasn't meant to be. Certainly Katie can see that. She'll snap out of it by morning.*

Christy's prediction was wrong. Katie didn't snap out of it. Christy lingered in bed, hoping to talk to Katie when she woke up, but Katie pretended to be still asleep.

"I don't know what to do," Christy confided to Uncle Bob at the breakfast table where only the two of them sat. "I think Katie's not just hurt because Doug didn't pay much attention to her last night, but I think she's mad at me for even suggesting she flirt with him."

It was easy for Christy to pour her heart out to her uncle. This morning she did it as if the confession would release her from the guilt she felt for pushing Katie into something she wasn't convinced she should do.

"You can't do anything," Bob said. "You tried to do something yesterday by coaxing her toward Doug, and that didn't work out. There's not much you can do or say at this point until her feelings mend some. It'll happen. It just takes time. Until then, leave her alone."

Then with a smile and a sip of his coffee, Bob added, "Trust me. When it comes to advice on women getting over being mad at you, I'm talking from experience." He gingerly nodded toward the closed bedroom door down the hall, where Christy could hear her aunt humming as she got ready for the day. Apparently Bob had taken his own advice and had allowed his wife time to be alone last night so she could mend from the trauma of the previous day.

Marti emerged bright and smiling, ready for a fresh start. "Good morning, you two. Beautiful day, isn't it? I thought we could all relax a little today. Take it easy, soak up some sun. What do you think? Are we all ready to enjoy ourselves?"

Christy thought her aunt was a little too perky, but she preferred perky over sulky any day. Besides, she agreed with Marti's advice on taking it easy. Maybe that would be the best thing for Katie and Doug, too.

For two sun-drenched, gentle hours, Christy sat by Todd's side on the top of the houseboat, reading while he fished. It was wonderful to be together without feeling they had to be doing or saying something to fill the time. Todd caught two medium-sized trout, which he cleaned while Christy watched.

Meanwhile Katie was off by herself, swimming for a little while, then kicking back on the deck while Bob and Doug worked on the rudder. Bob thought it needed some attention, so he had Doug in the water while he gave directions from the boat.

"Why don't we fry your fish for lunch?" Marti suggested once Todd had them cleaned.

"There's only enough for about one bite per person," Todd said.

"That's okay. It's all part of the experience of being on the river, don't you think?"

They were really on a lake, not a river, but no one mentioned this to Marti. It was nice to have her in a good mood.

*You really can be a sweetie when you want to be, can't you, Aunt Marti? Now if only Katie would perk up a little, Doug could see what a sweetie she can be.*

"Who's up for some water skiing?" Bob asked after lunch. "The rudder is as good as new. Katie? You want to go out with me?"

Katie gave him a wry smile and said, "I guess I'd better take you up on the offer. You may be the only male who ever asks me to go out with him."

Bob gave Katie a friendly hug and said, "I want to see you up on one ski again. You're very good, you know."

Katie shrugged. Christy interpreted the gesture to mean Katie would give up her athletic ability in a second if it meant a guy would be interested in her.

"You coming too, Christy?" Bob asked. "Or how about you guys? I made sure the tank is full, Todd."

"Good thinking," Todd said. "Sure, I'll go."

"How about you, Doug?" Bob asked, sounding like a coach trying to get all the cool guys to sign up for his team.

"Actually, I told Natalie I'd go out on the Wave Rider with her at two." Doug looked a little sheepish. "I'll stick around here. You guys go have fun. Maybe I'll see you out there."

When Christy, Bob, Todd, and Katie headed out for a good skiing spot, the awkwardness Christy felt with Doug the day before returned, only this time it was with Katie. She could feel her best friend's snubbing as if it were a chill wind.

*Why is it that everything started to go bad with all my friends the minute Todd and I started to go together? Is there some unwritten rule that once you have a boyfriend everyone else is commanded to turn against you?*

What hurt Christy the most was that she had been so eager to talk to Katie about Todd and how they had decided they would go together. Now that was the last thing Katie wanted to hear.

"Hit it!" Katie called from her position in the water sometime later. It was the last run of the day, and Christy had spent the afternoon mulling over her thoughts while she held up the ski flag whenever Todd, Bob, or Katie had gone down in the water.

"Do you want to try after Katie's run?" Bob asked Christy. "It looks as though we'll be leaving fairly early in the morning, so this may be your last chance."

Christy thought of the pep talk she had given herself after her last attempt at water skiing and decided she needed to give it one more try.

After Katie successfully completed a perfect run, she let go of the tow rope and dropped into the water. She seemed surprised to see Christy coming into the water.

"You're not going to try skiing again, are you?" Katie asked.

"I think I need to give it one more sincere effort before giving up," Christy said, trying hard to sound confident.

Katie shrugged, climbed back into the boat, and tossed Christy the rope. Don't you want these skis?" Katie asked, holding up the two skis while Christy struggled in the water to fit both her feet into the single ski.

"No, I think I'll try this one."

"Most people learn how to ski on two before they try one," Katie reasoned.

"Well," Christy said, feeling foolish and noble at the same time, "I guess I'm not like most people."

She positioned the ski toward the boat, tightly gripped the tow rope, and tried to remember everything Todd had told her. Then she bellowed, "Hit it!"

The rope edged across the face of the water as the boat pulled it taut. The instant she felt its tug, Christy began to lean back and let the boat do the work. The ski seemed to bounce and wiggle, making it difficult for her to find her balance. Then it happened. Miracle of miracles, she was standing up! She was skiing. And on one ski, no less.

"All right, Christy!" she could hear Todd cheering.

The boat slowly turned to the right. It was just enough of a shift to make her lose her balance. Christy wobbled and then tumbled into the water.

She must have been up on the ski for forty seconds, but to

hear Todd tell Doug back at the houseboat, it sounded as though Christy had broken a world record. Maybe it was, for her. Maybe she was, as Katie had said, "athletically impaired," but at least she had tried. And in that effort she had experienced enough achievement to make her feel like an Olympic medalist.

Christy was the first to shower and change while the guys secured the boat. Bob had decided they needed to camp closer to the marina that night so they could get an earlier start in the morning for their long ride home.

"I heard you experienced a great success this afternoon," Marti said when Christy emerged from the bathroom.

"It was a pretty big deal for me," Christy admitted. "But you should have seen Katie. She's incredible on skis!" Christy flashed a smile at Katie, who was helping to get dinner ready. Christy hoped it might mend some of the holes in their communication line.

Katie took the compliment and looked over her shoulder at Christy. It was the first time their eyes had really met all day. "You inspired me, Christy, to keep trying at the things that don't come easily for me."

"I can't imagine there would be very many things that don't come easily for you, dear," Marti said.

"Guys don't come easily for me. Particularly guys like Doug."

"Why didn't you say so?" Marti asked. "How silly of me not to have noticed! Well, if you're serious about taking Christy's inspiration to keep trying, then I have a plan."

Marti motioned for the two girls to come closer so she could fill them in on her scheme. Marti whispered, pointed outside, looked at her watch, and then gave Katie strict instructions to take a shower and not to come out "until you look and feel as pretty as a picture."

It was an ironic analogy for Katie, who worked for a photographer and often told Christy the secret touch-ups used on all the best pictures in the shop. Christy thought maybe Marti would be just the right touch-up artist to get things going between Katie and Doug.

Perhaps the best part was that Katie was willing to try. It made Christy feel as if they were being drawn back together as friends to work on Marti's project.

Christy noticed that the water Katie had started on the stove was boiling, so she added the measuring cup of rice, put on the lid, and turned the flame down low.

"Now, the chicken is already in the oven. It looks like we need to get this salad going," Marti said. "I'll have Bob set up the card table on the back deck."

Marti busied herself with her dinner arrangements while Christy made the salad and watched Todd and Doug out the window. They both had dark tans after a summer of endless surfing and looked relaxed in their T-shirts and swim trunks, helping Bob tie up the boat. Marti joined them and gave firm instructions on what time they were to be ready for dinner and how they were to look and smell when they showed.

Christy sprinkled a bag of croutons on top of her finished salad and smiled at her determined aunt. With Marti back in her "cruise director" mode, there was no telling how their dinner might turn out.

# CHAPTER FIVE

# Moonlight and Noses

"We need one more chair," Marti instructed.

Christy pulled the last folding chair from the closet and carried it to the back deck, where Marti stood by the card table. Not just any card table. This table had been transformed into an elegant dining spot for Todd, Christy, Doug, and Katie, complete with tablecloth, candles, and Marti's handsome name cards at each place. This was all part of her surefire plan to bring Doug and Katie together, a romantic sunset dinner on a floating restaurant.

"There," Marti said, tucking the last chair into its spot. "The boys should be done with their showers soon. Where's Katie? You two lovely young ladies should be standing out here by the deck, casually waiting for them to arrive. And remember, neither of you is to sit down until the boys pull out the chairs for you."

Christy nodded at all her aunt's "charm school" instructions. She had to admit, this was fun.

"How does this look?" Katie asked, stepping out on the deck wearing an oversized white T-shirt and shorts.

"Oh my!" Marti said, looking concerned. "Is that the best you can do?"

"Well, this was originally an invitation to go houseboating, not to the prom," Katie said sarcastically. "I would have brought my black sequined evening gown with matching gloves and mink stole, if you would have told me."

Christy glanced down at her own jeans shorts and the rolled-up, long-sleeved denim shirt with a torn pocket. *I wonder why Aunt Marti didn't criticize my outfit? Does she think a person only has to look good when she's trying to get a boyfriend?*

"Let's do this," Marti said, fussing with the long ends of Katie's T-shirt and tying them into a knot at her right hip. "Much more flattering. Shows off your flat stomach."

Katie laughed, startling Marti. "Thanks for the tip, but I'm not much of a knot-on-the-hip type of person." Katie untied it and let the now-wrinkled shirt hang naturally. "I did put on some makeup. Did anyone notice?"

In the dimming light of the evening sky, Christy hadn't. She and Marti both moved in closer to examine the makeup. It was hard to tell, but in a subtle way Katie's green eyes looked larger and more sparkling.

"There's always your personality," Marti said, stepping back and giving Katie another up-and-down scan. "You have a wonderful personality. Use it to your advantage, dear."

Then excusing herself to find the boys, Marti waltzed past Christy and Katie and into the bright lights of the houseboat kitchen.

" 'Use your personality, dear,' " Katie mimicked. "I think I just got slammed big time. What do you think?"

"I think we should both relax a little here and enjoy my aunt's game of Enchanted Evening. What do you think?"

"I think . . ." Katie hesitated. "Never mind what I think. You're right. This could be a lot of fun. Just the four of us. No unexpected 'angels' dropping by, I hope."

"I don't think so. Natalie's houseboat pulled out while you were in the shower."

"So we just stand here and act casual until the guys show up?"

Just then the motor to the houseboat started, and Bob began to maneuver their way out of the cove and into the main part of the lake.

"What's going on?" Katie asked.

"My uncle wanted to be closer to the marina so we can check in earlier in the morning. Aunt Marti is going to serve our dinners while Bob floats our restaurant under the stars. Pretty fun, don't you think?"

Katie started to brighten up a little. "Yeah, I guess this could be kind of fun. It'd be even more fun if I didn't feel like such a fashion degenerate."

Christy laughed. "You look fine. Look at me, though; I'm the slob of the year!"

"Hardly. You always look cute. Even in grubbies you look cute. How do you do that?"

"Do what? I don't do anything."

"That's what I mean," Katie said. "You're one of those people who looks good in anything."

Before Christy had a chance to return a compliment to her insecure friend, the guys entered the kitchen, filling the compact area with their presence. They immediately evoked Marti's laughter.

"What's so funny in there?" Katie asked, trying to peer through the mesh in the screen door.

The guys turned toward them and headed for the back deck. Apparently they had taken Marti's grooming threats to heart. Both guys had parted their hair in the middle and watered it down so that it stuck to their heads. They both had on T-shirts and shorts, but they had constructed bow ties out of paper towels and had somehow fastened them to their T-shirts at the neckline.

"Come meet your dates," Marti said with hints of laughter still tickling her voice. "Right this way, gentlemen."

Marti ushered them out to the deck, where Katie and Christy stood waiting. The guys smiled, and Christy noticed something dark on Doug's upper lip.

"Good evening," Doug greeted them, twitching his face a little and drawing attention to his painted-on moustache. "I'd like to thank whichever one of you left your mascara in the bathroom. I found it very useful."

They all laughed. Todd pulled out his chair and sat down. Doug followed his example. Under Marti's firm glare, Katie and Christy remained standing, waiting for the guys to pull out their chairs.

"Oh, I beg your pardon, miss," Doug said, catching on before Todd and rising to pull out Katie's chair. "May I?"

Katie graciously lowered herself into the folding chair and played right along. "Oh, thank you ever so much, kind sir. There's nothing like a man with a moustache to add that festive touch to any occasion."

"That's me," Doug said, pretending to twirl his moustache, "the man with the festive touch."

Todd pulled out Christy's chair, and Marti said, "Please make yourselves comfortable. Your salads are before you, and I shall return momentarily with a basket of bread sticks."

The houseboat slowly motored across the lake as the sun slid behind the hills. A gentle evening breeze rose from off the water.

"Look over there," Todd said, pointing to the hills to the left. As they watched, the moon rose like a prize-winning harvest pumpkin and lit their table the way a paper lantern lights up a garden party.

"Awesome," Doug said.

"Isn't it beautiful?" Katie asked. "What a perfect night. A *'bella notte,'* as they say. All we need is spaghetti and meatballs and a couple of Italian waiters to sing to us."

"Why?" Doug asked.

"Because it feels like the night in that movie when the dogs are eating spaghetti, and the boy dog uses his nose to push the last meatball over to the girl dog."

"Why didn't you say so?" Doug asked, playfully using his nose to nudge the cherry tomato from his salad off his plate and toward Katie. The tomato made it about halfway to Katie's plate before it toppled over the side of the card table and hit the deck with a splat.

"Now we know why they used a meatball in the movie," Doug said dryly.

They all laughed, and Christy felt happy. Very happy. She wondered if Todd were enjoying all this as much as she was. He looked downright silly with his slicked-back hair and paper towel bow tie. She would expect this kind of goofing off from Doug. It was a nice surprise to see Todd acting a little crazy.

*Just one more reason to like him so much*, Christy thought. *I wonder if Todd enjoys being around me as much as I enjoy being with him? The way Doug is teasing Katie, I wonder if he's starting to get more interested in her?*

Todd prayed for their food, and they dug in, chatting and dining under the moon. Marti appeared right on cue with two dinner plates steaming with the main course of rice, broccoli, and chicken with some kind of lemon-butter sauce and sprinkled with slivered almonds. Marti served Christy and Katie first and then returned with two plates for the guys.

"Is everything to your liking?" Marti asked.

"Great," Todd said.

Christy thought it looked great except for the nuts. She hated nuts. She'd tried some in the past and had thought they were okay. But now she was back to disliking them. Maybe no one would notice if she discretely scraped off the almonds and pushed them to the side of her plate.

"Do you happen to have any meatballs?" Doug asked. Christy could tell Marti was a little perturbed that they were being so silly and not acting mature and romantic as she had planned.

"I'm going to put some music on these outside speakers," Marti announced. "Some soothing, evening dinner music to help set the mood for you young people."

A few moments later, the strains of sweet violins surrounded them.

Katie burst out laughing. "It's the Italian music we ordered!"

"I like it," Christy said, quickly defending the classical music.

"Are you serious?" Katie asked.

"Of course I'm serious. I love this kind of music. Don't you?"

"Sure, in an elevator or at the dentist's office!"

"I like it," Todd said, reaching over and giving Christy's arm a tender squeeze. "This is music to touch the heart." He smiled at Christy, and she smiled back.

"Do you kind of get the feeling these two might want to be alone?" Katie said to Doug. "We could always take our dinner plates up on the roof. What do you think?"

Doug seemed to have sobered quickly after all the laughter. Instead of answering Katie, he lifted another bite of chicken to his mouth and said, "Good dinner."

"I made the rice," Katie said. "Well, actually I boiled the water."

No one seemed to think that was as funny as Katie did. They ate quietly, aware of Marti's ever-watchful gaze on them. She seemed pleased that the music had apparently tempered their silliness, and she tiptoed in and out as she served dessert.

The quiet must have been too much for Katie, because when the brownie with a cloud of whipped cream on top was served to Doug, Christy spotted a mischievous glint in her friend's eye.

"Eww," Katie said, looking at Doug's dessert and then at hers. "Can you smell that?"

"What?" Doug asked.

Katie daintily sniffed at her whipped cream. "I don't think we should eat this. Can't you smell it?"

"Smell what?" Doug said, sniffing his dessert. "I don't smell anything."

"Then smell mine," Katie said. She lifted her dessert plate with one hand on the bottom and held it up for Doug to smell. Doug leaned forward. Then Katie let loose with her sweet revenge and shoved the whipped cream and brownie into Doug's unsuspecting face.

"Gotcha!" Katie squealed with delight as Doug peeled the goo off his face. "That's for flipping Christy and me off the raft the first day. Now we're even."

Doug licked at the whipped cream and felt the table in search of his napkin.

"Here you go," Todd said, removing his bow tie and offering it to Doug. "I knew these things would come in handy."

Katie was still laughing. Marti hurried outside to see what was going on. "What happened here? How did this happen?"

"Just a little accident," Doug said good-naturedly. Half of his pretend mustache had been wiped off by Todd's bow tie. The other half of his face still sported chunks of chocolate and whipped cream. "Could we order one more dessert and maybe a few paper towels out here?"

Katie had dropped her fork during her attack, and as she bent down to pick it up, Doug lifted his empty plate to hand it to Marti. Somehow, the moment Katie's head came up, Doug's long arm swung out, connecting with Katie's face. The plate and his hand slammed into Katie's nose. The plate crashed to the ground, and Katie let out a wail and grabbed her nose. Christy sprang from her chair.

Doug, still wearing his dessert, jumped up and frantically said, "I didn't mean that, Katie. It was an accident. Really. Are you okay? You guys, tell her it was an accident!"

Katie seemed to be trying not to cry, but the tears came and so did a gush of blood from her nose.

"Don't tilt your head back," Todd said, jumping up and grabbing a corner of the tablecloth to apply to Katie's nose. "Here, put your hand on this and press right here."

Christy stepped back and let Todd take over. The sight of blood on Katie's white T-shirt made Christy feel kind of woozy. It all had happened so fast. The classical music still played in the background in cruel contrast to the frenzied activity around the table.

"Don't hold your breath," Todd said, his voice calm and steady. "Try to breathe normally through your mouth. Christy, could you bring me some ice in a plastic bag?"

"Sure," Christy sprang into action and slid past her aunt, who seemed to be frozen in place next to the screen door. Christy grabbed a plastic bag from the cupboard and filled it with ice cubes. She was glad Todd knew what to do. He had probably seen lots of bloody noses during his years of surfing.

"Everything okay back there?" Bob called from the captain's seat at the front of the boat.

"Nothing major," Christy called down the hallway. "Katie got a bloody nose. It's under control, I think." She slipped out to the deck and handed the bag of ice to Todd. "Can I do anything else?"

"No, thanks. This ought to do it. Hold this ice right here, Katie, with one hand. Good. Now give me your other hand." Todd guided her finger to a pressure point on the gum under her top lip. "Press here. That's good. It should stop bleeding in a minute."

Todd was right. Within a few minutes the crisis had passed. Doug wiped the rest of the brownie off his face and said, "Hey, it was totally an accident, Katie. Honest. I didn't see you there."

Katie said in a garbled voice, "That's probably because you had brownies in your eyes."

Everyone let out a short, relieved spurt of laughter. Everyone but Marti. She seemed completely undone. They had ruined her plans for a perfect evening.

"Do you want to share my dessert?" Christy asked, not sure what to say to Katie.

"I'm not exactly hungry anymore," Katie said, wiping her cheek. "I think I'd better go change."

Even though no one told them to clear the table, the three remaining dinner guests started to gather up the dishes and tear down the romantic dinner for four. The moon was now high above them as Christy blew out the candles and wadded up the soiled tablecloth.

The *bella notte* had not exactly turned out the way she had hoped.

CHAPTER SIX

# *Michael and Fred*

"No, it's me," Katie whispered to Christy in the darkness. "I know it is."

"No, it's not," Christy immediately responded. "It's the circumstances, or the guys, but really, Katie, it's not you."

The two of them had traded sleeping quarters with the guys for their final night of the trip and were lying in their sleeping bags on the roof of the houseboat. Nothing was above them but the inky sky flung with thousands of diamonds. The moon had taken its curtain call for the night and slipped behind Mount Shasta.

"I know you're saying all this to be nice to me, Christy, but I'd like to think our friendship is past the point of us lying to each other in the interest of being polite."

"I'm not lying. You don't have a boyfriend, not because of anything you're doing or not doing. The right guy hasn't come along yet. That's all."

"In almost eighteen years not one 'right guy' has come along, and you think it's *not* because of me? Think again."

It was silent for a few minutes except for the lulling sound of the water lapping on the houseboat's sides and a few late-night crickets and frogs saying good night to each other.

"Maybe we should pray about it," Christy suggested meekly.

"You mean the way you pray for your future husband and have a shoe box full of letters to him stashed under your bed? I don't think so, Christy. That's not me. I could never write a letter to someone I don't know. And what am I supposed to pray? 'God, bring me a man—now'? I thought really spiritual Christians prayed for patience and stuff like that. Not for boyfriends."

"But, Katie, if God knows all about us and if He cares about everything that happens to us, then of course you should pray about everything. Even about a boyfriend. God already knows what would be best for you, too."

"I hope you know how easy it is for you to say all that," Katie said quickly. "You have *the* perfect boyfriend of the universe. Of course you believe God is giving you His best. It's harder to believe stuff like that when you're like me and no answer to your prayers is sitting next to you holding your hand. I mean, what if God's best for me is that I don't get a boyfriend?"

"God still cares, Katie."

"How do you know that? I mean, don't you wonder sometimes how much of what we believe about God is real and how much of it we say simply because we want to believe it?"

Christy propped herself up on her elbow and looked at Katie. "What do you mean? It sounds as if you're saying you don't trust God."

"I don't know. It just seems God has forgotten about me when it comes to boyfriends, that's all. Not that I hold it against Him. After all, God must be rather busy these days—earthquakes, pestilence, famines, wars. What's a plea from Katie for a boyfriend when He has so much else to tend to?"

"God is big enough to handle all that and your feelings, too.

Please don't think He's forgotten you."

"If you say so," Katie said with a sigh.

It was quiet for a few moments before Katie asked, "So what time are we leaving in the morning?"

"I don't know," Christy said. "Pretty early, I guess. I'm sure the rest of them will wake us when they get up."

"Then we'd better get some sleep. Good night." Katie rolled over on her side with her back to Christy. In minutes, the only sound that came from her was the deep, slow, rhythmic breathing of someone lost in dreamland.

Christy was unable to enter dreamland herself for quite some time. She lay on her back in the stillness, watching for shooting stars and thinking about Katie. It bothered her that Katie had sounded as though she were doubting her faith in God. What bothered Christy even more was that she didn't have any really good answers for Katie.

*Not that I have to defend You, God. You are God. You can do what You want. But I do wish sometimes that You and Your ways were easier to understand. Sometimes all I know is that You're there. Maybe sometimes that's all I need to know.*

Christy noticed a trail of thin, iridescent clouds moving slowly across the night sky. *The dust beneath His feet*, she thought. *You are here, and You do care, don't You, God? Please help Katie to see that and to understand You.* Christy closed her eyes and drifted into a deep, sweet sleep.

When she awoke, the first thing Christy saw was Katie's face, which made Christy gasp. Katie had two black rings around both her eyes, a result of the blow she took to her nose the night before.

"Katie," Christy called softly, nudging her on the shoulder. "Katie, wake up."

"What?" Katie answered, sounding groggy and irritated.

"Just five more minutes, okay?"

"It's time to get up, Katie. We're on the houseboat. We have to get going. And you need to look in a mirror." Christy said the last part in a low voice and bit her lower lip, wondering how Katie would react to what she would see in the mirror.

Christy knew that if it had happened to her, she would be devastated and would probably try to find a way out of going to school the next morning. How could anyone begin her senior year with two black eyes?

Amazingly enough, the prize fighter look only bothered Katie for about two seconds. She looked in the mirror, screamed, then laughed and laughed until everyone else couldn't help but laugh along with her.

"You wait, Doug! I'm really going to get you back for this one!" she threatened him. She was still threatening when they arrived home from their trip late that evening. As Doug unloaded Katie's gear from the back of his truck, Katie reminded him, "When you least expect it, I *will* get you back, Doug. You can count on it."

Christy would have expected the jovial attitude to be long gone by the next morning. But when Christy picked up Katie for school, the first thing Katie said as she bounced into the car was, "What do you think of laxatives?"

Christy looked blankly at her friend. Katie had not even tried to cover up the black and blue with makeup. She looked awful. "What do you mean, laxatives?" Christy asked.

"You know the way Doug will eat anything. Why don't we make him some cookies and fill the dough with laxatives? He'd never know what hit him!"

"Katie, I can't believe you're even suggesting such a thing! That is so cruel. You would never really do anything like that, would you? You know when he hit your nose it was an accident. He felt awful about it. I think he apologized to you every five minutes on the drive home."

"Good. If you ask me, a little guilt is good for a guy."

Christy pulled into the parking lot on the back side of Kelley High and slowly proceeded up and down the rows in search of a parking place. "Did everybody decide to be early today, or what? This seems like a lot more cars than last year."

"You know how it is on the first day," Katie commented. "Everyone wants to make a good impression and all that. Besides, there are a lot more seniors this year than last. You know what I think?"

Christy found a remote parking spot and carefully eased the car in between the narrow white lines.

"I think," Katie continued, "since you're on yearbook staff you should put a picture of the parking lot in the yearbook. Nobody ever does that. I think a parking lot is as important as a locker. Maybe more so. Especially your senior year."

"You could be right. That's a good idea, Katie," Christy said, carefully locking the car and gathering the few things she had brought with her.

Even though she had been at this same school for three years and she liked Kelley High, Christy still felt as if a load of bricks had just been dumped in her stomach. It didn't matter that this was her senior year. She felt the same way she had the first day of kindergarten back in Wisconsin. Terrified.

"I think it's a really good idea," Katie chattered on cheerfully as they entered the main building. They merged into a stream of people who were all yakking and laughing and bumping each other with their backpacks slung over their shoulders. "Hey, Danny, how's it going?" Katie greeted a guy who passed them.

Danny waved back at Katie. He had on shorts and a T-shirt, and he wore sunglasses, even though he was inside the building.

"Did you see who Danny was with?" Katie said, grabbing Christy by the wrist.

The two of them looked over their shoulders at Danny and the slim, dark-haired girl he had his arm around. "That's Lynn! Can you believe they're together?" Kate said. "Actually, if you ask me, they make a good couple. I've known Danny since second grade. We used to get into trouble together when we went to Myers Middle School. I can't believe even Danny has a girlfriend!"

Christy felt relieved that Katie was by her side, breaking the ice, overshadowing Christy's timid feelings with her bold, friendly personality. Apparently first days didn't bother Katie a bit. And with two black eyes, no less!

Christy wished she had the right words at that moment to tell Katie what her friendship meant to her. How much she appreciated having someone beside her who could so easily lighten the brick load in her stomach.

"This is where I get off," Katie said, stopping in front of a classroom. She flashed a confident smile. "I'll see you at lunch? Same old spot?"

"Okay," Christy smiled back, trying to siphon one more burst of self-assurance from Katie before heading down the hallway to her first class. "See you!"

At 11:42 the bell rang for lunch, and Christy hurried to their meeting spot under a tree on the grass. Last year they had decided not to eat at the picnic tables or to rush out to their car and hurry through some drive-through, fast-food place like a lot of the other students did. Instead, Christy and Katie met at this remote spot.

But today their routine was interrupted. Sitting under "their" tree was a guy Christy didn't recognize. His sandaled feet were stretched out in front of him, and he looked a little too comfortable. A little too permanent. Christy stood back and watched. The guy pulled an apple from his brown leather backpack and chomped into it.

How could she tell him he was in their space?

"Hi!" Katie called out. She stepped up beside Christy and eyed the intruder.

"Who's that?" Katie said, almost loud enough for the guy to hear.

"I don't know," Christy whispered, turning back to him and scrunching up her nose at Katie. "Why don't we find a new spot?"

"Why?" Katie asked. "We can still sit there. There's more than one side to a tree, you know. Besides, once he overhears the kind of stuff we talk about, he'll probably leave in a second."

Katie boldly marched over to the tree as the guy watched. She planted herself like a flag of victory. Christy followed her lead, fully aware the guy was observing their every move.

As if nothing were out of the ordinary, Katie opened a bag of chips. "So how did all your classes go?" she asked Christy.

It was a little more difficult for Christy to jump right into their lunch routine and act as if they weren't being observed by this stranger.

Before Christy could answer, the guy spoke up. "Have you tried vitamin C?"

Christy noticed his accent. She guessed it was British.

"Excuse me?" Katie said, making eye contact with him.

"For the eyes," he said, motioning to Katie's obvious bruises. "Vitamin C with bioflavonoids three times a day. Have you tried it?" Katie looked at the guy, then at Christy. She seemed about to burst out laughing.

"Cabbage is a good source. Potatoes and tomatoes are as well."

He said 'potatoes' and 'tomatoes' funny, and Katie did start to laugh.

"Where did you come from?" she asked.

"Belfast."

Katie looked at Christy blankly. "Belfast. That's in Ireland, right?"

"Northern," the guy said quickly. "Northern Ireland. There's a vast difference, you know."

Apparently Katie and Christy didn't know. At the moment they were both captivated by this fair-skinned, dark-haired, green-eyed stranger.

"The name is Michael," the guy said, introducing himself with a smile. "And who might you be?"

"I'm Christy."

"Katie." The minute Katie said her name, Michael burst out laughing.

"What?" Katie wanted to know. "What's so funny about 'Katie'?"

"Nothing's wrong with being a Katie. It's a daft thing that I should leave a school brimming with Katies in Belfast, and the first person I meet in this California school is a Katie!"

"A 'daft thing'?" Katie repeated. The previous summer, she had started using an original expression, a "God thing," and every now and then Katie would inform Christy that Todd was doing a "Todd thing," but Katie had never heard of a "daft thing."

" 'Daft.' You know, 'daft.' You don't say that here?"

Christy and Katie both shook their heads.

"It means crazy or silly."

"Oh," both the girls said.

"So, Mike—" Katie began.

"Michael," he corrected her. "It's Michael."

"So, *Michael,*" she continued, "you're giving vitamin prescriptions to a complete stranger, and you think *we're* daft? Perhaps I should tell you right up front that you're quoting vitamins to the wrong person. Unless your vitamin C with whatever-noids is found as a natural source in Twinkies, there's a pretty good chance it won't find its way into my blood system."

Michael smiled. Christy noticed that his whole face lit up when he did. He seemed harmless enough. A new guy looking to meet some people. A foreign exchange student, perhaps. Still, this friendly flirting didn't come as easily to Christy as it did to Katie.

The rest of their lunch time, Christy sat back, quietly eating her sandwich and listening to Michael and Katie's playful banter about junk food versus health food. It appeared that Michael was winning, which was a first with Katie. Christy had rarely seen a guy overpower her in any category.

"Saved by the bell," Katie said as the loud buzzer echoed across the school yard. "I haven't given up, though. I'll prove to you why my way of eating is just as good as yours."

"We'll see," Michael said with a twinkle in his eye. Pulling a piece of paper from his backpack and scanning the computer printout, he asked, "Do you happen to know where I might find room 145?"

"You're kidding!" Katie said. "That's my next class. Government with Mr. Jacobs, right?"

"I suppose I should thank my lucky stars. I'll be needing some friendly assistance when it comes to your American government." Michael slung his backpack over his arm and offered a hand to Katie to help her stand up.

"Shouldn't that be your 'Lucky Charms'? You know, that leprechaun cereal with the little colored marshmallows? Never mind," Katie said, responding to the blank look on Michael's face. "You obviously need an education in more than just American government. American breakfast cereal is a very important subject, too, I hope you know."

"Oh, is it now?"

"See you later, Christy," Katie called over her shoulder as she and Michael took off together for their class, walking close, deeply involved in their conversation.

Christy watched them for a minute before heading to her yearbook class. Michael was about the same height as Katie, and from the back, Christy could see that his thick, dark hair had reddish highlights enhanced by the sun. The back of his T-shirt had a whale on it and some kind of slogan about saving the whales. He seemed like a decent sort of guy, even though he was so different.

*What am I thinking? He's a complete stranger, and he's totally captivated by Katie. This all happened too quickly. She's too eager for a boyfriend right now. How do we even know if this guy is a Christian?*

Christy entered her yearbook class and felt even more uneasy. Not just about Katie, but about being with this close-knit group of students. She hadn't worked on the yearbook staff the way most of them had last year. When she sat down at a desk in the back of the room, no one even seemed to notice she was there.

*Why did I ever take this class?*

"Hi, Christy," a guy said, coming through the door as the bell rang.

It was Fred, the school photographer who had caught her in

several embarrassing poses last year and made sure those shots made it into the yearbook. Part of her reason for signing up for yearbook was to prevent any more embarrassing photos this year, although she would never admit that to anyone.

Fred plopped down on top of the desk next to her. Reaching for the camera hanging around his neck, he pointed it at Christy and said, "Nice big smile for your ol' pal Freddy."

Christy did not smile. Calmly she said, "I don't want you to take my picture, Fred. Not today, not tomorrow, not ever. Okay?"

Snap! The bright flash went off in Christy's face.

"I don't think you're listening to me, Fred. I said *no pictures.*"

Fred's face appeared from behind the camera. His front two teeth were crooked, and his complexion wasn't the best. His hair clung to the top of his head like the skin on a pear. Katie had once said Fred was the kind of guy who should be arrested for using hair spray without a license.

"I had a dream about you last night, Christy," Fred said. "You were a famous model on location in Greece, and I was your photographer. You do believe that dreams can come true, don't you?"

*I can't believe this is happening!*

"I've already asked Miss Wallace if she'd make you my assistant this year so we can spend lots of time together. We'll have to go out on lots of photo assignments. Like every weekend for football games." Fred smiled, and she noticed a piece of something orange left over from lunch wedged between his two crooked teeth.

"Fred, I have a boyfriend." Christy never would have guessed how relieved she felt to be able to say those words aloud.

"Not that slime Rick Doyle, I hope!"

"No. His name is Todd. Todd Spencer. He's in college, and I'm sure I'll be spending all my weekends with him. So you see, I won't be able to go on any photo shoots with you."

Fred's enthusiasm seemed only slightly dampened. "Not a problem. I'll be with you every weekday, and Schmoddy-Toddy will only have you on weekends. We'll see what happens by the end of the school year. As I always say, 'May the best man win!' "

# CHAPTER SEVEN

# *She Brought Raisins*

"Oh, that wasn't the worst of it," Christy said, leaning against the kitchen counter that evening while her mom washed off a head of lettuce. "He took at least five pictures of me while I was sitting there listening to the teacher, and then Miss Wallace said I was assigned to take pictures with him at the football game Friday night."

"So what did you tell Fred?" Mom asked, her round face looking soft and interested.

"I told him I had a boyfriend, and if he didn't leave me alone Todd was going to beat him up."

"You didn't!"

"No, of course I didn't tell him that. I did tell him I had a boyfriend, though, and that I worked Friday nights and Todd and I had plans for Saturday nights."

"And do you and Todd have plans?"

"Well, not yet. But I'm sure we will. You know Todd is sort of a last-minute, spontaneous kind of guy."

"Christy, this is not the time to get in the habit of stretching the truth," Mom said as she sliced up a cucumber and added it to the salad in the big wooden bowl.

Christy snitched a cucumber slice. "I know. You're right." Pointing to the tomato, she said, "Did you know that tomatoes are full of vitamin C and something-noids?"

"Is that what you learned in science today?"

"No, that's what I learned from Michael." Christy gave Mom a rundown on how they had met Michael at lunch. "Then after school, if you can believe this, I waited for Katie at the car for at least ten minutes. She finally shows up with Michael in his beat-up little sports car, and she says she's taking him to 31 Flavors to introduce him to all the vitamins in jamoca almond fudge ice cream."

Mom chuckled and shook her head. "This could be a very interesting situation for Katie. Does she seem to like this Michael as much as he seems to like her?"

"I'm afraid the rest of the world has ceased to exist when he's around. It's kind of scary, though, Mom. She doesn't know anything about this guy. He's different. Not in a bad way, just unique. And he seems really interested in her—black eyes and all. I don't know. It doesn't feel right to me."

"Well, now's not the time to abandon her. Keep up with her in this new relationship, and keep those channels of communication open."

"I will," Christy said. "Are we ready to eat? Where are Dad and David?"

"Dad is in the garage, and your brother should be out front riding his bike. Could you call them both in while I put dinner on the table?"

Christy stepped out onto the front porch of their small rental home and called for David. A moment later the red-haired eleven-year-old came pedaling fast up their tree-lined street with his bike aimed at his homemade wooden bike jump. Up went the front tire as David let out a hoot and sailed through the air a full five seconds before landing on the grass.

"David, time for dinner."

"Okay, after one more jump," David said, pushing up his glasses.

"Mom said to come now."

"All right, all right! You don't have to get bossy."

"I'm not bossy. You just never come to dinner on time. And don't forget to wash your hands and put away your bike."

In a squeaky voice, David mimicked, " 'Wash your hands! Put away your bike!' Bossy, bossy, bossy!"

"David!" came a deep voice from inside the garage. That was all Christy's dad ever had to say to get either of them to straighten up. In his firmest, strictest, growling voice, he would call out their names, and both Christy and David knew they had better straighten up right then.

"I'm coming," David answered, sheepishly wheeling his bike into the garage.

"Tell your mom we'll be right there," Dad called out to Christy.

He was a large man who had worked on a dairy farm nearly all his life. Moving to Southern California had been a big change for him, and Christy knew it had taken him quite a while to make the adjustment. Now that they had been in Escondido for several years and things were going well for him at the Hollandale Dairy, Christy thought he seemed a little more settled. They still didn't have a lot of money, and her dad still wore his overalls in public, which embarrassed Christy, but in a lot of ways she knew she was blessed to have the parents she did.

Christy had some of those same thoughts later that week in English class. Their assignment was to describe someone they knew well and to use all five senses in the description. Her dad was the first person who came to mind. Christy jotted down some descriptive words the way the teacher had instructed them to. She wrote about how her dad's hands felt big and rough and how he smelled like cows a lot of the time, but on Sunday mornings on the way to church he always smelled like a forest, green and mossy. Sometimes the car would still smell like that on Monday mornings when Christy drove to school.

Her dad chewed Dentyne gum, which Christy listed under the sense of taste since she had chewed many pieces along with him over the years and that strong cinnamon tang on her tongue always reminded her of her dad. His bushy eyebrows and thick brownish-red hair made him look like an elf inside a giant's body.

For the sense of hearing, Christy wrote about the way his deep laughter tumbled from his huge chest and how, whenever he laughed, it made Christy's mom smile.

The last line of her description read, "Even though he comes across kind of gruff, my dad has a teddy bear heart. I've never doubted that he loves me, although I don't think I'll ever fully understand how much."

Feeling pleased with her conclusion and glad she had it done before class was over, Christy handed in her paper and used the rest of the class time to finish some of her Spanish assignment. It was due Friday, and she wanted to take home as little homework as possible.

As soon as school was over she would have to go to work at the pet store. She worked all day on Saturdays and went to church Sundays. That didn't leave much time for Todd and left even less time for homework.

When the final bell rang, Christy hurried to her locker and saw Fred standing there waiting for her. "Hi, Miss Chris. What time shall I pick you up for the game?"

"Fred," Christy said, impatiently spinning through the combination on her lock, "I told you I work tonight. I can't go to the game, and I can't take yearbook pictures with you."

"Sure you can! After the game. We could meet at one of the pizza joints where all the football players hang out and catch them with their mouths full."

"I don't think so, Fred."

"Come on, Miss Chris. We're in this together. Besides, your camera is nicer than mine."

"Would you like to borrow my camera?" Christy pulled it from the corner of her locker and offered it to Fred. It had been a Christmas gift from her Uncle Bob. She knew it was a nice one, but she didn't know how nice until Fred had drooled over it the first time she had brought it into class.

"Are you sure?"

Christy hesitated. Maybe it wasn't a good idea to loan such an expensive gift to this guy. Still, it would keep him out of her hair for a while. "Yes, you can borrow it on one condition."

"Wow, thanks! Anything. What's the condition?"

"That you promise to stop taking pictures of me and not to take any more for the rest of the year."

Fred made a face. "I can't promise that."

Christy reached for the camera. "Promise me, Fred, or else you can't borrow the camera."

"I can't promise that," Fred said, sadly handing the camera back to Christy. He looked dejected.

"Oh, all right," Christy said, pushing the camera back into his arms. "You can borrow it, and you don't have to make any promises. Just don't break it or lose it or hurt it, okay?"

"Not a problem. I promise I'll take perfect care of it, Christy."

Fred flashed her a big smile. "You're the best, you know. Anyone ever tell you that?"

"Just take good care of it, okay?"

As Christy drove to work, she wondered if she would regret her decision to loan Fred her camera. She decided to ask Jon, her boss at the pet store, what he thought. He tended to be a pretty good judge of character, or in Fred's case, judge of *a* character.

It felt strange going to work without Katie. Ever since last Christmas when Katie had landed a job as one of Santa's elves, Katie and Christy had shared rides to work. Katie had stayed on with the mall photographer and worked pretty much the same hours as Christy. Now with Michael to drive her around, Katie didn't seem to have much use for a best friend anymore.

It bothered Christy more than she had admitted to anyone. Especially since Katie was beginning to change. Not in any huge, obvious ways, but Christy noticed little things, like the way Katie had started to wear funky sandals like Michael's and how yesterday at lunch she drank bottled water instead of a Coke.

Jon was on the phone when she arrived at the pet store, so Christy went right to work, checking on the fish in the large aquarium section in the back of the shop. The soothing sound of the bubbles in the tanks and the gentle motion of all the fish made this hideaway Christy's favorite spot to go when she arrived at work and tried to make the transition from school to pet shop.

"Christy," Jon called from the front, "could you come up to the cash register, please?"

Christy slid the cover over a tank of angel fish she was feeding and hurried to the front. She had a feeling it was going to be one of those nonstop nights.

What she didn't count on was becoming one of the customers. By the end of the evening, she had a new pet to take home.

Christy tried to quietly open the front door around 9:15 when she arrived at home. The screen door didn't cooperate, and a loud screech announced her arrival. The eyes of both her parents were instantly on her, focusing on the rather large animal cage she held gingerly in front of her.

"Guess what? I got a bonus. From Jon. See, he thought I should have a pet since I worked at a pet store and didn't own any animals. He gave me everything free. There's even a big bag of food out in the car."

"What is it?" Christy's mom asked, rising from the couch and coming closer to inspect their new houseguest.

"A rabbit. I had a hard time choosing. You see, there was this little girl who came into the store with her mom, and she said she would pick whatever kind of pet I had. Since I didn't have a pet, Jon told me to pick a pet, any pet, and he would give it to me. So Abbey and I both picked rabbits."

"And what are you going to name it?" Mom asked, still appearing calm.

"Hershey. Because he's so dark, like chocolate. I can keep him, can't I?"

Mom and Dad exchanged glances. When Dad gave Mom a slight nod, Christy knew Hershey had passed the test.

"Not in your room, though," Dad said. "Keep the critter in the garage until we can come up with a hutch for it in the back."

"Hi there, little Hershey," Mom said, peeking in the cage. "What a cutie. Good choice, Christy."

"I'm glad you think so," Christy said, letting out a sigh of relief. "I felt as though I had about five thousand pets to choose from. It was so hard to decide! I'm glad you guys like little Hershey."

"Your brother will be thrilled, you know."

"I know. I'm hoping I can talk him into pellet-patrol when I'm real busy." Christy noticed her Dad smirking at the unrealistic goal. She knew it was a fat chance, but she could always hope.

"Todd called earlier," Mom said. "He's coming down tomorrow for the day."

"But I have to work," Christy said with a groan. "What time is he coming?"

"Before noon probably. Do you get off at six as usual?"

"Yes. I wish I could get off earlier. Tell him to come see me at work."

"David talked to him about some kind of skateboard park he wanted Todd to take him to. Maybe they can stop by the mall afterwards."

"Nothing like sharing your boyfriend with your little brother," Christy muttered on her way to the garage with Hershey.

Deep down, she knew she shouldn't be jealous of David spending so much time with Todd. It seemed to be good for both of them, since Todd was an only child and David looked up to him as the big brother he had never had. Any girl would be thrilled to have a boyfriend who got along so well with her family. And Christy *was* glad. It was just that she wished she could spend more time with Todd.

Todd and David didn't show up at the pet store the next day until after five. David wore a huge smile as he told Christy all about the skateboard park and how Todd had taught him some new, totally cool tricks.

"He's a natural," Todd said confidently.

"Hang on a second," Christy said, leaving Todd and David in the dog food section and slipping behind the counter to wait on a customer.

"Are you ready?" she asked the woman, who held out a dog leash and collar.

"Yes," the woman replied, "unless you happen to have the latest copy of *Gun Dog* magazine.

"All our magazines usually come in the last week of the month. We probably still have some of September's issue, but October's won't be here until sometime next week."

"Fine. Just this, then."

Christy reached for the leash to find the price tag. She noticed the woman seemed to be paying particular attention to Christy's hands.

"That's a charming bracelet," the woman said, looking at Christy's "Forever" ID bracelet. "Very unique design. Did you buy it here at the mall?"

Christy was about to say, "No, my boyfriend gave it to me." Then she realized that, yes, she had bought it *back* from one of the jewelry stores at the mall after Rick had stolen it and traded it in for a silver bracelet engraved with his name. But that wasn't what the lady was asking.

"Actually," Christy said, lowering her voice, "it was a very special gift from my boyfriend." With her eyes she motioned over to Todd, who was too far away to hear their conversation.

The woman followed Christy's visual gesture and turned back toward Christy with her face lit up in approval. "You are a very lucky young lady!"

Christy could feel herself blushing. "Thank you. I think so, too."

After she had placed the leash and collar in a bag and handed it to the woman, Christy remembered a detail about the bracelet she hadn't thought about in a long time. Last year when she was making weekly payments at the jewelry store to get back her bracelet, Todd was still in Hawaii. Yet some guy had come into the jewelry store and paid off the remaining balance so Christy could have her bracelet back. It still remained a mystery as to who that guy was.

For a while she thought it had been her boss, Jon, but he had denied it more than once. She even thought it was Rick since she thought she saw him at the mall the day she got her bracelet. It might have been, but Rick didn't seem to fit the profile of a benefactor who could keep a secret, especially when his silver substitute bracelet and his ego were involved.

It also occurred to Christy, as she rang up the next customer's purchase on the register, that she had never told any of this to Todd. Did he even know that the bracelet had been off her wrist for weeks while he was gone? Should she tell him?

Christy thought about the bracelet mystery again after dinner while Todd and she drove to the movies in his old Volkswagen, Gus the Bus. She wasn't sure how to bring up the subject. Todd was still talking about skateboarding and his adventure with David that afternoon. A heart-to-heart talk about the ID bracelet, the symbol of their relationship, didn't seem to fit in at this particular moment.

She decided to wait until after the movie. Maybe if it would be a real mushy one it would help Todd get into a more serious mood.

"Looks like we have a choice," Todd said, scanning the list of movies at the ticket window. "It's great when they're not all 'R's.' Do you think they're getting the hint in Hollywood that people want something other than blood and guts?"

Long lines had formed, and Christy and Todd slipped into one, even though they hadn't decided what they were going to see yet.

"Could be," Christy said. "What sounds good to you?"

"That second one on the list starts in five minutes," Todd said. "I don't know much about it, but the rating is right. What do you think?"

"Sure. Sounds fine. I don't know anything about it either."

"Christy!" came a loud voice from across the parking lot.

Todd and Christy turned around and saw Katie and Michael jogging toward them, holding hands.

*They're holding hands! Why are they holding hands? Katie and Michael are really together. Katie, do you know what you're doing? You met this guy five days ago, and here you are, obviously on a date, and you're holding hands!*

"Can you believe this?" Katie said breathlessly as she joined them. Her face looked flushed but happy. She was wearing jeans and a T-shirt with a Save the Whales slogan on it. Christy noticed Katie's black eyes had greatly improved. And she wore a new necklace made from tiny, brightly colored beads. "Todd, this is Michael. Michael, this is Christy's boyfriend, Todd."

The two guys shook hands, and Todd said, "So how did you two meet?" Christy thought he looked a little surprised.

"At school," Katie said, giving Christy a startled look. "Didn't Christy tell you? It was a designed meeting."

*Designed meeting? Katie, a week ago you would have said it was a 'God thing.' What's happened to you? What's this 'designed meeting' stuff?*

By then Todd was up at the window, and Michael quickly pulled some money from his pocket and told Todd, "Two more of whatever you're buying."

Todd paid for the tickets, and the four of them entered the theater. Katie chattered on as they found four seats together near the front, right when the previews began to run.

"Just in time," Katie whispered to Christy. The two girls were wedged together, with the guys sitting on either side of them. "Isn't this the cheekiest thing?"

"Cheekiest?" Christy questioned.

"Oh, Michael says it all the time." Katie giggled. "Isn't he terrific? Don't you just love this? Do you realize you and I are finally doing what we always wanted to? We're finally on a double date together!"

Christy smiled warily in the darkened room. "Yeah, this is great!"

Michael put his arm around the back of Katie's chair, and she snuggled a little closer to him as the movie started. Christy slipped her right hand through Todd's arm, and he grasped her fingers and wove them around his.

Todd squeezed her hand as if to say "Relax!" She gave him a squeeze back and settled into her seat. Katie was right. This was what Christy had always dreamed of, going to the movies and holding hands with Todd, double-dating with Katie and . . . that's where the dream didn't seem to match up. Christy had never imagined anyone like Michael in Katie's life.

Now that he was here, she didn't feel settled about him. Why couldn't it be Doug or Glen? Or any other normal guy from church? Why did Katie have to get involved with this strange guy, who most likely wasn't even a Christian? What was going to happen?

"We brought our own snacks," Katie said, reaching for Michael's leather backpack and pulling something from it. "You want some?"

*Come on, Christy, relax. Enjoy this time with your friends. Sit back, eat some M&M's and try to act as if everything is the way it should be.*

"Sure," Christy whispered back. "What did you guys smuggle

in? M&M's? Snickers? Ding Dongs?" Christy tried to think of what other favorite junk food Katie might have brought with her.

"Raisins," Katie said, offering Christy a small box. "We brought raisins and unsalted sunflower seeds."

"Raisins?" Christy repeated. "You mean those chocolate covered raisins?"

"Nope. Just plain, ordinary, healthy raisins. Michael says they're full of iron and something else. They're good. Really! Here, have some." Katie plopped the little box in Christy's lap and tossed a handful of raisins into her own mouth.

*She brought raisins. Katie is eating healthy raisins! Oh, Katie, this is worse than I thought. You're really serious about this guy, aren't you?*

# CHAPTER EIGHT

# Mice on a Mission

"Do you have any bottled water?" Michael asked the waitress at Marie Callender's Pie Shop and Restaurant a few hours later when the foursome stopped in for an after-movie snack.

"Yes, we do. Would you like anything else?"

"No, thank you. Just water."

The waitress turned to Christy. "And for you?"

Christy felt a little embarrassed ordering pie after Michael ordered only water. "I'd like a piece of cherry pie, please."

"Would you like that with ice cream or whipped cream?" the waitress asked.

She thought ice cream sounded good but turned it down. "No, thanks."

"Would you care to have it heated?"

"No, thank you."

"Good choice," Michael said, leaning across the table and confiding in Christy. "It won't be until the next generation that we'll see the side effects of all this microwaving we've done to our food. Can't be good for humans, I think. Best to avoid it whenever possible."

"Right," Christy said with a slight smile.

"A small salad, please," Katie ordered. "No dressing."

After the raisins in the theater, nothing should have surprised Christy, but Katie ordering a salad did.

"Not the iceberg lettuce," Michael added to Katie's order. "It retains pesticides even after it's been washed."

"Would spinach be okay?" the waitress asked, looking a little annoyed at Michael, the "nature boy."

"Sure," Katie said. Then turning to Christy, she mumbled in a low voice, "I guess it wouldn't hurt to try spinach for the first time in my life. What do you think?"

Christy knew this was neither the time nor the place to tell Katie what she thought. Instead, she returned Katie's friendly smile and waited to see what recommendations Michael might have for Todd's order.

"Pumpkin pie with whipped cream and a glass of water."

"Is tap water okay, or would you prefer bottled water as well?"

"No, city water is fine. Hasn't killed me yet."

The waitress turned with a swish, and Christy felt certain she was miffed with them. Christy didn't like anyone to be upset with her. Not even a waitress.

"So tell me about Belfast," Todd said to Michael, who jumped right in and in his wonderful accent talked about the political unrest in his beloved city. He told of being in a grocery store as a child and leaving only minutes before a bomb exploded. The bomb sheared off the front half of the store, but Michael and his mother were unharmed.

Christy enjoyed listening to Michael speak with such passion about his homeland. She had to admit his accent was charming, and he spoke with beguiling animation. Katie looked so proud to be with him. He was nice-looking in his natural, earthy sort of way. His thick, dark hair fit well with his fair skin and green eyes.

Christy had to admit his personality and looks were intriguing. If only he would say he was a Christian, it would make everything perfect.

When the food arrived, Todd said, "Would you guys mind if I prayed before we eat?"

"Pray for a piece of pie?" Michael asked with a laugh.

"I like to give thanks to God whenever He provides me with something to eat."

Michael looked amused. "But the waitress provided it. The cook prepared it. It's the money from your own pocket that will pay for it. What has God done to provide your pumpkin pie?"

Now it was Todd's turn to look amused. "God made the pumpkin. I want to tell Him thanks." Bowing his head, Todd said in a jovial voice, "Thanks, Father, for making the pumpkin. Thanks, too, for making Michael. You did a good job on both of them. Amen."

Michael laughed aloud. "I don't suppose I've ever heard a prayer like that before. You sure God heard you?"

Todd nodded and gave Michael a confident smile. Just before the first forkful of pumpkin pie touched Todd's lips, he said with complete assurance, "Oh, yeah. He heard me all right. God hears."

Michael took a swig of his bottled water and, shaking his head, said, "Your friends are a bit daft, Katie. Anyone ever tell you that?"

"They're the best friends a person could ever hope for, Michael," Katie quickly retorted, moving the spinach around on her plate, apparently trying to work up the nerve to take her first bite. "You won't find better than these two anywhere."

"I found you," Michael said, facing Katie and looking deep

into her eyes. "It's the luck of the Irish I carry with me wherever I go."

Katie blushed. But she didn't turn away. Instead, she met Michael's gaze and locked into a silent, visual embrace with him.

Christy looked down at her cherry pie. It was awfully hard to act casual when Katie was falling in love right before her eyes. Had she acted like that when she had first met Todd? It seemed so long ago. She was so used to him now, so comfortable around him. She couldn't picture herself being entwined in such an intimate exchange with him in a public place. Still, it was amazing to see Katie so in love.

*Tomorrow,* Christy decided, *when Katie and I are working in the church's nursery, I'm going to lay it on the line with her. If this guy isn't a Christian, which he doesn't appear to be, then she needs to break up with him immediately before she gets too involved.*

But the next morning, Katie didn't show up for her commitment to work in the nursery. Christy had her hands full with fifteen weary and hungry three-year-olds.

"I just found out the teacher for the three-year-olds has gone home ill," the church nursery coordinator said, popping her head into Christy's room. "I have you and another high schooler scheduled. Do you need an additional helper?"

"Definitely!" Christy said, retrieving a truck from a little boy who was about to throw it at two girls quietly looking at books on the rug.

"Mine!" the boy wailed. He burst into tears and tried to retrieve the truck from Christy's raised hand.

"The other high schooler is my friend Katie. She hasn't shown up. I could use all the helpers you can send me!"

"I'll send three junior helpers in right away," the woman promised. "Here's the lesson book. If you don't mind, could you look it over? It looks like you'll need to teach the Bible story today. Snacks will be at the regular time, and I'll be right next door if you need anything."

A mixture of panic and anger washed over Christy. Katie was the one who was good with little kids. She could entertain them on a moment's notice. Katie would be great at doing the lesson, even if it was last minute. She was probably off with Michael somewhere and hadn't even bothered to let Christy know she wasn't coming. This was unfair!

Fortunately, the three middle-school helpers were right at home with toddlers. They busied the kids with crayons at the table while Christy peeked at the lesson book.

It seemed easy enough, a story about seasons and how God is in control of all the changes that take place in this world. Some verses appeared at the end of the lesson from Ecclesiastes about there being a time for everything. She thought she had heard a song about that before.

*I'm so mad Katie isn't here! She probably knows the song. She could have sung it for the kids. She should be doing this, not me!*

Christy stared out the window at the church parking lot while she thought about Katie's desertion. The leaves were changing color on one of the big shade trees; several floated down and landed on some of the car tops like giant yellow and orange confetti.

It was a memorable parking lot. Her dad had given Christy her first driving lesson there. Last summer they loaded the bus for church camp in the lot. It had been Katie's idea to go, but she had backed out at the last minute, leaving Christy alone as a camp counselor to a bunch of fifth-grade girls.

Then Christy flashed on another memory of that church parking lot. Two years ago she had given Rick Doyle a Christmas present out by his car, and he had unexpectedly kissed her. Come to think of it, the gift for Rick and going out to the parking lot with him had been Katie's idea, too.

Christy realized she had a memory for almost every season in that parking lot. Maybe she could make a memory for this little bunch of young hearts out in that same lot. They could go for a walk and each collect one of those autumn leaves. Then they would come in for story time. Christy would put all the leaves up on the board and talk about how it's God who makes the seasons change. It seemed simple enough.

"Okay, now everyone remember to hold onto the hand of your buddy. We're going to be very quiet." Christy placed her finger over her lips and motioned for the class to tiptoe behind her like little mice.

Except for a couple of creative youngsters who added some tiny mouse squeaks, they made it to the parking lot without incident. Christy led them to the tree at the side of the lot and said, "Now while you're still holding the hand of your buddy, everyone pick up one special leaf, and we'll take them back to class."

Two little boys near the fence spotted their "special leaves" in opposite directions and tried to retrieve them while still holding hands. They yanked hard on each other's arm. Before a major scuffle could break out, Christy stepped in and helped Tyler find his leaf while one of the junior helpers took Benjamin's hand and helped him find his.

"Okay, buddies, everyone holding hands? Show me your leaves in your other hand. Oh, those are all beautiful! You did a great job. Now we're going to be quiet little mice again and go back to our room."

The procession seemed much louder than on the way out. Christy had to stop them at the door and press her finger to her lips once more. "I want to see only quiet little mice tiptoeing down the hall. Which one of you is going to be my quietest little mouse?"

"Me!" they all said loudly.

Christy quickly pressed her finger to her lips again. "Shh! I don't want to hear any noise. Quiet little mice don't make any sounds at all."

With exaggerated tiptoe steps, Christy held her new buddy's hand and demonstrated how quietly she wanted them to walk. It was working. They held hands, still clasping their special leaves, and tiptoed to the classroom.

The nursery coordinator happened to be standing by their door and seemed delighted at what she saw. "I wondered why it was so quiet in here all of a sudden," the woman whispered to Christy. "It looks like you had a special adventure."

Christy nodded and led the sweet parade into the classroom. As the coordinator watched, Christy said, "Now all my little mice need to sit on the floor and carefully hold your leaf in your lap. These are special treasures! God made these leaves."

The children took their places and looked at their autumn leaves with reverent awe, awaiting their next instruction.

"I've never seen this class behave so well before," the coordinator whispered to Christy. "You're a miracle worker! I didn't know you had such a gift to work with children. You should become one of our regular teachers. I'll talk to you about it afterwards."

Christy felt warmed inside. She did kind of enjoy this, as long as the kids were cooperative. She didn't do well when they were fighting and screaming.

"Okay, my little mice, you're doing a good job! One of my helpers is going to come around and put a piece of tape on your leaf with your name on it so you'll know which one to take home with you after class. I'm going to put all the leaves up here on the board, and then I have a very special story to tell you."

Christy couldn't believe how sweetly the little faces looked at her. They followed instructions and waited expectantly for her story.

After she had gathered the leaves and arranged them on the board behind her, Christy sat on the teacher's stool and held up her Bible for all the children to see. "Do you know what this is?" she asked.

"The Bible!" they all yelled. A string of comments and pushing and tattling followed.

*Okay, so I don't ask questions unless I want a riot to break out.*

"That's right, the Bible. Now everyone listen. Quiet little mice listen to the story without making a sound." Christy waited a moment while her helpers calmed the children.

"The Bible tells us about God. The Bible says . . ." Christy quickly opened to Ecclesiastes 3:1 and began to read, "There is a time for everything, and a season for every activity under heaven: a time to be born and a time to die, a time to plant and a time to uproot."

Christy noticed the next verse said, "A time to kill and a time to heal." She didn't think a bunch of three-year-olds would understand that, so she skipped down a few verses and read, "A time to weep and a time to laugh, a time to mourn and a time to dance." Then thinking she might lose their attention if she read the entire passage, which went on for another four verses, Christy quickly summarized, "You see, there's a time for everything."

*I wonder if the person who wrote this lesson thought about how short the attention span of a three-year-old is?*

She spoke a few minutes to the now-wiggling bunch about

how God is in control of everything and how He knows when it's time for things to change.

"Right now it's time for the leaves to change color," Christy explained. "Everything happens according to God's plan."

Just then the helper from next door walked in with a tray of juice and crackers, and all concentration was lost. Still, Christy felt good about having taught her first lesson to preschoolers. Some eternal secrets were locked inside those yellow leaves, secrets about God's design and His proper time for everything.

Even if the kids hadn't learned much, Christy knew she had snatched a nugget of God's truth for herself and hidden it in her heart. This morning had been a time to try something new, a time to teach toddlers. To her surprise, she enjoyed it.

As the children filled in around the small tables, a few fights broke out in their eagerness to get their snacks. This was the part Christy wasn't good at, calming down the wild ones. She had seen Katie do it with ease and wished Katie were here now.

Then, remembering how the verses said there was a time for everything, Christy gritted her teeth as she pulled apart two squabbling toddlers.

*Maybe there is 'a time to kill,' and that time is this afternoon, when I get my hands on Katie for abandoning me!*

# CHAPTER NINE

# *Harder and Richer*

"Well, do you know when she'll be home?" Christy asked Katie's brother on the phone Sunday evening. She had tried all afternoon to reach Katie, but no one had answered the phone.

"I don't know," her brother said.

"If it's before ten, could you ask her to call me? Thanks."

Christy hung up the phone and was about to head for the kitchen to find something to eat when the phone rang.

"Hello?"

"Hey, how's it going?"

"Todd, hi. I wish you were here."

"Yeah? What's up?"

"Katie didn't show up at church today. I called her all afternoon, and she wasn't home. I just talked to her brother, and he doesn't know when she'll be back. She's out with Michael; I'm sure of it. This is *not* a good thing."

Christy could hear Todd chuckling on the other end of the line.

"What? You think this is funny? She's serious about this guy. What's so funny about that?"

"It's not funny, but you are," Todd said in his matter-of-fact way.

"So you think I'm funny?"

"You sound like a mother, not a best friend."

"Todd, I can't believe you're making fun of me and treating this relationship between Michael and Katie like it's nothing!" Christy said, letting her irritation show. "He's not a Christian; she's falling in love with him. It's obvious. She's going to get hurt, Todd, or worse. And excuse me, but I happen to care about what happens to my friends!"

"Then stick with her," Todd answered calmly.

"It's kind of hard to stick with her when she's out with him!"

There was only silence on the other end of the phone.

"What should I do, Todd? I am her best friend!" Christy didn't realize how loud her voice was until Mom poked her head around the corner and peered at Christy.

More silence on the other end.

"Todd, are you even interested in participating in this conversation? I feel as if it's awfully one-sided." Christy had lowered her voice, but she was aware the intensity of her tone had not diminished.

"I'm here, Christy."

"Well, I wish you'd tell me what to do about all this. It's not something to laugh about, and it's not something to ignore. Katie is headed for big trouble if we don't do something. Tell me what to do!"

Todd paused before saying, "I don't know what to tell you other than to keep with her. Keep loving her. Pray."

Now Christy felt really mad. Todd prayed all the time about everything, and Christy tried to, too. But right now her best friend was about to make the biggest mistake of her life! Todd's answer, obviously, was too simple.

"It's not that easy," Christy argued.

"Sure it is. You're the one who's making it so hard."

"I am not!" Christy's voice came out wobbly with emotion. "I can't believe you are being so insensitive, Todd Spencer. I don't want to talk to you anymore!" Before she knew what she was doing, Christy slammed down the receiver.

*What have I done? I've never had an argument with Todd like that. I've never hung up on him. He must think I'm awful! I can't believe I did that.*

Christy immediately dialed Todd's number, but the answering machine came on with his dad's voice saying, "We're not able to come to the phone right now, but if you'd like to leave a message, wait for the beep."

Christy waited for the beep and in halting words left her message. "I—I'm sorry, Todd. If you're there, please call me back. I'd like to talk to you about this some more. Thanks. Oh, it's Christy. Bye."

*That has to be the dumbest message in the world. What if his dad listens to it? Is Todd there and not answering, or did he call from somewhere else?*

Christy thought of how sometimes Todd would drive down to see her and not call until he was in town, only a few blocks from her house. He would call to see if it was a good time to come over. What if he were calling her from downtown? It was an hour and a half back to his house, so it was no small thing for Todd to come see her. She felt awful.

For the next hour Christy waited for the phone to ring. She tried watching TV, eating ice cream, and doing her nails. She went out in the garage and gave Hershey a carrot and stroked his soft fur for a while. She felt terrible.

At 9:15 the phone rang, and Christy sprang from the couch to answer it. It was the wrong number; the person didn't even speak English. Finally at ten Christy forced herself into bed, but she lay awake in the stillness for a long time, blaming herself for hanging up on Todd, and worrying about Katie. It was *not* a good night.

She tried to call Todd again at 7:45 the next morning, but she only got the answering machine again. She knew his dad left early for work and Todd had classes on Monday mornings, but she had hoped to catch him before he left. The thought of spending the day at school without having apologized to Todd depressed her. It almost diminished her concern for Katie. Until she saw Katie at lunchtime, that is.

Michael hadn't arrived at their lunch spot yet. Katie was sitting by herself under the tree, so Christy rushed to get to Katie before Michael showed up.

"Katie," Christy began breathlessly, "why weren't you at church yesterday? You left me with a whole bunch of rug rats all by myself. Where were you?"

"Michael and I went to the beach."

"All day? I called you all afternoon, and your brother didn't know where you were."

"I don't have to check in and out with him. And what's with you?"

Christy decided to get right to the point. "You've got to end this thing with Michael. You're going to get hurt; I just know it. He's not a Christian, is he?"

Katie looked incredulously at Christy. "I don't know. It's different in Northern Ireland than it is here. With the Protestants and Catholics there it's more of a political thing. Michael believes in God."

"Oh, great! He believes in God. That's terrific! Do you realize what you're doing, Katie? You're going back on every standard you ever set. Don't you remember in Sunday school class when you were 'Katie Christian' up on the chair and 'Peter Pagan' pulled you down? It's happening with Michael."

Katie laughed. "You crack me up, Christy! You should see your face right now." Katie imitated her with a wild, bug-eyed look, shaking her finger in Christy's face. Katie laughed again. "Relax, will you? I'm not doing anything wrong."

"You're dating a non-Christian. Don't you think that's wrong?"

Katie thought a minute and said, "When you went to Disneyland with Todd a couple of years ago, would you say that you were a Christian then?"

"Well, no, I wasn't a Christian yet, but that's different."

"How is that different? If Todd hadn't spent so much time with you, do you still think you would have become a Christian when you did?" Katie challenged.

"I, well, it's not the same, Katie. That was years ago. Todd and I weren't really dating, and I wasn't falling in love with him the way I see you falling in love with Michael."

"You're daft!" Katie said, boldly using Michael's word as if it were hers. "You and Todd were dating, and you did fall in love with him. Only he was the Christian and you weren't."

Just then Michael walked up. Christy turned on her heel, refusing to make eye contact with him. "I'll talk to you later, Katie."

"What's with her?" Christy heard Michael ask Katie.

As Christy marched away, she heard Katie say, "She must have had a fight with Todd."

Now Christy was really fuming. It was bad enough that she

had gotten nowhere with Katie, but to hear her crack about having a fight with Todd was even worse, especially since it was true.

Christy found an unoccupied corner of a picnic table and tried to convince herself she was hungry enough to eat her lunch.

"Hey, Miss Chris!" came an irritatingly familiar voice behind her. She was *not* in the mood to talk to Fred.

"I got some great shots at the game Friday. You should have been there. I love your camera. Are you going to be needing it the rest of this week? Because if you don't mind, I'd like to finish off this roll of film."

"Fine," Christy said without looking up.

"Thanks." Fred was about to walk away when he stopped. "Are you okay?"

"Sure. I'm fine."

"Then why are you sitting here all by yourself?"

"I need to get some homework done," Christy lied.

Fred sat down next to her. "You're lying, Christy. You don't have any books with you. You're a terrible liar, I hope you know. Boyfriend problems?"

Christy ignored him. She felt terrible.

"Problems at home?"

Christy unwrapped her sandwich and prepared to take a bite.

Fred wouldn't give up. He bent closer and in a low voice said, "You can confide in me, Christy. Your dad is beating you, isn't he?"

His question prompted her to crack a tiny smile since the thought of her dad beating her was so completely absurd. "No, Fred, my dad doesn't beat me," she answered.

"Mine does."

Christy looked up at Fred for the first time. He was serious.

"Your dad really beats you, Fred?"

"Well, he used to, before my mom divorced him. I haven't seen him since I was nine. I don't even know where he lives now. The only reason I said anything was because I used to sit by myself at lunch every day when I was a kid, especially after he had beaten me and I didn't want to hear another person ask how I got the black and blue marks."

Fred lifted Christy's right arm and checked both sides. "No welts. You must be telling the truth." He smiled as if trying to make light of the subject.

"Fred," Christy said softly, "I'm really sorry. I had no idea."

"It's not something you go around broadcasting, you know. Besides, he's long gone."

"But the memories take a little longer to go away, don't they?" Christy asked. She almost thought she saw Fred's eyes mist over.

"Yeah, well, life goes on. Nobody has it perfect, you know. I don't even know why I told you. It's not really something I'd like spread around, okay?"

Christy nodded.

Fred let out a sigh. "So you haven't told me what your problem is."

Christy had almost forgotten her problems with Katie, Michael, and Todd in the light of Fred's revelations. "Oh, it's nothing really. I'm glad you came by, though. I feel better. Thanks."

"There's the smile I was waiting for," Fred said. Before Christy could stop him, Fred lifted the camera and pointed it at her face for a close-up shot. "Big smile, Miss Chris!"

"Fred, don't take my picture." Christy put her hand in front of the lens and blocked the shot just as the camera clicked.

"Hey!" he protested. "That would've been a great shot. Why did you do that?"

"Because I've told you, I don't want you to take my picture."

"But it's part of our relationship. It's my way of documenting our year together."

"Fred, we don't have a 'relationship.' Our year together is based on us being in the same yearbook class. That's all."

"You can see things your way, I see things mine."

"Fred," Christy began, but she didn't know what else to say. She felt frustrated. He had opened himself up and told her about his dad, and that made her feel more tender toward him. However, Fred seemed to use her sympathy to assume their relationship was progressing.

She decided to try ignoring him. It had worked in junior high with guys like Fred. Maybe he would take the hint if she ate her sandwich and didn't talk to him.

Unfortunately, Fred seemed content to sit in silence. He dug into his own sack lunch. Every now and then he would look up and smile at people who happened to notice them, as if this were a planned lunch meeting and he and Christy were together by mutual choice.

"I need to go to my locker," Christy suddenly said, stuffing the unfinished half of her sandwich in her bag and getting up from the table.

"I'll go with you," Fred quickly offered.

"That's okay. I'm going to stop at the rest room, too. You can't come with me there."

"Then I'll see you in class in a few minutes."

Christy started to walk away when Fred said softly, "And thanks for having lunch with me. Nine years is a long time to eat lunch by yourself."

Christy kept walking but thought about how, apparently, things hadn't changed much for Fred over the years. Part of her felt sorry for him and wanted to make an effort to be nicer to him.

He wasn't that bad. He had a pretty nice personality. If only he weren't so annoying.

The more she thought about it, the more Christy realized Fred's appearance was his problem. However, she had enough of her own problems and began to plan how she would start calling Todd the minute she got home from school. She vowed she wouldn't go to bed that night until she had cleared things up with him.

She finally reached Todd at 9:45 that night. He seemed fine, completely unaffected by their tiff the night before.

"I'm really sorry, Todd. I can't believe I hung up on you."

"You were mad."

"I shouldn't have been."

"Why not?"

"Because I shouldn't have gotten so upset."

"You know what C. S. Lewis said?" Todd asked. "He said, 'Anger is the fluid that love bleeds when you cut it.' I just read that the other day. You love Katie, Michael is cutting into that relationship, you're bleeding anger. It's natural."

"So you think it's right for me to feel this way?" Christy asked.

"I didn't say it was right; I said it was natural. The right way is hardly ever the natural way. The right way is God's way, which is supernatural."

"How am I supposed to get from the natural to the super-natural?" Christy asked. As soon as she did, she had a feeling she knew what Todd was going to say.

"Pray."

"That's what I thought you'd say."

Todd let out a low chuckle. "It's hard, isn't it?"

"Yes, it is. I thought the longer I was a Christian, the easier it would become. It seems to only get harder."

"Harder and richer," Todd added. "I guess we shouldn't want it any other way. All true love relationships seem to become harder and richer the more they grow."

Christy wondered if Todd were referring to his relationship with God, with her, or both. She thought the harder-richer part certainly applied to both relationships in her life.

"Well, I still want to apologize for hanging up on you, Todd. And I still feel concerned about Katie. I'll try to pray about it more. If nothing else, I've learned I don't want to ever have to wait so long to apologize to you again. It was awful going a whole day without things feeling settled and right between us."

"Yeah, I didn't like the feeling much either. I was over at Doug's when I called you last night, and I have to admit that when you hung up on me I felt pretty weird about calling you back, especially with Doug right there. He told me to let it go. He even said it was probably good for our relationship to go through this. For a while I almost thought he seemed glad you were ticked off at me. He didn't happen to call you last night, did he?"

"No. I tried to call your house but only got your answering machine."

"You want to come up here this weekend?" Todd asked. "Can you stay at Bob and Marti's and go to church with me Sunday?"

"I have to work Friday night and Saturday. And I have one more week to volunteer at the church nursery. I wish I didn't have so many things going on. I'd really like to spend some time with you. More than just a quick Saturday night movie."

"I know what you mean. How about next weekend then, if you're done with nursery duty? Think Jon would let you off early on Saturday?"

"I'll work it out somehow, Todd. I need to spend more time

with you. It seems like there's so much going on, and we're so far apart."

"Next weekend," Todd said. "We'll get together then. I'll call you this weekend after you get off work."

Christy didn't even try to hide her disappointment when she replied, "You mean, you're not coming down this weekend? We could do something when I get off work Saturday or maybe Sunday afternoon."

"I'd better stick around here and get some studying done. This semester is taking off without me; I'm already behind. I'll call you, and we'll get together the next weekend."

*Two horrible, long weeks!* Christy thought. It was bad enough going twenty-four hours without feeling that things with Todd were settled. Now waiting two weeks to see him again seemed like an eternity.

It hadn't seemed so difficult in the past, before they were actually going together. Then it was a treat whenever he did show up. Now it seemed like it was mandatory that they be together whenever possible.

Christy determined she would get off work all of Saturday the following weekend, and she would have her homework done so nothing would interfere with their time together.

Everything seemed fine until the next evening when Christy ran the plans past her mom.

"That's Dad's birthday weekend. I thought we'd do something together as a family," Mom said. "Maybe go to the mountains for a picnic."

"Todd could come with us, couldn't he?"

"Well, I don't know, Christy. It's your dad's weekend. He should be the one to choose who comes with us."

That didn't concern Christy. Dad liked Todd. Although Todd

had been included on lots of outings with Bob and Marti, he hadn't done much with Christy's parents. Certainly now was the time to start.

"I think we'll just have a birthday cake here at home," Dad said later that evening. "I'm not much for gallivanting around the countryside."

"It's okay if I invite Todd over, isn't it?" Christy asked. She could immediately tell by the look on Dad's face that the thought of including Todd in their quiet family celebration had never crossed his mind.

"Maybe not, Christy," Mom said, also interpreting Dad's expression. "Let's just keep it the four of us, and you and Todd can spend some time together the following weekend."

*Three weeks!* Christy thought it seemed like a lifetime. How could she contentedly wait three weeks to spend time with her boyfriend? Something had to change.

The first thing she thought of was her job. She would change her hours so she could have Saturdays off. Maybe she could work one or two weeknights besides Fridays, especially since Todd was busy with classes and wouldn't be coming down on weeknights anyway. That way they would have all their Saturdays free to spend together.

That Friday when Christy arrived at work, she approached Jon with the request. He looked thoughtful. "Perhaps if I can get someone to cover the Saturday hours I can give you Saturdays off, but I don't have any open shifts on weeknights right now. If you want to give up your Saturday hours, it most likely will mean all you'll have for a while will be your five hours on Fridays. Is that going to be enough money to put gas in the car?"

Jon was right. Five hours on her minimum-wage salary was not much money compared to the expenses she had, especially with all the added expenses that came with her senior year.

"I don't know," Christy told Jon. "All I know is that I have too much going on and something has to give. I have no time for a social life."

Jon made a clicking noise. She had heard him use that sound to get the attention of the birds and guinea pigs when he was about to feed them. Now he seemed to be using it to comfort her. "Time is a funny thing, isn't it? There never seems to be enough of it when you have something to do, and when you have nothing to do, there's too much of it."

"You're right," Christy said, looking as forlorn as she felt.

"Don't worry about it. We'll work out something. You might as well make time to enjoy your only senior year in high school." Then with a wink and grin, he added, "Let's *hope* you only have one senior year in high school!"

What was it that Todd had said? Harder and richer. He might be right about the richer, but right now things just seemed harder.

# CHAPTER TEN

# Thirty Percent Off

As Christy drove home from work that Friday night, she knew she needed to get a few things in order in her life. First on the list was to make peace with Katie.

The next morning she called Katie to ask if she wanted to ride to work together and plan to have their lunch breaks together, the way they used to. When Christy called, Katie obviously wasn't up yet.

"What time is it?"

"A little after eight. Did I wake you?"

"Yeah, but that's okay. I didn't get home until almost two," Katie said with a huge yawn. "I'm really tired. But I'm glad you called. I was kind of wondering for a while there if you were going to ignore me forever."

"Why didn't you get home until two? Where were you?" The instant Christy said it, she realized she sounded like a nagging old hen and was defeating her plan to rebuild bridges.

Katie paused and then in an irritated voice said, "We were at a concert in San Diego."

"I didn't mean to sound like that," Christy said. Then trying hard to change her tone, she asked, "Did you and Michael have a good time?"

"Yes, we did. Michael and I always have a good time."

Christy tried to sound encouraging. "That's great, Katie."

"Do you really mean that?" Katie asked.

Christy knew she couldn't lie. How could she get around this? She paused and found she couldn't answer.

"That's okay," Katie said. "You don't have to answer that. I know how you feel about Michael. I don't want you to lie to me, ever. I won't lie to you, and you know that. I want you to be happy for me. I have never felt so wonderful in my whole life, Christy. I feel as if it's finally okay for me to just be me. Michael likes me. Can you believe that?"

"Of course I can. There's plenty to like. You're a treasure, Katie."

"Do you understand what I'm saying? Michael *likes* me, Christy. He's the first guy who has ever been really interested in me, and it's killing me that you won't be happy for me."

"I just wish he were a Christian," Christy said.

"Why does that make such a big difference to you? I'm not going to marry him! We're dating, that's all. He's very open to God and to spiritual things."

Christy paused and chose her words carefully. "But Katie, you and Michael are getting so close so fast, and I'm worried about you. He doesn't have the same standards you do."

"Yes, he does," Katie quickly defended. "You don't know him, Christy. You don't know what he's like. You're too self-righteous to even get to know him because he doesn't fit your little perfect Christian standard. Let me tell you something. Michael has been more of a gentleman to me than Rick Doyle ever was, and Rick was supposed to be some hotshot Christian. Rick kissed me, and it meant nothing to him. Another conquest. A game. When Michael kisses me, I can tell he means it from the bottom of his heart. Our relationship means as much to him as it does to me."

"He's kissed you?"

"Of course he's kissed me. You and Todd kiss. Why are you being so judgmental? I haven't done anything you haven't done. I'm not doing anything wrong!"

Christy could tell Katie was fully awake and on the defensive. It would be difficult for Christy to accomplish much bridge mending now. Instead she chose to redirect the conversation.

"Is there any way we can take our breaks together at one today and meet at the Food Park in the mall? I've really missed spending time with you, and I think if we're going to talk, we should do it in person."

"I can't today. I already have plans," Katie said, sounding as though she was calming down some.

"How about after work? We could get together then. Do you still get off at six?"

"Well, actually, I don't work at the photographer's any more."

"You don't? Since when? What happened?"

"I kind of got fired."

"Katie, when did this happen? Why didn't you tell me?"

"You haven't exactly been available for small talk this past week," Katie said.

"What happened?"

"My boss didn't like me taking so much time off, so he let me go. It's for the best. I wouldn't have had any time for a social life with all the hours I was scheduled to work."

Christy knew exactly what Katie meant, but still, being fired was a horrible thing. "Are you going to get another job?"

"I don't think so. At least not right away. It's not a big deal."

"Not a big deal? Katie," Christy scrambled for the right words, "you're changing. What's happening to you?"

"I'm finding myself," Katie answered confidently. "And the good part is, thanks to Michael, I really like what I'm finding."

It was silent for a moment.

Katie spoke softly. "You know, Christy, I think of all the changes you've been through since we've been friends, all the guys, all the difficult situations. During those times I tried to be there for you, and I tried to understand. It would really help if you could take a turn now and support me a little. If you could try to understand and be even a little bit happy for me, it would mean a lot."

"Katie, I do want to support you. I *have* supported you in a lot of stuff over the years. Maybe more than you even know. The problem is that I'm watching you fall in love with a guy who isn't a Christian, and there's no way I can feel good about that."

"Well," Katie said with a sigh, "I guess I misjudged you, and I misjudged our friendship. I thought you cared about me more than you cared about your pious little Christian rules. It's exactly like Michael said, religion and politics are about the same things. They're all a matter of taking sides and taking shots at those who aren't on your side."

"Katie . . . it's not like that."

"Yes, I think it is. I need to go, Christy; there's a call on the other line. Think about what I've said, and let's talk again when you're ready to be a little more open-minded."

Christy had a hard time at work acting as if nothing were wrong. Everything she had ever felt about friendships, dating, and Christianity had been shaken in that phone conversation. How could things have changed so much and so fast?

During the next week, Christy pursued Katie and continued

trying to wedge back into their friendship. Somehow Michael kept interpreting the wedge as something to divide Katie and him.

After four tense lunches under their tree that week, Christy decided it would be best to leave Michael and Katie alone on Friday and pick up again on Monday. She felt she was doing the right thing sticking by Katie in this way. Todd had encouraged her to do exactly that and had warned her about getting her feelings hurt.

"Remember what happens with love when you cut it?" Todd had said. "The fluid it sometimes bleeds is anger."

That seemed to be exactly what was coming from Katie and flowing all over Christy—anger in the form of cruel remarks and defensive arguments.

"So is it just on Fridays and Mondays, or what?" Christy heard Fred's voice behind her only minutes after she had taken a lonely seat at the picnic tables. "Sort of a random first-of-the-week, end-of-the-week ritual?"

"Excuse me?"

"The last time you sat here was on a Monday, remember? Not this week but last week. I'm trying to figure out if there's any kind of pattern here. Do you only eat by yourself on bad hair days, or what?" Fred sat down beside her and popped the top on his can of Dr. Pepper.

"No, I only eat by myself when I don't have anyone else to eat with." As she heard her own words, Christy realized how pathetic she sounded. The awful truth was that she had spent so much time with Katie over the last few years, she didn't have any other close friends at school. At least no one who invited her to make a run to Taco Bell at lunch time.

"Not a problem," Fred said confidently. "I happen to be available today, and I don't mind eating with you a bit."

"Thanks, Fred," Christy said, her sarcasm showing through. She hoped no one would see her with him. His constant attention was beginning to bug her. He seemed to always be at her side, not only in yearbook class but also here at lunch.

Christy ate her sandwich in silence, aware of Fred's noisy slurping from his soda can.

"You know, Fred, you would be a lot more, well . . . attractive if you didn't make such loud noises while you're eating and drinking."

"Good point," Fred said without seeming offended. "I hadn't realized I was doing that, but you're right, it is kind of uncouth."

Christy gave him a slight smile and continued eating her lunch.

"What else?" Fred asked.

"What do you mean?"

"What else would make me more attractive? I mean, I'm not stupid. I know I'm not the kind of guy a girl like you would be interested in, no matter how much I hope and dream that I could have a girlfriend like you someday."

"Fred—"

"Don't worry, I'm not trying to compete with your boyfriend like I said I was at the beginning of school. I've given it a lot of thought. I'm not your kind of guy, and I know that. What I guess I'm trying to ask is, how can I improve myself so that I could one day attract a girl like you?"

Christy felt awkward. "I'm not sure, Fred."

"Yes, you are. You know what girls like in a guy. Pretend you're my big sister. What would you tell me? I mean, I'm a senior, for pity's sake, and I've never been on a date, never even called a girl without her hanging up on me. Could you sort of give me a crash course in self-improvement?"

Christy wasn't sure how to respond. No one had ever asked her anything like this before. Still, Fred was sincere, and he really did have a lot of potential. She realized that since his dad left when he was nine, he probably didn't have any strong male role models.

"Well, you might want to try doing something different with your hair."

"Like a haircut?"

"Sure. Why don't you go to one of those places that advertises they style your hair for what looks best on you and ask them to do whatever they think would look good on you."

Fred's expression brightened. "That's a great idea! My mom's been cutting my hair ever since I was a kid. Maybe it's time for a change."

"Sure," Christy said enthusiastically, "let your mom have a little break. Ask them to show you how to style your hair while you're there. You know, you don't need a lot of hair spray or anything."

"I use my mom's gel."

"You might want to pick up some of your own hair care products, too. They might even have a line for men, which would be good, because you don't exactly need the same stuff on your hair that someone, say, with a perm would need."

"This is great, Christy! You don't know how much I appreciate this. Maybe you'd like to come with me. We could go today right after school. You can tell the stylist what you think looks good on me."

"I have to work right after school, Fred. But thanks for asking."

"At the pet store at the mall, right? Not a problem. I'll come in afterwards and show you the transformation."

"Don't you have to go to the football game and take pictures?"

"Not a problem. I'll ask one of the other people on the staff to go this week. I would certainly think the future of my image is more important than a few football photos. I've deprived myself too long. The time has come to take bold steps!"

In a way Christy wanted to laugh at Fred. He was acting so exuberant, yet all she had done was suggest he do something normal with his hair. She could tell it meant an awful lot to him, though. And she was kind of curious to see how it all turned out.

Even though she wouldn't admit it to Jon or anyone else that evening at work, Christy was glad when she saw Fred pop into the pet store. Only he looked exactly the same. No transformation of any kind had taken place.

"Take one last look at the old Fred," he said when he approached the counter where Christy stood behind the cash register. "In an hour I will return, and you won't even recognize me."

"Have fun!" Christy said cheerfully as Fred waved and left the store.

A little more than an hour later, Fred returned right when Christy was getting ready to go on her fifteen-minute break. She planned to run down to the yogurt shop. Jon said earlier that they had Bavarian chocolate raspberry, which was one of Christy's favorites. Fred, however, had other plans.

"Well, what do you think?" Fred turned around slowly, showing off his very stylish haircut. It was the first time Christy had ever seen him without a lot of goop on his hair. The color had changed from a greasy margarine shade of yellow to a light blond. Along with the new hairstyle, the transformation make him look nice.

"It looks great. Fred, I like it. How do you like it?"

"I feel like a different person! And I have you to thank for making the suggestion. Now I need your advice on a shirt. They're holding it for me. When do you take a break? I'd really like your opinion."

Christy hesitated but then agreed. "I have a few minutes right now, if you promise it won't take very long."

"Not a problem. It's two doors down, and they're holding it at the front register." Fred headed out the door and waited for Christy to join him.

Jon exchanged places with Christy at the register. She began to explain where she was going.

"I heard," Jon said. Then in a lower voice he added, "If they're on sale, talk him into a couple of new shirts. Looks like his wardrobe could use a boost."

Christy hurried to join Fred. For the next fifteen minutes he directed her through the contemporary clothing store, pointing out an entire wardrobe of shirts, sweaters, pants, and even socks, asking Christy's opinion on everything.

"I really need to get back," Christy said. "I'm sure you can make these decisions on your own, Fred."

"Not a problem," Fred said. "I'm pretty sure I remember all the ones you liked best. You've helped me more than you'll ever know. Thanks, Christy."

"You're welcome, Fred. Oh, and if any of them are on sale, maybe you should get two. That's some advice a friend gave me."

"Good advice. I'll be back over to show you my final choices. Thanks again!"

Christy could have anticipated Jon's teasing reaction when she returned to her station behind the counter. "Perhaps you should consider fashion consulting," Jon said without looking up from the register where he was ringing up a subtotal. "Might pay more than pet store wages."

"All right, get all your jokes out now," Christy said. "I was only trying to be helpful. The guy asked me for my opinion."

"Let's face it, Christy. If you've discovered a natural flair for fashion consulting, perhaps we should consider opening a booth here for poodle owners. We'll supply you with swatches of colored yarn, and you can advise which color of puppy sweaters would look best on their little poodles."

Christy knew this was particularly funny to Jon because, even though he loved all kinds of animals, his respect for poodles had slipped through a crack. Jon thought all poodles were a freak of nature and not worthy to even be called dogs, let alone members in good standing in the animal kingdom.

"You know, it might help promote some business, Jon," Christy said. "It would be especially delightful for me to see long lines of customers in our store with each of them holding a poodle. Lots and lots of poodles. Yes, that's what this store needs. We could put a sign in the window: 'We Cater to Poodles.'"

A sly grin stretched across Jon's lips. "I'm going on a break. I'll be back in a few minutes."

Christy hoped Fred would pop in and out during the time Jon was gone, but Fred didn't show up. Jon still had his little grin on his face when he returned, and his hands were behind his back.

Trying to sound stern, Jon said, "Now I want you to take this, go in the back, and get busy marking all those jars of fish food. Don't come back up front until it's done." Then he produced from behind his back a large plastic cup from the yogurt shop bulging with a mountain of her favorite, Bavarian chocolate raspberry.

"Oh, if I must," Christy said with a sigh, accepting Jon's

thoughtful gift. "You really are too hard on me, you know. You keep treating me like this," Christy held up the yogurt for emphasis, "and I'll think you might be afraid that I'll quit on you one day."

"That's exactly what I'm afraid of," Jon said. Then snapping back to his teasing, he ordered, "Now get to work!"

Christy had just spooned the first mouthful of yogurt onto her tongue when she heard Jon say, "Sure, you can go see her. She's in the back."

A moment later, Fred—the new, improved Fred—stepped into the back room, decked out in a stylish outfit. Christy quickly swallowed the yogurt, nearly choking on it, and said, "Fred, you look great!"

"You like it? This was the blue shirt you liked. I bought it in green, too."

Fred truly had gone through a transformation. Now, standing before her was a nice-looking, stylish guy. She knew this was a breakthrough for him, and in a way she felt pleased with herself for helping in the metamorphosis.

"I owe it all to you, Christy," Fred said enthusiastically.

Just then Christy heard Jon say, "Go on back. Christy is receiving all her guests in the back parlor this evening."

Before she could turn her head, Fred, in his exuberance, threw his arms around her and said, "You'll never know how much you mean to me, Christy!"

Startled by the hug, Christy pulled away and turned to see Doug standing behind her with Jon right behind him.

"Hi," Christy said, turning to greet Doug. She could feel her cheeks burning. "What are you doing here?"

"Uh-oh," Fred said, taking a step backwards. "Is that brick wall your boyfriend?"

"Only in my dreams," Doug said.

"Oh, you too," Fred said, relaxing his posture and extending his arm to offer Doug a handshake. "I'm Fred."

"Doug," Doug said, returning the handshake. "I should mention, in all fairness, though, that Christy's boyfriend is my best friend. He's the brick wall you should be worried about."

Christy couldn't believe all this was happening. Did Doug think something was going on between her and Fred? He wouldn't say anything to Todd, would he?

"Fred is on the school yearbook staff with me," Christy said, hoping Doug would forget he ever saw Fred hugging her. "He was here doing some shopping and stopped by to see me."

Fred beamed a crooked-tooth smile at Doug. "She's transformed me into a new person!"

At that moment, Christy had to admit Fred's transformation didn't seem too evident. He still had the same personality and the same way of grinning so close to your face that it made you want to turn away.

"New hairstyle, new clothes." Fred stretched out his arms for them to get a full view. A price tag still hung from the inside of the right sleeve. "I'm a brand-new me."

"Looks like you're still thirty percent off, buddy," Christy heard Jon say. She wasn't sure if Jon was referring to the price tag or making a subtle hint to Fred that he still was a little bit off.

Picking up a box knife, Jon sliced through the plastic line on the price tag and handed it to Fred. "You know, this price tag reminds me of something. Now what was it? Does it happen to remind you of anything, Christy?"

"As a matter of fact, it does. The fish food. I'll get right at it, Jon."

Jon smiled at the guys and said, "Fish food. I know it's a rather demeaning task for our oh-so-popular fashion consultant. But the truth of the matter is I pay her to do this sort of thing."

Jon made his remark in a light voice, which made Christy feel relieved. Still, she knew that even though he was easygoing, he could get upset when there was a lot of work to do or if he was short of staff. She also knew it hadn't helped that she had asked to have next Saturday off. Jon had given it to her even though he hadn't hired anyone to take her place.

"Not a problem," Fred said. "I need to get going anyway. I saw a sale sign in the window at the Foot Locker. I'd better buy a pair of shoes now before I add up how much money I've spent. I might end up looking for a job labeling fish food, too, to pay for my new image!"

Christy and Jon exchanged glances. The thought flashed across Christy's mind that if Jon hired Fred it wouldn't be a problem for her to get Saturdays off permanently. Jon's look clearly said, "Don't even think about it!"

Picking up the sheet of already-marked price stickers, Christy began to affix them to the little round containers of fish food. Jon returned to the front, Fred bustled out with his packages, but Doug remained.

"Want some help?"

"Sure, thanks, Doug. You want some of my frozen yogurt?" She knew that was a pointless question. Doug loved to eat anytime, anywhere, any kind of food. Of course he would like some of her yogurt.

*Good thing I took a spoonful when I did!*

Christy was about to ask Doug what he was doing there when a voice with a familiar accent called through the doorway, "Excuse me, but is your name Doug?"

Christy recognized Michael right away and then realized that

Michael and Doug had never met. Why would Michael be looking for Doug?

"Yes, I'm Doug."

"And is it true that you were houseboating on Lake Shasta over Labor Day weekend?" Michael looked serious.

"Yes." Doug glanced at Christy for some explanation as to why this stranger would know they had gone houseboating.

Before Christy could let Doug know who Michael was, Michael continued with his volume escalating. "Are you the one who went Wave Riding with my little sister, Natalie?"

"Well, I . . . yes, I did go Wave Riding with Natalie, but . . ."

"Then put up your fists, man. I've come to defend my sister's honor." Michael played the part of an enraged Irishman in such a convincing manner that for a moment Christy forgot this must all be a joke.

Then she caught a glimpse of Katie hiding behind a bird cage, with her hand over her mouth. Katie seemed to be enjoying this immensely. Christy knew then that this was Katie's sweet revenge on Doug for the bop on the nose.

Doug had lifted his clenched fists to defend himself from the advancing, fiery-faced Michael. "Honest, man, I didn't do anything! Natalie and I went Jet Skiing. That's all! I'm telling you the truth!"

"That's not the story I heard from Natalie. She was a sweet, innocent wee lass until she met the likes of you! Men like you need to be taught a lesson, and I'm just the one to do it."

Michael's fists were up, and he was in a boxing stance. With a swing of his right arm, slicing the air between them, Michael showed Doug he meant business.

Doug looked flabbergasted. "I'm telling you, nothing happened!" Beads of sweat were forming on his forehead.

Christy wanted to break up the whole scene before it went too far. Her idea of a joke and Katie's idea were quite different.

"Wait," Christy said, stepping forward, prepared to explain everything to Doug.

Just then Michael took another staged swing at Doug. Doug, in an involuntary reaction to Michael's swing, lifted his right forearm to block the blow. Instead, he connected with Christy's jaw and knocked her to the floor.

CHAPTER ELEVEN

# *Truce or Consequences*

"Christy, are you all right?" Doug dropped to her side and gently touched her jaw.

"Oww," was all she could say. It was more of a groan than a word, since her mouth felt too numb to form any accurate sounds. Her eyelids felt as if they weighed a hundred pounds each. Although she could hear everything going on around her, no matter how hard she tried, she couldn't open her eyes.

"She's unconscious!" Katie squealed. "Doug, what did you do?"

"Katie!" Doug shouted. "Where did you come from?"

"She's with me," Michael said. "We saw you coming into the pet store, and we thought we'd have a bit of a go-round with you. Didn't count on this. Can you hear my voice, Christy? Can you open your eyes?"

She could hear Michael as clear as could be, but her eyelids refused to cooperate. "Ohh," was the only sound she could form with her mouth.

"What happened?" Now it was Jon's voice. She knew he would be ticked off with all the goofing around. She wouldn't blame him if he became so upset he fired her. She felt certain this whole thing was her fault. The thought made her cry. Tears slid from under her closed eyelids, and Christy had no power to stop them.

"Look, she's crying!" Katie sounded panicked. "You guys, we'd better call 911!"

"Christy," Doug and Jon called her name at the same time. She could feel a strong hand lifting her head and someone else dabbing a tissue at the tears chasing down her cheeks. Then, as if the lock on her eyelids had been released, she was able to slowly open her eyes.

Blinking a few times and trying to steady her voice, she said, "I'm fine. Really. I'm okay." It came out garbled because of her throbbing jaw.

"I'm so sorry, Christy," Doug said softly, his face only a few inches from hers. "Let me help you up."

Doug took one arm, and Jon held the other. Christy rose to her feet and, feeling embarrassed by all the attention, said, "I'm okay, you guys. Really. I'm fine."

"Then how come you sound like a truck driver?" Katie said.

Christy tried to smile. "Ouch."

"You know, Doug," Katie started in, "it's not a surprise you don't have a girlfriend with the winning way you keep leaving your mark on any girl who comes too close to you."

Michael laughed along with Katie. "I'm Michael," he said, "Katie's boyfriend. I suppose I should actually thank you for giving her the black eyes. That's the first thing I noticed about her. If it weren't for the eyes, we might not have started a conversation."

Doug seemed more interested in Christy at the moment than in Katie's boyfriend or the cheap shot she Katie had taken at him. "You'd better sit down, Christy." Doug held her arm and directed her to a folding chair at the table. "I guess we'd better find some ice for that. Here," Doug said, handing her the plastic cup, which was now half full of melting yogurt. "Hold this on your cheek until I can find some ice."

"I already have it," Jon said, returning with an ice pack. "Put this paper towel between you and the ice. Otherwise it will be too cold."

Christy gingerly held the cold pack against her sore jaw. It was a doozy, and she knew she would be feeling it for quite some time to come.

"Can we call a truce?" Doug asked Katie once Christy had the ice firmly in place. "I have to tell you, Michael was very convincing. I'd say you've won, Katie. I don't think I could top that, and I don't think I'd want to try. Besides, it isn't fun when someone keeps getting hurt, especially the innocent bystanders." Doug gave Christy a sympathetic look.

"Sure, we can call a truce," Katie said, offering her hand to shake on it with Doug. With a hint of glee in her voice, she added, "But you have to admit that was a good one! Michael, you were award-winning in your performance of a big brother defending the honor of his baby sister!" Katie offered Michael a high five, and he cheerfully slapped his hand against hers.

"Had you going, didn't we?" Michael said to Doug.

Doug nodded and tried hard to push a grin onto his face.

"The funniest part, I think," Katie said, "was accusing Doug of being involved with a young girl when the truth is, he's never even kissed a girl before."

The room became silent except for Katie's laughter. Christy could feel all eyes on Doug. She knew he must be terribly embarrassed in front of Michael and Jon. Doug had made a vow that the first girl he ever kissed would be his wife, at the altar on their wedding day. Christy saw it as a noble, honorable goal. She especially admired that he had kept to that standard, and as a guy over twenty, he had never kissed a girl. The way Katie blurted it out made Doug sound like some kind of freak with a serious disorder.

"I think we should call a truce all around," Christy said, working hard to form the sloppy words that seemed to stumble off her lower lip. "Enough people have been hurt."

Katie sobered, and everyone focused back on Christy.

"We actually stopped by to see if you wanted to go out after work," Katie said. "Doesn't look like you'll be up for it now."

Christy shook her head. "But thanks for stopping." She sounded as if she had a mouthful of marbles.

"Are you doing anything, Doug? You want to do something with us?" Michael invited.

"I need to get going. This was supposed to be a quick stop to say hi to Christy. Maybe another time."

"We'll get going, then," Katie said, "before we cause any more damage. Bye, you guys. We'll see you later, hopefully under less bizarre conditions."

Jon joined Katie and Michael in the exit, saying, "Take it easy, Christy. If you want to cut out early, that's fine. I am counting on you to work tomorrow."

"I'll be here," Christy promised.

"Why don't you go on home?" Doug suggested. "You need to take some aspirin and get to bed. That jaw is going to hurt more in the morning."

"I'll go after I finish marking this fish food."

"I can do it for you," Doug said. "I'm sure Jon won't mind. Do you feel strong enough to drive home by yourself? I could follow you if you want."

"No, I'm sure I'll be fine. It's not very far, and I feel okay, really. A little sore, maybe."

"As long as you're sure you'll be okay."

"I'm sure. Thanks, Doug."

"Yeah, right. Thanks a lot for almost breaking your jaw, you mean."

Christy stood up and placed a comforting hand on Doug's arm. "It wasn't your fault. Please don't blame yourself, okay?"

Doug looked down at his feet and then almost shyly into Christy's eyes. "I feel really bad about this, Christy."

"Please don't. I don't blame you a bit. Don't feel bad about it."

Doug's grin returned. "Thanks, Christy. You're a sweetheart." Then carefully, tenderly, he slipped his arm around her shoulders and gave her a gentle side hug.

"What is this, the Annual Hug Christy Miller Fest and we forgot to put up signs in the window?" Jon said, sticking his head in the back room. "Hey, I checked with Beverly, and she can stay the rest of the night. Why don't you go on home?"

"Okay, thanks, Jon," Christy said, grabbing her purse and heading for the back door. "I'll try to be here a little early tomorrow."

"Mind if I finish labeling these for Christy?" Doug asked.

"Do I mind? Not a bit!"

Just as the door was closing behind her, Christy heard Jon say to Doug, "You wouldn't happen to be looking for a Saturday job, would you?"

Christy knew it was out of the question since Doug didn't even live in the area. He must have been passing through on his way home from college for the weekend. She never did ask him why he had stopped by.

Doug might talk to Todd before Christy did. She wondered how this whole escapade would be interpreted to Todd.

"Doug still feels real bad," Todd told Christy the next night on the phone. "He keeps blaming himself."

"I told him not to. It wasn't his fault," Christy said, propping her bare feet up on a kitchen chair and leaning back against the wall.

"I'll tell him again tomorrow."

"I wish I were there and could go to church with you tomorrow."

"You'll be here next weekend," Todd said.

"I know, but it seems like forever," Christy said with a sigh.

"Your dad's birthday is tomorrow, isn't it?"

"Yes. We're going to have his birthday lunch after church. Bob and Marti were supposed to come, but they're at a golf tournament in Palm Springs. He goes every year. It'll just be our family. I wish you were coming."

"What did you get your dad?"

"A flashlight. I know it sounds kind of lame for a birthday present, but that's what he wanted. It's a certain kind with an emergency flasher and a built-in radio. My mom said he'd like it. Doesn't seem real personal to me."

"Then why don't you make your card personal?" Todd suggested. "Didn't you tell me you wrote a description of him for your English class? Include that with your card. That's personal. He'll like it."

"You think so?"

"Sure. Dads like to hear they're doing something right every now and then."

Christy took Todd up on his idea and rewrote the essay on a piece of flowered stationery. This time she added at the end,

"Daddy, I love you, even though I don't think I'll ever be able to tell you how much." She signed it, "Forever, your daughter, Christina Juliet Miller."

When her dad opened his gifts the next afternoon, Christy started to feel a little flip-floppy in her stomach. *What if he doesn't like the letter? What if the part about him smelling like cows hurts his feelings? The ending is kind of sappy. What's he going to say?*

Her dad opened the card and read the page silently as she bit her lower lip and tried to ignore her mother's questioning glances. To her amazement, her dad didn't say a word. He folded up the paper, carefully placed it back in the card, and put the card back in the envelope.

"What did it say?" David wanted to know.

Dad didn't answer. He looked up at Christy, and she saw two teardrops start to race down his cheeks. She couldn't remember ever seeing her dad cry before.

"Did you like it?" It was barely a whisper emerging from Christy's still-sore jaw.

"Christina," he said, placing his big, rough hand under her chin and gently cupping her face. "You have given me the greatest reward a man can ever hope for in life. I'm so proud of you, baby."

Now Christy was crying, and her mom was crying, too. David kept looking at each of them, saying, "What? What's going on? Why is everybody crying?"

Christy had never expected this reaction. Todd had said all dads like to know they're doing something right, but this had turned into much more than a pat on the back for her dad. Somehow, Christy's dad had taken her feeble words and embraced them as a wonderful treasure.

It was a surprising and memorable experience, and Christy decided to write about it in her journal that night. She described the scene at lunch and her dad's reaction. Then she added, "It made me think about my heavenly Father. I don't often tell Him how I feel about Him. I know He loves me, even though I don't think I'll ever understand how much. And I love Him, even though I don't think I'll ever be able to fully tell Him how much."

Then Christy had an idea. If it touched her dad's heart so much for her to write out her feelings for him, how much more would it touch the heart of her heavenly Father if she tried to express her love for Him on paper?

For the next hour, Christy filled two pages of her journal with her heartfelt attempt at telling God how much she loved Him. In the same way that her dad's birthday lunch had turned into an emotional time between Christy and her dad, this hour of pouring out her heart to God on paper did something to Christy. She felt warmed and secure and closer to God than she had ever felt before. It was as if He were right there beside her, His heart listening to her heart, His eyes filling with tears the same way her dad's had.

Christy tried to explain it all to Todd later that week on the phone. He listened with understanding and simply said, "You know, if anger is the fluid love bleeds when you cut it, there must be something opposite that comes out of love when you nurture it. Some kind of sweet fragrance or something."

"Todd, do you realize how poetic that is?"

"Yeah, I guess it is. Are you surprised?"

"What?" Christy asked. "Surprised that deep down you're a romantic? No, not really. I've known all along that's how you think and feel, even though it doesn't come out very often."

"It's there, all right," Todd agreed. "I'm saving it."

There was a pause, and Christy wondered what he meant. Was he saving all his romantic expressions for her or for the future or

. . . (she didn't like the thought) . . . saving them for someone else?

"There's a time for everything," Todd said. "A time to keep your innermost feelings to yourself and a time to share them. It hasn't yet been the right time for me to share a lot of my innermost feelings with you. But I'm sure you know they're there."

"And when will it be the right time?"

"I don't know. How do the leaves know when to change color? It's something supernatural that they do in a natural way when God puts all the right elements in place. Right now it's a time for us to . . ." He didn't seem to have the right word.

"To enjoy today?" Christy ventured, remembering her uncle's advice on the houseboat.

"I suppose. More than that, though. I'll have to think about that one."

Christy thought about it, too. She especially thought about Todd's words as she drove to school on Friday. A few of the trees along the way were changing into their autumn wardrobe and dancing about in the morning wind. She thought of Todd's question, "How do the leaves know when to change color?" and she thought about how there's a right time for everything.

*And the time for me to finally see Todd is tonight! I can't wait to get off work and go up to Newport Beach with him. It's a good thing Bob and Marti are going to be home from their golf tournament today and they don't mind my staying with them for the weekend.*

With a cheerful bounce in her step, Christy breezed through her morning classes and determined she would have a good time at lunch with Michael and Katie. The last few days had been pretty rough. It seemed whenever Katie tried to make a move to improve the friendship with Christy, Christy was in a critical mood. Whenever Christy tried to be patient and understanding,

Katie or Michael would say something that would set her off, and she would have to walk away before she said something she would regret later.

Today Christy wanted peace.

"Guess what we're doing this weekend?" Katie asked the minute Christy joined her under the tree. Michael wasn't there yet. "We're going to San Diego tonight, and tomorrow morning we're going out on a boat to go whale watching! Doesn't that sound like fun?"

"Where are you staying?"

"Remember that girl, Stephanie, we stayed with last spring when we went to the God-Lovers Bible study? Well, I got her number from Doug. She's still in the same apartment, and she invited Michael and me to stay with her. Isn't that great?"

"You're both going to stay at her apartment?" Christy asked.

"I suppose. She has two rooms, you know." The delight seemed to be draining from Katie's face. "I thought you'd be excited for me. Is that too much to ask? Why are you so critical?"

"It sounds a little strange, the two of you going off for the weekend and staying in the same apartment. Don't you think so, too?"

"I can't believe this, Christy. Why won't you take my word for it? Michael is a total gentleman. We're not doing anything wrong. His morals are as strong as mine."

Christy could tell that Katie was starting to get heated up. Her freckled face served as a clear thermometer of what was going on inside, and right now the red was creeping to the top of her head.

"You're really starting to get to me, Christy! Here I go and set this whole thing up with a bunch of Christians so that Michael can be around them and maybe even go to the God-Lovers group on Sunday night, and you make me feel guilty, like I'm doing something wrong!"

"I'm sorry," Christy said defensively.

"No, you're not. You've got your own set of standards, which I might add, seem to me to be a double standard, since you're going to spend the weekend with Todd."

"I'm staying at my aunt and uncle's. You know that."

"And I'm staying at Stephanie's. It's the same thing. You and Todd are going to be together the whole time. Why is it so wrong for me to try to introduce Michael to some Christians? Christians, I might add, who aren't as judgmental as you!"

Katie's words were piercing, and Christy felt her tear elevator quickly approaching the top floor, where all the wet drops would soon fill up her eyes.

"I need to go," Christy said, getting up and excusing herself when she saw Michael approaching. "I really do hope you have a good weekend, and I really do hope Michael becomes a Christian. I'm sorry I'm the way I am, Katie. I guess I just care about you too much, and I don't want you to get hurt."

Christy snatched up her uneaten lunch and was about to turn to go when Katie said, "I know that. Don't you remember what I said when we were on the raft? There are no guarantees. I know that. I know it's too late for any kind of a guarantee that I won't get hurt. The same thing applies to you and Todd, Christy. Or are you not willing to see that?"

Christy couldn't look at Katie. She couldn't talk to her when things got this tense between them. Trying to hold back the tears, Christy stepped away and greeted Michael with a fake "Hi! How you doing?" She kept on walking, heading for the lonely spot at the picnic table that had often been her refuge recently.

Today, of all days, Fred had taken her spot and was joined by two freshman girls, one on either side. He was wearing one of his new outfits, and as Christy approached, she overheard the girls asking how they could get their pictures in the yearbook.

"I'd say for freshmen your best bet is to do something out of the ordinary in cooking class. If you know when you're going to be baking a cake or something, you two can add some, say . . . green dye, and simply let me know ahead of time. I'll come to your class and record it on film."

He sounded so official. Christy had confused feelings. She didn't exactly want to join them, especially now that Fred had this new image that seemed to help him attract girls, even if they were freshmen. Still, the sad part was that now she had no one to eat lunch with.

At this moment, more than ever, she realized how few friends she had at school. Teri had graduated last year, and Brittany and Janelle, two girls she used to hang out with during her sophomore year, had both moved. Katie was the only person Christy had spent lunchtimes with for the last two and a half years. Except for Fred. Now even Fred had other friends.

"Miss Chris," Fred called out, spotting her as she tried to slide past him, "come here!"

Christy sighed, blinked back the renegade tears, pasted a smile on her face, and joined Fred and his fan club.

"What's wrong?" Fred immediately asked when he saw her.

*I must be the worst faker in the world. I can't even hide my emotions from Fred.*

"My jaw is still a little sore," Christy said. It was true. She involuntarily had been clenching her teeth while she was talking to Katie, and her jaw did hurt. "Makes it kind of hard to eat."

"Why don't you try some pudding or Jell-O from the food machines?"

Christy nodded her appreciation for the suggestion and noticed her camera sitting on the table. She thought it would be
good to have it back so she could take it with her this weekend.
"Are you done using my camera yet, Fred?"

"There are about four more shots on the roll."

"Mind if I take it back?" Christy picked up the camera and
removed the lens cap so she could look through the viewfinder.
"You didn't mess it up or anything, did you?"

"Of course not!" Fred looked shocked that Christy would ask
such a question. She could see him clearly through the small box
and had a sudden inspiration to snap his picture so he could see
what it felt like. A sneaky idea came to her.

"Did you girls know that Fred sort of got a makeover last
weekend?"

Fred looked pleased that Christy was still noticing and com-
menting on the vast improvements. She had him centered perfectly in the viewfinder. Now to get both the girls to move in just
a little closer.

"Yeah, he got his hair cut, and he even got his ears pierced!"

Both girls cooperated beautifully by leaning in to get a closer
look at the ear nearest them. They had expressions of curious
amazement on their faces. Fred's mouth opened, and his eyes
bulged at the exact instant that Christy snapped the photo.

"This will be perfect for the yearbook," Christy said.

The two freshmen looked at each other in delight. Their wish
had been granted. Fred jumped up and tried to snatch the camera
away from Christy. She held it over her head out of his reach and
said, "Now, Fred. That's the only picture I have of you so far, and
you have at least a dozen candid shots of me. Don't you think it's
only fair that I get to keep this one?"

Fred plopped down hard on the bench. "Okay, okay. I get the

picture, Christy. Har-har. Just a little joke there. We can deal on this one. You give me that photo, and I'll give you back the ones I've taken of you."

"I don't think so, Fred. I think this picture will cancel out only the one from last year at the pizza place that Rick so easily persuaded you to take of me. That means I have about a dozen more of you to take before the year is over."

"That one last year was Rick's idea, not mine. Come on, Christy, have a heart!"

She was about to hold out to even the score when she remembered how things had turned out between Katie and Doug as the two of them had played their game of sweet revenge. As innocent as it had seemed in the beginning, someone kept getting hurt as their game progressed. Christy surrendered.

"Okay, Fred. Truce. I do need my camera back, though. When we get the roll developed, you can decide what you want to do with the picture."

Fred broke into a toothy smile. "Thanks, Miss Chris. You're the best."

Christy walked away with her uneaten lunch and her camera, deciding to shoot the last few pictures of the parking lot like Katie had suggested at the beginning of school. Something inside her felt right for having made peace. Maybe it was that fragrance Todd talked about, the fragrance that comes when you nurture love instead of cut into it.

*Great!* Christy heard a condemning voice inside her head. *I have this wonderful relationship I'm nurturing with* Fred *of all people, while nothing but anger keeps bleeding out between my best friend and me. It's time for a truce, Christy. How are you going to do it?*

# CHAPTER TWELVE

# A Handful of Regret

"Jon, I'm leaving," Christy called out to her boss at one minute after nine on Friday night as he began to lock up the pet store.

"Have a great weekend," Jon called back. "Say hi to Todd for me."

"I will. Thanks! And thanks for letting me have tomorrow off." Christy closed the door behind her and hurried to her car in the dimly lit parking lot.

Todd should be waiting for her at her home. She had her bags all packed so they could leave right away for the drive to Bob and Marti's.

She was so excited about seeing Todd that the keys trembled in her hand. On her first attempt to put the key in the lock, she dropped her ring of keys and bent to pick them up. Straightening, she tried the wobbly key again.

"Need some help?" a deep voice behind her asked.

Christy spun around and practically screamed. "Todd, I didn't see you!"

He opened his arms, and she wrapped her arms around his middle and pressed her cheek against his broad chest. She could hear his heart beating. Was it racing as fast as hers, or was it her imagination?

Todd held her for several minutes, pressing his cheek against her hair. "It's so good see you, Kilikina," he whispered.

Christy felt like crying, she was so happy and so excited to finally be with him, to feel his strong arms around her.

"I thought you'd be waiting at my house," Christy said as he let go and held her at arm's length, carefully examining her face. She wondered if he noticed the slight black and blue mark on her lower jaw, a fading souvenir of her collision with Doug's arm last week.

"I only got into town a few minutes ago. I knew you'd be getting off work, so I thought I'd come here and surprise you."

"You surprised me, all right! Where did you park Gus?"

"Over there," Todd said, motioning with a chin-up gesture over his shoulder. "Why don't I follow you?"

"Okay," Christy agreed, laughing at her trembling hand as she tried once more to get the key in the lock. "If I can ever get this door open."

"Allow me," Todd offered, sounding like her private knight in shining armor. He placed his hand over hers. It felt warm, strong, and confident. Together they unlocked the door.

"Thanks!" Christy beamed. "I'll see you at home."

Her hope had been that they could leave for Newport Beach right away. Todd seemed less eager to leave. He had brought a present for Christy's dad, which she had to admit was a very thoughtful gesture. It took a while before her dad opened it because Mom offered Todd some pumpkin bread she had just baked, and she kept asking him questions about school.

David, of course, had stayed up to see Todd and was trying to coax Todd into taking him skateboarding again.

"Okay, dude. How about if I come down next weekend on Sat-urday?" Todd suggested.

"Cool," David said. "Wait till you see all the new tricks I can do."

"Oh, yeah? Can you block a punch yet?" Todd playfully swung at David's right ear, and a wrestling match broke out be-tween them on the living room floor. Mom quickly moved the cof-fee table out of the way and watched the two of them wrestle like brothers.

*Nothing like sharing your boyfriend with the rest of your family!*

It was after ten o'clock before Todd finally tossed Christy's weekend luggage into the back of Gus. Christy's mom and dad stood outside with them and gave the usual list of "to do's," end-ing with Mom's most important request that Christy call them as soon as she arrived at Bob and Marti's.

Christy climbed up onto the torn passenger seat of the Volk-swagen bus. Todd used to have a beach towel over the seat to help keep the stuffing from coming out, but tonight it was missing. Christy had to find just the right position so she wouldn't get poked by the torn vinyl.

Soon Christy forgot about the uncomfortable seat and was busy chattering away. "I think my dad really liked that book you gave him. That was so thoughtful of you, Todd." She had to talk loudly because of the rumbling inside the van.

They talked back and forth nonstop for the first hour of the drive. Christy realized her throat hurt from talking so much and so loudly. She settled back a little and let Todd carry the conver-sation for a while. It felt so good just to be with him and to finally have their weekend together.

As soon as they arrived at Bob and Marti's, Todd headed for the refrigerator to pour himself a glass of orange juice. "You want some, Christy?'' He obviously felt at home here since he was over all the time, even when Christy wasn't around.

"Definitely."

"Ice?"

"Yes, please. I'm going to call my mom and dad."

After letting them know the trip was uneventful and they had arrived safely, Christy was about to hang up when her mom said, "Have fun, dear. We sure find it comforting to know that we can let our seventeen-year-old daughter take off for the weekend and know that you're making good choices."

Christy hung up and thought of how different the warnings from her parents had been several years ago. It felt good to know that, despite all the up-and-down times, she had managed to earn their confidence. With their confidence came fewer restrictions and greater freedoms.

"I guess I'll get going," Todd said when Christy hung up. He placed his empty glass in the sink and said, "What do you want to do tomorrow, Christy?"

"Let's go out to breakfast," Christy suggested.

"Good idea," Marti interjected. She had entered the room a few minutes earlier. "I know just the place for the four of us."

Christy had meant that only she and Todd would go out to breakfast. How could she *un*invite her aunt? Maybe it didn't matter. What mattered was that she would be with Todd.

"Around eight?" Marti suggested.

"I'll be here at eight," Todd agreed and waved goodnight as he let himself out.

"He didn't kiss you good-bye," Marti said as Christy finished off her juice. "Why didn't he kiss you?"

"I don't know."

"Don't you two kiss?"

"Yes, sometimes."

"And what else?"

"Nothing else. Well, except hold hands and hug."

Marti looked to Bob and then back at Christy. "That certainly doesn't sound natural, dear. At this point I would have thought you two would be much farther along physically. I was planning to have a heart-to-heart talk about the physical dimension of your relationship, but you're not giving me much to discuss with you."

"I think things are right where they should be," Christy answered. "I have no regrets now, and I don't want to, ever."

"Very noble," Bob said. "Your aunt and I respect and support you two for your standards, don't we, Martha?"

Christy watched her aunt's expression change from critical to compassionate. Marti had Christy's best interests at heart, Christy knew, even if her methods were a little off sometimes.

"Yes, Christina, I have to agree. Your morals are quite commendable. Not at all the norm for most teens your age, I suppose. You are both intelligent people. I guess we can be glad that your school's sex education programs have been so successful."

Christy wanted to laugh. The open discussion she had experienced in her school had taught her about the complications and consequences of going too far, but she knew it was her relationship with the Lord that made her want to do the right thing.

"Actually, what makes the difference for Todd and me is that we're both Christians, and we're both trying to obey God."

"Oh."

"You know," Bob said, changing the subject, "I'd kind of like to sleep in tomorrow morning. Why don't you and Todd go out for breakfast, and the four of us can eat dinner together."

"That's fine with me," Christy said. "Is that okay with you, Aunt Marti?"

"Of course, dear. You two would most likely enjoy spending the time together alone. Knowing Todd's preference, it will probably be a casual sort of breakfast, anyway. We can make plans for something a little nicer for dinner."

Todd showed up a few minutes after eight the next morning. Marti was right—he had on his usual beach wear of shorts, sandals, and hooded sweatshirt. Mr. Casual himself.

Christy had ended up rising at six to shower, fix her hair, and dress. Even though she had on cutoff jeans and an oversized chambray work shirt with a white T-shirt underneath, she had spent as much time on her appearance as if she were going to the prom. Her makeup was light but precise. She had worked hard to get the mascara even on both eyes. Her hair, clean and combed, hung naturally without any of the clips or barrettes Marti urged her to use. Christy felt fresh and pretty, ready for whatever this day might hold.

"It's just you and me," Christy said softly when she answered the front door. "I'll explain on the way."

Todd led her out to Gus and opened the passenger door for her. Christy noticed the beach towel was back in place, covering the seat. Something deep inside her warmed, knowing that Todd had noticed and done something to make her seat more comfortable. She got in. Todd started the engine.

"Ah, Todd," she said, "by any chance, is this towel a little wet?"

"Oh, man. Sorry, Christy! I went surfing this morning and laid my towel there to dry. Here," he said, tugging it off the seat, "but the seat is still wet, right?"

"That's okay," Christy said.

"No, it's not. Hey, I know what we can do," Todd said, slipping the car gears into neutral. "You drive, and I'll sit on the wet seat."

"I don't know, Todd." The only other time Christy had been in the driver's seat and Todd in the passenger's seat was in Maui when he had been stung by a bee and she had to drive a Jeep on the precarious Hana road.

"You can do it! Compared to Hana, Newport will be a breeze." Todd hopped out and jogged around to her door, urging her to trade places before she had a chance to protest.

Christy slid into the driver's seat, buckled her seat belt, and popped Gus into gear, and down the street they chugged.

"I don't know where your aunt wanted to go for breakfast, but since I'm paying now, is Carl's Jr. okay?"

"Sure. Show me where to turn."

"Take a right at our intersection."

Christy looked at him out of the corner of her eye while slowly coaxing Gus down the street. She couldn't believe he had said "our intersection." It was the intersection where he had first kissed her and where he had given her the ID bracelet. She had thought of it as "their" intersection before, but she had never heard Todd refer to it that way.

A smile tickled the corner of her lips. She and Todd were really going together. Even Todd realized some of the things that had happened between them were sacred. Things like "their" intersection.

Christy turned right, and Gus rolled into the parking lot at the Carl's Jr. fast-food restaurant. She parked the van and turned off the engine, proud of herself for getting them there without incident.

"Looks like Gus recognizes an old friend when he sees one. He doesn't perform that well for just anyone, I hope you know,"

Todd said as they approached the cash register and placed their orders for two Sunrise Breakfasts.

The food was soon brought to their booth next to the window, and Todd reached over to hold Christy's hand while he prayed.

"So what was the deal with your aunt and uncle?" Todd asked.

Christy gave him a summary of what had happened after he left last night, including the part about Marti asking why he hadn't kissed her good-bye.

Todd looked thoughtful then, and leaning closer to Christy, he said in a low voice, "It's not that I don't want to kiss you anymore. You know that, don't you?"

Christy felt her cheeks blush. She hoped no one else in the restaurant had heard him.

"There's a time for everything," Todd said, still keeping his voice low. "It's kind of my agreement with God, to keep my life balanced by doing only what I'm supposed to do when He says it's time to do it. I'm not saying it's easy."

Christy sipped her orange juice and kept her eyes fixed on Todd. His silver-blue eyes were only inches away as he leaned closer and said, "There's something I've wanted to tell you, Christy. I hope you'll take this the right way. One of the things I really appreciate about you is that you don't come on to me. Do you know what I mean?"

"I'm not sure," Christy said, her eyes still locked onto his.

"You let me make the first moves, and that really helps."

Christy nodded, not exactly sure what he was saying, but agreeing that she did let him make the first moves.

"Girls have no idea what they do to a guy when they come on to him. Not only by touching him but also by what they wear. I love the way you dress. You always look good. Really good. Yet you don't try to show off or, you know, tease a guy."

Christy felt as if she were getting an education into the way guys think and, although she had heard some of this before, hearing it from Todd made it real and personal.

"I want you to know," Todd continued, "you've been helping make our relationship what it is by letting me be the initiator and by having so much . . . 'dignity' is the only word I can think of. You treat yourself like a gift. A treasure. And that comes across. It makes you so absolutely beautiful, Christy. You have no idea."

*You're right. I have no idea what you're saying. I'm only being myself. I can't believe you're sitting here telling me I'm beautiful! This is a dream come true.*

Christy felt the same way now with Todd as she had on the phone last night with her parents. Many times in the past she had wanted to run ahead of Todd and speed up their relationship. Now she was glad she had let everything develop at its own pace and in its right time. If she hadn't been patient, Todd might not be saying these things to her right now.

They ate for a few minutes in comfortable silence. It almost seemed to Christy that the air around them had turned fragrant. There was no mistaking a sweetness lingering in her heart after Todd's words.

"I have something else I've been wanting to ask you for a long time," Todd said as they returned to the van. "I keep going back and forth because I'm not sure it's my place to ask."

"You can ask me anything," Christy said, climbing up into the passenger seat.

"Is it still wet?"

Christy touched the seat before sitting down. The sun had baked that side of the vehicle while they ate. "No, it's dry enough. It's fine."

Todd started the engine and drove out of the driveway. "I thought we'd go over to Balboa Island. Is that okay with you?"

"Sure. What was it you wanted to ask me?"

"I guess I should just come out and say it."

"Yes, you should."

"Christy, I know it probably shouldn't bother me, but I've wanted to ask you about Rick. When you were dating, what actually went on between you two? I've tried not to let it bother me, but Rick said some things when we were rooming together last year that didn't sound like the Christy I know. I wanted to hear it from you. If you don't feel comfortable talking about it, I understand. I probably shouldn't even be asking."

"Of course you should. There's not much to tell. We went out a few times, I broke up with him. It wasn't the best of relationships. I got closer to God after we broke up. Why? What was Rick saying?"

Todd hesitated and then let out a heavy sigh. "Rick said you were easy. That you did whatever he wanted you to."

"That is a lie!" Christy said, raising her voice. "Rick said that about me? He is such a jerk! How could you believe him? Todd! I can't believe you thought—"

"Hey, relax. I didn't say I believed him. I know you. Like I said, it's been bothering me, so I wanted to talk with you about it."

"Todd," Christy began with a lower, calmer voice, "Rick is the kind of guy who seems to get whatever he wants. For some reason, he decided he wanted me. It's all a lot clearer to me now that I know what kind of guy he is, but at the time I have to admit I was a little misty-minded. I thought he really liked me just because I was me. He has a way with words. I know now that some guys can manipulate girls by what they say. At the time, I don't know, I guess I really wanted a boyfriend. I thought I needed one. You were leaving for Hawaii, and Rick was so nice to me. . . ."

"Hey, you don't have to apologize for anything, Christy. I'm not asking you to give me an account of your relationship with Rick. That's between God and you. I guess I needed to hear from you that he didn't take advantage of you."

"He tried more than once. We kissed a few times, but I always pulled away. I know it made him mad. It just didn't feel right to me."

"That's all, then? Some kissing?"

"And a few hugs," Christy said. "Nothing else. I can't believe he made it sound like more than that."

"I'm sure with some other girls it has been. Maybe it sort of bent his ego out of shape since it wasn't more than that with you," Todd said.

They had reached the ramp to the Balboa Island Ferry, and Gus's tires clanged loudly up the metal incline. Todd stopped the engine and suggested they climb out for the short ride across to Balboa Island.

Christy stood by the side, gazing out at the blue water in the bay. The October morning breeze chilled her, and she crossed her arms to keep warm. Todd came and stood behind her, wrapping his big arms around her and burying his nose in her hair.

A sudden flash of a memory came to her of a time when Rick had held her like this and whispered sweet words in her ear. Now it made her mad that she had ever gone out with Rick. If only she had waited, she could have shared all these boyfriend-girlfriend moments and feelings with just Todd.

"Hey," Todd said softly, "why are you all tensed up?"

"I'm mad. Mad that I ever went out with Rick. Mad at myself for not waiting for you. And before you say that this anger is bleeding out of love that's been cut, it's not! Love was not even a part of my relationship with Rick. Not real love."

"Christy, you're being too hard on yourself. Think back on when you were with Rick. There were some good times, too, weren't there? A few fragrant memories?"

Todd was right. There had been some special moments with Rick—on the swings at the park, flying kites at the beach, their first date at the fancy Villa Nova Restaurant.

"Yes, there were some good times. It wasn't all bad, and he didn't do anything to ruin my life forever."

"Here," Todd said, letting go of Christy and coming around to face her with his hands cupped together in front of her. "Put all your regrets in here."

"What?"

"In my hands. Put all those regrets and bad feelings in here. Sort out the good stuff and keep that part in your heart. Put the rest in here."

Christy gave Todd a wary look. Then playing along, she held her fingers over his hands and pretended to be sprinkling all the bad stuff into his open palms. "There. Now what are you going to do with my little pile of ashes?"

"Same thing God says He does with all our sins," Todd said, pretending to toss the handful of regrets into the wind and out to the ocean. "He separates them from us as far as the east is from the west, and He buries them in the deepest sea."

Then looking into Christy's eyes, Todd's silver-blues shot straight to her heart as he said confidently, "God doesn't hold this against you. I don't hold this against you. Why should you hold it against yourself? It's all gone, Christy. Choose to remember only the good parts, okay?"

Christy drew in a deep breath of the chill morning air. "Okay."

Todd smiled, and she could see the dimple in his right cheek. "God likes giving us beauty for our ashes when we let Him," he said.

The ferry motored into the harbor, and the two cars behind Gus started up their engines. "Time to go," Todd said as he opened the door for Christy to get in. They drove off the ferry and down the narrow street. On the second corner to the left, a fun-looking yard sale was in progress.

"Let's stop," Christy said. "Is there any place to park?"

"Looks pretty tight. Why don't you hop out, and I'll circle the block."

Christy did, and the first thing she saw was an old bookshelf. The sticker said five dollars. Before she had a chance to change her mind, Christy reached in her purse for a five-dollar bill and bought the bookshelf. Todd turned the corner, and she flagged him down, proudly pointing to her purchase. He double-parked Gus, popped open the back, and slid in the bookshelf. Then they jumped back in Gus and sputtered down the street.

"Isn't it cute! I needed something in my room for all my junk. This will be perfect. Of course, it needs some paint. You want to help me paint it?"

Todd had a wide grin across his face. "That had to be the fastest shopping spree on record! Sure, I'll help you. We can stop by the paint store and paint it today so it'll be dry enough to take home tomorrow."

"Perfect!' Christy said excitedly. "It's so cute. Don't you think it's cute?"

"If you say so," Todd said, the grin still flickering across his face.

# CHAPTER THIRTEEN

# *To Cherish*

"How's it going?" Todd asked when he stepped out to the front of Marti's house, where Christy had her bookshelf balanced on a carpet of newspapers. Uncle Bob had sanded it down for her with his electric sander, and now it was ready for the paint.

Christy had been stirring the paint while Todd was inside making sandwiches. He handed her a paper plate with a huge turkey sandwich and a mound of potato chips.

"You must think I'm going to work up a pretty big appetite," Christy said.

"I figured whatever you didn't eat I would," Todd said, chomping into his equally large sandwich. "Marti said she had made reservations somewhere for the four of us for dinner. That's several hours away, though."

"Well, I'm ready to start painting," Christy said. "If you want some of my sandwich, go ahead. Leave me about three bites, though."

"I can do this," Todd said, sitting on the steps and taking another bite of sandwich. "You work; I'll supervise."

Christy dipped the brush into the bucket of paint and started with the inside.

"Good thinking, doing the inside first," Todd praised. "Don't forget to do the undersides of the shelves, too."

"Todd, do you think white is the best color? I'm wondering if I should have done it in a soft yellow or maybe a real faint, dusty rose."

"White is good."

"No, really, don't you think we should have picked something a little more exciting? Maybe a pale, sky blue."

"White is good."

Christy turned to face Todd and waved the wet paint brush at him. "You don't really care, do you?"

"I think white is good." He bit into his sandwich. "Goes with everything, it's easy to, ah . . . match with anything. White is good."

Christy gave him a little smirk and went back to work. "I really like this bookshelf, I hope you know. It's going to be a new home for a lot of old mementos. Most of them from you."

"From me? All I ever gave you was a bracelet. Oh, and maybe that coconut I mailed you from Oahu."

"Keep thinking," Christy said. "Remember the flowers you gave me?"

"Oh, yeah. Those little white ones when you were leaving to go back to Wisconsin."

"Carnations, Todd. They were carnations. I dried them and saved them in a Folgers coffee can. It was all I could find to put them in when we moved out here to California. I still have them."

"Amazing," Todd said, stuffing in the last bite. "That had to be like three summers ago."

"Yep. The same summer we went to Disneyland, and you bought me the stuffed Winnie the Pooh. Remember?"

"Oh, yeah. Disneyland. I remember," Todd said, leaning back

in his chair and folding his arms across his chest. "I wanted to impress you so much, I let you think I was paying for everything. Then when I gave you back your aunt's money at the end of the night, I thought you were going to kill me!" Todd laughed. "Didn't you throw your shoes at me or something?"

Christy laughed. "Yes, can you believe it? Here I thought you were going to kiss me good night, and instead, you hand me this wad of money and tell me the only reason you took me was because my aunt talked you into it."

"You thought I was going to kiss you?" Todd looked surprised.

"Of course I did!"

"No way, man, I was too chicken! I'd never kissed a girl before. I have to admit, I thought about it all day, but when the moment came, there was no way."

"Do you remember the first time you did kiss me?" Christy asked.

"Of course. I'll never forget it," Todd said. "It was only two days later, but everything had changed. Tracy told me you'd given your heart to the Lord and that you were leaving to go back to Wisconsin. So when I caught up with you at our intersection, I remember thinking, 'Okay, Todd, it's now or never.'" He looked so content as he said it. "And it was 'now.' I'll never forget it."

"Me neither," Christy said. She painted a bit more on the inside and said, "So are you going to help me with the rest of this?"

"Sure. Hand me a brush. You want me to do the front or the back?"

"Whatever you want."

Todd squatted down right behind Christy and put his arm out next to hers. "How about if we do it side by side? I'll come along and clean up all your mistakes."

"Oh, getting a bit overly confident of ourselves, aren't we?"

Christy teased. "And what makes you so sure I'm going to make any boo-boos?"

"Just a precaution," Todd said.

She loved feeling him this close, with his broad shoulders hovering over her. Christy tilted her head back and leaned gently against his chest. "Now this is what I call teamwork," she said.

Just then Christy heard a familiar, but not so favorite, sound—a camera clicking. This time it was Bob, not Fred, who hid behind the lens.

"Thought I'd see how the camera was working," Bob said, his merry eyes twinkling. "Don't let me bother you two."

"Christy was just asking me how I thought she'd look with a bit of paint on her nose, and I was about to show her," Todd said, lifting his paint brush and playfully preparing to make his mark.

"Fine, fine," Bob said, positioning the camera closer. "Don't let me stop you."

"Wait!" Christy squealed as she heard the camera click. "The paint goes on the bookshelf, not me!"

"Oh, right. Now what exactly does a bookshelf look like? Oh, here's one." With that, Todd dabbed a bit of paint on the end of Christy's nose.

"That's not a bookshelf! This is," Christy said, and with that, she dotted Todd's right cheek. "Oh, that wasn't a bookshelf. That was a dimple. Now where did that bookshelf go?"

"I don't have any dimples," Todd said, touching his cheek.

"Oh, yes you do. I noticed it the first time we went to Balboa on the tandem bike. Remember? We bought Balboa Bars."

"That's right," Todd said. "And you got a streak of chocolate right there on your face." He outlined the memory with a stroke of the paint brush. "And it stayed on the rest of the day!"

"You asked for it, *dude!*" Christy teased. "This is for never writing to me *ever!*" She painted a stripe up his arm.

*Click* went the camera.

"Hey, I sent you a coconut!"

"And this is for all the times you've thrown me in the ocean!" Another stripe went up his other arm.

"Whoops!" Bob said. "That was the last shot. Guess you'll have to call a truce."

Christy and Todd looked at each other. They each had their paint brushes poised and ready to strike.

"Truce?" Christy suggested.

"Truce," Todd agreed, and as if they were slapping high fives, they whapped their paint brushes together and were instantly showered in a spray of tiny polka dots.

"Look at us!" Christy said, cracking up at the sight of Todd with paint in his face, hair, everywhere. "Do I look as funny as you?"

"No, funnier."

After they finished laughing and wiping the paint from their eyelashes, Todd and Christy set to work. Within an hour they had transformed the bookshelf into a white home for all of Christy's mementos.

Standing back to admire their work, Christy said, "I don't know. A dusty rose would have been nice."

"White is good," Todd assured her. "After it dries, you'll see."

Todd drove the few blocks to his house to shower and change while Christy went to clean up in the bathroom off her guest room. Little flecks of paint clung to her arms and to her eyebrows. It was a tedious process, getting herself back to normal, and she needed an extra dose of lotion when she was done. She changed into a pair of jeans and a white cotton shirt, rolling up the long sleeves.

Todd was already downstairs, watching TV with her uncle. "Did you check on it yet?" Christy asked.

"Check on what?"

"The bookshelf. I want to see if it's dry."

"It won't be dry until tomorrow," Bob said. "Did Marti tell you we're going out to dinner in about an hour? She's made reservations at a new place in Huntington Beach."

Todd rose from the couch and said, "Sounds like we have enough time for a walk on the beach."

Christy smiled at the good-looking, bronzed young man walking toward her. His short, sandy blond hair was still wet. His blue eyes met hers, and he held out his hand, inviting her to take a walk. She slipped her hand into his, and they walked together out the sliding door. Kicking off their shoes, they let their feet sink into the cool sand.

"It's going to be quite a sunset tonight," Todd said. "See how the clouds are sort of puffing up there on the horizon? Wait until the sun hits the ocean. They'll all turn pink and orange."

"The dust beneath His feet," Christy said.

"You remembered," Todd said, squeezing her hand. "Yeah, those clouds are going to turn into some major mounds of dust tonight. Looks like God has been busy walking around our side of the earth today."

They made their way through the sand, hand in hand, down to the firm, wet sand along the shoreline and walked together in silence. Todd's thumb automatically rubbed the chain on her Forever bracelet.

That reminded Christy she had never asked him if he knew who paid for her to get it back. "Todd, I want to ask you something. You had some stored up questions for me this morning; now I have one for you. I guess the first thing I should ask is, did you know Rick sort of stole my bracelet?"

Todd stopped walking and faced her. "What do you mean?"

Christy explained how she had taken off her bracelet, left it in her purse in Rick's car, and then thought it was lost. She later found out he had used it as a trade-in on a new bracelet—a clunky silver one that said "Rick." Christy figured out he had taken it, and after breaking up with him, she tried to buy it back from the jewelry store where he had hocked it.

"I didn't know any of this," Todd said, still standing in one spot as the tide rose and lapped up, burying their feet in the sand.

"My next question was if you had been the one who paid the balance so I could get it back. All the jeweler would say was that it was some guy."

"It wasn't me. I didn't even know. Do you think it was Rick?"

"I did for a while, but the more I think about it the more I doubt it."

"Your dad maybe? Bob?" Todd suggested.

"Maybe. Although I don't think either of them knew about the whole incident. I guess it'll remain a mystery."

Todd wiggled his feet out of the sand and started down the beach, holding even tighter to Christy's hand. "I don't mind it being a mystery as long as you have the bracelet back."

"I guess I can live with a little mystery, too," Christy said. "The whole thing only makes me madder at Rick."

"Wait a second. Wasn't that part of the regrets we tossed out to sea this morning?" Todd motioned out to the ocean. "You want to try swimming out there and gathering up all the ashes again? It's not worth it, Christy. Let it go."

"You're right," Christy agreed, nestling her head against Todd's shoulder. Then after a brief pause she added, "I wish I could let this whole thing with Katie and Michael just go, too."

"That's different," Todd said. "You can't let that go. You have to hold on tighter than ever."

"But when I tell her he's not a Christian and she should drop him, she turns on me. I hate causing all this conflict."

"So are you going to change your opinion on dating non-Christians?"

"No. I can't. I feel too strongly about it," Christy said.

"Then what can you change?"

Christy thought. She wasn't sure. When Todd said, "change," it reminded her of when he had said, "How do the leaves know when it's time to change?" His answer had been that it's something supernatural that God brings about in a natural way.

"I guess I can't change anything. Only God can. I can ask Him to do something supernatural in a natural way."

Todd squeezed her hand again. "And you can ask Him and ask Him and ask Him again. Really good answers come from persistent prayers."

"But in the meantime, everything is different between Katie and me."

"Yes," Todd agreed.

"It's impossible for me to change how I feel about her dating Michael."

"Yes."

"I wish it weren't so hard and that it didn't take so long for God to answer prayers."

"I agree."

"How can you take it so lightly?" Christy asked.

"I don't take it lightly. I've been praying for Katie and Michael ever since that night we met up with them at the movies. The only thing that gives me hope is that God said there is a time for everything. This is a time for Katie to make some major choices, and this is a time for you to stick close to her. Then, depending on how her choices go, you two will probably soon have either a time to mourn together or a time to dance. For me, it's a time to pray."

"Could we do that right now?" Christy asked.

Todd led her a few feet up to the drier sand, and the two of them sat close together, holding hands and praying for Katie and Michael. When they looked up, the sun had dipped its toes into the ocean. As Todd had predicted, the "dust of His feet" clouds were ablaze with California sunset colors—ambers, tangerines, lemons, and dusty rose.

Although Christy couldn't explain how, she felt everything with Katie was going to turn out okay. Maybe it was simply because Christy had finally released the situation to the Lord as she and Todd had prayed. Or maybe it was because of the incredible sunset. It made everything else seem small compared to God's display of magnificence. If God could tell the sun when it was time to set, certainly He could tell Katie when it was time to break up with Michael, with or without Christy's input. Christy silently vowed to pray for Katie and Michael every day, and she hoped she would always be able to see things in perspective— from God's point of view.

Todd slipped his arm around Christy and drew her close. "You know what, Kilikina? I've prayed a long time about us being together just like this."

Resting her head on his shoulder, Christy said, "I've prayed the same thing, Todd. You know how the other day you said that for us, right now, this is a time to enjoy?"

"I remember," Todd answered, his voice sounding low and mellow.

"I think I know a better word."

"Yeah? What's that?"

"Cherish. For us, right now, this is a time to cherish."

Christy could hear Todd's echo of agreement from her snuggled-up position against his chest. "I like that," he said, "a time for us to cherish."

Together they watched the sunset, each hearing the other's steady breathing and feeling the warmth of being so close.

"Look at the color of those clouds," Christy said softly as the last tinges of pink faded from the sky. "Did you see it? It was a sort of dusty rose, wasn't it?"

Todd must have caught her hint. "White is good for a cloud too, you know."

"But don't you think dusty rose is more of a forever, cloud kind of color?"

"You know what," Todd said, grasping Christy's hand and leading her back toward the house. "I think we have enough time to go to the paint store before dinner and buy ourselves a can of dusty rose paint. After all, what other color would you paint a 'cute,' five-dollar bookshelf?"

"Well, white is good," Christy said, teasing him right back. "But not for this one. This one is a dusty rose."

"Because this is one to cherish."

"Right," Christy agreed, gazing into the great forever beyond the sunset. "This is one to cherish."

"And so are you, Kilikina," Todd said, stopping in the sand and wrapping his arms around her. "You are the one I cherish."

# Two Captivating Series from Robin Jones Gunn

*Sweet Dreams*

# Sweet Dreams

## ROBIN JONES GUNN

**BETHANY HOUSE PUBLISHERS**
MINNEAPOLIS, MINNESOTA 55438

*Sweet Dreams*
Revised edition 1999
Copyright © 1994, 1999
Robin Jones Gunn

Edited by Janet Kobobel Grant
Cover illustration and design by the Lookout Design Group

This story is a work of fiction. All characters and events are the product
of the author's imagination. Any resemblance to any person, living or
dead, is coincidental. Text has been revised and updated by the author.

A Focus on the Family book published by
Bethany House Publishers
A Ministry of Bethany Fellowship International
11400 Hampshire Avenue South
Minneapolis, Minnesota 55438
www.bethanyhouse.com

Printed in the United States of America by
Bethany Press International, Minneapolis, Minnesota 55438

**Library of Congress Cataloging-in-Publication Data**

Gunn, Robin Jones, 1955–
    Sweet dreams / by Robin Jones Gunn.
       p.  cm. — (The Christy Miller series; 11)
    Summary: Christy Miller learns to be a friend by letting go of both
her best friend, Katie, and her boyfriend, Todd, when he takes a short-
term mission assignment.
    ISBN 1–56179–732–4
    [1. Friendship—Fiction.  2. Christian life—Fiction.]  I. Title.
II. Series: Gunn, Robin Jones, 1955–    Christy Miller series; 11.
PZ7.G972Sw    1994
[Fic]—dc20                            94–6239
                                          CIP
                                          AC

99 00 01 02 03 04 05 / 15 14 13 12 11 10 9 8 7 6 5 4 3 2

*For my brother,*

*Dr. Kevin Travis Jones*

# Contents

# CHAPTER ONE

# *What Else Could Go Wrong?*

"We need to have the team captains in the very front," Christy Miller called out to the girls lined up for the yearbook picture of the Kelley High volleyball team.

Flipping her nutmeg brown hair over her shoulder and closing one eye, Christy sized up the group in her camera's view-finder. This would be her last photo for the yearbook, and she was eager to finish.

"Where's Katie?" she asked. "And who's the other captain?"

"I am," said a tall girl kneeling in the front.

"Squeeze in on the right, you guys," Christy directed. "There, that's good. Does anyone know where Katie is?"

"She's not in the locker room," one girl said. "I was just there."

"She's probably off with Michael," a girl in the middle row observed.

"Yeah, well," said another girl, "if I was going to fall in love, that's who I'd want to do it with, too."

"Did you see them today?" a girl with sandy blonde hair asked. "They had on matching 'Save the Rain Forest' T-shirts. And yesterday Katie said Michael was applying to go on a trip to the Amazon this summer with some environmental group. I bet she goes with him."

Christy's heart began to pound faster. This was her best friend they were talking about. Katie wouldn't run off to the jungle without telling Christy about it. At least, six months ago she wouldn't have. But ever since Michael had entered Katie's life, Christy and Katie had grown farther and farther apart. It felt like a stab wound to hear these girls display more knowledge of Katie's life than Christy had.

"Just take the shot," one of the girls said. "We have to get back to class."

"Okay," Christy said, focusing the camera. "Can you squeeze a little closer in the back row? Great. Perfect. Okay, you guys, smile!" She snapped the picture, and the girls immediately dispersed.

Hurrying back to her class, Christy thought, *This silence thing has gone on long enough. I'm going to talk to Katie today and do whatever it takes to get our friendship back on track.*

In a few months they would be graduating from high school. They had had so many great times together. It couldn't end with this icy standoff between them.

Everything had changed the day Katie met Michael, and Christy had done little to hold on to their friendship. Of course, Christy had been busy with her own boyfriend, Todd. That was a relationship she had waited a long time for. Now, nearly every weekend she and Todd were together, and she hadn't felt the need to work things out with Katie until the girls on the volleyball team displayed their superior knowledge of the events in Katie's life.

Right after school, Christy began to carry out her plan. She knew where Katie parked her car in the school lot, so Christy decided to wait by Katie's car. When she showed up, Christy would say, "I've been a horrible friend for not being supportive of your relationship with Michael. I've missed your friendship, and I want us to find a way to be close again." *That's* what she would say.

Christy found Katie's car and waited nearly twenty minutes. There was no sign of Katie anywhere. Dozens of cars zoomed past her, leaving the parking lot looking like an emptied pizza box with the few remaining cars scattered around like leftover chunks of pizza toppings. She was about ready to give up and leave when she heard Michael's slightly beat-up sports car roar into the parking lot.

*I'll say, 'Hi, Michael,' and I'll smile at him and be nice,* Christy told herself. But she barely had a chance to look at him.

The passenger door of his car opened before Michael had even come to a complete stop. Katie lurched out, slamming the door. Michael popped the car into gear and bolted past them, leaving a puff of exhaust to envelop Christy and Katie's first face-to-face encounter in more than two months.

"Hi," Christy said shyly. "How are you doing?"

Katie stared at Christy, her eyes swollen and red. "Why are you here?"

"Well, I, um . . . you missed the yearbook picture with your volleyball team."

"You waited here to tell me that?"

"No, actually, I waited here because I wanted to talk to you."

"I don't believe this," Katie said, shaking her head so that her short, straight, copper-colored hair swished like silk tassels.

"Believe what?" Christy asked, shrinking back. Katie had no problem speaking her mind, and it looked as though she was in the mood to let someone have it. Christy didn't want it to be her.

"I can't believe this," Katie said again, groping in her backpack for her car keys. "I don't think I can talk to you right now. This is too weird."

"What's too weird?"

Katie stood still, her green eyes narrowing into slits, scrutinizing Christy's expression. "This is just too much of a God thing for me right now. I have to go." Then, jerking her car door open, she climbed in and started up the engine.

Christy didn't know if she should knock on the window and try to get Katie to pay attention to her or if she should run across the parking lot, jump in her own car, and chase Katie. Before Christy had time to decide, Katie jammed her car into drive and squealed out of the school parking lot.

" 'Too much of a God thing'—what's that supposed to mean?" Christy muttered as she picked up her belongings and lugged them across the lot to her lonely-looking car. "Do I have bad timing, or what? She and Michael obviously had a fight. Maybe after she's had some time to cool down, I'll try talking with her. Why did I wait by her car anyway? I should have called her. It's easier to talk on the phone."

"Christy!" came a familiar voice across the lot. It was Fred, one of the other yearbook photographers. Fred was okay in a let's-just-be-friends kind of way. Still, something about him bugged her.

"I'm glad you're still here," he said. "Did you take the picture of the volleyball team?"

"Yes, and I know it's due tomorrow."

"Why don't you and I drop it off at the one-hour photo place together? I'll treat you to a Coke while we're waiting."

"No thanks," Christy said, unlocking her door and getting inside.

"Okay, then an ice cream," Fred amiably suggested.

"I really need to get home, Fred. I have a ton of homework. I'll drop it off on my way home and pick it up tomorrow."

"You're planning on staying after school tomorrow to finish the layout, aren't you?"

"Yes, I'll be here."

"I did it!" Fred said, his face full of glee. "I finally got you to say yes to something I asked. We're on a roll, Christy. It can only get better from here. So do you want to go to the prom with me?"

"No!" Christy said. This was only the fifteenth time he had asked her.

Fred looked undaunted. "Not a problem. You still have six weeks to change your mind."

"I'll see you tomorrow, Fred," Christy said.

"I'll be looking forward to it," he responded cheerfully. He waved and smiled so that his crooked front tooth stuck out. Jogging to his car parked on the other side of the lot, he drove off on his merry way.

Christy stuck her key in the ignition to start her car. Nothing happened. She jiggled the key and tried again. Nothing.

*I don't believe this! What else could go wrong?* Christy thought, climbing out of the car and slamming the door. With deliberate steps she marched back to the school building to call her dad.

About fifteen minutes later, he pulled up in his white truck. He still had on his overalls from the Hollandale Dairy. He was a large man with reddish hair and bushy red eyebrows. It was embarrassing to have to call her dad to come start her car. She was glad no one was around to see the rescue.

"Did you leave your lights on?" Dad asked when he hopped out of the truck with jumper cables in hand.

"I don't think so."

"Go ahead and pop the hood. We'll try giving the battery some juice."

Christy's dad connected the two car batteries, letting his truck run for a few minutes before saying, "Get in and start her up."

Christy turned the key, and the engine immediately turned over. She smiled her relieved thanks to her dad. Embarrassing or not, it was nice to have a dad who came to the rescue.

"I'll follow you home," Dad said after he had disconnected the cables and slammed down her hood.

They reached home with no problems. Christy thanked her dad and then went straight to her room and flopped on her bed. At nearly the same instant, the phone rang.

"Christy," Mom called from down the hallway, "telephone."

Christy forced her long legs down the hallway and picked up the phone. She heard Todd's familiar "Hey, how's it going?"

"Don't ask," she said.

"Bad day?"

"It didn't start out that way, but the last hour or so has been pretty frustrating." Christy ran through the details, deleting the part about Fred asking her to the prom. "The worst part is," she said, "I feel as if I don't know how to make things right with Katie. Everything I try blows up in my face. I guess I should call her or go over to her house. I hate things being unsettled like this."

"Good idea. Let me know how it goes."

"That's all the advice you have for me? Aren't you going to tell me what to say?"

"No."

"Todd, it's not going to be that easy."

"Sure, it will."

"She'll probably yell at me."

"So she yells at you. At least it'll get you two communicating."

"But then what do I say? Do I go over the stuff I've told her before about how she shouldn't be dating Michael because he's not a Christian? She won't listen to me. I've tried before to get closer to her and help her see that what she's doing is wrong, but she only pushes me away."

"Then let go," Todd said.

"Let go?"

"Listen, Christy," Todd began. His direct yet gentle tone made her relax a little. "I think sometimes the test of true love for a friend is found not in holding onto that person tighter but in letting them go. Sometimes when we step back and let go, it gives God room to do what He's been trying to do all along. It's like He's been waiting for us to get out of the way."

"So you think I've been in God's way?" Christy asked, feeling a little defensive.

Todd paused before saying, "I think you need to let go. Then you'll know for sure that you're not in the way."

Christy let out a sigh. "Okay, I'll call her and tell her . . . I don't know what I'll tell her. But I'll call her. Pray for me, okay?"

"I always do," Todd said. Then with his familiar "Later," he hung up.

Christy closed her eyes and pictured Todd, her tall, broad-shouldered boyfriend. She could see his screaming silver-blue eyes crinkle at the corners and his chin automatically tilt up like it always did whenever he said "Later." She knew she was lucky to have him. Perhaps "blessed" was a better word.

Christy quickly dialed Katie's number before she had time to think about it. Katie answered on the second ring.

"Hi, it's me. Do you have a minute?"

Dead air filled the space between them.

"Why?" Katie finally said.

Christy wished she had taken the time to plan her words before calling. She spouted off the first thing that came to her mind. "Katie, I want you to know that I'm not going to try to tell you what to do anymore. I know I've been critical of Michael, and I'm sorry. Will you forgive me, Katie?"

Christy hadn't expected to cry, but she did. The tears dripped off her cheeks. She stared at the water droplets on her jeans and waited for Katie to respond.

"I can't talk to you right now," Katie said solemnly.

Christy wanted to argue and somehow convince Katie they needed to talk *now*. That's what would make Christy feel better. Apparently, that wasn't what Katie needed. Did letting go mean not pushing Katie to talk things through?

"Okay," Christy said. "That's fine. Could we maybe talk another time?"

"I promise we'll talk later. I'm just not ready yet."

"All right."

"Okay," Katie said. It sounded as if she was crying, too. Then right before she hung up, she said, "Thanks, Chris."

Christy sat with her back against the hallway wall for a long while after hanging up the phone. This was all so complicated. Everyone had told her that her senior year would be her best year of high school. And true, there had been lots of wonderful things, like being with Todd, working on the school yearbook, and having her job at the pet store.

Yet this unresolved conflict over Michael had taken a chomp out of Christy's heart. She had lost her best friend to a dark-haired exchange student from Ireland who, for the last six months, had occupied Katie's every spare moment. Christy brushed her hair back and wiped her blue-green eyes with the palm of her hand. She felt as though she had lost her best friend. And maybe she had.

# *The Organic Tomato*

The next morning Christy spotted Michael at his locker. Sucking in a deep breath, she approached him with a smile. If she couldn't make peace directly with Katie, maybe somehow she could open up the communication lines through Michael.

"Hi, Michael," she said.

"Morning," Michael returned. His Irish accent made him sound naturally cheerful, but his face told Christy the opposite. He looked as if he had just gotten up, with his dark hair twisted in uncombed curls at the nape of his neck. He was wearing his favorite baggy shorts, leather sandals, and his overly familiar 'Save the Whales' T-shirt.

"Have you seen Katie yet today?"

"No." His answer was curt.

Christy hesitated and then said, "I don't know if it's even my place to ask, but are you guys okay?"

"What did Katie tell you?"

"Nothing. That's the thing. I haven't talked to her, and I know she was upset yesterday after school. I just wanted to see if everything was okay."

"Look," Michael said, cocking his head and sounding mellow

but looking stern, "you haven't the right."

"The right?" Christy ventured.

"Let's be straight. I know you haven't been favorable toward me since Katie and I started to date. Now that Katie somehow believes your prayers have worked against her, you haven't the right to step in like a vulture, waiting to pick at my bones."

Christy was shocked. "What?" she stammered, but it was too late. Michael had already turned and was maneuvering his way through the congestion in the hallways.

*I haven't the right? What do you mean I haven't the right? I'm Katie's best friend!*

The bell rang loudly right above Christy's head. She felt like yelling back at it.

*Why would Michael say such a thing to me? Why would he say I'm like a vulture? And what does he mean my prayers have worked against her? What's going on here?*

Hurrying to her locker, she threw her books inside and wished somehow she could curl up inside, too. She wished it even more when she heard someone call out, "Miss Chris." She knew it had to be Fred.

"Hey, what's with Katie? She was all over my case this morning because she heard we took the volleyball team photo without her."

"What did you tell her?"

"I told her you took it. Wasn't my fault she didn't manage to show up."

"Oh, that's just great. Thanks a lot, Fred. Now she'll never speak to me again!" Christy slammed her locker door and marched down the hall to her first class.

"Sure, she will," Fred said, briskly trotting beside her. "I told her if she wanted to reschedule another photo to talk to you, and you would contact the rest of the team."

"And how am I supposed to do that?" Christy blurted out. "The pictures are due today." Christy suddenly remembered the roll of film was still in her purse.

"Oh, didn't you hear? We have two extra weeks. Miss Wallace found out we're four pages short, so she asked if you and I would work on photo collages. I told her we would work together day and night until we got it just right."

"Why did you tell her that, Fred?"

Fred looked as if he were venturing a wild guess. "Because I'm such a cool guy, and you're dying to spend quality time with me?"

"Guess again, Fred!" Christy spewed and ducked into her classroom just as the final bell rang. She dropped into her chair, feeling horrible. She never should have talked to Fred like that. She wouldn't want anyone treating her that way. And Michael had, that morning. Maybe that's why she turned on Fred.

*I'll apologize to him just before yearbook class*, Christy decided, trying to focus on the handout the teacher had placed in front of her.

It was a quiz. She had forgotten all about it and hadn't studied at all. This day was not shaping up any better than yesterday.

It didn't get much better until that afternoon. She found Fred in their yearbook class, bending over a table covered with candid photos.

"Fred," Christy said, walking up beside him and gently touching his arm, "I want to apologize for what I said this morning. It was rude, and I'm sorry. I'm kind of under a lot of stress, but that's no excuse."

"It's okay," Fred said without looking up.

There was a pause, and then Christy said, "Should we start working on those collage pages?"

"Sure. I started to look for a few larger ones to sort of get us going, and then I thought we could fill in with some smaller shots."

Miss Wallace walked up and held out a picture of a toddler wearing cowboy boots, a hat, a holster, and a diaper. "Can you guess who this is?"

Fred and Christy looked at the photo and both shook their heads.

"Hal Janssen," Miss Wallace announced.

"You're kidding! Has anyone on the football team seen this?" Christy asked.

"No, Hal's mom brought it in this morning. Won't it look great next to his Cougar of the Week shot when he scored the most points against Vista High?"

"This is perfect!" Fred said, holding up the picture. All his gloom had evaporated. "Now all we need are pictures of Aaron Johnson and Adrian Medina, and our baby hall of fame will be complete."

"This was really a good idea, Fred, collecting all these baby pictures of this year's outstanding students," Miss Wallace said.

"It wasn't my idea," Fred replied quickly. "It was Christy's. I just agreed with her."

Miss Wallace smiled at Christy. "You've done a terrific job, Christy. I think you're a natural at this sort of thing."

Christy could feel a rush of pink to her cheeks. It felt good to know she had finally done something right.

For the next week and a half, Christy kept busy with the yearbook, homework, and her job at the pet store. Over the weekend Todd came up from San Diego, where he was attending college. They went miniature golfing with her eleven-year-old brother and then sat close together on the couch that night, eating popcorn and watching an old black and white movie with Christy's parents. Everything was great. Wonderful. Everything except that she was still waiting for Katie to contact her.

Christy saw Katie and Michael one time at school. They were holding hands, and everything between them seemed perfect. Why, then, wouldn't Katie call Christy or come over and tell her all was well? What had gone on between Katie and Michael that had caused the tension in the parking lot?

When Christy walked into the yearbook class on Thursday, Miss Wallace said, "Christy, I've arranged for you to take another picture of the volleyball team in about ten minutes. They said some of their team members didn't make it for the last shot. Fred offered to take it if you didn't want to, but I thought you would since you've been working on this one all along."

Christy looked over at Fred, who stood a few feet away. He shrugged and said, "Whatever. I didn't know if you were okay with Katie yet."

Christy didn't know either. What would be best for Katie? Would she smile for the picture if Christy was the one behind the camera? Would it be easier if Fred took it?

"Do you mind, Fred?"

"Not a problem. I'll take the picture if you'll pick out Adrian Medina's baby picture and figure out where to put it."

"Oh, we got it?"

"His stepmom mailed us three pictures," Miss Wallace explained. "Wait until you see them! One with spaghetti or something all over his face."

Fred grabbed his camera and was about to hurry over to the gym. Christy caught him before he went out the door, and looking him in the eye, she said, "This is really nice of you, Fred. Thanks."

"Does this mean you'll go to the prom with me?"

"Fred!" Christy said, laughing.

"Never hurts to try." He gave her one of his toothy grins. "I do want to ask you something when I come back, though, okay?"

Christy felt a little nervous that he would put her on the spot for something. "You'd better hurry," she said. "You wouldn't want to have to try to assemble that bunch again."

"Right." Fred hustled out the door.

Christy went to work on the layout, playing with all the pictures and the copy as if it were a jigsaw puzzle. She didn't hear anyone come up behind her, but she then became aware that someone was looking over her shoulder. She turned around and saw Katie.

"That's Adrian?" Katie said, examining the photo of Adrian as a toddler splashing in a plastic kiddie pool that lay next to the one of him holding up the trophy the polo team had won this year. "He got his start in water sports early, I see."

"Cute, isn't it?" Christy said, feeling natural and at ease with Katie, as if no strain existed between them.

"Are you busy after school?" Katie asked.

"I don't think so." Christy knew work needed to be done on the yearbook, but then, the yearbook always needed work. She wasn't about to brush Katie off, since she apparently was now ready to talk.

"Can you meet me by my car? We'll grab a snack. My treat."

"Oh, well, if you're paying, then of course," Christy said with a smile.

Katie seemed to be fine. Maybe they wouldn't have that much to talk about. A few misunderstandings, some bruised feelings. Maybe they could move on from this point, and Christy would have a chance to really get to know Michael. Maybe she and Katie could renew their friendship and redeem what was left of their senior year.

Christy met Katie at her car right after school. Katie drove out of the parking lot in silence. Then they both began sentences at the same time.

"Oh, I'm sorry. Go ahead," Christy said.

"No, you go."

"I was just saying, so where do you want to go?"

"I thought you'd like to see my new hangout."

"Sure," Christy said. "And what were you going to say?"

"I was going to say it seems you're doing a good job on the yearbook and you really enjoy it."

"I do. I never would have guessed it would be so much fun. You know, I really only signed up because I needed one more class and, because I thought if I was on staff, I could make sure Fred didn't put in any of those embarrassing pictures like he did last year."

"Now you're the one putting in the embarrassing photos, so that makes it okay." The criticism in Katie's voice was evident.

"What do you mean?" Christy knew she sounded defensive.

"Nothing. Forget I said anything. That's not why I wanted to get together today. You have to do whatever you have to do. I'm not your judge. Too many people judge other people these days. Especially Christians."

Christy could guess what Katie was hinting at.

Silence ushered them down the main street of Escondido and sat beside them at a red light. When the light turned green, it was as if a signal went off, and both of them began to talk at the same time.

"We seem to be conversationally impaired today," Katie said, with her light laugh returning. "Here's the place."

She pulled into the driveway of a strip mall and parked in front of a small restaurant called The Organic Tomato.

"The Organic Tomato?" Christy asked.

"Don't worry. They serve a lot more than tomatoes," Katie said as she led Christy into the tiny cafe.

Christy struggled to believe this was Katie, the person who used to identify her four basic food groups as fat, sugar, preservatives and salt. Michael, who was into vitamins and health food, obviously was a powerful influence on Katie.

The small cafe was brightly lit. A dozen small, round tables with bright, flowered tablecloths were positioned around the room, making Christy feel as if she had stepped into a kaleidoscope. At any moment the tables might begin to spin, and she would be caught up in the swirl of repositioning colors. No one else was in the restaurant.

"Are you sure they're open?" Christy whispered.

"Oh, sure. Michael and I come here all the time after school." Katie walked to the back where a small window opened up to the kitchen.

"Hi, Janice. How's your day been?"

A slender, blonde woman with glowing skin and beautiful blue eyes stepped out, wearing an apron with a big red tomato on the front. "Great, Katie. How are you doing, Michael? Oh, that's not Michael."

"This is my friend Christy. Christy, this is Janice."

"Nice to meet you."

"And you."

"So what's your special for today?" Katie asked.

"It's the southwest tofu burger, with blue corn chips and fresh squeezed carrot juice."

Christy wasn't sure what all that was, but just hearing the

names made her want to gag. How could Katie stand this place?

"Sounds great," Katie said. "I'll have that. You want the same, Christy? Remember, it's my treat."

"Well, I was wondering if maybe I could see a menu."

"Sure," Janice said. "Here you go. There's a spinach and sprout salad you might like. The eggplant lasagna is also a favorite."

Christy nodded and accepted the flowery menu. She followed Katie to a table and said, "I had a lot for lunch. I was thinking of maybe just a soda."

"Soda?" Katie said.

Christy realized then that no one would walk into a place called The Organic Tomato and order a Coke.

"They have some all-natural sparkling beverages," Katie explained. "But mostly they serve juice. It's all squeezed fresh, right here."

"Oh, I'm sure it is," Christy said cautiously. "Maybe just an orange juice then."

"I heard," Janice called from the back. "Carrot juice and o.j. coming right up."

Christy didn't feel comfortable. It wasn't just the "organic" atmosphere. It was knowing that everything they said would he heard. Plus, none of the food on the menu even sounded familiar. At least she *thought* they were foods. Bulgar wheat salad, tofu scramble, lentil soup, bean curd. It looked as if a little kid had mixed up all the letters on the menu and put them back in the wrong places.

Janice appeared with the smallest glass of orange juice Christy had seen since she had ordered a kid's breakfast from Denny's a decade ago. The juice was so full of pulp she was tempted to use her spoon and eat it like soup. Somehow she thought that might upset Katie, so she took tiny sips and ran her tongue across her front teeth after every swallow, checking for stray pulp pieces.

Katie's tofu burger looked normal enough. Christy guessed the bun was made from organic, whole-grain something. It was a bit disturbing that the chips were a navy blue. But Christy decided that if she concentrated on Katie's face instead of her plate, she could pretend they were eating regular hamburgers and French fries at McDonald's like they used to before Katie met Michael.

"You want a bite?" Katie offered.

"No, thanks. I'm fine."

Katie took two or three bites and motioned for Christy to try a blue chip. She took a tiny one, and it tasted like a normal corn chip. Janice turned on some airy harp music, and Christy felt a little more at ease.

"God wants me to break up with Michael," Katie blurted out.

"Where did that come from?" Christy almost felt like laughing at Katie's abruptness.

"Please don't make light of this, Christy. I'm serious." Katie took another bite. Her expression grew sad. "And I've been disobeying God."

A dozen questions ran through Christy's mind. But she chose to remain silent and let Katie do the talking.

"I've known it for a couple of weeks now," Katie said. "All along I've been praying that Michael would surrender to the Lord. I thought that's why God brought him into my life, for me to show him how to become a Christian. And I've tried. Believe me! The six and a half months we've been together I've talked to him, given him books to read, taken him to Bible studies, introduced him to other Christians. And you know how I gave him that Bible for Christmas."

Christy nodded. She remembered shopping with Katie and looking at what seemed like every Bible ever made until Katie found one she thought Michael would read.

"He just won't believe. It's not that he can't believe that Christianity is the right way or that he doesn't believe in God, because he does. It's that he won't surrender his life to Christ."

Christy could see the pain in Katie's eyes.

"I told God that if He wanted me to break up with Michael, I would. And then God told me to break up with him. Don't ask me how I know. Michael wanted to know how God talks to me. I can't explain it. It's just that deep inside my heart I know what the Holy Spirit is telling me."

Katie took another bite of her burger and motioned for Christy to have another chip. She obliged.

"So two weeks ago when you saw us in the school parking lot, I had just told Michael. I said we had to break up."

"Oh, Katie, I didn't know."

"That was the thing. See, on the way back to school I prayed for a sign. I know you're not supposed to mess with God like that, but I was so upset. I said, "God, if I did the right thing by breaking up with Michael, then make me run into Christy on the way home.""

"You're kidding."

"No. It was such a God thing, I couldn't believe it. When I prayed that, I knew you would either be working at the pet store or on the yearbook. Then there you were, standing by my car! After that I don't know what happened. Michael said some mean things, and I got really mad at God because He was making me do this."

Katie waved her hand at Christy's confused expression. "I know, it's dumb, but it was like God did what I asked by putting you there, and then I got mad. I couldn't even talk to you."

"Yes, I noticed," Christy said softly.

"It was as if you were on God's side, and somehow you were both against me. I don't know, Christy. I was a mess for a couple of days. Then Michael and I got back together. He's happy. I'm happy. Everything is normal, except I know I'm disobeying God. So I'm ignoring Him." Katie chomped into her burger and ate silently for a moment.

"Why are you talking to me now?" Christy asked. "Does it seem like I'm not on God's side any more?"

"No!" Katie said quickly. "You are. That's why I thought I needed to talk to you face to face. I want you to tell me to break up with Michael."

"I can't do that," Christy said. "That's between you and God and Michael."

"Thanks a lot," Katie muttered.

"What do you mean?"

"I mean, all along you kept warning me about him not being a Christian, and now that I want you to tell me to break up, you won't do it."

"I can't," Christy said. Then using Michael's words, she added, "I haven't earned the right. I'm not your personal Holy Spirit. You have to listen to what God tells you to do and then choose to obey or disobey."

"I'm disobeying," Katie admitted sadly. "It's a creepy feeling."

"Then why don't you break up with him for good this time?"

"There's only one problem."

"What's that?"

"I'm in love with him."

# CHAPTER THREE

# *Blessed Are the Peacemakers*

"You're in love with him," Christy repeated. "What does that mean?"

"It means," Katie said, putting down her burger, "I'm in love with him. Do you know how hard it is to push someone out of your life when you're in love with him? It's impossible! Christy, there has never been any other guy in my life. There might never be any others! For six months the center of my universe has been Michael, and it's been wonderful. Why would I give that up?"

"Because God told you to?" Christy ventured.

"Exactly! But I want a human to tell me so I'll know it's the right thing to do. You have to help me out here, Christy."

Christy remained silent, confused as to what to say. It would be easier if she could have time to think all this through. Would it be okay for her to go ahead and say, "Yes, Katie, God has told me to tell you to break up with Michael?" Or should she stick with her gut feeling that this was a decision Katie had to make, with or without a cheering section?

"You're not going to help me on this one, are you, Christy?"

"Katie, you already know what I think about all this. I think Michael is a great guy, and he's been the perfect boyfriend for you. But unless he becomes a Christian, the only areas you have in common are the emotional and physical. The spiritual part of you will never connect with him, and that's the part of you that's going to last forever."

"You sound like Todd," Katie said.

Christy took that as a compliment.

"So go ahead, Christy, finish your speech. Tell me what to do."

Christy hesitated. "Katie," she said firmly, "you have to do what God tells you to."

"You make me so mad!" Katie spouted, pushing away her plate. "You have no idea how hard this is, Christy."

"I know," Christy said softly.

"No, you don't!" Katie yelled. "You've never gone through anything like this. This is the hardest thing I've ever done. I love him, yet I'm breaking up with him because God told me to! That's the only reason. Do you have any idea how stupid that sounds to Michael? All that witnessing. All those books. All those Bible studies. And now I'm telling him God is so mean that He won't let us go out anymore!"

Christy didn't know what to say.

"Come on," Katie said. "Let's get out of here." She left enough money on the table to cover the meal and marched out to the car. Christy hurried after her and jumped in just as Katie backed up sharply and swerved into the flow of traffic. "God is so totally unfair!"

Christy grabbed onto the side of her seat as a car cut in front of them. Katie laid on the horn and yelled, "Why did God bring Michael into my life only to jerk him away? I am so mad right now I could scream!" And Katie promptly screamed.

Christy had always admired Katie's ability to express her feelings. But she had never seen Katie this upset.

Katie sped into the school parking lot and pulled up next to Christy's car with a screech.

"Are you okay?" Christy asked before getting out.

"No, of course not. What a stupid question! I'm dying here, Christy. Have a little sympathy, will you?"

"What can I do?" Christy felt flustered.

"Nothing. I asked you for help, and you wouldn't give it to me. If I'm going to do this, I'm going to have to do it without any human affirmation. So just leave me alone."

"Do you want to call me later?" Christy asked.

"Maybe."

"Call me," Christy urged, hopping out of the car. She wasn't sure Katie heard her, because Katie started to speed away just as Christy closed the door.

Christy felt awful as she drove home. Her stomach didn't seem to like the pulpy orange juice, plus a flood of accusations swept over her.

*You're a terrible friend, Christy. You're so chicken, you couldn't even tell Katie the right thing to do. All you could do was hide behind God and force Katie to make her own decision. Is that the compassionate, Christian thing to do?*

The minute Christy arrived home, she grabbed the phone and called Todd. To her relief, he answered on the first ring. Christy spilled out all the events of the past hour.

"You did the right thing," Todd said. "Don't listen to all those doubts and accusations. Those aren't coming from the Lord. You pushed Katie closer to God. You made her responsible for her choice. You did the right thing."

"Then how come I feel so terrible?"

"Maybe because you would like everything to be smooth and easy, and it isn't always like that. You're a peacemaker, Christy. I like that about you. God says the peacemakers will be called His sons and daughters. How do you feel about that? Christy Miller, daughter of the King! Should I start calling you Princess now?''

Christy let out a gentle laugh. "Only if you want me to call you Prince Todd.''

"I can live with that.''

"Well, Prince Todd, thanks for listening. You're a peacemaker for me, I hope you know. I appreciate you so much. Thanks for always being there.''

"You're welcome, Princess. So what do you want to do this weekend?''

"I don't know. Should I see if I can get off on Saturday and stay at my Uncle Bob and Aunt Marti's? You and I could spend some time on the beach." Christy's imagination began to swirl with dreams of walking hand in hand on Newport Beach at sunset.

"Sounds good to me. Call me after you figure it all out.''

"Okay, I will. Thanks again, Todd. I don't know what I'd do without you.''

"You would probably be closer to God, because you would have to talk to Him more," Todd said. Then with a quick "Later," he hung up.

*What did Todd mean by that? Does he think I don't talk to God very much or that I'm not close to God? Oh, well. I'm not going to worry about it. One thing Todd is right about, I do like things calm and peaceful. Looking for hidden meanings in his words does not make me feel peaceful!*

Christy quickly dialed her aunt and uncle's phone number. They lived only a few blocks from Todd's dad in Newport Beach, and over the past few years Todd had become like a son to them. There should be no problem inviting herself to visit for the weekend. But the answering machine picked up her call on the fourth ring. She left a message and then called Jon, her boss at the pet store.

"Hi, Jon. It's Christy. I wanted to see if I could have Saturday off."

"Saturday, as in the day after tomorrow?"

"Yes."

"You're asking me now? And you think I should give you the whole day off?"

"Yes." Christy thought she knew Jon well enough to know he was teasing her. At least she thought he was teasing her.

"Big date with Todd?" Jon asked.

"Well, kind of. I'm probably going to go up to Newport for the weekend. I could work another evening next week if you need me to make up the hours."

"No, it's okay. You haven't had any time off for the past few months. I'd say you're ready for a break. You'll still be here to-morrow for your regular hours, won't you?"

"Yes, of course. Thanks, Jon. Did anyone ever tell you what a nice boss you are?"

"No," Jon said plainly.

"Then let me be the first. You're a very nice boss, Jon!"

"You don't have to schmooze me anymore, Christy. I already said you could have the day off."

"I know, but I might want to ask another favor someday."

"Well, next time I'll say no."

"Thanks for saying yes this time, Jon. I'll see you tomorrow."

The minute Christy hung up the phone, it rang again. Star-tled, she jumped and then answered it.

"Okay," the voice on the other end said. "I did it. It's for good this time. Now I'm going to go crazy. I am absolutely going to go crazy!"

"Katie," Christy said cautiously, "tell me what happened."

"I went right over to his house and told Michael that I loved him, but I had to break up with him, and the only reason was because I knew that's what God was telling me to do. He said, 'You know that I love you, Katie, and now I love you more, because you're one of the few women I know who would make such a decision because of her convictions.' Then he kissed me on the cheek, and I ran out the door."

Christy could tell that Katie was crying. She let Katie sob a few moments before trying to comfort her.

"You did the right thing, Katie."

"Then why does it hurt so bad?"

"I guess the good feelings don't always come in the same envelope as the right answer."

Katie burst out laughing. "Did you hear yourself? What is that supposed to mean?"

"It's the first thing that popped into my head. What I mean is, for now, all you can know is that you did the right thing. I think the feelings will catch up eventually."

"I hope you're right. I can't believe I did it. I'm going to hate myself tomorrow. Oh, no," Katie groaned. "Tomorrow is Friday. What am I going to do?"

"What do you mean?" Christy asked.

"For the past six months Michael and I have always been together on the weekends. I have to have something else to do. Promise me you'll spend the whole weekend with me, Christy. I'll go crazy if I'm by myself."

"Well, I . . ."

"I know you have to work, but that's okay. I'll go to work with you. I'm sure Jon can find something for me to do in the back room. He doesn't have to pay me or anything. I just can't stay home by myself."

"Sure," Christy said boldly. "We'll work something out. I was trying to make plans to go to Bob and Marti's. I'm sure they wouldn't mind if you came, too."

"Oh," Katie said, sounding depressed. "You probably wanted to be with Todd. You don't need me in the way."

"No, Katie, it's fine. Really. You know Todd; he won't mind a bit. I'd love to spend the weekend with you. It's been so long since we've done anything together. It'll be great. You'll see."

"Well, if you're sure."

"Yes, I'm sure. I'll give my aunt another call, and then I'll call you back. You might as well start packing, Katie. I'm sure it'll work out."

"I broke up with Michael." Katie sounded like she couldn't believe her own statement. "I really did it. I broke up with him for good."

"Katie, are you okay?"

"No," Katie said somberly. "But I will be. Someday. Not to-morrow. But one day, I will be. Call me back. Bye."

Christy listened to the dial tone and wondered if Katie really would be okay. She hung up and tried to sort out all the events of the past few hours. After weeks—no months—of stifled tension between Katie and her, in the last two and a half hours everything had changed.

In a way, Christy wished Katie's big breakup with Michael hadn't come until Monday. That way, at least Christy and Todd could have had a fun weekend together. The minute she thought it, she felt bad.

She and Todd had enjoyed months of terrific weekends to-gether, and during many of those weekends they had discussed

Katie and Michael's relationship. Over and over Todd had told Christy to wait and be patient, to stick with Katie through this whole thing. He had told her there was a time for everything. Apparently now was the time for Christy to come alongside Katie and support her and cry along with her. Todd would understand.

And he did. When she called him later that evening to tell him that she had reached Bob and Marti and they were delighted to have Katie and Christy come up for the weekend, Todd said, "I'll see if Doug can come home from college this weekend. We'll all have to go to Disneyland or something."

"That would be fun," Christy agreed. "You know, you and I haven't been to Disneyland since our very first date. When was that? Three years ago?"

"Yeah, I'd say it's time we go again. Doug's great when it comes to cheering up brokenhearted women. He'll be a good companion for Katie."

"Doug doesn't have a girlfriend yet?" Christy asked. "I thought he would have met somebody by now."

"Nope. He told me once that he thought he knew whom God wanted him to marry, but he was waiting for the girl to figure it out. He wouldn't tell me who it was."

"You think it might be Tracy?" Christy asked. "They went out for a while."

"I don't know. He wouldn't give me any hints. Could be Katie, for all we know. Doesn't matter, though. Doug's sure that God will work it all out."

"I guess Katie and I will drive up together on Friday night as soon as I get off work. We'll get to Bob and Marti's after ten. Is that too late for you guys? I mean, do you want to get together on Friday night, or wait and do something on Saturday?"

"Whatever," Todd said amiably. "We'll take it as it comes."

"I'm looking forward to seeing you," Christy said softly.

"Yeah, I'm looking forward to seeing you, too."

"Bye," Christy said.

"Later."

Christy made a quick phone call to Katie and filled her in on the plans. Even though Katie sounded tired at first, she spoke up when Christy mentioned Doug.

"I don't want charity," Katie said. "Doug is not interested in me, he never has been, he never will be. I don't want him coming along just to give me all his little hugs and try to make me feel better."

"Okay, fine. Doug might not even come. But we're still going to Disneyland, and that will be fun," Christy said, trying to sound cheerful.

"Yeah, right. You, Todd, and me. What a fun day that will be. Is Todd going to hold hands with both of us so I won't feel left out?"

Christy was beginning to get irritated. "Katie, will you stop it? We're going to the pet store tomorrow after school, and then you and I are going to drive up to Newport, stay at my aunt and uncle's, probably go to Disneyland on Saturday and then church with Todd on Sunday, and you are going to have a wonderful time. Got it?"

"Sorry," Katie said. "I'll try not to be a brat this weekend. I appreciate your making room for me in your plans."

"It'll be fun, Katie. You'll see. I'm really looking forward to it."

"Me too," Katie said with a sigh. "I wonder what Michael is going to do this weekend? I guess it doesn't matter, does it?"

Christy didn't answer.

"Well," Katie said, snapping back to a more positive tone of voice, "I have some more homework to finish. I'll see you to-morrow. Thanks again, Christy. This is the true test of a best friend. Thanks for sticking with me through all this."

"There's nothing to thank me for, Katie. I'll see you after school. Good night."

Christy hung up, thinking, *If you only knew how selfish I'm feeling right now about having to share Todd with you this weekend, you wouldn't be thanking me.*

CHAPTER FOUR

# Just Let Me Hurt

"Oh, Miss Chris," Fred said the minute Christy walked into yearbook class on Friday. "May I have a moment of your time?"

"What do you want, Fred?" Christy was not in the mood to deal with him.

"Do you remember yesterday, right before I left to take the photo of the volleyball team, I said I wanted to talk to you about something?"

Christy didn't remember, but she wanted to speed this conversation along, so she nodded and waited for Fred's reply, expecting another invitation to the prom.

"I wanted to ask you something."

"What, Fred?" she said, her irritation showing.

"I wanted to ask you what church you went to."

"Why?" Christy asked, surprised.

"I kind of wanted to try going sometime."

"Why?" Christy asked, and the minute she did, she realized how rude she sounded.

"It's a free country," Fred said, puffing out his chest a little. "At least, the last time I checked, it was. I've never been to church before. I thought I might like to try it sometime."

33

"That's great, Fred," Christy said, quickly changing her tone. "I think you'll like it. It's a really good church." She gave him directions and specifics on when the high school group met and when church services were held.

"Thanks," Fred said. "I'll see you there this Sunday."

"Oh," Christy said, "is that why you wanted to go to church? Just because I do?"

"No!" Fred answered defensively.

"Well, I'm not going to be there this Sunday. I'm going to be at my aunt and uncle's for the weekend." Then, trying to sound nice, she added, "Some other people from school go there, though, so I'm sure you'll see somebody you know."

"Like Katie," Fred said.

"Actually, Katie is going to be with me. There are other people, though. I think you'll like it; you should go."

"I will," Fred said. "Are you ready to work on these last two collage pages with me? We have to have everything done by next Wednesday. That's the final, final, drop dead deadline."

"Are you sure?"

"Yes, I'm sure."

Christy couldn't help but wonder about Fred's interest in attending church. She would have liked to believe he was becoming interested in Christianity. Maybe somehow she had been a witness to him, although she wasn't sure how. Most of the year she had been rude to him, and she had never tried talking to him about spiritual things. Somehow, she couldn't help but wonder if it was one of his tactics to spend time with her, especially since they would be done with their mutual projects by next Wednesday. They wouldn't have too many other reasons to talk to each other after the yearbook was done. That is, unless Fred started going to her church.

She told Katie about it on the way to work after school that afternoon. It had been months since Katie and Christy had talked like this, and Katie said she didn't even know Fred had been chasing Christy.

"Only all year," Christy said.

"Man," Katie said with a sigh, "we've missed a lot this year, haven't we? I mean, our whole senior year is almost over, and you and I barely know what's going on with each other."

"I know," Christy said.

"I regret that, Christy, and I know it's all my fault because I was so wrapped up in Michael."

"It's not all your fault. I didn't exactly make things comfortable for either of us. I could have done a lot more to keep our friendship close, but I didn't. I'm sorry I didn't try harder."

"Let's promise each other that we'll never do that again," Katie said, looking solemn. "Let's promise that we'll never in our whole lives let a guy come between us. Even when we're old and senile, we'll still be best friends."

"Promise," Christy said. "Although, if I'm senile, I can't promise that I'll exactly remember who you are from day to day."

"Then we'll just have to make sure they check us both into a rest home where all the patients wear name tags," Katie said, and the two friends laughed together—something they hadn't done for months.

The evening at the pet store zipped by. Christy had quietly let Jon know that Katie and Michael had broken up, and Jon made sure Katie kept busy in the stock room, helping him rearrange supplies. Jon kept her laughing, too, with all his stories about crazy customers.

Just as the two girls were about to leave the store, Christy sidled up to Jon and said, "Remind me to do something nice for you someday."

Jon smiled and whispered, "She's not through the worst of it yet. It'll hit her pretty hard. Probably sometime this weekend. Anyone who's had a broken heart knows it gets worse before it gets better."

Jon's expression and tender words made Christy wonder who had once broken his heart. Maybe he had never recovered, since he was in his early thirties and still not married.

"You want ice cream or frozen yogurt or something before the long drive up to Newport Beach?" Christy asked as she and Katie headed for the car. "We could stop by Baskin-Robbins on our way out of town."

Katie didn't answer.

Christy unlocked the passenger door, and Katie got in, fastened her seat belt, and looked straight ahead, as if in a daze.

"Hello, Earth to Katie. Do you want to stop by 31 Flavors or not?" Christy asked. Then she noticed a stream of tears pouring down Katie's cheeks.

"That's the first place we ever went together. Remember? It was the day we met. Right after school, I told Michael I was going to educate him on how many vitamins could be found in a scoop of Jamoca Almond Fudge ice cream."

Christy swallowed hard. Things had been going so well at work. She hadn't expected this kind of sorrow attack. "We don't have to stop there. We don't have to stop anywhere. We can just drive straight to Bob and Marti's. Forget I suggested it. Bad suggestion."

Maneuvering the car out of the parking lot, Christy checked Katie's face each time they passed a street light to see if the tears were letting up.

"Do you realize," Christy said, "this is the first time since we went to San Diego about this time last year that you and I have gone anywhere together, just the two of us? And can you believe my parents actually let me take the car for the whole weekend? This is really a first, Katie."

Katie leaned back against the headrest and closed her eyes. In a choked voice she said, "Take me home, Christy. I can't do this."

"Sure you can," Christy said cheerfully. "We're going to have a great time together this weekend. You'll forget all about Michael."

"I don't want to forget about Michael!" Katie said, raising her voice. "There are no bad memories to try to forget. Everything was wonderful. You don't get it, do you? I loved him. I still love him!"

Christy drove silently onto the freeway and moved into the middle lane. They passed the off-ramp for Katie's house, but Katie said nothing. Christy assumed Katie didn't really want to go home. She just needed to get away. Christy decided it was up to her to convince Katie that they were going to have a good time.

Christy drove a little faster. The farther Katie got from home, the less realistic it would be for them to turn around and go back, and the more enthusiastic she might become about the weekend.

They continued in silence. Christy felt relieved that traffic was light. They should make it to Bob and Marti's in about an hour and a half. She wondered if she should turn on the radio. No, a song might come on that would remind Katie of Michael, although Christy didn't know what song that might be. She realized how little she knew about Michael and Katie and the things that were special to them. Maybe they should talk about anything unrelated to Michael.

"Did I tell you we have until Wednesday to finish up everything on the yearbook? I think it turned out really well. It's been a lot of fun. Maybe I'll take some courses like that in college. That reminds me. I never heard what you decided about college next year. Did you hear back from any of the ones you applied to?"

Katie pursed her lips. "I was accepted at the Queens University in Belfast. That's where Michael is going next year."

"Belfast? You mean in Ireland? I didn't know you even applied. Are you still going there? What am I saying? Of course you're not. What's your next choice?"

"I don't know," Katie said. "I didn't have any backup plans."

Christy could see the tears starting to slide down Katie's freckled cheeks again. She knew she'd better start talking fast. "I guess I'm going to Palomar Community College, at least for my freshman year. My aunt wants me to go to a state university. You know they started a college savings account for me several years ago. Well, there's probably enough for my first year. But my parents think I should wait until I have a better idea of what I want my major to be before I go to a university. That way I can get all the general ed. courses out of the way. Palomar is pretty good, from what I hear. Why don't you go to Palomar with me? It'd be great, Katie. We could even take some classes together."

By now they were well on their way down the freeway and were driving past Camp Pendleton Marine Corps Base. Katie stared blankly out the window.

"Maybe I'll join the army," Katie mumbled.

"The army?" Christy questioned with a laugh.

"All right, then, the air force."

"Katie, you crack me up," Christy said. "You belong in a drama class."

"I'm not being dramatic," Katie said, facing Christy. Katie's eyes looked puffy in the dim light.

"What I mean is, you seem like you would be great as the star in a school play. I can see you going to college and majoring in acting much more than I picture you in the cockpit of a fighter plane."

"Acting, huh?" Katie said.

"I think you would be great in drama. You have a natural flare for it. I always said you would be the next Lucille Ball."

"I don't feel like I'm going to be the next anything. I hurt so bad, Christy. You can't imagine how bad this hurts."

"That's because you keep thinking about it. Try to get your mind on something else. Let's play a game or something. I know. I'm thinking of an animal that starts with the letter 'G.'"

"It's giraffe, and I don't want to play."

"How did you know it was a giraffe?"

"You pick a giraffe first every time we play this stupid game."

"Okay," Christy said, still trying to move the conversation off Michael, "your turn. You pick one."

"Christy," Katie said sharply, "you don't get it, do you? I don't want to play any stupid games. I'm hurting. Just let me hurt, will you!"

Christy recoiled, trying hard not to let her wounded feelings show. Now *she* was the one who wanted to turn around and take Katie home. With Katie so set on feeling sorry for herself, it was bound to be a miserable weekend.

*If only Katie and Michael hadn't broken up. What am I thinking? I prayed for this for months, and now I wish she was still with him? I'm so confused! What am I supposed to say to cheer her up? I can't under-stand why she's hurting so much—she did the right thing, and she knows it.*

"Katie," Christy began softly, "you're right. I don't totally understand what you're feeling. I'm trying to say the right things here, and I don't seem to be helping at all. Maybe you can help me understand. I mean, you broke up with Michael because you were convinced God told you to break up with him. Tell me what you're feeling now."

Katie shook her head. "There's no way of explaining it. It's like a death, Christy, a loss of something precious. It doesn't matter how prepared you are for that death, it still hurts. It just really, really hurts."

"I'm sorry," Christy said. "I wish I could do something."

"Just let me hurt."

Christy remembered a conversation she had had with Todd several weeks ago after Katie had acted so strangely in the school parking lot. Todd's advice had been to release her and wait. What was that other part he had said about the true test of love? Something about how the strength of love is when you can let go.

Katie showed incredible strength when she let go of Michael. Now it was Christy's turn to let go of her goal of making Katie feel happy. If Katie needed to feel sad for a while, then she needed to be released by Christy to feel sad.

Biting her lower lip, Christy determined to try to understand what would be best for Katie, to somehow release her and not take her angry words personally.

"Okay," Christy said, "I'm trying to understand. I want you to know that you're free to feel whatever you feel and say whatever you want to say around me. I know I won't always understand it all, but I want to try. So please don't think you have to act a certain way this weekend. Just be whatever you need to be. And I promise I'll stop trying to cheer you up."

"Thanks, Chris," Katie said, releasing a giant sigh. "I don't want to mess up this weekend for you and Todd."

"You won't. Besides, it's our weekend, too—yours and mine.

And you need to be free to feel whatever you're going to feel."

"I hope you never go through this, Christy. You can't imagine how powerful your emotions can be. I think I'd rather have my toenails pulled out one by one by an army of ferocious snapping turtles."

Christy laughed, and Katie cracked a smile.

"I don't know why," Katie said, "but I feel a little better."

"Good," Christy said, flashing Katie a comforting smile.

When they arrived at Bob and Marti's, Todd's old VW bus, Gus, was parked in the driveway. Christy felt warmed inside just knowing he was there waiting for her.

The girls hauled their weekend luggage to the front door and were met with a round of hugs from Todd, Doug, Bob, and Marti. To Christy it seemed like a "welcome home" party. Katie looked a little wary, as if she were suspicious of everyone's warm affections.

"You ladies hungry? Something to drink, perhaps?" Uncle Bob, always the gracious host, looked as if he had just come from the golf course. He had on a light blue knit shirt, khaki shorts, and white deck shoes with no socks. For a man in his early fifties who had never had children, he looked and acted like one of the college boys.

"Sure," Christy said, "I could go for something. How about you, Katie?"

Marti, Christy's petite aunt, grasped Katie's arm with her long, perfectly manicured nails and said, "I heard you've become quite the healthy eater. I'm so pleased! Wait until you see what I bought just for you and me this weekend." Marti led Katie through the swinging door into the kitchen, and the rest of them followed.

"Look!" Marti said with glee. "Organic carrots that I just ran through my juicer." She poured a tall glass of the thick, very orange juice and handed it to Katie.

Katie graciously accepted and lifted the glass to her lips. Christy felt shivers just looking at the gloppy juice. She didn't know how Katie could manage to drink it.

Katie took a sip and said, "It's very good, Marti. Thanks."

Christy thought she detected tears glistening in Katie's puffy eyes.

"Here, Christy," Marti said, pouring another glass. "You'll have to try some."

"I really don't think I can, Aunt Marti. Thanks, but I'd like a glass of water, if that's okay."

Marti looked disappointed, but only for a moment before she turned her attention back to Katie, who had taken another swig of the juice. "I have spinach quiche for us for breakfast, and to-morrow for lunch I'll make you some of my jicama, alfalfa sprout, and currant salad. You'll love it."

"Don't go to any trouble on my account," Katie said.

"Are you kidding? This is a dream come true for me! I've been trying to get Christy to eat like this for years. Goodness knows, Robert will never try my food. I'm thrilled to have someone to share my recipes with."

"And if you get tired of rabbit food," Bob said with a twinkle in his eye, "you can share my recipes for some real food like do-nuts, bean dip, and pork chops."

"And that's just for breakfast," Doug said, and they all laughed.

Doug was the kind of guy who seemed to always be in a good mood. Tall, with sandy blond hair and a little boy smile, he was famous for his big hugs.

Christy was laughing until she looked over at Katie. Katie had placed the half-empty glass on the counter, and now tears were trickling down her face. She quickly wiped them with the back of her hand and blinked away their companions. Then, with her head down, she quietly slipped out of the kitchen.

"Is she all right?" Marti asked. "It wasn't something I said, was it?"

"No, she's okay. She's just hurting," Christy said.

"Well, then, go after her and cheer her up!" Marti said.

"I already tried that," Christy said. "I think she just needs to be alone for a bit. She'll be okay."

"Why don't I take her things up to her room," Bob offered and left the kitchen.

The rest of them stood in silence, looking at each other. None of them seemed to know what to do or say.

"She'll be okay," Christy repeated. "She'll be better tomorrow."

Christy could only hope she was right.

CHAPTER FIVE

# *The Happiest Place on Earth*

At 8:45 the next morning, Todd, Doug, Christy, and Katie piled into Gus the Bus and cheerfully waved good-bye to Bob and Marti.

"Say hi to Mickey Mouse for me," Bob called out.

"I'll save the rest of the spinach quiche for when you come home, Katie," Marti said.

Todd popped Gus into gear, and they sputtered down the road.

"Boy, does this feel like a time warp," Christy said, reaching over and giving Todd's arm a squeeze. "Remember the last time you took me to Disneyland, and Bob and Marti sent us off?"

"I still remember what Bob said," Todd replied with a grin that made his dimple appear. " 'Have fun. I won't worry about you unless it's after midnight and we haven't heard from you yet.' I thought for sure you would turn into a pumpkin if I didn't have you back by midnight!"

"All I remember is that Tracy was sitting right here," Christy said, pointing to where she sat in the front seat. "And I thought you had invited her to go with us, but you were only giving her a ride to work."

"That's right," Todd said, looking as if it was hard for him to remember that part.

"I felt horrible because I snapped at Tracy, and then she sweetly handed me a birthday present."

"What was it?" Katie asked.

"My Bible. It was actually from Todd and Tracy, but she made the fabric cover on it."

"I never knew that," Katie said. "A lot of Christians were nice to you before you came to know the Lord, weren't they?"

Christy interpreted that as a little jab that she hadn't been nicer to Michael. She realized Katie was right. She was about to answer with an apology when Todd stopped at a red light. He hopped out of the van and jogged around to Christy's door.

"What's he doing?" Katie asked.

Christy couldn't answer but let out a bubble of delighted laughter. This was their intersection. This was where Todd had first kissed her and where he had given her the gold "Forever" ID bracelet she wore on her right wrist. Todd opened Christy's door, and practically scooping her up in his arms, he helped her out of the van. Together they ran to the front of the vehicle, and in front of Doug and Katie and the whole world, Todd wrapped his arms around Christy and quickly kissed her. Then he let go as fast as he had embraced her, and they each ran to their side of Gus and hopped in just as the light turned green. Todd slid the van from neutral to first gear and drove on as if nothing unusual had happened.

"So how about those Dodgers?" Doug said to Katie.

"I don't see anybody doing any dodging," Katie quipped back.

Doug laughed and kept laughing all the way down the freeway to Anaheim. Christy realized the little encounter at the intersection was probably embarrassing for Katie and Doug, but to Christy it meant everything. It meant that Todd valued their special memories as much as she did and that he didn't care if the whole world knew they were going together. It was a wonderful, warm, delicious feeling, and Christy hoped it would last all day.

They parked Gus and took the tram to Disneyland's entrance. Christy had her camera looped over her arm and a sweatshirt wrapped around her waist.

That morning she had remembered the peach-colored T-shirt she had worn on her first Disneyland date with Todd and wished she had brought it to wear just for the memories. Instead, she had on a cream-colored T-shirt and jeans. Katie wore jeans, too, and a green cotton shirt. Both the guys had on shorts, and they all had brought along sweatshirts for the cool of the evening. Their first stop inside the park was at the lockers to leave their sweatshirts.

"Where to first?" Doug asked. "I'm a Tomorrowland kind of guy. You might as well all know that right up front."

"What I hear you saying," Todd said, "is that Space Mountain is calling your name. Am I right?"

"What can I say? I have the need for speed."

"My kind of guy," Katie said, flashing Doug a big smile.

Christy's stomach started to feel a little queasy, thinking about all the roller coaster rides these three would want to go on. She preferred the gentle boat rides like It's a Small, Small World. Last time Todd had talked her into the bobsleds, and that was about the wildest ride she had ever been on. Apparently, it was tame compared to some of these others.

"Tomorrowland it is," Todd said. "As long as we make it to Adventureland before it's dark, I'll be happy."

"My favorite is Thunder Mountain," Katie said.

She had been doing a great job of keeping cheerful all morning. Perhaps letting her alone last night to cry herself to sleep had been the best thing for her.

"What's your favorite, Christy?" Katie asked.

She didn't dare say It's a Small, Small World, so she said the first thing that came to her mind. "I like the Swiss Family Robinson Tree House."

Todd stopped walking and looked at Christy with pleased surprise. "Really? That's cool." Then he took her hand and gave it a squeeze.

"She just said that because she knows it's your favorite spot, Todd," Doug said over his shoulder. He and Katie were leading the way, blazing the trail down Main Street as they headed toward Tomorrowland.

If she had thought about it, Christy would have remembered how Todd had turned into a free-spirited Tarzan in the tree house when they had climbed through it on their first visit here. Todd's dream was no secret to anybody who knew him well. He wanted to be a missionary and live off the land in a jungle somewhere. He had never wavered from that goal, and more than once Christy had questioned whether or not she had what it took to be a missionary as well.

Fortunately, that question didn't need to be answered for a long time. For now, she and Todd were together. Things had never been better. She had never been happier.

The line for Space Mountain was long, and they had to wait about forty minutes before it was their turn. But the time went fast, with Katie and Doug chattering away.

Christy was relieved to see Katie doing so well emotionally. Doug was a great encourager. If anyone could make Katie feel better, it was Doug. Good ol' Doug. Christy decided she was going to try and find some way to let him know how much she appreciated him.

Soon they were stepping into the cars that would take them whirling through the darkness on this inside roller coaster. Christy climbed in and immediately curled up against Todd's chest. He circled her with his arms and whispered, "Scaredy-cat?"

Christy answered with a little "meow" just as the car lurched forward and the ride began. Squeezing her eyes shut, she clung to Todd's arm and clenched her jaw to keep from screaming. She could hear Katie shrieking and Doug laughing from the seats in front of them. She wondered how many other adrenaline-pumping rides they would coax her onto before the day was over.

The answer was five. They went on every fast ride they could find. The only comforting part was that each time she could cuddle up with Todd, close her eyes, and feel his strong arms around her. She had never felt this close to him before. It was as if Todd was sheltering her, protecting her, and letting her lean on him for strength. She wondered if he felt the closeness, too.

Each time they stepped off one of the wild rides, Christy kept her arm around Todd's waist. She wanted to feel his arms circling her all day. All week. All year. The rest of her life. This was where she belonged.

"Anyone hungry besides me?" Doug asked around noon.

"I think your stomach has a timer," Katie said. "It goes off about every hour, doesn't it? I mean, it couldn't be much more than an hour since you had that popcorn."

"Hey, I'm a growing boy," Doug said.

"I'm just giving you a hard time," Katie said. "I'm hungry, too. What do you guys want to eat?"

They were near the center of the park, by Sleeping Beauty's

Castle. Todd suggested they grab a hamburger at the Carnation Plaza.

"Did you know they have Fantasia ice cream here?" Doug asked as they stood in line to order their hamburgers a few minutes later. "I think this is the only place in the world you can get it."

"What is it?" Katie asked.

"It's kind of hard to describe. It has maraschino cherries in it and other stuff."

"Did you know there's enough red dye in a jar of maraschino cherries to kill a laboratory test rat?" Katie asked. The minute she said it, everyone looked at her, including people standing in the line next to them. "At least, that's what I've heard," she said in an apologetic way.

It was her turn to order at the small window. Katie asked the girl in the striped apron if they had whole wheat buns.

"No, sorry."

"Okay, well, this is what I want. I want a hamburger with extra tomatoes, lettuce, pickles, and onions and no meat."

"No meat?" the girl asked. "I think it's still the same price."

"That's okay," Katie said.

"Hey," Doug said, sliding in next to Katie and bending to address the girl inside, "put her hamburger patty on mine. I'll eat her meat."

"I'm not sure we can do that. Maybe you two could swap your own meat."

"Fine with me," Doug said.

"Okay," Katie agreed. "Are your french fries prepared in pure vegetable oil by any chance?"

"Are they what?" the girl asked.

"Never mind," Katie said. "No french fries. Just the burger with all the extras."

Once they had ordered and found a place to sit, Christy thought she noticed a cloud beginning to form over Katie's countenance. Did her attempt to order healthy food make her think too much about Michael?

"Slap that baby right here," Doug said, opening the bun of his double cheeseburger and waiting for Katie to slip her meat inside. "You want my tomatoes?"

"Sure," Katie said. "I'll take your lettuce, too, if you don't want it. I don't care about the pickles."

Doug swapped his lettuce and tomatoes for Katie's hamburger. She patted the top of her "veggie burger," looking pleased with the trade.

"Don't they remind you of a nursery rhyme couple?" Todd asked Christy. "You know, that one about the Jack guy who couldn't eat any fat and his wife who was totally into carbohydrates. Only these guys have it in reverse."

"Katie just doesn't know what's good for her," Doug said. He lifted his bulging burger up to her mouth and said, "Come on, just one little bite. You can't go organic the rest of your life."

Katie turned her head away and playfully said, "Get that thing away from me, Michael."

The instant she said "Michael," everything stopped.

"I mean, Doug," Katie said sheepishly, her bottom lip beginning to quiver.

"Hey, that's okay," Doug said calmly.

Christy could tell that Katie was trying not to cry, but it seemed impossible for her to hold back the tears. Doug's tender words were equivalent to the thumb of the little boy plugging the great sea wall in Holland. Perhaps Doug realized that, because he pulled his chair over next to Katie's and putting his arms around her, he offered her his broad chest to cry on.

"Go ahead," Doug said, gently pulling Katie closer. "You can cry. It's okay. Go ahead."

Christy thought Katie would pull away, but to her surprise, Katie fell into Doug's embrace and began to cry. Actually, she began to wail like Christy had never heard anyone cry before. She glanced around, aware that they had an audience of all the tourists sitting close to them in this open air patio. Dozens of people who thought they were spending their day at "The Happiest Place on Earth" seemed dying to know what was wrong with the wailing redhead.

"Come here," Doug said, tenderly helping Katie to her feet while her face was still smashed against his chest. "We need to step inside my office."

Then, making eye contact with Todd, he said, "Keep the birds out of my french fries. I'll be back in a few minutes."

Christy and Todd, along with the rest of the lunching tourists, watched as Doug led Katie away from the crowd and under some trees over by the swan-filled moat that surrounded Sleeping Beauty's Castle. He sat down with her on a bench away from the main path of vacationers. With his arms still around her, Doug let Katie cry. She wasn't wailing anymore; at least Christy couldn't hear her.

Christy turned to Todd, aware that people were watching them, and said, "I hope she's okay. Do you think I should go over there?"

"Probably not. She's in good hands with Doug. He has the gift of mercy. That's what she needs right now."

Just then, a small, brown bird hopped up onto the back of

Doug's vacated chair and cocked his head, eyeing Doug's french fries.

"He wasn't kidding about protecting his fries from the birds," Christy said. "Come here, little guy. You leave Doug's fries alone. I'll share mine with you."

She broke off the end of one of her fries and tossed it on the ground near Katie's chair. Immediately the eager bird was joined by his brothers, sisters, aunts, uncles, and cousins, all pecking at the one scrap of french fry.

Christy smiled and began to feed the whole flock. As she did, Todd prayed aloud, with his eyes open, and thanked God for the food and prayed for the Holy Spirit to comfort Katie. Then he added, "I know You care, Father. Your Word says You care about even the smallest bird that falls to the ground, and You provide for all Your living creatures. I know You care about what Katie is feeling. I know You will provide for her emotional needs. Thanks, Papa."

Over the years, Christy had become accustomed to Todd's open way of talking with God. It felt natural and comfortable, even here, out in a patio restaurant in the middle of Disneyland. She felt God's presence, and she felt hopeful that the worst might be over for Katie. She couldn't explain why, but Christy felt strangely comforted and confident that her heavenly Father would always take care of Katie.

Todd and Christy had both finished eating and were tossing their last fries to the birds when Doug and Katie returned. Katie looked red-faced but much more peaceful.

"I'm sorry about that, you guys," she said quietly as she slid back into her chair.

"No need to apologize," Todd said.

"Did you keep the birds out of my fries?" Doug asked.

"It wasn't easy," Christy said. "We had to lure them away with our fries. But it worked."

"Your food is probably cold by now," Katie said sympathetically. "Let me buy you another lunch."

"Since when did a little cooling off stop me from eating anything?" Doug asked, chomping into his big burger. "This tastes fine to me," he garbled through a mouthful of meat.

Katie nibbled at her veggie burger.

Todd asked, "Where to next? You guys think you can handle something a little tamer, like maybe the Jungle Cruise or the Pirates of the Caribbean?"

Doug squinted one eye and in his best pirate accent said, "Me thinks the bloke has Adventureland in his plans."

"We could split up," Christy suggested. "I mean, if you guys don't want to go in the tree house and all that."

"No, I like the tree house," Katie said. "And we have to go to New Orleans Square."

"That's right," said Todd. "I want to get a mint julep and an apple fritter."

"More food?" Doug said. "Count me in!"

It seemed as if nothing had happened. Katie appeared mellow; apparently, releasing the pent-up tears had helped. Doug seemed his happy self and quite unaware that he had single-handedly saved the day.

They finished their lunch without incident, and then Doug turned to Katie and with genuine compassion asked, "If I bought you a Fantasia ice cream cone, would you eat it? Or do you just want a bite of mine?"

"Maybe a bite of yours," Katie said. "I haven't had real ice cream in so long, it might make me sick."

"Wait here, then. I'll be right back. Anyone else want one?"

"I'm too full," Christy said.

"Sure, I'll try anything," Todd said, reaching for the money in his pocket. "How much do you need?"

"My treat." Doug jogged over to the ice cream line. He returned a few minutes later with two huge scoops of what looked like a greenish rocky road ice cream.

"You want the first bite?" Todd said, offering his cone to Christy.

"What? Am I your guinea pig? If I gag on it then you'll know you should accidentally drop it for the birds to clean up?"

"It does look a little weird, doesn't it?" Todd agreed.

"Trust me," Doug said. "It's great stuff. Gourmet. This is the only place you can get it."

"Since when did Doug become a gourmet? He'll eat anything!" Katie said. "Here, let me try it."

Doug held out his cone, and Katie took a dainty bite. Christy and Todd watched.

"That's good," she said. "Let me have another bite. I only got a little bit."

"I'll be glad to get you your own cone, if you want."

"No, just a bite." Katie took another nibble and said, "I'm not kidding, you guys; this is really good!"

Todd and Christy leaned into Todd's cone at the same time and almost bumped noses as they each took a bite. They both leaned back laughing, and at the same time said, "It *is* good!"

"Told you guys," Doug said. Looking at Katie, he asked, "Would you hold this for me for a second?"

Katie took the cone, and Doug popped up and headed for the ice cream window. "Protect that cone from the birds for me, Katie. The only way to do it is to eat the whole thing and don't let a single drop fall to the ground."

"Very tricky," Katie said. "Forcing me back into an addiction to sugar. You should be ashamed of yourself, Doug!"

"Don't get one for me," Christy called out. "I'll share Todd's."

"Oh, you will, huh?" Todd said, taking a big chomp out of the side of the cone.

"This is really good," Katie said. "What are all these little chunks?"

"Cherries," said Todd, taking another bite. "And chocolate chips, I think."

"Wait," Christy said, reaching for her camera. "I have to get a picture of this for the yearbook. Nobody will believe I caught Katie eating ice cream during her senior year. Smile!"

Katie held up the cone and willingly smiled for the camera.

Just then Doug appeared with another cone in each hand.

"I said don't get one for me," Christy said.

"Who said this is for you?" Doug teased.

"What, you think you're going to eat both of those?" Katie asked.

"No, one is for Todd since Christy demolished half of his."

"I did not!"

Doug handed the cone to Todd, and Todd handed the half-eaten one to Christy. "Sounds good to me," Todd said, and he took a man-sized bite out of the new cone.

"Isn't this great stuff?" Katie said. "I love it!" Katie eagerly licked around the bottom of her cone where it was beginning to drip. "This is so good, you guys!"

Doug and Todd looked at each other as if to say, "It's good, but not that good."

"You've been away from sugar for too long," Christy teased. "Welcome back, Katie!"

"You know what?" Katie said with a glimmer of joy returning to her green eyes. "It's good to be back."

# CHAPTER SIX

# *If Only You Knew*

"So you really think you would like to live like this?" Doug asked Todd as the four of them crowded into the very top of the Swiss Family Robinson Tree House and surveyed the fake jungle below them.

"Oh, yeah! Can't you just hear the tropical birds and smell the fragrance of the rain-washed leaves on the banana trees?" Todd said.

"Those are mechanical birds with little tape recorders inside their bellies," Katie informed him. "And that's not the scent of rain-washed banana trees. It's the smell of mint julep on Doug's breath. He had three, remember."

"They were small," Doug said. "Besides, Katie, I didn't see you having any trouble putting away your entire apple fritter."

"I know," Katie said with a giggle. "Those were so good!"

Christy was the only one who didn't make fun of Todd's dream to live in the jungle. She saw something wild and wonderful and terrible in his eyes. What was it? The call of God on a man's life? It seemed to Christy that something deep inside was calling to Todd, and he would not rest until he had responded to this mission that for years had whispered to him deep in the night.

"Your turn to pick the next ride, Todd. Jungle Cruise or Pirates?" Katie said.

Todd was leaning over the railing of the tree house, staring at the clumps of scurrying people below. He didn't seem to hear Katie's question.

Christy moved closer to him and put her arm around his shoulder, looking down at whatever it was he was staring at. She tried to imagine what he was thinking. Was he dreaming about jungle life? Sleeping in a hammock? Paddling in his canoe to a neighboring tribe, taking along only his Bible and a spear to catch a fish along the way?

"You know what, Kilikina?"

She loved it when Todd called her by her Hawaiian name. She leaned her head against his shoulder and listened with all her heart.

"There are more lost people in the city than in the jungle today."

Christy pulled back. Where did that come from?

"We're going on down, maties," Doug said in his pirate voice. "We'll be waitin' on ye at the line for the Pirates. Look for us on the starboard side."

"Let's go," Todd said, quickly shaking himself from his daydream and taking Christy by the hand.

She wanted to ask him what he meant by his comment. Was Todd thinking God was calling him to something other than being a missionary in the jungle? After all these years of knowing Todd, she still didn't have him figured out.

*Will I ever?*

The Pirates of the Caribbean was fun. It reminded Christy of when they had gone on that ride last time and had eaten at the Blue Bayou Restaurant.

When they went on the Jungle Cruise, she noticed that Katie and Doug seemed to be almost cuddled up together. At least they were sitting close. Well, everyone in the boat was, she had to admit. But Doug had his arm across the back of the seat, which made it convenient for Katie to lean up against him. Katie seemed in great spirits. Either she was over her mourning for Michael or she was on a sugar buzz. Or maybe both.

Next they went exploring on Tom Sawyer's Island. Katie seemed to have more fun than the other three put together. They ran across the wobbly bridge, hid in the rock caves, teetered on the balancing rock, and then went on the canoe ride around the island.

Christy took her place in the canoe and held her paddle like an expert. "This is where all my experience from canoeing at summer camp last year is going to pay off," she said.

"But are you sure you can paddle fast without your buns being covered with red ant bites?" Katie said loud enough for everyone on the canoe to hear.

"Doesn't sound like the kind of summer camp I'd like to go to," a large man in front of Christy said over his shoulder.

Christy felt her face turning red and looked down, pretending to adjust her camera.

"Is that getting heavy?" Todd asked. "I can carry it for a while if you want."

"Actually, I should be taking some pictures." Christy took the camera from its case and snapped a couple of shots of Doug and Katie and then two of Todd.

"Here," Doug said, laying his paddle across his lap while everyone else paddled through the water. He reached for the camera. "Let me get one of you and Todd."

Christy leaned against Todd's chest and turned halfway around to face Doug. Todd and Christy smiled. Christy already imagined the kind of frame she was going to buy to put this picture in, a heart-shaped one with flowers around the border.

After the canoe ride, the foursome seemed to be exploring at a slower pace. It was soon dusk, and Todd and Christy left Doug and Katie in the long line for Splash Mountain in order to go retrieve their sweatshirts. They made plans to meet in an hour in Bear Country. Todd and Christy walked hand in hand all the way to the lockers, gathered up the sweatshirts, and headed back down Main Street.

Todd stopped in front of one of the stores and said, "I want to buy something for you."

"You don't have to," Christy said, surprised at Todd's sudden pronouncement.

"I want to. The last time we came here I bought all those things for you with your aunt's money. Ever since then I've wished I had bought something for you with my own money. Something special, just from me to you."

As far as Christy could remember, this was the most tender Todd had ever been. With his arm around her, they browsed through the shop and examined shelves and bins loaded with Disney paraphernalia. Then Christy saw it. It was perfect.

"I'd like this," she said, reaching for the porcelain, heart-shaped frame. It was exactly what she had in mind. "I'm going to put the picture of us in the canoe in this. You know, the picture Doug just took."

"Cool," Todd said. "See anything else you can't live without?"

"Yes," Christy said with a sly grin creeping onto her face, "you."

Todd seemed surprised but honored. "You could live without me, Christy," he answered.

"But I wouldn't want to," she said softly.

Before she knew what was happening, Todd took her face in both his hands, tilted it up, and kissed her. When he drew away, Christy caught her breath and noticed a single tear caught in the corner of his eye. Todd blinked quickly and wrapped his arms around her in a tight hug.

Into her hair he whispered, "Kilikina, if you only knew. If you only knew."

"Knew what?" Christy whispered back. She was aware that people in the crowded store were looking at them, but after Katie's wailing at lunch, this seemed mild.

"Come on," Todd said, letting go and quickly wiping his eyes with the cuff of his blue hooded sweatshirt. "Let's pay for this and then go someplace where we can talk."

Christy slipped her hand into his and followed Todd to the cash register, where he paid for her heart frame. The woman in the ruffled apron carefully wrapped it in tissue, tucked the gift in a bag, and handed it to Christy.

Todd then led Christy down Main Street as if he knew right where he wanted to go to talk. Her curiosity was stampeding through her mind.

*What did he mean? If only I knew what?*

She didn't like the queasy apprehension bouncing around in her stomach. Was something wrong? Had she done or said something she shouldn't have?

Weaving their way through the crowds in Frontierland, Todd directed Christy toward the big white steamboat docked and ready to take on passengers. The huge Mississippi River replica twinkled with strings of tiny white lights, and on its lower deck a Dixieland jazz band played music to set a person's heart to dancing or at least toes to tapping. Todd didn't seem interested in doing either. He headed up the stairs and made his way over to two empty chairs in the corner of the nearly vacant top deck.

As they sat down, the ship blew its loud whistle and embarked on its journey around Tom Sawyer Island in the coolness of the evening.

"Todd," Christy began, as she faced him, "what's wrong? You're so serious. Was it something I said?"

Todd shook his head and released a puff of a laugh. "No," he said, and then changing his mind, he said, "well, yes, but there was nothing wrong with what you said. It was good. Too good, actually."

"I don't understand. I only said I wouldn't want to have to live without you, and you said if only I knew. Knew what?"

Christy stopped breathing, and all the blood drained from her face. "Todd," she forced the words from her tightening throat, "you're not going to die or something, are you?"

Now Todd really laughed. He tilted his head back and guffawed into the star-filled sky. "No, Kilikina, I'm not going to die. Well, I mean, I am someday. We all are. I don't know when, though, and I don't have any plans to in the near future."

"Then what did you mean?" Christy demanded to know. Her heart was pounding, and she felt flustered. She realized how much she cared for Todd and how much it would hurt if she lost him for any reason.

"I don't know if I can explain it. I want to try, though. Just listen and see if this makes any sense to you."

Christy looked at Todd with wide eyes.

He pressed his lips together and then began slowly. "You know how I'm an only kid and my parents divorced when I was pretty young?"

Christy nodded.

"I sort of grew up by myself and never had anyone to care for or anyone who cared for me. I know my mom and dad both love me, but I would have given anything when I was a kid if they would have decided to love each other again. You know what I mean? It was great that they loved me, but I wanted them to love each other."

Christy thought she saw another tear about to escape from Todd's eye. She squeezed his hand and with her expression urged him to go on. He had rarely talked about his parents, and she wanted him to know he could trust her with the secrets of his heart.

"When I came to know the Lord, it was like God gave me all the love I had missed out on as a kid. It was a secure kind of love. Total acceptance. Grace. God's love changed me. Totally. And I believe God called me to be a missionary. You know, go to the ends of the world and tell people who have never heard about God's love. And it was going to be so easy. I had nothing to give up. No family or anything. And then you came along."

Christy wasn't sure if Todd meant she was interfering with God's plan for his life or what. "Are you saying I'm keeping you from God?"

"No, not at all. You challenge me to grow in my relationship with God. You always have. It's just that you really, truly care about me. You want to be with me. You said in the store you wouldn't want to live without me."

"That's not a bad thing, Todd. I meant it. I care about you more than you can even begin to imagine," Christy said.

"I know," Todd said softly. "You're the first person who ever has."

He didn't say it as if he was trying to feel sorry for himself. It was as if he had made a precious discovery when he realized just how much Christy meant to him.

"That should make you feel good, Todd. Why do you seem bummed out about knowing how much I care?"

The steamboat had completed its circle around the island and was now docked to unload passengers and take on new ones. Todd and Christy remained in their seats, holding hands, locked in their own private world.

"I'm not bummed out. Amazed would be a better word. There's just never been anyone in my life who has cared about me as much as you do. I've pulled away from you in the past, like when I went to Hawaii. Maybe I was afraid of getting too close or caring too much. I don't know." Todd drew in a deep breath as the whistle sounded again, and the ship set out. "I don't know why it's all hitting me so hard or why your words pierced my heart in the store. All I know is that I don't want to live without you either, Kilikina. You are the most precious gift God has ever given to me."

Tears welled up in Christy's eyes, and she felt her lower lip tremble.

Todd stood and moved his chair next to hers so they both faced the front of the boat. He stretched his arm across the back of her chair. Christy nestled her head in the curve of his shoulder and felt his strong jaw resting against her hair.

Without words, they watched the steamboat move into the night as the bright music of the Dixieland band played below them. Above them glittered a thousand night stars, and Christy could hear the steady rhythm of Todd's heart.

Never before had Christy felt so close to Todd and so close to God and so sure that He would keep all of His promises. For perhaps the first time in their relationship, Christy didn't have to wonder if Todd felt the same way she did.

CHAPTER SEVEN

# Sunday Best

The shrill sound of the alarm clock roused Christy at 7:30 on Sunday morning. She rolled over, slapped the top of the clock, and let out a groan. "Katie, we have to get up."

"Not yet," Katie mumbled from her rollaway bed on the other side of Bob and Marti's guest room. "Let me sleep five more minutes, okay?"

"I'll hop in the shower first," Christy said, stumbling out of bed. "Church is in an hour."

"I think churches would have much better attendance if they had afternoon services," Katie muttered, pulling the pillow over her head.

"I have a headache," Christy groaned as she stepped into the adjoining guest bathroom. "My feet hurt from walking so much yesterday. I want to go back to bed."

"So go back to bed. We'll meet the guys later this afternoon."

Christy considered hobbling back to bed and diving under the covers, but only for a minute. "No, this is the Lord's day. We need to honor Him and worship with His people."

"I'm worshiping Him in silent praise." Katie's words sounded mushy as she spoke into her pillow.

69

"I don't think there is such a thing," Christy said, turning on the shower. While waiting for the water to warm up, she examined her face in the mirror. "I look like raw hamburger meat."

"I feel like raw hamburger meat," Katie responded.

"My eyes look like two blowfish caught in a head-on collision," Christy stated, opening her eyes wide and trying to count all the bloodshot lines.

"Christy," Katie said, propping herself up on her elbow and squinting her eyes, "will you and your little blowfish take a shower and let me sleep another five minutes?" She immediately dropped back down on her bed and pulled the covers up over her head.

Giving up any further evaluation of her Disneyland-wearied body, Christy closed the bathroom door, stepped into the shower, and in five minutes was finished. "Your turn," she said brightly to Katie as she opened the door and breezed out in a cloud of steam.

"Already?" Katie groaned, rolling to the edge of her bed in an effort to get up. "Why did we ever say we would go to the first service?"

"I left the shampoo and conditioner in there," Christy said, unwrapping the towel from her wet hair and blotting it dry. "And my curling iron is plugged in on the counter."

"You're acting a little too perky for me, missy," Katie said, plodding her way into the bathroom. "There's nothing worse than watching your best friend fall in love right before your eyes."

"I know," Christy called back as Katie closed the bathroom door. "I did that once, remember?"

For a second she paused, hoping the reference to Michael wouldn't set Katie off emotionally. But then a smile spread across Christy's lips as she slipped into her dress. *Is that what I'm doing?*

*Falling in love? Or have I been in love with Todd all along, but neither of us realized it until last night?*

She felt like humming. Everything in the world seemed wonderful. Absolutely perfect. It could only get better. In less than an hour she would see Todd. She would slip her hand into his, he would squeeze it tight and hold on to her. They would sit together in church—Todd's church—and sing praises to God. Yes, this morning was definitely a morning to sing.

"Christy?" Bob's voice called out from behind the closed bedroom door and was followed by four gentle taps.

"Yes?"

"Just wanted to make sure you girls were up. I have breakfast ready for you, if you're interested."

"Thanks, Uncle Bob. We'll be down in a few minutes."

"Katie," Christy said, opening the bathroom door and fanning her hand to clear away the steam, "I'm going downstairs. My uncle said he has breakfast ready. Then I'm coming back to do my hair."

"If it's donuts or waffles, save me one."

Christy danced down the stairs. She found Uncle Bob in the kitchen pouring orange juice into tall glasses and placing them next to a platter of fresh cut fruit and assorted muffins and croissants.

"Good morning, Bright Eyes," he said, offering Christy a glass of juice. "How was your day in the Magic Kingdom?"

"Wonderful," Christy said, taking a swig of juice and reaching for a blueberry muffin. "Absolutely wonderful."

"Glad to hear it," Bob said with a smile. "Sounds like a vast improvement over the last time you and Todd went."

"There's no comparison," Christy said. She felt like letting her bursting heart sprinkle its joy all over the kitchen by telling her uncle she was fully in love and had no doubt Todd felt the same way about her.

But just then Aunt Marti walked in. To Christy's surprise, Marti wasn't wearing her Sunday morning robe and slippers. She had donned a becoming blue knit dress, and her hair and make-up were done to perfection. Then Christy noticed that Bob was looking more dressed up than usual.

"You're going to be late," Marti pointed out to Christy. "You can't go to church with your hair still wet."

Christy swallowed her bite of muffin and brushed off her aunt's comment. "Where are you guys going?" she asked.

"With you. To church," Bob said. "It's sort of a favor to Todd. He helped me clean out the garage last week and wouldn't accept any money. Said the only payment he wanted was for us to visit his church. Looks like today is the day."

Christy couldn't believe it. Todd had succeeded in accomplishing what no one else in Christy's family had been able to do. Bob and Marti were going to church.

"I'll dry my hair," Christy said, swallowing another gulp of orange juice and dashing back upstairs.

Katie had just finished drying her hair when Christy entered the room. "Katie, you'll never guess what. Bob and Marti are coming to church with us!"

"That's good," Katie said calmly.

"It's not good," Christy spouted.

"It's not?"

"No, it's better than good. It's unbelievable! It's fantastic. This is a total God thing, Katie. I'm so excited!"

"I can tell," Katie said, scanning Christy's exuberant face. "That's great! Are they ready to go?"

Just then the girls heard the doorbell ring.

"That's probably Todd," Christy said. "I have to hurry!"

Katie stepped away from the sink and let Christy finish getting ready. Katie slipped her shoes on and scrounged in her suitcase for her Bible.

"I'll have to share with you," she called to Christy over the whir of the blow dryer. "I guess I didn't bring my Bible."

"Would you grab mine? It's over on the night stand. And get my purse, too."

"Yes, your majesty. Will there be anything else?"

"Yes, go downstairs and stall for me. Tell them I'll be there in two seconds."

Katie obliged and left Christy with a toothbrush in her mouth, a mascara wand in one hand, and a hot curling iron in the other. "Come on, hair," Christy garbled, her teeth clenching the foaming toothbrush. "Work with me, here. Oh, forget it!" She plopped the curling iron down, gave a few quick swipes of the mascara wand to each eye, and pulled the toothbrush from her mouth, took a quick drink, and swished out her mouth. Then she bent at the waist and tossed all her hair in front of her face, stood up, jerked her head back, and gave her head one more shake. "It's the natural look today," she told her reflection in the mirror and then hurried down the stairs.

Todd stood at the front door waiting for her. The minute they made eye contact, she knew something was different between them. He felt what she felt. For an instant she was sure she was Cinderella, gracefully descending the stairs to meet her Prince Charming.

"Let's go," Marti said briskly, entering the room at top speed. "Is Christy ready yet? Oh, there you are."

As Christy joined Todd, he smiled and took her hand in his. She was delightfully aware that he kept glancing over at her as they hurried down the walkway.

"Is Doug going to meet us there?" Marti asked, letting herself into the front seat of Bob's luxury car.

"Yes," Todd said. "Would you like me to drive my car, too?"

"You three can fit in the back seat," Marti directed.

Katie was already seated next to the far window. Christy slid in next to her, and Todd squeezed in next to Christy.

"Oh, I should have let you sit in front, Todd," Marti said as Bob pulled into the street. "You can sit here on the way home. There's much more room."

Marti chattered all the way to church, apparently wanting to prove she was comfortable in this new experience. Todd's church was big and open. The people were friendly and casual. Many of them wore shorts to church, which seemed to shock Aunt Marti.

Doug had saved a row of seats for them. Marti kept chattering even after the service began, and Christy felt sorry for Katie, who was sitting next to Aunt Marti.

Todd and Doug had no trouble participating in the worship. Christy loved standing between the two of them and hearing their deep, rich voices blend on the praise choruses. She sang her heart out, too. On the last song, Doug and Todd each held one of her hands. Christy was surprised at first, but then she noticed a lot of people were joining hands across the aisles. She peeked over at Bob and Marti. They were holding hands, but neither was singing.

*I hope this church isn't too contemporary for them*, Christy thought. She noticed that the congregation was a mixture of older and younger people. Plenty of people were Bob and Marti's age. She would love for them to become involved in the church and come to know the Lord personally. It had been her longtime prayer, and now they were actually here, in church, and she didn't want anything to turn them off.

After the singing, everyone sat down, and the pastor took his place on the platform. Instead of standing behind a podium, he perched on a stool and held his open Bible in one hand. His words of teaching were strong, yet compassionate. He spoke with gentle authority. Christy closed her eyes for a moment and pictured Jesus teaching this way, urgently, lovingly coaxing people to turn their lives toward God.

She could imagine Todd being the same kind of teacher as this man. And she could imagine her aunt and uncle responding to the message and giving their hearts to Christ.

During the final portion of the message, the pastor read a verse about how there's no greater love than when a man lays down his life for his friend. He said that was what Jesus did for us, and we show we are truly His disciples when we obey God to the point of giving up that which is most precious to us.

Christy immediately thought of Katie giving up her relationship with Michael because she knew God wanted her to. Christy hoped Katie would be encouraged by this pastor's words and know that she had done the right thing. She also thought the message should be particularly convincing to Bob and Marti.

At the end of the service, the pastor prayed. He said if any individuals wanted to give their lives to the Lord, this was a good time to silently pray, confess their sins, and invite Christ to take over their lives. Christy prayed for Bob and Marti like she had never prayed before.

When they all went out to lunch afterwards, Christy couldn't wait to ask how they liked the service. As soon as they were seated at the large booth, Christy turned to Marti and said, "Did you like the church? Wasn't the message great?"

Marti studied her menu and gave a noncommittal grunt.

"It was different than I expected," Bob said. "He's not the usual black-robed, pulpit-pounding kind of preacher."

"And what kind of church music was that?" Marti asked, peering over the top of her menu and shaking her head. "Guitars and drums! The church I grew up in had an organ. That's proper church music. And that so-called pastor didn't even wear a tie! How does he think people are going to respect his position as a clergyman when he stands up there—or sits up there—looking like one of the original Beach Boys?"

Christy and Todd exchanged glances. Apparently Marti had heard none of the message. She was too distracted by the music and the pastor's appearance. Something inside Christy's heart sank all the way to her big toe. This had been the perfect opportunity for her aunt and uncle to become Christians. But the prospect of either of them making such a decision seemed doubtful. It depressed her. She glanced at her menu but didn't feel hungry for anything now.

"They have a Lighter Fare column here," Marti said, directing Katie to the back of the menu. "I can recommend any of their salads. Be sure to order your dressing on the side, and don't order the house dressing. I understand it's made with sour cream. Terribly fattening."

Katie skipped the Lighter Fare column and stuck with the hamburger column. When the waitress came to take their order, Katie went first. "I'll have the double cheeseburger, fries, and a chocolate shake."

Marti started to laugh. "You have such a fresh sense of humor, Katie, dear."

Katie remained straight-faced.

"She'll have the Hawaiian fruit salad," Marti told the waitress. "And I'll have the same. Dressing on the side for both of us."

"I'm having the cheeseburger," Katie said to the waitress, ignoring Marti's shocked stare. "And could you please add some bacon to that?"

"Katie's come back to the real world," Doug said, leaning across the table and confiding in Bob loudly enough for Marti to hear. "It happened yesterday. I admit, I led her to this destruction with a Fantasia ice cream cone."

"You should be ashamed of yourself," Marti said. She was taking this loss of her health-food comrade seriously. "Do you realize, Doug, it will take her a week to detox from what you let her eat yesterday, and now this—beef and pork and sugar all in one meal!"

Before Marti could rage anymore, the waitress asked, "Would the rest of you like to order, or should I come back?"

"No, we're ready," Bob said. He ordered a patty melt with extra onions. Doug ordered a french dip with a side of onion rings. Todd ordered a turkey sandwich with potato salad, and then it was Christy's turn. She still didn't know what she wanted.

"What is your soup today?" she asked, stalling for time.

"Cream of mushroom and vegetable beef barley."

Both of those gave her the shivers. Now she really didn't know what she wanted, and everyone was waiting for her. Christy hated making decisions; this kind of situation had never been her strength. The worst part was, the only thing that sounded good to her was the Hawaiian salad. But how would it appear if she ordered that after Katie refused it?

"I guess I'll just have the, um . . ." Christy hesitated. *Oh well. What does it matter?* "I'll have the Hawaiian fruit salad."

"Dressing on the side?" the waitress asked.

"Sure. That's fine." Christy closed the menu and handed it to the waitress, fully aware of her aunt's puzzled look.

Christy's choice must have thrown Marti for such a loop that she didn't continue her lecture when the waitress left. Doug jumped right in and began to tell Bob about the highlights of their Disneyland excursion. Katie joined him, and soon a spirited conversation was in full swing around the table.

Todd reached over and grasped Christy's hand under the table. He squeezed it, and she squeezed his back. Instantly, the warm feelings she had experienced at Disneyland returned. An invisible bond seemed to encircle Todd and Christy in their own private bubble. Nothing, Christy was confident, could ever burst it.

# CHAPTER EIGHT

# *Fasten Your Seat Belts, Please*

"Good-bye, now," Bob said, patting the side of Christy's car as she and Katie waved at him, ready to drive home after their full weekend.

"Call us when you get home," Marti added. "And drive safely. Do you both have your seat belts on?"

"Yes," Christy called out from her open window. "We're all set. We'll be fine." She slipped the car into gear and eased away from the curb.

"You really don't want to leave yet, do you?" Katie questioned as Christy glanced at her waving aunt and uncle's reflection in the rearview mirror.

"The weekend went too fast," Christy answered with a sigh. "I wish I could have spent some more time with Todd."

"He's coming down to your house next weekend. You can live till then," Katie said.

Christy couldn't tell if Katie was teasing or being sarcastic. Katie seemed to have made considerable progress in recovering from the loss of Michael after her emotional release at Disneyland. Still, Christy couldn't help but wonder if a few more tears weren't left inside Katie. Christy decided to redirect the conversation.

"There are some CD's in a box under the seat. Do you want to find us some traveling music?"

Katie reached for the box. "What do you want to listen to?" Then, before she lifted the lid, Katie said, "Oh, wait! I have a new CD in my backpack. Doug gave it to me."

"Doug gave it to you?"

"Yeah, this morning in the parking lot after church. He said it had some songs he really liked, and he thought I might like them, too. Wasn't that nice of him?" Katie unlatched her seat belt and knelt on the front seat, reaching into the luggage in the back.

"Careful," Christy said, checking her rearview mirror, which was filled with the reflection of Katie's backside. "Try to hurry, okay?"

It was dusk. Christy turned on her lights and gingerly merged into the traffic on Pacific Coast Highway.

"Where is that thing?" Katie leaned farther into the backseat.

Christy wanted to say to Katie, as if she were a child, "Sit back down right this instant! Do you realize how dangerous that is?" But instead she nibbled on her lower lip and checked her side mirror. To her horror she saw blue flashing lights.

"Katie . . . is that a policeman behind us?"

Katie popped her head up, checked the car behind them, and with a friendly wave said, "Yep, looks like he's trying to get your attention. Hey, Mr. Policeman!"

Just then the siren went on, and Christy felt her heart stop. "What do I do? What do I do?" she sputtered.

Katie twisted around and plopped back in her seat. "Relax! You didn't do anything wrong. Pull over to the right. Where's your registration? In here?" She opened the glove compartment and began to shuffle through the papers as Christy nervously pulled the car over to the side of the road and rolled down her window before turning off the engine.

"Now what do I do?"

"Wait and be cool. He'll come to you."

"Should I get out my license? Where's my purse?"

"Relax! It's right here," Katie said, handing Christy her purse. "And here's Mr. Policeman."

Christy turned to face a stern-looking man who leaned on the window rim and peered in the car, taking a good look at Katie.

"Good evening, officer," Katie said with a smile.

The policeman then looked at Christy and said, "May I see your license and registration, please?"

"It's right here," Christy handed him her whole wallet.

"All I need is your license," he said. "Would you mind taking it out?"

"Oh, sure. Sorry." Christy fumbled with her wallet while Katie thumbed through a small stack of papers she had pulled from the glove compartment.

"Here's the registration," Katie said, holding out the paper to the officer before Christy had managed to pull her license out of her wallet.

The officer waited.

"I almost have it," Christy said with a nervous laugh. Her hands were shaking so badly she could barely get a grip on the slick piece of paper. "There." She handed it to the officer. He looked the papers over and then pulled a pad of paper out of his back pocket.

Just then a garbled message came over his car radio. He said something about staying put and walked back to his car. Christy closed her eyes and let out a heavy sigh.

"Why are you so stressed?" Katie said. "You probably have a taillight out or something. It's nothing. Relax."

When Christy opened her eyes, she was aware of all the cars zooming past them. She felt certain all those people were laughing at her, snickering at her embarrassment. This was awful.

"Okay, Miss Miller," the officer said, striding up to her car. "You lucked out. I have to respond to this call right away." He handed her papers back and quickly looked into the car, making eye contact with Katie. "I suggest you put your seat belt on and keep it on. The next officer might not be in such a hurry." He rushed back to the patrol car, turned on the lights and siren, and pulled out into the traffic.

Still quivering, Christy crammed the papers and wallet into her purse and turned the car on.

"What was that supposed to mean?" Katie said.

"You didn't have your seat belt on," Christy said sharply. "I almost got a ticket because you didn't have a seat belt on."

"It was only for a minute. I was going to put it back on after I found the CD."

Christy took her time pulling back into the traffic flow.

"Are you sure that's what the problem was?" Katie asked defensively.

"Yes."

"Well, then why didn't you tell me there was a policeman behind us? I wouldn't have been so obvious about retrieving the stuff in the backseat."

"It doesn't matter if a policeman is there or not. You're supposed to keep your seat belt on," Christy snapped back.

"Okay, okay, it's on." She clicked it hard for added emphasis. "Man, you would think you actually got a ticket the way you're acting!"

"But I could have."

"But you didn't!"

"But I almost did!"

"But," Katie spoke each word firmly, "you didn't."

Several minutes passed before Christy broke the stubborn silence. "I'm sorry, Katie. I was nervous. It really freaked me out."

"No, it's my fault," Katie said. "You're right. Just because we didn't suffer a consequence this time doesn't mean I did the right thing by taking off my seat belt. Like the guy said, we lucked out. Or should we say it was a God thing?"

Christy shot a smile at Katie. It was nice to hear Katie use her old favorite phrase and call something a God thing. It was good to have Katie back.

"Pull in there," Katie said, pointing to a convenience store on the right side of the road.

Christy made the turn and parked in front of the brightly lit store. "Good idea. I should call my parents and tell them where we are."

"I need something to drink. How about you?" Katie asked.

"Sure. I could go for some juice."

"I'll get it for you," Katie said, pushing open the store's door and greeting the clerk with a friendly hello as if she knew him.

Christy dialed her home. She decided to save the part about being stopped by a policeman until she got home, and only told her mom they were just past Laguna Beach. Mom gave all the usual instructions about being careful, and Christy said, "Don't worry, Mom. We will."

"Ready?" Katie asked, exiting the store with a bottle of orange juice in one hand and a bag in the other.

Christy nodded and unlocked Katie's door. They crawled in, and as Christy started up the car, Katie said, "I picked up a few supplies for the rest of the journey home. Are you ready for a Twinkie?"

"A Twinkie? Do you know how long it's been since I've seen you with a Twinkie in your hand?"

"Yes," Katie said, tearing off the clear wrapper and sinking her teeth into the yellow sponge cake. "Too long." There was a dot of white frosting on her top lip.

Christy laughed. "It's nice having you back, Katie. I'll take one of those Twinkies, if you have enough."

"Enough?" Katie said, opening the grocery bag and holding it up so Christy could see inside. At least eight packages of a variety of non-Michael-approved junk food lurked inside.

Katie handed Christy an opened Twinkie. She then pulled out a bag of chips for herself. "Let's hope my next boyfriend, if there ever is one, is a connoisseur of the finer things in life. Like Doritos. Ranch flavored." With that she chomped down on the chip in her mouth.

"Are you going to be okay seeing Michael tomorrow?" Christy asked cautiously. "I mean, he's in your government class, right?"

"I'll be okay. I think. I don't know. I don't want to think about it. I don't trust any of my emotions at this point. I wanted to tell you, though, that being with you guys this weekend really helped. I had a great time. Doug went above and beyond the call of duty in helping me feel better. He's a great guy. I think he should be a counselor."

"Well, if it gets rough this week, I'm here for you."

"Thanks, Christy." Katie snapped another chip and said, "Do you know what's weird? I feel that while I was with Michael I was in a time warp. I'm outside of it now, so I feel normal. But when I was with him, being in his world seemed normal. Does that make sense?"

"Sort of."

"The thing is, I don't think I did anything wrong. I mean, I know I didn't do anything wrong morally. Michael's standards were just as high as mine. That wasn't really a problem. Who knows? It might have been a problem eventually, if we had gone together longer. You want some chips?"

"No, thanks." Christy licked the last Twinkie crumbs from her lips and urged Katie to keep talking while she kept her eyes on the road.

"Do you think it's possible that it was really God's will I go out with him just to tell him about the Lord, even though Michael didn't make a commitment to Christ? At least now he's heard. Maybe I was the only one God could use to tell him."

"Maybe," Christy said cautiously.

"And maybe he'll become a Christian soon, and we'll get back together." Katie turned in her seat to face Christy and wiggled to get comfortable in her seat belt. "Maybe the whole reason we broke up was to force him to look at the Lord without me there to bug him about it."

"Maybe," Christy said.

"I don't know," Katie said. "I don't know what I think. All I know is when I first started going out with him I knew somewhere deep inside my heart that it wasn't right. But I didn't think we would be together for very long, and I knew I wasn't going to do anything wrong. What would it hurt? Then one date turned into two, and then three and, well, you know the rest."

Katie crumpled up the empty bag of chips and tossed it in the sack, rummaging around for a bag of candy. "So my question is, did I do anything wrong by dating a guy who's not a Christian? Everyone always tells us not to, but sometimes it's okay, isn't it? Like when it's just a short time, and nobody gets really hurt. I mean, I came out of this whole relationship fine. Sure, I still hurt a little, but I think I'm going to be okay. I'm a better person. I obeyed God when He told me to break up. It was okay this one time, wasn't it?''

Christy had strong opinions about only dating Christians, and she and Katie had talked about it before. Of course, as Katie had pointed out, it was easy for Christy to say that when she was dating Todd. But it was a lot harder to say those same things when no decent Christian guys were around.

"I think the guideline exists for a reason," Christy said.

"Right, I know. So you won't marry a non-believer and end up 'unequally yoked.' But don't you think it's okay if it's for a short time and nobody gets hurt? Just a friendship. Don't you think that stuff about not dating unbelievers is totally, grossly overemphasized?''

Christy tried to think of a way to tell Katie what she thought yet somehow tone it down so it didn't come out as intensely as she felt it. Suddenly a peculiar analogy came to her. "Actually, Katie, I guess with Michael you lucked out. It would have been different if the officer didn't have another call or if we'd actually gotten in an accident.''

"What are you talking about? Are we having the same conversation here?''

"You know, all that talk about wearing your seat belt is grossly overemphasized. You're not planning to get in an accident. You guys only went out for a little while. Still, I'd say you lucked out.''

"Are you talking about my dating Michael or my taking off my seat belt?''

"Both.''

Katie let the full meaning of the analogy sink in. "Oh" was all she said.

Christy immediately felt bad. "I'm sorry, Katie. I shouldn't have said that. That was judgmental of me. You're right, I was too self-righteous and judgmental the whole time you were dating, and that wasn't right."

"No, you don't have to apologize. I deserve all your words and more. I live too much on the edge. I take off my seat belt and think it's okay as long as I don't get caught. I become involved emotionally with a guy who's not a Christian and think it's okay just because we're not going beyond my standards." Katie took a deep breath. She rested her bag of M&M's on her lap. "But you're right, Christy. There's a higher level of accountability that's not based on whether or not you get caught."

Katie crumpled the candy bag and stuffed it back in the sack. Sitting up straight, she made a declaration. "Hear ye, hear ye. From this day forward, the new, improved Katie is going to strive for integrity in all things. Even in what I eat. That's probably the best thing that came out of my relationship with Michael, an appreciation for healthy food. I'm going to go back to eating right. And I'm going to keep exercising regularly and start reading my Bible every day, and I am not going to gossip ever again."

They were now approaching the interchange with the freeway that would take them back to Escondido. Christy signaled in plenty of time, got in the right lane, and followed the curve in the road up, over and onto Interstate 78. She needed to concentrate on changing lanes, so she held back from responding to Katie until they were securely in the middle lane.

"You're a good influence on me," Katie said. "You do everything right."

"No, I don't."

"Yes, you do. You're much more conscientious than I am. Much more concerned about doing the right thing."

"I don't do the right thing any more often than you do."

"Oh, yes you do. You have a certain quality. Anyone can see it by just looking at your face. You're without guile, Christy."

"Whatever that means. It sounds like a curse," Christy said with a laugh.

"Not at all." Katie shook her head. "I'd say it's a blessing. Just look at your life. Everything is perfect. You've never hit a wall with God. I mean, what's the worst thing that could ever happen to you?"

"I don't know. I guess my parents could die."

"Then you'd go live with Bob and Marti and be pampered to death. And the only other awful thing would be if Todd broke up with you."

There was a moment of jaw-clenching silence.

Then Katie said, "But that would never happen. Don't you see? You are living with the reward of having your relationships according to God's way and in His time. I want that kind of blessing on my life, too."

Christy wasn't sure it all worked as neatly as Katie claimed.

# CHAPTER NINE

# Sweet Dreams

It was the fastest week on record, Christy was sure. She couldn't believe it was Friday already. She was driving to the pet store after school, but she wished she was going home instead. She could use a nap.

Every night that week Christy had stayed up until after eleven, studying. The worst part was, everyone said it would be like this for another three weeks until finals. She didn't think she could keep up the pace. But she had no choice. What kept her going was knowing Todd would come up tomorrow.

"Wonderful," Christy spoke into the stillness of the car. "No, marvelous. No, no, no. Delicious. Fantastic. Unbelievably terrific!"

*No, that's still not it,* she insisted. *How can I describe what I'm feeling? How do I put my thoughts about Todd into words? It's too good to be true. This must be love. But how do I describe it?*

As Christy parked her car and took quick steps into the mall, she realized her problem was a common one. What was it her English teacher had said last year? Through all the generations, poets, composers, and artists have tried to describe love. Yet no one has completely captured it, so the world is still full of poets, composers, and artists who continue in the footsteps of their fore-fathers, attempting to portray love, yet never with complete success.

"Hi, Jon," Christy said, taking her position behind the cash register.

"Hi. I've been meaning to ask you how your bunny is."

Christy thought Jon said "honey." It seemed strange that he would ask about Todd that way.

"He's fine. I'm going to see him tomorrow."

Jon gave her a puzzled look and said, "Has he been eating well?"

Christy laughed. "Of course. He eats all the time. Why do you ask?"

"No reason. It's just that if they're not feeling well, they tend to stop eating. What about spending time with him? You still hold him a lot, don't you? Give him lots of snuggles and love?"

Now Christy really laughed, only it was an embarrassed laugh. She glanced around to make sure no customers in the store could hear their conversation.

"Yes, I give him lots of snuggles. Why in the world are you asking?"

"Because I know how easy it is to end up neglecting the little guy when you're not around him all the time."

"The little guy?"

"Don't your parents make you keep him in the garage?"

"In the garage?" Christy questioned.

"Isn't that where Hershey's cage is? In the garage? You know, Hershey, the rabbit I gave you a couple of months ago."

"Oh, Hershey! Yes, his cage is in the garage." Christy tried to stifle her laughter.

"Why? Who did you think I was talking about?" Jon asked.

"Never mind," Christy said, grateful and relieved that a customer had stepped in front of Jon and placed an aquarium filter on the counter.

Christy smiled at the woman and said, "How are you today?"

"Fine, thanks. Is this one on sale?"

"Yes," Christy said, double-checking the price sticker. "This one is twenty percent off."

"Yeah, well, it's not the only one," Jon said loud enough for Christy to hear.

She shot him a quick glance and then focused back on the customer. "That's fifteen cents change for you." Christy placed a dime and a nickel in the woman's open palm and, handing her the bag, said, "Thanks a lot. Have a nice afternoon."

The woman smiled and left. Another customer stepped up to the counter. Christy went through the process of scanning the merchandise, ringing it up on the cash register, and making change. She had done this so many times she could almost do it in her sleep, which was a good thing. She was incredibly tired. She had a hard time staying alert until closing at nine.

"You look as if you're all ready to go," Jon commented as Christy began to pull down the metal cage door that closed the pet store off from the rest of the mall. "We still have two more minutes."

"Do you want me to put the door back up?"

"No, that's fine. You go ahead and leave. You look beat. I'll close up."

"Preparing for finals," Christy offered by way of explanation. "Get used to this walking-in-my-sleep look. I'll probably be like this for the next few weeks."

"Do you want to take some time off? I have a new guy starting next Wednesday, and he was asking for more hours than I could give him. It would just be until you want the hours back," Jon said.

"I'd miss the money, but it would sure help right now." Christy thought a moment and then said, "You know, if it would be okay, I could use the next few weekends off. Maybe the next three?" In the back of her mind she was trying to calculate when the prom was. She wanted to be prepared in case she and Todd decided to go. It was almost too late to buy tickets, but she wanted to leave every door open.

"Okay," Jon said, reaching for the clipboard behind the register. "Let's say you work tomorrow and then again on Friday a month from now. Is that too much time off?"

"It sounds like a lot."

"It's up to you."

"I think it's fine. Go ahead and give the other guy my hours. I need to make it through this next intense month of school. Thanks for being so understanding, Jon."

"It's part of my managerial role. Besides, who says I'm too old to remember how stressful the end of your senior year can be? You take it easy. And try to get some sleep, okay?"

"I will. Thanks, Jon. See you tomorrow morning."

Christy barely remembered her head hitting the pillow that night. On Saturday morning her mom came in to wake her up at 10:15.

"Christy? Time to get up, honey. You need to leave for work in half an hour."

"Ohhhh," Christy groaned. "My head is pounding."

"Are you feeling all right?"

"My throat is swollen. I feel awful!"

Mom placed her cool hand on Christy's cheek. "Feels like you're running a temperature. When did this start?"

"I was tired yesterday." Christy swallowed. It felt as if she had a wad of gum stuck in her throat. "My throat didn't hurt, though. And I didn't ache this much, either."

"I think you'd better stay in bed. Do you want me to call work for you?"

"I guess," Christy groaned. "Tell Jon I'm going to sleep some more, and if I feel better, I'll work this afternoon."

Mom left the room, and Christy rolled over and kicked off her sheets. She felt as though she was burning up. She could hear her pulse pounding in her inner ear.

*What happened to me? I feel awful.*

"Okay," Mom said a few minutes later, entering Christy's room. "Jon said he doesn't want you to come in at all. He has someone to cover your hours, and he didn't want you to bring any flu bugs into work."

"Thanks, Mom."

"Jon also told me about your arrangement to take time off for the next few weeks. I think that was wise of you. Perhaps you should have started sooner. Do you feel like taking a bath? That would be the best thing for the aches."

"I guess," Christy said feebly. Ever since she was a child she was used to special treatment when she got sick. Her mom seemed like a natural nurse, bringing Christy juice, taking her temperature, and scanning the vitamin book to find a natural cure for every ailment. It was easy for Christy to surrender to her mom's babying.

"I'll go run the water in the tub."

Christy slowly sat up in bed. The room felt as if it were spinning. Today reminded her of one of her greatest fears: One day she would be mature and self-sufficient, living in a college dorm room or an apartment. She would come down with some kind of killer flu, and she wouldn't have her mom to take care of her.

Standing on wobbly feet and inching her way across the carpeted floor, Christy shuffled to the bathroom, where Mom had already placed a tray with ice water in a glass with a straw, several vitamins, and two aspirins on a napkin. Christy noticed an unpleasant fragrance rising from the steaming tub.

"I've put some apple cider vinegar in the water," Mom said. "The book said it helps to draw out the toxins. Soak in there for at least twenty minutes, okay?"

"You're starting to sound like Katie," Christy said, realizing that it hurt her throat to talk. She twisted her hair up on top of her head and secured it with a clip.

"I'm going to change the sheets on your bed and air your room out." Mom closed the bathroom door. Christy could hear her humming as she went about her nursing tasks.

Gingerly lowering herself into the stinky, steaming water, Christy closed her eyes and imagined what it would be like to get sick if she were Katie's roommate. She could picture Katie popping her head into Christy's room and saying, "Oh, you're sick? Well, don't worry about answering the phone. I'll put the machine on. There's some leftover Chinese take-out from a couple of days ago. I won't be back until late tonight, so don't bother to wait up for me."

Yes, the image of independent life made her grateful still to be at home and to have her mom to take care of her. Even the water didn't smell so bad, once she snuggled all the way in and grew used to it.

She soaked until the water felt cool and her fingers felt wrinkly. But when she stood up, she didn't feel much better. Only dizzy. Mom had delivered a clean set of sweats to the bathroom, which Christy put on. Even her feet hurt as they plunged into the legs of the sweatpants.

Glancing in the mirror, Christy thought, *Scary! Look at the dark rings under my eyes. I'm glad Todd isn't here to see me looking like this.*

Then it hit her. Todd was coming today!

"Mom!" Christy called out hoarsely, opening the bathroom door and making her way back to her bed by the most direct route possible. She found her room looking fresh and her sheets changed with the corner of the covers turned down, inviting her to crawl in. Even the clutter on her floor had been picked up. On her nightstand stood another glass of ice water with a bent straw and a box of throat lozenges. Christy slid in between the sheets and felt as if a million pounds had been lifted from her when her head touched the soft pillow.

"How are you feeling?" Mom said, entering the room carrying a tray adorned with a cup of tea and some dry toast. "You want to try to eat something?"

Christy shook her head. "Todd," she whispered, trying not to strain her sore throat. "Call him and tell him not to come."

"Oh, dear," Mom said. "I hope he hasn't left yet. I'll call him right away."

Christy felt exhausted from the hot bath. Her bed was clean and comforting, and her room smelled fresh. The fragrance from Mom's can of Lysol was a vast improvement over the apple cider vinegar bath. Christy sniffed, thinking she could still smell some of the vinegar. Then she fell asleep.

Sometime later, she felt a cool hand on her forehead. Without opening her eyes, she whispered, "Todd?" as a question to see if Mom had called him.

"I'm right here," Todd's deep voice answered. He removed his hand from her forehead and took her hand in his. "How are you doing?"

"I . . . but, you . . ." She tried to express that she was sorry he had come all this way when she was sick. But the words were caught in her swollen throat, and she swallowed them.

"Hey, don't try to talk. You should drink something, though. Here, let me hold this for you." Todd lifted the glass of ice water to her lips, and she obediently sipped from the straw. The coldness felt good on her raw throat, and she drank nearly half the glass before letting go of the straw.

"Good job. We'll do that again in about five minutes. Your mom gave me strict orders to make you drink water and take all your pills. Think you can manage this one?" He placed a small vitamin between her lips and held the glass of water for her. She swallowed the pill, even though it hurt going down, and drank most of the rest of the glass of water.

"Want some more water?"

Christy shook her head.

"Go back to sleep. I'll be here," Todd said. "I have some reading to do. You have some recuperating to do."

"I'm sorry," Christy forced out the words.

"Sorry for what? Sorry you're sick? I'm sorry you're sick, too. That doesn't change anything. I wanted to spend some time with you, and that's what I'm doing. You rest. Don't worry about me. I have finals to study for, and there's no place I'd rather sit and study than by your side."

As Christy slipped off into a dream, she thought of how those were probably the sweetest words Todd had ever said to her. No, the sweetest words anyone had ever said to her. Even though she still felt sick, her heart soared.

It was late afternoon when Christy began to wake up. She

remembered the feel of Todd's hand on her forehead and thought it must have been part of her dream.

He had placed his hand on her forehead like that once before. It was early morning on the beach a year and a half ago. Todd was about to leave for Hawaii, and Christy had begun to date a guy named Rick. As Todd's farewell, he had placed his cool hand on Christy's forehead and blessed her, saying, "The Lord bless you and keep you. The Lord make His face to shine upon you and give you His peace. And may you always love Jesus first, above all else."

Surely Todd's hand on her forehead had been just a memory evoked by her feverish dreams. She now had only to open her eyes to verify if it was a dream. She hesitated. Keeping her eyes closed, she decided it would be better to continue in her lovely dream than to see nothing but thin air beside her bed.

But the sound of someone moving in a chair prompted her to open her eyes. And there he was. For real. A dream come true. Todd's blond head was bent over a thick textbook, a notebook was draped on his lap, and a pencil was in his mouth. Christy tried to lie as still as she could, watching Todd without his knowing she was awake.

That's when she realized her throat didn't feel quite so swollen anymore, and her head wasn't throbbing, either. She actually felt a lot better.

Just then her bedroom door squeaked open, and Christy snapped her eyes shut and pretended to be asleep.

She heard her mom's voice whisper, "How's our patient?"

Footsteps followed closer to the bed.

"Still sleeping," Todd answered. "Her fever seems to be down."

"Good," Mom whispered back. "You know, Todd, this is

above and beyond the call of friendship to spend your whole day here with her."

"I'm getting a lot done," Todd said and then added with a hint of teasing in his voice, "since it's quieter here than in the library. Besides," now his voice turned serious, "what I feel for Christy is above and beyond the call of friendship."

Christy couldn't believe Todd said that to her mom. Her heart began to beat a little faster. It was one thing for Todd to reveal his feelings to Christy at Disneyland, but it was quite another to say something to her mother. She never would have imagined such a moment.

"You know you have our blessing in that area," a deep voice said.

*My dad is in here, too? Todd said that in front of Dad, and he said Todd has his blessing? This has to be a dream!*

Christy stretched her long legs beneath the covers and pretended to be stirring from her sleep. With the finesse of an actress, she let out a slight sigh and fluttered her eyes open.

Her dad and mom were standing beside her bed, and Todd was still seated at the foot. As soon as she opened her eyes, Todd leaned forward and reached for her hand, giving it a squeeze.

"Well, Sleeping Beauty, did you have sweet dreams?"

She felt like telling him the conversation she awoke to was sweeter than any dream ever. Their eyes met, and she wondered if Todd knew she had overheard their conversation.

"Your fever seems to be gone," Mom said, feeling Christy's forehead. "You look better around the eyes. How's your throat?"

"It's lots better."

"Good! Now you should eat some soup. I'll get it."

Christy's dad brushed his large, gruff hand across her flushed cheek. "Glad you're feeling better."

"Thanks, Dad." Christy smiled at him. She was amazed that she could be in bed, holding hands with her boyfriend while exchanging tender, meaningful smiles with her dad. It all seemed natural. Sweet. In every way, a dream come true.

# CHAPTER TEN

# Weird and Tweaked

"You're here!" Katie said, coming up behind Christy at her locker on Monday morning. "I called this weekend, and your mom said you were sick. Are you better?"

Christy closed her locker, and the two of them maneuvered their way through the crowded hallway. "I'm getting there. I might go home after lunch, but I didn't want to get behind in my classes. I have something to tell you at lunch, though. Can you meet me out at the tree?"

"Sure. And I have something to tell you that you won't believe!" Katie's eyes sparkled as she waved and called out, "Ta-ta!" before ducking into her classroom.

*I wonder what's up? Does it have something to do with Michael?*

It was torture sitting through her classes, waiting for lunch so she could find out what Katie's secret was. Finally the lunch bell rang, and Christy hurried out to their meeting spot.

"You go first," Katie said, sitting on the ground beneath the tree where they usually ate. It was also the spot where Katie had first met Michael at the beginning of the school year.

"No, you go. My curiosity is overflowing."

"It's about Fred," Katie said excitedly.

"Oh," Christy retorted flatly. "Maybe I should go first. My news about Todd is definitely more exciting than anything you could tell me about Fred."

"Not necessarily," Katie said coyly.

"Okay, go ahead. What about Fred?"

"He came to church yesterday," Katie said. "He sat next to me."

Christy wasn't impressed. She bit into her apple and said, "He asked about church. I told you that, didn't I? I'm glad he went. Now, do you want to hear about Todd?"

"I have more," Katie said. "After church we walked out to the parking lot together. When we got to my car, Fred said, 'So, how do I give my heart to God, like that minister talked about?' "

Christy lost interest in her apple. "Really? That's great! What did you tell him?"

Katie looked as if she were about to bubble over with excitement. "I just told him that God knew his heart. If he wanted to get things right between him and God, all he had to do was ask God to forgive him for everything wrong he had ever done and then invite the Lord to take over his life."

"And?" Christy said.

"And he and I prayed right there in the parking lot by my car. Fred gave his heart to the Lord."

"I don't believe it."

"I know. What a God thing! It was so incredible. He was so ready, I felt as if I just stood there and watched. All these months of trying to convince Michael to give his life to God. All our long conversations, and all my explanations and pleadings, and here Fred, of all people, follows me to my car and gets saved!"

Christy laughed with joy. "That's great! It was kind of the same way with Alissa. I mean, Todd and I had been praying for her, but then one afternoon on the beach she said 'I'm ready,' and her life has never been the same since."

"I don't understand why it was so easy for Fred and impossible for Michael," Katie commented, opening her sack and looking inside.

"Who knows. God is weird," Christy said reverently. "Not weird like goofy, but weird like unexplainable."

"Yeah, God is weird, and we are tweaked," Katie surmised. "That's my philosophy of life. God's way of doing things is never our way, and we're bent. Tweaked. We always want to do things in a way that's twisted from God's."

"I like that," Christy said. "Only you could put it so eloquently."

"So when you see Fred in yearbook next period, act real excited for him."

"Don't worry! I won't have to act; I *will* be!"

True to her word, Christy was excited for Fred when she told him, "I'm so glad you've become a Christian! That's the best thing that could ever happen to you, Fred."

Fred beamed his toothy smile and said, "And the second best thing would be if you went to the prom with me. I already have the tickets, you know."

Christy's enthusiasm stopped cold. Is that why Fred started going to church and said he became a Christian? Was it all part of a scheme to become involved in Christy's world? And how could she ask him without sounding accusatory?

"Fred," she began, "I am not going to the prom with you. Not even because you've become a Christian."

Fred's face fell. "You think that's why I did it?"

"Well, no. I just want you to know I really can't go with you. I have a boyfriend. If I do go, it will be with him."

Fred turned and walked away. Was he hurt? Mad? Finally giving up? She wondered if she should follow him to the other side of the classroom. But then, what would she say?

Instead, she slipped into her desk and breathed out a heavy sigh. *At least now Fred knows I won't go out with him. I'm sorry to hurt his feelings, but his bugging me about the prom has gone far enough. He'll be okay. He'll bounce back. He always does.*

She and Todd needed to decide tonight if they were going to the prom. That would settle the matter once and for all. She tried to concentrate on her reading, knowing this free class time would enable her to lessen her homework load. But all she could think about was Todd.

He had been wonderful to stay with her all day Saturday. Then he had called and talked to her for almost two hours on Sunday. Their conversation had been full of plans for the upcoming weeks and even into the summer. Christy hadn't brought up the prom, though, and she didn't know if Todd was even interested.

She called him that night and started out by asking what he thought about the prom.

"It's a poor imitation of the real thing."

"What?" Christy asked, not following him.

"It's like pretending you're at the wedding feast. It's a poor imitation of the real thing."

"You mean, you think people who go to the prom are pretending like they're getting married?" It had a certain ring of truth, Christy thought. She had heard from some of the girls how much they were spending on their dresses. Then there was the whole extravaganza of flowers, tux, and the limo.

"You see, I think that what every human soul longs for, whether that person knows it or not, is to be at the marriage feast of the Lamb," Todd explained.

"You lost me," Christy said.

"Christy. You know, when this world comes to an end and we all stand before God, He's going to bring all those whom He's prepared to be the Bride of Christ—the Church—into the marriage feast, where the Believers and Christ will be united forever. It's going to be the biggest, wildest party ever."

Christy guessed Todd must be talking about prophecies from the Bible, from the book of Revelation. It was an area she didn't know a lot about.

"So deep within the heart of every person is the desire to be invited," Todd continued, "to be dressed like royalty and treated the same, and to be included in the celebration. Something like a prom is a hollow imitation of the real thing you and I will experience one day."

Now Christy felt annoyed. It was one thing to have an opinion about the prom. It was another thing to have the blessed hope to spend eternity celebrating around God's throne. But to overlap these two and invalidate the prom in light of heaven was ridiculous.

"Todd, I know you like to see something spiritual in everything, and I think that's great. But this is just the prom. It's a human, earthly celebration, and I don't see how it has anything to do with heaven. May I rephrase my original question? Would you like to go to the prom with me?"

"If you really want to go."

Christy hated answers like that. It wasn't an answer; it only put the question back on her. "I don't know what I want. That's why I'm asking what you want."

"Let's talk about it, then," Todd said. "How much does it cost? Do we want to go with some others or by ourselves? Do you want to go out to dinner first? Do you have a dress or money to buy a dress? And most importantly, why do you want to go?"

For twenty minutes the two of them tossed back and forth the pros and cons. In the end, Christy said, "I don't know. I still feel as if I could go either way. It would be fun and wonderful and romantic to get all dressed up and go with you, but it would take all our money, and I'm not into dancing."

"It's up to you," Todd said, putting the decision back in her lap again. "If we do go, you need to know that even if you don't see a parallel between the two, while I'm at the prom I'm going to be thinking about heaven and our ultimate celebration there one day."

After Christy hung up, she wasn't sure how to take Todd's comments. Did he mean that he wouldn't be focusing on her that evening or admiring her or enjoying being with her because he would be centering his thoughts on eternal things? Why did Todd have to be like that? God was always first in his life.

Then Christy realized that was a compliment, not a slam. It was a rare thing to be so focused on God. Todd seemed to see God's perspective on everything.

Christy decided to let go of the prom question and focus on her homework so she could get some sleep. Her flu bug had passed, but she felt weak and ready for bed at 5:30. She decided to put all her energies into studying this week. When she saw Todd over the weekend, they could come to a conclusion about the prom. That would still give them two weeks to make any arrangements. She could come up with a dress by then—couldn't she?

Even though she thought she had set the prom question aside for the week, it kept popping up in her mind. After all, she would remind herself, this was her senior year. She was graduating. She had a boyfriend. It was only natural they should go to the prom. Secretly, she would love to show off Todd to all the other girls in her class. More than that, though, she would love to have a reason to dress up and be with Todd in a formal setting. He was always so casual. She had only seen him dressed up a few times, and she had never danced with him.

Not that Christy was sure she knew how to dance. She had never been to a dance and had never really learned how to dance.

The more she thought about it, the more complicated the whole thing became. She had almost $450 saved up from work, and it killed her to think that if she did go to the prom, it would cut deeply into her savings. And Todd didn't have much money. How much was she expecting him to pay for the tux, flowers, dinner, and the tickets?

The more she thought about it, the more frustrated she became. Two years ago, Rick had asked her to his prom, and her parents had said absolutely not. She was a sophomore then. Now she was a senior. Her parents hadn't been fond of Rick. They liked Todd. Still, what would they say if she told them she wanted to go?

CHAPTER ELEVEN

# *I'll Be Here*

"Are you sure you don't want to come to Newport Beach with me this weekend?" Christy asked Katie over the phone on Thursday night. "We had such a good time a couple of weeks ago. I have the weekend off work, and I'm taking my books to study with Todd. You know you're welcome to come."

"I know, but I feel like staying home. Can you believe I just said that?" Katie said. "I feel I need time to sort things out. I talked to Michael yesterday."

"Was that the first time?"

"Yeah. It was awful. He's such a sweetheart. I love him. I truly do. Do you think it's possible to genuinely love someone even though that's not the person you'll marry?"

Christy gave it some thought. "I think it is possible, Katie."

"Do you suppose that for the rest of your life in some small way you remain in love with him?"

"Maybe. I don't know. That would sure hurt for a long time if you did. Maybe you grow out of love the more you're away from that person. You then grow in love with someone else, and it dims the memory of that first love."

"Do you really think so?"

"I don't know."

"Well, if I am going to grow out of love with Michael, all I know is that it's going to take longer than two weeks."

"Are you sure you want to stay home this weekend? It seems like you'll be depressed the whole time."

"That's sort of what I want," Katie admitted. "I want to lock myself in my room and put on the CD Doug gave me. It has this one song that gets me every time. I need to put away all my Michael souvenirs and have some time to cry out the rest of my tears in a less public place than Disneyland."

Christy thought about her next words and then decided to go ahead and say them. "Would you like me to stick around with you? I will if you want me to."

"No, you need to see Todd. You guys only have the weekends, and you were sick last weekend. Really, I'm fine. You go. Call me when you get back, okay?"

"Okay. And Katie?"

"Yeah?"

"I think you're doing great. You amaze me the way you put your mind to something and stick with it. I'm sure it would be a lot easier to get back together with Michael and let go of all the hurt. Instead, I see you willing to keep the hurt and let go of Michael. You're incredible. I love you, Katie."

Christy could hear Katie sniffling and felt bad for her.

"Thanks, Chris," Katie said in a wobbly voice. "I really needed to hear that. I love you, too. And I appreciate you more than you will ever know."

"Listen, Katie, if you want to talk any time this weekend, just call me at Bob and Marti's, okay? I mean it. Any hour of the day or night. You have the number, don't you?"

"Yes, I do. And thanks. I might do that. You have a fun

weekend, okay? Say hi to Todd for me. And if you see Doug, tell him I really appreciated the card he sent me last week. It cheered me up a lot."

"Okay, I will. Bye." Christy hung up and sat still for several minutes, thinking about Katie. She wished she could do something to make this Michael withdrawal easier. She thought about how every country-western song she had ever heard was true. Love hurts. Bad.

Friday after school, Christy hurried home to throw her stuff together for the weekend. Todd was coming to pick her up. She knew he would probably stay for dinner, but she wanted to be ready to leave whenever he was. She planned to discuss the prom during their ninety-minute drive to Bob and Marti's. If they did end up going, she would probably have a better choice of dresses at one of the big malls near her aunt and uncle's, and this would be the weekend to buy one.

Todd arrived a little past six o'clock, and Christy's mom had dinner all ready. Todd seemed like such a natural part of her family. Most of the dinner conversation flowed between Todd, Christy's little brother, and Christy's dad. As she cleared the table and served her mom's apple crisp for dessert, she realized there hadn't been even a pinch of a letup in the conversation. It was nice, really. Familiar. Secure.

For a brief instant, Christy wondered if life would be like this if she and Todd were married and invited her family over to their apartment for dinner. There was only one thing wrong with this picture. The apartment in her mind was the Swiss Family Robinson Tree House, and her parents and brother came by canoe. Even then, Christy couldn't quite picture herself wearing animal-skin garments with a bone in her hair, serving apple crisp in bowls carved out of gourds.

The jungle was Todd's dream, not necessarily hers. And that was a long, long way off. For now, there was a prom dress to worry about.

They didn't get on their way until after nine. As Christy crawled into the passenger seat of Gus, she felt more like stretching out in the back and taking a nap than initiating a lively conversation about the prom.

"Is it okay if I move these?" Christy asked Todd, holding up a handful of mail that was strewn on the passenger seat.

"Sure. Toss 'em on the floor."

"They might get lost," Christy said. "Are these letters supposed to be mailed?"

"No. It's my mail. I hadn't picked it up for almost a month, so there was a bunch."

They waved to Christy's mom and dad, who were standing on the front porch under the arched trellis covered with fragrant jasmine. Christy smiled with memories of the front porch and of Todd.

Todd cranked Gus into gear, and they puttered down Christy's quiet, tree-lined street and headed for the freeway. "You still feel up for going to the beach early tomorrow morning? You were looking a little tired after dinner."

"I am tired. I can't seem to get my energy back."

"Why don't you take a nap? I have a new tape from Doug. I'll put it on, and you can crash."

Christy knew Todd was right. She should sleep. They would be together lots more during the weekend. They would have time to talk about the prom later. Grabbing her jacket from off the back seat, she wadded it up into a pillow and leaned against the window.

Todd popped in the tape, and the mellow music came tiptoeing out, oblivious to the noisy rumble of the Volkswagen bus engine.

"This is nice," Christy said with her eyes closed. "Who is it?"

"It's a collection of different Christian artists. It's Doug's latest favorite."

"I wonder if this is the same CD he gave to Katie. She said she liked it and was going to lock herself in her room and listen to it all weekend." Then with a half smile she added, "I almost got a ticket when she took off her seat belt in the car and started rummaging through her pack, trying to find it on the way home from Bob and Marti's.

For the next hour or so, Christy dozed while Gus rumbled up the freeway. She didn't fully wake up until they arrived at Bob and Marti's.

"Kilikina," Todd said softly when he turned off the motor and it was suddenly quiet, "we're here."

"How are you doing?" Christy asked, stretching her stiff neck.

"I'm a little tired from driving, but I'm okay. You ready to go in?"

"Sure." Christy yawned and put on her jacket, ready to brace herself against the brisk chill off the ocean. She noticed something white on her lap. Holding it up to the light, she realized it was one of the letters tucked on the dashboard that had slipped off during the trip.

Todd came around and opened her door.

"Here," Christy said, handing him the letter. "It fell in my lap." She hopped out and zipped up the front of her jacket.

"Thanks," Todd said, taking the letter and placing it on the vacated passenger seat without even glancing at it.

*Guys are weird*, she thought. *No sense of curiosity. I'd never let my mail go for a month.*

"Let's walk on the beach," Christy said, feeling awake and alert, especially when the salty ocean scent hit her.

"Okay. We'd better tell Bob and Marti we're here, though," Todd suggested. He carried Christy's bag to the front door and knocked before turning the unlocked doorknob and walking in. "We're here!" he called out.

"Come on in," Bob answered. "I'm in the den."

Bob was pedaling away on his exercise bike, which was set up in front of the wide screen TV. "How was the ride up?" he asked, puffing for breath.

"I slept," Christy admitted.

"We're going for a walk on the beach," Todd said. "Just wanted to let you know we were here."

"Great! Beautiful night. Marti's in bed. I'll be turning in as soon as the news is over. How about if I leave the back door un-locked?"

"Thanks," Todd said. "See you tomorrow."

Todd reached for Christy's hand and led her out the back door and across the patio. They slipped off their shoes and dug their toes into the sand, running hand in hand down to the water.

Even though it was late, other people were out, riding bikes, walking along the beach, and hanging out on their patios, talking and laughing. Some partied with the music cranked up. None of this was unusual for a weekend in a beach community. The only thing a little out of the ordinary was the moon.

It was full, but not tinted the icy blue of winter and spring. Tonight it glowed with an amber hue. It hung right in the middle of the night sky, reflecting off the ocean. The face of the man in the moon appeared to be jovial, about to burst with some secret he hid behind his back.

Christy knew what the secret was. The tawny, golden promise of summer. She couldn't wait.

Todd and Christy stood close together, their feet burrowed in the cold sand at the edge of the foaming night waves. The water rushed up to tickle their ankles and then ran away before anyone could catch it in its game. Todd looped his thick arm around Christy's shoulders and rested his face against the top of her head.

"Oh, Kilikina," he whispered into her hair, "it feels so good to be with you, to hold you. You're in my thoughts day and night. I hold you in my heart."

This was not how Todd usually talked. Something deep inside Christy felt like weeping for joy. She had yearned to hear Todd say these things to her. She had waited a long time. And now it seemed as if she had only met him yesterday, and they would be together forever. She wanted to turn around, look him in the face, and say, "Todd, I love you."

But the memory of something Todd had said once stopped her. He had said he thought men should be the initiators, and women should be the responders. Christy knew that if the words "I love you" were ever to be spoken between them, they needed to come from Todd first.

She did her best to keep a guard on her heart. "I love being here with you," she said, nestling her head against his shoulder.

She felt like praying, the way Todd always did. In a rare, bold move, Christy spoke to her heavenly Father, sending her words into the night winds.

"Father, You made the heavens and the earth and all that is in them. You are such an awesome God! Thank You for making this perfect moon and this perfect night and for letting us be to-gether." She was about to whisper her "Amen," when a strong, clear thought came to her. Without questioning it, she added, "And, Father, please prepare us both for what You have planned for our lives. We want to serve You and honor You in whatever You want us to do. Amen."

"Amen," Todd added, kissing Christy on the top of her head. "I'm going to get up early to go surfing tomorrow morning. You want to come with me?"

Christy couldn't believe Todd could switch gears so quickly. "Sure. When?"

"Around six. Will that give you enough sleep?"

Still startled by his abrupt switch, Christy said, "Six is fine. Where do you want me to meet you?"

"Out on Bob's patio." He released her from his hug and reached for her hand, slipping his fingers in between hers. "Ready to head back?"

"Okay," she said. She wasn't really. She could have stood wrapped up in Todd's arms for hours watching the moon, listen-ing to the waves, feeling the cool water on her ankles, and dream-ing with her eyes open.

They walked hand in hand back to Bob and Marti's patio, where Todd stopped and planted his feet in the sand. He turned Christy around so she faced him. Taking her face in both of his hands, he tilted her head up and looked into her eyes without saying a word. What did she read in his silver-blue eyes? Some-thing powerful and intensely honest. Something stronger than she had ever seen before.

What did Todd read in her eyes? Did he see in her, as she had seen in the moon, a promise of summer, all warm and glowing with hope?

With a kiss as tender as rose petals across her lips, Todd said softly, "Meet me right here when the sun comes up."

"I'll be here," Christy promised. "Right here."

Todd let go. It seemed a hard thing for him to do.

Christy opened the back door and then locked it before quietly tiptoeing up the stairs to her prepared guest room. With a smile still on her freshly kissed lips, she set the alarm for 5:30 A.M.

# CHAPTER TWELVE

# Salt on Her Lips

The irritating buzzer seemed to be going off inside Christy's head. She turned over in bed and woke up fully, realizing the noise was coming from her alarm clock.

She squinted to see the time. "5:30? What was I thinking when I set this noisy thing for 5:30?" And then she remembered. With a clear purpose and distinct joy, Christy rolled out of bed and let her now-singing heart lead her reluctant, weary body into the shower.

The next time she checked the clock, it was 6:01 and she was ready. Quietly padding down the stairs, she left her prepared note on the entry table by the front door. Once before she had left for an early morning walk on the beach without telling anyone and had worried her aunt and uncle. That wouldn't happen this time.

Slipping out the back door and scanning the patio, her heart sank when she found no sign of Todd.

*Maybe my clock is a little fast. Or maybe he's running behind. I know he wouldn't go out without me.*

Christy made her way across the patio, her bare feet feeling the brunt of the concrete's cold. She walked to where she and Todd had stood last night and where he had said to meet him.

Christy searched for that exact spot. And there she stood, straight and tall, unmovable, eagerly scanning the horizon for a glimpse of Todd or his orange surfboard. She found neither.

Since Todd lived so close, she knew he would be walking. So she kept her eyes fixed to the left, the direction from which he would be coming. A few early risers were scattered here and there across the wide beach. It was a clear, chilly, glorious spring morning.

A guy with a white surfboard under his arm came riding by on a wide-tire beach bike. He did a double take when he noticed Christy standing there like a statue, so purposeful and yet, she suspected, so silly-looking.

She gave up the fantasy of waiting on the exact spot and took a seat at the patio table, facing the south and waiting.

Her feet were cold. She thought about going inside to put on some shoes and socks. Then when she came back, Todd might be standing there waiting for her. She hurried inside, grabbed her shoes and socks, slipped quietly downstairs, and went out the back door. Still no Todd. Now she was worried. The clock in her room had said 6:20.

*Maybe I misunderstood. He must have said 6:30, and I thought he said 6:00. He'll be here any minute. Brrr! I'd love a cup of hot tea to warm up my hands.*

Thinking she had ten more minutes, Christy went back inside, made herself and Todd some tea, and carried the mugs outside, one in each hand. Still no Todd. She sat down at the patio table and placed Todd's tea in front of the empty chair. Wrapping her fingers around her hot mug, she blew at the steam rising off the top and took a tiny sip. This experience was too painfully familiar. She had been through these kinds of ups and downs with Todd before.

After last night, Christy had felt certain she would never be left guessing where she stood with him again. She was in his heart. He had said so. He wouldn't forget and leave her. He couldn't.

Christy waited a few more minutes before taking the next sip. She looked down into the mug and saw a dark reflection of her doubt-filled eyes. There was something penetrating about seeing her own reflection. It was as if she was facing her own thoughts.

*Let go.*

The thought came to her as clearly as if it had been spoken aloud. Immediately she responded with a silent prayer.

*You're right, Lord. I'm holding on to these fears and doubts when I should be holding on to You. I do let go now. I want to embrace Your truth.*

She breathed in a fresh peace and looked up. Todd was standing there.

"Hi," he said. He looked awful.

"Are you okay?" Christy asked, putting down her mug and standing up.

"Yeah, sure, fine," Todd answered.

"Do you want some tea? I just made it. It's still hot."

"Thanks." Todd leaned his surfboard up against the lounge chair and sat down in the chair next to Christy. His wet suit made a slippery, rubber sound as he slid onto the vinyl chair pad. "I like tea," Todd said.

"Me too," Christy said, taking a sip and studying Todd's eyes. He hadn't looked directly at her yet.

"What is it?" Christy asked, leaning forward and placing her hand on top of Todd's. He responded by grasping her hand and entwining his fingers with hers. He squeezed her hand tightly. Almost too tightly. Then lifting her hand to his lips, he kissed her hand twice before placing it gently back on the table.

Forcing a smile, he looked at her and said, "Ask me again later, okay?" He took a sip of tea and looked into his mug, as if scrutinizing his reflection the way Christy had.

*Ask you again later? When? In five minutes? In five months? What's wrong, Todd? I want to know now.*

Christy remembered feeling this same way with Katie in the school parking lot when Katie wouldn't tell her what was wrong. Todd had advised Christy to wait until Katie was ready to talk. He said the test of true love was found not in our trying to hold our friends tighter but in the strength to let them go. Christy would now, with great determination, apply Todd's advice to his own situation. She couldn't begin to imagine what was wrong.

They walked down to the water with their arms around each other. She had never felt him hold on to her this closely before. They stopped at the crest in the dry sand, right before it turned wet from the persistent morning tide.

Todd scanned the water and then let go of Christy. He reached for the leash at the end of his board and pulled apart the Velcro strap. It sounded like fabric ripping. Todd fastened the leash to his ankle and zipped his wet suit up to his chin. Then marching down to the water, he walked right into the first wave, ducking under and getting himself soaked before bobbing up, shaking the wet from his hair, and mounting his surfboard. He paddled out to a cluster of about a dozen other surfers and took his place sitting on his board with his legs dangling in the water.

*This is hard*, Christy thought. *How long will I have to wait before he tells me what's bothering him? I thought I had Todd all figured out, and now this morning, I feel as if I don't even know him.*

For the next half hour, Christy watched, prayed, and waited. Todd caught maybe three waves during that whole time. There weren't very many big ones, and Christy knew enough about surfer etiquette to know that Todd would never cut off another guy if he took the wave first. She felt relieved and a tiny bit nervous when she realized he had caught a wave and was riding it all the way to shore.

Todd emerged from the water, scooped his board under his arm, and jogged up to where Christy sat. When he was still several yards away, he stopped, tilted his head back, and shook his sun-bleached hair. She had watched him shake out his hair like that a dozen times. Watching him now, it made Todd seem familiar once again.

"I made a decision," Todd said, planting his board upright in the sand and sitting down next to Christy in the sand. He reached over and took her hand. She responded by slipping her small hand into his cold one and giving it a squeeze. Todd's thumb rested on Christy's gold ID bracelet, and she could feel him instinctively rub his thumb back and forth over the word "Forever" engraved on the bracelet.

With his gaze fixed out on the ocean, Todd squinted his eyes against the brilliant blue. Turning back to face Christy, he looked directly at her. Now the brilliant blue was in his eyes.

"Kilikina, I made a decision." He paused. "You know that letter you showed me last night in the van? I opened it when I got home. It was from a mission organization. You see, I wrote to them last summer and sent in an application for a short-term mission assignment. Three to four years. They wrote back to tell me I was accepted. They want me there in two weeks."

For Christy, it was as if the whole world had just stopped. She couldn't hear the waves or feel the ocean breeze on her face. All she heard were Todd's words frozen in the air between them. She couldn't think or feel or breathe.

"I was pretty amazed," Todd went on. "Everything appears to be set up and ready for me to walk right into the position after the training. It's what I've always wanted to do.''

Christy could feel the numbing effect of Todd's words begin to thaw. As it did, she felt as if a thousand needles were piercing her heart.

Todd took a deep breath. He let go of Christy's hand and turned to face her more squarely. He leaned closer and said, "I prayed all night. I didn't sleep at all. When I thought about leaving you, it tore me up inside. When I thought about staying, I had peace. That's how I knew what my decision was. I'm going to call them on Monday and tell them I can't take the position.''

"You're going to what?" Christy couldn't believe she had heard correctly.

"I'm turning it down. I can't go now. Not with us being so close. A year ago I could have gone. Six months ago, maybe. But not now. It's like I told you at Disneyland, I've never had any-body. Now I have you. I don't take that lightly. You are God's gift to me, Kilikina. I can't leave you. Not now. Not ever.''

Christy closed her eyes and caught her breath. Her heart was pounding wildly. This whole conversation seemed like a bizarre dream. She tried to take in all that Todd had said. She felt relieved that he had made his decision based on what would be best for them. She couldn't bear the thought of being separated from him any more than he apparently could stand the idea of being away from her. But did he mean it deep down inside?

"Todd, are you absolutely sure? You've always wanted to be a missionary.''

"And I always wanted," Todd paused, searching for the right words, "well, I've always wanted other things, too.''

"Todd, are you sure you want to give up this opportunity?" Christy asked, looking him in the eye.

"Yes, I'm sure.''

"And you're giving it up because of me or because of us?"

A smile crept onto Todd's face, causing his dimple to appear on his right cheek. Christy had never seen him look so vulnerable. "Yes, because of you, because of us. You mean more to me than anything, Kilikina." Then he leaned over and kissed her.

When he drew away, Christy could taste the salt on her lips. She had tasted the salt of her own tears before, but she wasn't prepared for the taste of ocean water in his kiss. It seemed different than any of Todd's other kisses. This had a bit of a sting to it.

"Come on," Todd said, standing up and offering Christy his hand. "Let's get some breakfast. We have the whole day to spend together. What would you like to do?"

Christy rose to her feet and brushed the sand off her backside. "I don't know. Give me a minute here. This whole thing has hit me by surprise. First, I imagined all the possible things that could be bothering you, then you tell me you've been offered a position with a mission for three to four years, and then you say you're not going. It's a bit much for me to digest in one bite."

"You're right," Todd said. "I had all night to think it over. I feel so relieved that I told you. I wasn't going to. I was going to act as if I'd never received the letter. I'm glad I told you."

Christy couldn't exactly say the same.

When they reached Bob and Marti's, Todd hosed off his board and his wet suit and left them to dry on the patio.

"Do you think Bob would mind if I borrowed a pair of shorts and a T-shirt?" Todd indicated the stack of freshly laundered clothes lying on the dryer in the laundry room.

"I'm sure it would be fine; you know how easygoing Uncle Bob is."

Helping himself to a pair of khaki shorts and a white T-shirt,

Todd went into the downstairs bathroom to shower and change.

Apparently Bob and Marti weren't up yet. The house was still quiet. Christy noticed it was almost eight o'clock.

Todd emerged from the bathroom and joined Christy in the kitchen. "Do you want to eat here or go out?"

"Let's stay here," Christy suggested. "Does cereal sound okay?" She pulled two boxes from the cupboard.

"Sure." Todd opened the refrigerator and pulled out a gallon of milk. "Is it okay if we eat by the TV?"

"I guess," Christy said.

"Didn't you grow up watching Saturday morning cartoons while you ate your cereal?"

"No, we weren't allowed to eat in the living room."

"Must be one of the advantages of being an only child raised by one parent who was never home. There weren't too many things I wasn't allowed to do."

Christy and Todd carefully carried their cereal bowls into the den and switched on the TV with the volume low so they wouldn't wake anyone up. Christy finished eating first and placed her empty bowl on the floor. Then she grabbed one of her grandmother's crocheted blankets out of the basket by the wall and stretched out on the plush love seat. She curled up with a pillow under her head. With heavy eyelids and a heart full of emotions, Christy tried to pay attention to the cartoon while listening to Todd's rhythmic crunch of cereal. Before long, Todd's crunching ceased, and Christy gave in to the sleep dust that had collected on her eyelids. She couldn't possibly keep her eyes open when her lids weighed so much.

Aunt Marti's voice woke Christy some time later. Christy lifted her still-groggy head and looked around for Marti's location. She was standing directly behind the love seat. "How long have you two been sleeping here?'' Marti wanted to know.

"I don't know," Christy mumbled. She noticed Todd was asleep, too, stretched out on the couch. He had slept through Marti's entrance.

"Shh," Christy said, pressing her finger to her lips. "He didn't get much sleep last night."

"And why was that?"

"It's a long story," Christy said.

"Could it be because he never went home last night?"

"Aunt Marti!" Christy said sharply. "He didn't stay here all night. We both got up early because Todd went surfing while I watched him. We came in a little while ago, and I guess we were both super-tired."

"Oh," Marti said with a twittering laugh. "Then by all means, don't let me bother you. I'll turn off the TV so you can get some more sleep."

The minute the sound went off, Todd opened his eyes and said, "What's going on?"

Christy thought it was funny. She had seen her dad respond the same way. As long as the TV was on, he could snore away, sound asleep in his recliner. The minute the TV was turned off, he would wake up.

"Go back to sleep," Marti said. "Would you like a blanket?"

"No, I'm fine," Todd said, sitting up and running his fingers through the sides of his hair. "Man, I really conked out."

"It's only 10:30," Marti said. "Why don't you sleep some more? It's Saturday, you know."

"We must have slept for two hours! Did you sleep too, Christy?"

"I think I fell asleep before you did," she said, yawning and sticking her bare feet out from under the crocheted blanket.

"Well, as long as you're both up, would you like to join Robert and me for a leisurely brunch?"

Twenty-five minutes later, Christy and Todd were following Bob and Marti through the buffet line at a nearby resort hotel and loading their plates with a variety of fancy foods. To be specific, Todd was loading his plate. Christy was picking and choosing carefully. She didn't feel hungry. Instead, she felt more like she had an upset stomach. When she sat down to eat, she realized her queasy stomach was because of Todd's letter and his turning down the opportunity.

Christy lifted her fork to her mouth and bit into a ripe strawberry. Swallowing the small bite, she licked her lips. They tasted salty.

She took another bite of the strawberry, fully expecting it to taste sweet this time. Again, it tasted salty. Was it the strawberry? Or was it the acid from her grumbling stomach tainting the strawberry?

Todd's news had been unsettling. But when Christy considered the alternative, his decision was good news. She should be happy. Relieved. Delighted.

She tried to silently pray and ask God to give her His peace the way Todd said he had peace. Even though Todd seemed settled with his decision, she wondered if one day he might resent her for holding him back from his dream. On the other hand, would Christy end up resenting God if someday He took Todd away?

# CHAPTER THIRTEEN

# *Let Go*

"Bob said he would go with me to the men's prayer breakfast on Tuesday morning," Todd said enthusiastically. "Did I tell you that?"

Their weekend together had flown by, and Todd and Christy were now chugging down the freeway on their way to Christy's house.

"I think my aunt enjoyed church this morning a little more than she did a couple weeks ago. At least she wasn't as critical. Uncle Bob said he liked it," Christy said. Her voice quavered as they went over a rough spot on the freeway. Gus passed every bump along to his passengers. "You have a great church. I think they would be comfortable there, if they decided to be involved."

"Hopefully not too comfortable," Todd said. "We want them to squirm when the reality of heaven and hell is presented. They need to get saved, not just churched."

Christy agreed. They drove on down the freeway, each enveloped in private thoughts. It had been a difficult weekend for Christy ever since Todd had made his announcement on the beach. Todd seemed normal, relaxed, and content. Christy hadn't yet found the peace he had.

Last night her sleep had been sparse. What little sleep she did get was punctuated by fitful dreams. The worst was a nightmare she had had once before, and in that same room.

It was during the summer of the year she gave her heart to the Lord, just before she had made that big decision. She had dreamed she was in the ocean and seaweed had become tangled around her legs and in her hair, pulling her farther and farther down to the bottom of the ocean. That's when the dream had ended the first time she had dreamed it.

But last night it had kept going. She had struggled against the seaweed, pulling and kicking. But she rapidly ran out of air. Then she had heard a voice say, "Let go." She relaxed, and immediately she was released, and her body had floated to the surface, where she drew in the sweet, fresh air.

Christy didn't know what it meant.

*Maybe what's bothering me is that we haven't talked about the prom. I have to know by tomorrow, since the prom is only two weeks away. Once we decide, I'll feel more settled and secure.*

Christy tried to think of how to bring up the subject. She could talk to Todd about anything. Why did she feel so tongue-tied about this?

Todd talked a little about school ending next week for him, and how he needed to find a summer job. "I might even take a class or two in summer school, since I'm not going anywhere."

Christy thought she detected a hint of sadness or disappointment in his voice. But then, summer school never sounded interesting to Christy.

Anxious to keep the plans for their future together headed in a positive direction, Christy said, "I feel relieved about finally deciding to go to Palomar in the fall. I'll still be at home, which will save money. I'll still work at the pet store, and we'll have lots of time to spend together. I think Katie's going to Palomar, too."

"Cool," Todd said calmly. "It's going to be great being to-gether this summer, isn't it? Long, sunny days on the beach."

Suddenly Todd turned off the freeway. "I have an idea. Let's go down to the beach and watch the sunset. If we hurry, we can make it."

He turned right and then left and then left again as if he knew where he was going. Todd had told Christy before that there was a favorite spot for surfers somewhere along here.

They pulled into San Clemente State Beach and stopped at the small booth where a uniformed park ranger checked cars in and out. Fees were posted on the window for day use, camping, etc.

"How much will it cost for us to go down and watch the sun-set?" Todd asked.

The ranger pushed up his wire-rimmed glasses and glanced at Todd, then smiled at Christy. "For you two, how about free?"

"Cool," Todd said.

"Here, let me give you a half-hour pass. Stick it on your win-dow."

"Thanks," Todd said, and he gave the ranger a Hawaiian surfer "hang loose" gesture. The ranger returned the universal sign, and Gus puttered into the campground.

"This is a great place to go camping," Todd observed. "We should get a bunch of us together this summer and rent a spot for a week."

"Sounds like fun," Christy said.

"We could have a huge campout the last week of summer. Surf all day. Sing around the campfire at night. Wouldn't that be great! We could call it Summer Fall Out."

Christy had to smile at Todd's enthusiasm. He was definitely a visionary. Yet she wondered if he wasn't trying a little too hard to speak their future into being, to plan his own adventures to take the place of the ones he would have had in Papua New Guinea.

They parked in the day-use lot, and Todd led Christy down a wide but steep dirt trail to the beach.

"It's a long way down there," Christy said. "Is this the only trail?"

"This is the main path," Todd said. "It's the safest way to go."

They passed several people who were walking up, burdened with armloads of beach gear. They all seemed to be huffing and puffing from the climb.

*That's going to be us going back! Good thing we're not carrying beach chairs and surfboards.*

Todd continued to hold Christy's hand when they reached the bottom of the trail. They climbed over a railroad track and down a sand dune before they were actually on the beach.

The sight that greeted them was worth the hike. Mr. Sun was just beginning to dip his sizzling toes into the cool, blue ocean. The sky all around the sun looked like a huge, pastel beach towel lovingly wrapped around him to brace him from the chill of the water.

"It's beautiful," Christy whispered.

Todd wrapped his arm around her. They stood together in silent awe, watching the sunset. All Christy could think of was how this was what she had always wanted, to be held in Todd's arms as well as in his heart.

Just as the last golden drop of sun melted into the ocean, Christy closed her eyes and drew in a deep draught of the sea air.

"Did you know," Todd said softly, "that the setting sun looks so huge from the island of Papua New Guinea that it almost looks as if you're on another planet? I've seen pictures."

Then, as had happened with her reflection in her cup of tea and in her disturbing dream, Christy heard those two piercing words, "Let go."

She knew what she had to do. Turning to face Todd, she said, "Pictures aren't enough for you, Todd. You have to go."

"I will. Someday. Lord willing," he said casually.

"Don't you see, Todd? The Lord is willing. This is your 'someday.' Your opportunity to go on the mission field is now. You have to go."

Their eyes locked in silent communion.

"God has been telling me something, Todd. He's been telling me to let you go. I don't want to, but I need to obey Him."

Todd paused and said, "Maybe I should tell them I can only go for the summer. That way I'll only be gone a few months. A few weeks, really. We'll be back together in the fall."

Christy shook her head. "It can't be like that, Todd. You have to go for as long as God tells you to go. And as long as I've known you, God has been telling you to go. His mark is on your life, Todd. It's obvious. You need to obey him."

"Kilikina," Todd said, grasping Christy by the shoulders, "do you realize what you're saying? If I go, I may never come back."

"I know." Christy's reply was barely a whisper. She reached for the bracelet on her right wrist and released the lock. Then taking Todd's hand, she placed the "Forever" bracelet in his palm and closed his fingers around it.

"Todd," she whispered, forcing the words out, "the Lord bless you and keep you. The Lord make His face to shine upon you and give you His peace. And may you always love Jesus more than anything else. Even more than me."

Todd crumbled to the sand like a man who had been run

through with a sword. Burying his face in his hands, he wept.

Christy stood on wobbly legs. *What have I done? Oh, Father God, why do I have to let him go?*

Slowly lowering her quivering body to the sand beside Todd, Christy cried until all she could taste was the salty tears on her lips.

They drove the rest of the way home in silence. A thick mantle hung over them, entwining them even in their separation. To Christy it seemed like a bad dream. Someone else had let go of Todd. Not her! He wasn't really going to go.

They pulled into Christy's driveway, and Todd turned off the motor. Without saying anything, he got out of Gus and came around to Christy's side to open the door for her. She stepped down and waited while he grabbed her luggage from the backseat. They walked to the front door.

Todd stopped her under the trellis of wildly fragrant white jasmine. With tears in his eyes, he said in a hoarse voice, "I'm keeping this." He lifted his hand to reveal the "Forever" bracelet looped between his fingers. "If God ever brings us together again in this world, I'm putting this back on your wrist, and that time, my Kilikina, it will stay on forever."

He stared at her through blurry eyes for a long minute, and then without a hug, a kiss, or even a good-bye, Todd turned to go. He walked away and never looked back.

The next day Christy stayed home from school. Her mom understood and let her have the day to cry alone. That's all she did. The more she cried, the more she hurt and the more utterly exhausted she felt.

At about four o'clock there was a gentle tap on her bedroom door. "Hi," Katie said, poking her head inside. "I heard. Doug called me this morning."

She sat down on the side of Christy's bed and with extra tenderness said, "I'm sorry, Christy."

"I can't believe I did it, Katie. Why did I? I keep going over the whole thing in my mind, and I think I must be crazy."

"Weird," Katie corrected her. "Remember? God is weird. We are tweaked. Whenever you do something weird, you're becoming a little more godly. And believe me, what you did was weird!"

Christy reached for a tissue and dabbed her swollen eyes.

"Doug said Todd told him last night that you loved him enough to let him go and that you motivated him to obey God's call when he was ready to forget it. That's incredible, Christy. That's like that verse about there being no greater love than to lay down your life for your friend. I don't know how you did it. I couldn't have."

"What do you mean? You did. You're the one who broke up with Michael, remember?"

"That was different."

"I don't know, Katie. A broken heart is a broken heart."

"If I hurt so much over Michael, I can't imagine how much you must be hurting over Todd. What can I do?"

"Nothing. Tell me I did the right thing."

Katie let out a laugh. "How can you have any doubts? Of course you did the right thing! You gave nobility a face, Christy."

"Nobility a what?" Christy propped herself up on her arm and scrutinized Katie's expression.

Katie smiled. "Can I just say, yes, Christina Juliet Miller, you did the right thing. You gave God a gift: Todd, free and clear. And there's one thing I know for sure. You can never out-give God. I can't wait to see what God is going to give you!"

"I wish I could have your optimism, Katie."

"You will. It just takes a little time. What's that bit of wisdom you told me several weeks ago? Oh, yes. The feelings don't come in the same envelope. They'll catch up. Until then, here's Doug's CD. It'll help. My favorite song is number seven. It's a good song to cry along with."

"Thanks. You know, Katie, I keep thinking what I had with Todd wasn't real. It was too perfect. He was too perfect. It was a sort of dream and now it's time for me to wake up and grow up. I'm a different person now at seventeen than I was when I met him. But I'm still too young to be as serious as I was becoming with him. This is all probably for the best."

"Keep telling yourself stuff like that," Katie said with a knowing smile. "The only part I'll agree with for now is that with God, things do tend to turn out for the best. Think you'll be back in school tomorrow?"

"Yes, I have a final in Spanish. Thanks for coming over."

Katie gave Christy a hug and said, "That's what best friends are for. Now listen, I'm going to pick you up for school tomorrow morning. Wear something you really like so you'll feel good about yourself. I'll bring an extra Twinkie for you for lunch."

Katie kept her word, and at lunch she presented Christy with a Twinkie.

"I thought you were done with Twinkies," Christy said.

"Not completely. I have to admit I'm still trying to find a balance between Twinkies and Tofu."

Christy laughed.

"Did I tell you that Fred was at church again yesterday?" Katie asked. "He bought himself a Bible, and I saw him carrying it to school today. Isn't that incredible? Who would have ever guessed?"

"Katie," Christy asked cautiously, "are you really, truly over

Michael? You seem to be doing so well, but are the feelings really gone?"

Katie turned solemn. "Maybe I'm still working on a balance there, too. I don't think the feelings will ever be gone completely. It's still hard when I see him, even though I know I did the right thing. Remember when we talked about being in love? I think what we decided is true. You can be in love with someone and yet never marry him. A little part of that person will always be hidden somewhere in a secret garden deep inside your heart."

As Katie spoke, the tears welled up in Christy's eyes. It still hurt so much.

"The thing is, Christy, I never compromised my standards or morals with Michael, and so in that area, I have no regrets. You should never have any regrets with Todd, either. You loved him. Face it, you always will. Now go on with your life. God is near to the brokenhearted, and it just so happens that you and I both qualify for that position."

Between her tears and her Twinkie, Christy forced a smile.

"And," Katie added, holding her head high, "I just so happen to think that being near to God is a wonderfully safe place to be."

Christy thought of Katie's words often as she went through the motions of life that week. Nights were the hardest. She lay awake for long hours in the darkness, exhausting her imagination as she hoped her circumstances would change and fighting off the unanswerable questions. Whenever the phone rang, her heart froze. Each day she checked the mail. But Todd had never written to her before. He wouldn't now. And he wouldn't call, either. He was gone for good.

# CHAPTER FOURTEEN

# *The Secret Revealed*

Christy made it through the weekend with Katie's help and even went to church on Sunday. Fred sat with them during the service. Afterward they walked out to the church parking lot together, and Fred followed Christy to her car.

Right in front of her parents and her brother, he said, "Christy, as you know, the senior prom is this Friday. I would be honored if you would go with me."

Christy had to give the guy credit for perseverance. "Thanks for asking me, Fred. I really mean that. I just can't go. Not with you. Not with anyone. You need to find someone fun to go with and have a great time. You deserve it."

Fred hung his head and said, "I guess I can take a hint." With that, he left.

A short time after they had reached home, Katie called. "Go ahead. Guess," she said.

"Guess what?"

"Guess what I'm doing this Friday?"

"I give up."

"I'm going to the prom. With Fred."

There was complete silence.

"Well?" Katie prodded.

Christy burst out laughing. It was the first time in more than a week that she had laughed, and it felt good.

"I think it's great. You'll have so much fun!"

"At least he's a Christian," Katie said. "That's a step in the right direction for me."

"He'll treat you like a queen," Christy predicted. "I'm glad you're going with him. Fred deserves the best, and that's what you are."

It wasn't until that night that Christy felt the impact of Katie's call. As long as they were both staying home from the prom, it felt okay. The two of them could rent old movies and commiserate. Now Katie had a date, and it was a date with someone who had initially asked Christy.

On Thursday night a phone call came for Christy. It was Doug.

"How are you doing?" he asked tenderly.

"Sometimes okay, other times not so okay," she answered.

"Would you be willing to do me a favor?" Doug asked. "Would you let me take you out to dinner tomorrow night? You see, I'm at the airport right now, and Todd just left. I feel as if I lost my best friend, and I was wondering if you could cheer me up."

Something inside Christy froze all over again at the news that Todd was gone. All her fantasies of Todd not really leaving disappeared. She felt the bitter sting of reality.

"You would have to wear something nice," Doug was saying. "The restaurant I'd like to go to is kind of fancy. So how about it? Could you do me this one favor?"

"All right," Christy said. That was about the extent of the words she could find.

"Awesome," Doug said. "I'll pick you up at 6:30, okay?"

"Okay. Bye."

Christy crawled into bed, still feeling numb, and cried herself to sleep.

The next morning she woke up feeling almost relieved. As long as Todd was still in California, she had held on to some thin strands of hope that something would change. Now he was gone. Tonight was the prom, and although she wasn't going, she would be dressing up and having dinner with Doug at a nice restaurant. That wasn't such a bad thing.

She left school at noon and went to Katie's house to help her dress for the prom. Katie seemed so excited. But after Christy finished applying Katie's makeup, Katie turned somber.

"You know," she said, examining her image in the mirror, "I've been wondering if Michael will be there tonight. I really wish I was going with him instead of Fred. I did spend nearly all of my senior year with him."

Christy cast an understanding smile at Katie's pretty reflection. "I know exactly what you're feeling."

"You wish you were going out with Todd tonight instead of Mr. Counselor-to-All-Brokenhearted-Women, don't you?"

"Well, yes, but . . ."

"But you have to take what you can get, right?" Katie said.

"Something like that."

Katie turned and faced Christy, examining her through narrowed green eyes. Christy knew Katie was looking for something that couldn't be found on the surface. "Do you think Todd is going to come back? Or do you think he's really gone for good?"

Christy couldn't turn from her friend's intense gaze, so she met it head-on and let Katie see the tears in her eyes. "Yes," Christy said, "I think he's really gone. For good."

Tears welled up in Katie's eyes as she said, "I'm so sorry, Christy."

Forcing a smile, Christy said, "Don't you dare start to cry, Katie! You'll ruin the perfect job I did on your makeup."

Her expression still serious, Katie said, "You did the right thing, Christy. God will have someone else for you. I know I didn't want to hear that right after Michael, but I believe it now. For both of us. God has a couple of peculiar treasures, like that Bible verse says, for us. What do you think?"

A giggle bubbled up inside of Christy, and she said, "I think if you're looking for peculiar, look no farther! Fred definitely qualifies."

Katie laughed and said in a game-show-host voice, "The qualifications are 'peculiar' and 'treasure.' Contestants who only fall into one category and not both are automatically disqualified."

Christy laughed and said, "And maybe Fred does qualify."

She was still smiling ten minutes later when she left Katie's to hurry home and begin her own beautification ritual. She had to admit, it was kind of exciting and mysterious to think of who her peculiar treasure might be if it wasn't Todd.

Humming to herself, Christy showered and washed, dried, and curled her hair. When she combed it out, she started playing with it, trying to come up with a new hair-style. Something fun and different. She needed a fresh start. She ended up taking two small portions of her hair from right behind each ear and braiding them. Then taking the two braids and crisscrossing them over the top of her head and securing the ends with hidden bobby pins, she created a hair headband. It looked kind of cute, she decided.

Choosing a dress was easy. Aunt Marti had bought one for her before Christmas, assuming she would have lots of Christmas parties and dances to go to. In the end, Christy had only worn it on Christmas Eve when her family went to the candlelight service at church. It was black velvet, and she liked the way it fit.

Doug arrived right at 6:30, wearing a striking black suit. He handed her a corsage and said, "If you don't want to wear it, that's okay. You can just hold it if you want. It smells nice."

Christy lifted the white gardenia from the plastic box and sniffed its rich, sweet fragrance.

"I do want to wear it," Christy said. "Right here so I can smell it all night."

Doug pinned on the corsage, and with his little-boy grin lighting up his face, he said, "You look absolutely gorgeous. Did you know that?"

Christy felt herself blush, mostly because her parents were standing close enough to hear Doug's compliment.

She felt a little awkward when her mom wanted to take pictures, and Christy wasn't sure what to do with her hands. She ended up clutching her beaded purse in front of her with her hands crossed at the wrists. Doug stood next to her but didn't touch her. It all felt a little strange, a little like going out on a first date.

But it was a nice awkwardness. Much nicer than staying at home alone on prom night.

Doug helped Christy up into the cab of his yellow Toyota truck and apologized for not renting a limo. Christy laughed and said she felt more at home in his truck anyway.

All the way to the restaurant in San Diego, Doug and Christy reminisced about the things they had done together over the past three years. Doug was with Todd the day Christy met him on the beach at Newport. A wild wave had seized her gangly fourteen-year-old frame and had tumbled her ashore, draped with sea-weed, right at Doug and Todd's feet. It was Doug's body board she had then used to master the waves that had dumped her onto the beach.

"I'll never forget the night we had a campfire on the beach," Doug said. "We were all going around the circle praying, and you were sitting next to me. In your prayer you thanked God for coming into your life. That was the first any of us knew you had become a Christian."

"That was the first time I ever had the wind nearly knocked out of me by one of your hugs!" Christy said. "Oh, and remember the time you came over to my aunt and uncle's, and when I answered the door with that basketful of laundry, I tripped and you and I both ended up in a tumble with all my dirty clothes?"

Doug laughed. "Do you remember when you and Katie came down to San Diego, and we were doing the dishes at Stephanie's apartment? We were throwing something up on the ceiling."

"It was that little Mr. Gizmo you got out of the cereal box," Christy said.

"All I remember is it dropped off the ceiling into your hair."

"That was a fun time," Christy agreed. "And remember the houseboat trip when you went jet skiing with that girl, Natalie? And then a couple of weeks later Katie and Michael tried to set you up at the pet store. Michael said he had come to defend his sister's honor, and his sister was supposedly Natalie?"

Doug nodded as he drove into the Mission Bay area of San Diego. "But that wasn't such a great memory. I accidentally knocked you nearly unconscious."

"It wasn't your fault," Christy said. "It's funny now."

She realized they had been talking and laughing the whole way. She felt unexpectedly lighthearted.

"What about that time," Doug continued, "when we all went ice skating, and you skated with me to make Todd jealous, and

Todd ended up skating with those two junior high girls?"

"Wait a minute. You knew I was trying to make Todd jealous?"

"Christy," Doug said, shooting her a knowing glance, "yeah. And did you know I was trying to make Todd jealous that time I buried my nose in your hair to smell your green apple perm, right when Todd drove by?"

Christy was shocked. "You did that on purpose?"

"Not at first. I really was only going to sniff your hair. Then when I heard ol' Gus chugging down the street, I decided to linger a little longer."

"You beast!" Christy said, playfully swatting Doug with her purse.

"Oh, that's nothing," Doug said. "My favorite was being your valet when Rick took you to the Villa Nova. I loved the look on his face when I gave you a hug."

"I forgot about that night," Christy said. "Did you know that Rick actually stole the bracelet Todd gave me and hocked it at a jeweler's? Did he ever tell you that when you were roommates last year? I paid every week to get it back. Well, that is until some mystery guy went into the jeweler's and paid more than a hundred bucks for me to get it back."

"Yeah, I knew that," Doug said, his voice quieting down.

Christy's heart stopped. For some reason Doug's response made her blurt out, "It was you."

Doug looked straight ahead and kept driving.

"All the jeweler would tell me was it was some guy. And it was you, wasn't it, Doug?"

"Yep. It was me. You weren't ever supposed to find out."

"Why?" Christy asked, still overwhelmed at Doug's kindness, not only with the bracelet but also in all the other situations they had been reminiscing about. And he had been so sweet and understanding with Katie at Disneyland. Not to mention being so nice to her tonight.

Doug pulled off the freeway and stopped at a red light. "Christy, do you remember when we went to the Rose Parade, and you asked if I was just being nice to you because Todd asked me to keep an eye on you?"

She sort of remembered. Doug seemed to be studying her expression before giving her his explanation.

"I guess," she said.

Doug looked away and let out a deep breath. "Well," he said, his cheerful disposition blowing away the momentary dark clouds, "let's just say I knew how much that bracelet meant to you."

"Thanks, Doug" was all Christy could find to say as he pulled into the parking lot of a gorgeous restaurant that looked like an old clipper ship. "I appreciate you being here for me, especially tonight. You're a very special friend."

"A very special friend," Doug muttered. "Just friends."

"What?" Christy asked, not sure she had heard what he said.

Doug turned off the engine. "Nothing," he said. "Enough of the serious stuff. Let's have some fun."

Doug came around and opened the door. Taking Christy's hand, he helped her down from the truck. "Think of tonight as your very own private prom night with your special friend. And enjoy every minute of it, okay?"

"I will, Doug. I will."

As Doug and Christy walked arm in arm into the restaurant, a smile tiptoed onto Christy's lips. She felt a peculiar happiness, but she wasn't sure why. All she knew was that deep inside, the forever part of her heart was still very much alive.

# Don't Miss These Captivating Stories in
## THE CHRISTY MILLER SERIES

# THE SIERRA JENSEN SERIES

If you've enjoyed reading about Christy Miller,
you'll love reading about Christy's friend Sierra Jensen.

**#1 • Only You, Sierra**
When her family moves to another state, Sierra dreads going to a new high school—until she meets Paul.

**#2 • In Your Dreams**
Just when events in Sierra's life start to look up—she even gets asked out on a date—Sierra runs into Paul.

**#3 • Don't You Wish**
Sierra is excited about visiting Christy Miller in California during Easter break. Unfortunately, her sister, Tawni, decides to go with her.

**#4 • Close Your Eyes**
Sierra experiences a sticky situation when Paul comes over for dinner and Randy shows up at the same time.

**#5 • Without A Doubt**
When handsome Drake reveals his interest in Sierra, life gets complicated.

**#6 • With This Ring**
Sierra couldn't be happier when she goes to Southern California to join Christy Miller and their friends for Doug and Tracy's wedding.

**#7 • Open Your Heart**
When Sierra's friend Christy Miller receives a scholarship from a university in Switzerland, she invites Sierra to go with her and Aunt Marti to visit the school.

**#8 • Time Will Tell**
After an exciting summer in Southern California and Switzerland, Sierra returns home to several unsettled relationships.

**#9 • Now Picture This**
When Sierra and Paul start corresponding, she imagines him as her boyfriend and soon begins neglecting her family and friends.

**#10 • Hold On Tight**
Sierra joins her brother and several friends on a road trip to Southern California to visit potential colleges.

**#11 • Closer Than Ever**
When Paul doesn't show up for her graduation party and news comes that a flight from London has crashed, Sierra frantically worries about the future.

**#12 • Take My Hand**
A costly misunderstanding leaves Sierra anxious as she says goodbye to Portland and heads off to California for her freshman year of college.

# A Promise Is Forever

# A Promise Is Forever

## ROBIN JONES GUNN

**BETHANY HOUSE PUBLISHERS**
MINNEAPOLIS, MINNESOTA 55438

*A Promise Is Forever*
Revised edition 1999
Copyright © 1994, 1999
Robin Jones Gunn

Edited by Janet Kobobel Grant
Cover illustration and design by the Lookout Design Group

Unless otherwise identified, Scripture quotations are from the HOLY
BIBLE, NEW INTERNATIONAL VERSION®. Copyright © 1973,
1978, 1984 by International Bible Society. Used by permission of
Zondervan Publishing House. All rights reserved. The "NIV" and
"New International Version" trademarks are registered in the United
States Patent and Trademark Office by International Bible Society. Use
of either trademark requires the permission of International Bible
Society.

This story is a work of fiction. All characters and events are the product
of the author's imagination. Any resemblance to any person, living or
dead, is coincidental. Text has been revised and updated by the author.

International copyright secured. All rights reserved.

A Focus on the Family book published by Bethany House Publishers
A Ministry of Bethany Fellowship International
11400 Hampshire Avenue South
Minneapolis, Minnesota 55438
www.bethanyhouse.com

Printed in the United States of America by
Bethany Press International, Minneapolis, Minnesota 55438

---

**Library of Congress Cataloging-in-Publication Data**

Gunn, Robin Jones, 1955–
    A promise is forever / by Robin Jones Gunn.
        p.   cm. — (The Christy Miller series; 12)
        Summary: Eighteen-year-old Christy Miller goes on a missionary
trip to Europe with her friends Katie and Doug and is reunited with her
old boyfriend Todd.
        ISBN 1–56179–733–2
        [1. Missionaries—Fiction.   2. Christian life—Fiction.
3. Friendship—Fiction.]   I. Title.   II. Series:  Gunn, Robin Jones,
1955–      Christy Miller series ; 12.
PZ7.G972Pr      1994
[Fic]—dc20                                                      94–19929
                                                                    CIP
                                                                    AC

---

99  00  01  02  03  04  05 / 15  14  13  12  11  10  9  8  7  6  5  4  3  2

*To Ross, young Ross, and Rachel,*
*my wonderful family.*
*I hold the three of you in my heart—forever.*

# Contents

# Acknowledgments

Writing this series has been a great joy to me. Many "peculiar treasures" have joined me in this adventure, and I'd like to say thanks to all of you.

Thanks to my friends at Focus: Janet, Beverly, Rolf, Al, Gwen, Nancy, Bruce, and David.

Thanks to my friends in Great Britain: Noel, Linda, Andrea, Robin, Charles, Jennie, Avril, Ruby, Norman, Lynn, and Mark.

Thanks to my friends in other parts of Europe: Merja, Satu, Leo, Mike, Stephanie, Jakobs, Vija, Mary, Donna, and Wendy Lee.

Thanks to all the young princesses around the world who have become friends with Christy Miller and have written me so many encouraging letters.

And, above all, thanks to the Author and Finisher of my faith, who was and is and is to come.

# CHAPTER ONE

# *The Adventure Begins*

"Do you think we're going to make it?" Christy Miller breathlessly asked her best friend, Katie, as the airport tram rumbled toward the terminal.

"We have to make it!" Katie said, looping her backpack over her shoulder. "The very second this tram comes to a stop, we're out of here. Grab your bag so we can be the first ones off."

Christy pulled her black shoulder bag off the luggage rack and moved closer to the tram door, right behind her determined, red-headed friend. "Do you remember which gate we're supposed to go to?"

"Fifty-four," Katie called over her shoulder just as they came to a bumpy stop. The dozen or so other passengers rose to their feet. "Come on!" Katie flew out the door with long-legged Christy right behind her. They trotted across the runway asphalt at San Francisco International Airport and took the terminal's steps two at a time.

"This is Gate 87," Christy said, scanning the signs above them as they entered the building.

"Which way to gate 54?" Katie loudly called out so anyone nearby could hear.

"At the end of this concourse turn left," a uniformed desk clerk responded. "Go past concourse E and keep going until you reach the International Central Terminal."

Christy was about to ask for clearer directions, but Katie was already hustling her way through the crowds. "Wait!" Christy yelled, and she hurried to catch up.

It was bad enough their flight from the Orange County airport had been delayed more than an hour. She didn't need to be separated from Katie and miss their flight to London.

"We only have twenty minutes!" Katie said as Christy fell into step with her. "Doug was right. We should have taken that earlier flight with Tracy. This is crazy!"

"I hope Doug made his flight up from San Diego okay," Christy puffed. Her hair was tangled in the shoulder strap of her black bag. She yanked it off her right shoulder, and a few long, nutmeg strands came with it. "Ouch!"

"Left here," Katie directed at the end of the concourse. She broke into a jog, her green backpack bobbing up and down as she athletically maneuvered her way through the crowds as if she were running an obstacle course. Christy fell in line behind her, keeping her eyes on the bobbing green backpack.

*This is impossible. We're never going to make it. I can't believe I let Katie talk me into another one of her crazy adventures!*

Katie stopped in front of an opening to another concourse. "Is this the international terminal?" she asked a man in a business suit.

He shrugged and kept walking. Katie approached another man stepping off the escalator.

"Keep going that way. All the way to the end."

"Thanks." Katie burst into a full run. All Christy could do was follow. She felt the perspiration bead up on her forehead and wished she hadn't worn so many layers.

They had been instructed by the missionary organization in England to dress warmly for this January outreach trip, but right now Christy wished she had packed her coat instead of worn it. Her shoulder bag felt as if it weighed a hundred pounds, and she wished she had taken Katie's advice and brought a backpack instead. What else had she miscalculated? Was this whole trip a mistake?

"Come on!" Katie yelled over her shoulder when she noticed that Christy had fallen behind.

With one last burst of adrenaline, Christy pushed herself to catch up with Katie, fully aware that in this whole throng of travelers, they were the only ones running.

"Doug!" Christy heard Katie yell. "Over here!"

Doug stood by the entrance of the international concourse, head and shoulders above the rest of the crowd. His usually boyish grin was replaced by a frown, which Christy had rarely seen in the few months they had been dating. She wanted to fall into his arms and feel one of his reassuring hugs, but there was no time.

"Quick!" Doug said. "Get in line for the metal detector. Over there. Hurry! Our plane leaves in five minutes!"

Katie and Christy immediately followed his instructions and passed through the archway, fortunately without setting off any alarms.

"Tickets, please," the woman behind the check-in counter said. She looked unruffled. The girls scrambled for their tickets and passports. The attendant tore off a portion of their tickets and said, "Gate 54. To the right. They've already boarded."

"Come on, you guys, let's go!" Doug's coach-like holler was a stark contrast to the ticket agent's relaxed attitude.

Christy realized that Tracy must be sitting alone on the plane, waiting for them. They *had* to make this flight. The three of them ran to the gate just as the door began to close.

"Wait!" Doug sprinted ahead. "We're on this flight."

The man held the door open with his foot as another attendant reached for their tickets and quickly scanned them. "You just made it."

Only a few more pounding paces, and they were on the plane.

"I can't believe this," Christy said under her breath. She handed the flight attendant her ticket stub.

"Your seat is in row 34. That's all the way in the back."

"Naturally," Katie muttered. Clutching her backpack in front of her, she led the way down the narrow airplane aisle.

Christy was the first to spot petite Tracy, planted in the middle of row 34. Her heart-shaped face had taken on a stern, defender-of-the-seats look.

"That was *not* funny, you guys," Tracy said, scrunching up her delicate nose and trying not to look mean or terrified or both. "I almost got off the plane! I decided if you guys didn't show up in two more minutes, I was going to get off the plane. No way was I going to fly to London by myself!"

"We made it. A bit on the close side, I'd say." Doug popped open the overhead compartment and stuffed Katie and Christy's bags in next to his and Tracy's.

"You'll need to take a seat, please, sir," the flight attendant said with a definite British accent.

Doug lowered himself into the aisle seat next to Christy. Katie, on the other side of her, began to fill Tracy and Doug in on their morning's delay. Christy closed her eyes and drew in a deep breath. She felt like crying. Or laughing. Or something. Then she felt Doug's strong hand covering hers.

"You okay?" he asked softly.

Christy opened her eyes and looked into Doug's gentle, understanding face. "That was too close," she said. She was still thinking, *This is too much. This is crazy. Why am I here?*

"We made it. We're on our way to England," Doug said, wiping the perspiration from his forehead with the back of his shirt sleeve. The boyish grin returned. "Can you believe this?"

"No," Christy whispered, feeling Doug's hand squeeze hers. "I can't. It all happened so fast."

"Yeah, but we made it," Doug pointed out as the flight attendants began their presentation on the aircraft's safety features. "I wish more people from the God Lovers' group could have come. I'm glad the four of us made it."

"Doug, four and a half weeks was not exactly a long time for everyone to raise support and get passports and everything," Christy said. "If we would have waited until the summer to do this outreach, I'm sure a lot more people could have come."

Doug shrugged his broad shoulders. "I figure if the four of us return with great reports of the trip, everyone will want to go this summer, and we can do it all over again."

"If we do, I'm definitely taking the early morning flight like Tracy did, even if it does mean getting up at five in the morning! You were right about that one." Christy pulled off her coat and fanned her red face with her hand.

Doug smiled. She could tell he liked being told he was right. Not in an arrogant way, but in a big brother, Doug way.

The plane was now taxiing down the runway, about to take off.

"Did the mission send you the final information?" Christy asked. "That's the only part my parents were concerned about. I gave them the address we'll be at the first two nights in London and the place we'll have our training. But I think they were concerned I didn't know where our outreach assignment would be for the last two weeks of the trip."

"All I received from the mission in the fax yesterday were directions on how to get to Carnforth Hall for the week of training. Don't worry," Doug said as the nose of the plane tilted up and they took off into the wild blue yonder. "God will direct our paths. These next three weeks will be an awesome chance for us to trust Him."

Christy had to smile. She had known Doug since she was fourteen. In those four and a half years, he had hardly changed. As a matter of fact, he was saying "awesome" the day she had met him. He had grown taller and more muscular, but still, he looked the same, acted the same, and even dressed about the same.

But in those years Christy had changed a lot. She had grown up. Now eighteen and a half and a college freshman, she felt as if she were almost the same age as Doug, a twenty-three-year-old with only eight credits to go before completing his bachelor's degree in business.

"Doug," Tracy asked, leaning past Katie and Christy, "did you receive a confirmation for the Bed and Breakfast we're supposed to stay at in London tonight?"

"Yep."

"And did you get the train tickets for us to Carnforth Hall?"

"We buy them at the airport. I have all the information."

"What about the schedule?" Katie asked. "When do we have to be at Carnforth?"

"Friday afternoon."

"Did you get that tour book of London?" Tracy asked. "There's so much to see. How are we going to get to it all in only two days?"

"Will you guys relax?" Doug said. "I've got it covered. Once they turn off the seat belt sign, I'll get my tour book down and we'll make some plans."

Christy felt as if all she had been doing for the past month was make plans. It still amazed her that her parents had agreed to let her spend her semester break with her three closest friends on the other side of the world.

It was even more amazing that Katie's parents had agreed. They had never been in favor of her taking off on trips with the church youth group. But they saw it more as a cultural experience than a missions trip. Tracy and Doug were both older than Katie and Christy, and they both came from very supportive families. Christy's parents were supportive, of course, although they tended to be a little more on the protective side.

Her dad's final words last night had been, "I hope this trip helps you figure out what you want to do with your life. You know your mother and I will support you, whatever you decide. But you need to know it's time for you to decide."

At the time she had bristled at his words. Making decisions had never been her strong point. Christy had made plenty of decisions she had regretted later. The biggest one had to be last spring when she broke up with Todd, Doug's best friend. Todd had a once-in-a-lifetime opportunity before him, and Christy didn't want to hold him back. At the time, she knew it was the right thing to do, but it had taken her months to recover from the loss.

It had taken Doug even longer to convince Christy that she should go out with him. She had wavered in her decision all summer, and it was October before she finally agreed to be Doug's girlfriend.

The funny part was, nothing much had changed between

them during the three months they had been going together. They were close friends, but they always had been. He held her hand more, but he never kissed her. It was a comfortable, secure friendship, and one her parents felt good enough about to let their daughter fly to Europe with Doug.

Doug clicked open his seat belt, stood, and reached for the tour books in his backpack. For the next hour, the four of them made big plans about all they would see in London. To Christy, it still seemed like a dream.

Dinner was served—sliced beef with gravy, peas, fruit salad, and a piece of spice cake with chopped nuts, which she gave to Doug. Nuts had never been Christy's favorite. Tea was served with milk and sugar, and Christy sipped at the steaming brew, feeling grown-up and important. Maybe she could do this international thing after all.

As soon as their tray tables were cleared, the movie began. Christy couldn't see over the head of the guy in front of her, so she gave up on the movie and asked Doug to hand her bag to her from the overhead bin. She found her journal and began to write.

*The adventure begins! I'm on the plane now, between Doug and Katie, and we are actually flying to England. I still can't believe this. I feel as if everything in my life has been rushing past me these last few months, and I'm caught up in the current.*

*My dad was right in urging me to make some decisions about the future. I don't know what I want to be. I don't know if I like being grown-up. And when did that happen, anyhow? I must be grown-up if I'm on my way to England. I can't believe I'm in college. Sometimes I feel so independent, and other times I wish I could go back to the simpler days when I would spend the whole day lying on the beach, doing nothing but watch Todd surf. Oops. I did it again; I mentioned the "T" word. I wasn't going to do that anymore. I know that . . .*

"The 'T' word?" Katie asked, looking at the page.

Christy snapped her diary shut. "I thought you were watching the movie," she whispered harshly. She glanced at Doug. He had on his headset and seemed caught up in the action on the small screen in front of them.

"I can't believe you still even think about the 'T' word!" Katie whispered back. "It's been months—almost a year—since he left. The guy is gone. Long gone. Ancient history. You have absolutely no contact with him. He's most likely on some mosquito-infested tropical island serving God and loving it. If he still wanted you in his life, he would have written you. But then he's never written to you, has he, Christy? Ever. In your whole life. Think about it."

"Have you forgotten about the coconut he sent me from Hawaii?"

"Christy," Katie's piercing green eyes looked serious, "I couldn't tell you this if I weren't your best friend."

Christy looked away. She already knew what Katie was going to say. They had had this same conversation at the end of the summer when Katie tried to convince her to let go of Todd's memory and give Doug a fair chance.

"I know," Christy whispered, a tiny tear blurring her vision.

"No, I don't think you know, Chris. Otherwise we wouldn't be having this conversation." Katie sounded stern.

"Can we have it another time, Katie?" Christy said, blinking her blue-green eyes. "What I write in my diary is my business, not yours. You don't know what I'm thinking."

"I can make a pretty good guess."

"So what? I don't remember inviting you into my thoughts!" The instant Christy made the remark, she regretted it. This was not a good way to start off a three-week trip in which she and Katie would be together day and night. Especially when, in her

heart, she knew Katie was right. She knew that part of her growing up and making decisions about her future had been hindered
because she couldn't seem to get over Todd.

"Fine." Katie planted her headphones back over her ears and
fixed her attention on the screen.

Christy reached over and squeezed Katie's arm to get her attention. Katie slowly turned to face Christy and lifted the headset
off one ear.

"I'm sorry," Christy said.

"Don't worry about it. We'll talk later." Katie flashed a smile,
squeezed Christy's arm back, and returned her attention to the
movie.

Christy knew all was forgiven. She also knew Katie would
make sure they talked later.

Glancing over at Doug, Christy wondered if he had heard any
of their conversation. He had always been so patient and understanding with her.

The ultimate proof had been when Christy found out he had
bought back her gold ID bracelet from a jewelry store two years
ago. Todd had given her the bracelet. Then a sort-of-boyfriend,
Rick, had stolen it from Christy and hocked it at a jewelry store
so he could use the money to buy her a clunky silver one that said
"Rick."

Her relationship with Rick had quickly dissolved, and she had
begun to make payments to buy back the gold bracelet. Then one
day the jeweler gave it to her, saying some guy had come in and
paid for it in full.

It wasn't until last spring that Christy had found out Doug
was the one who paid for it. He did it simply out of his love for
Christy. It didn't matter to Doug that the bracelet was given to
Christy by another guy, another guy who just happened to be his

best friend and who had captured Christy's interest from the day she had first met them on the beach at Newport. During the years of friendship that followed for the three of them, Doug always took a backseat to Todd.

Anyone who knew them would be quick to say that Doug had waited patiently for Christy. He had never let his deep feelings for her come out until after she had broken up with Todd and had given the bracelet back to him. Not until Todd was on a plane headed for parts unknown did Doug let his feelings for Christy be known. Even then, he took it slow.

He had to be the most patient guy on the face of the earth. And, as Katie had pointed out last summer, since 1 Corinthians 13 described love as being patient, kind, not jealous, and always looking out for the best interest of others, then Doug must deeply love Christy.

Christy looped her arm through Doug's, which was balanced on the armrest between them, and leaned her head against his shoulder. Doug was a treasure. A treasure she should not take for granted. She knew girls who would do anything to have even a fraction of Doug's attention. And here she had it all. She knew she should appreciate him more.

Doug adjusted his position to make Christy more comfortable. She closed her eyes and told herself again that she was really, truly on an airplane on her way to London with the most wonderful—no, make that the most awesome—guy in the whole world and with her two best friends, Katie and Tracy. This trip would change her life forever. She had no doubt.

She vowed that nothing would ruin this trip for her or for her friends, especially not the memory of an invisible Todd.

CHAPTER TWO

# *Big Ben and Other Famous Stuff*

"Do you think I exchanged enough money?" Katie asked, adjusting the shoulder straps on her backpack.

The four friends stood on the platform with their luggage gathered around their feet. They were waiting for the next underground train to arrive.

"I don't know," Katie continued. "A hundred dollars doesn't look like much when it's turned into pounds. And their money is so weird-looking! It looks like play money."

"Katie," Tracy said softly, leaning closer and making sure the crowd of local people standing around them couldn't hear, "I think it's obvious enough we're tourists without our announcing to all these people how much money we have on us and that we think their money looks weird."

Katie's straight red hair swished as she glanced around, checking out the audience Tracy seemed so concerned about. Quickly changing the subject and lowering her voice just a smidgen, Katie asked, "Are you sure we know which train to take?"

Doug patted the folded map in the pocket of his jacket. "I got us this far, didn't I? I think I can find the hotel. Did you guys keep your tube passes handy? We'll need to run them through the machine again when we leave the station."

"This reminds me of the BART trains in San Francisco," Tracy said softly. "Except those are above ground. Have you guys ever been on BART?"

None of them had.

"This system is slightly older," Doug said. "Did you see in that one tour book that they used to run steam engine trains down here more than a hundred years ago?"

Christy looked up at the rounded ceiling and then at the many large billboard posters scattered across the brick walls of the underground tunnel. She couldn't imagine people and trains being in this same tunnel a hundred years ago.

"Isn't it freaky, you guys," said Katie, "to think that there's a city above us? I don't feel like we're in London yet. Maybe I will when I see one of those red double-decker buses."

Just then a loud rush of air sounded through the dark passageway. A moment later the underground train came to a halt. Before Christy had time to situate her suitcase so she could wheel it onto the train, people began to push toward the open door. Her luggage, with a pop-up handle and wheels, had been a present from her wealthy Aunt Marti.

"Can you get it?" Doug asked as he noticed her struggling.

"Yes, I have it now." Christy pushed her suitcase toward the door, feeling Doug right behind her, prodding her onto the train.

Tracy found a seat inside and plopped down her bag, motioning for Christy or Doug to sit next to her. Katie was behind Doug. Christy sat next to Tracy and didn't notice the doors closing until she heard Katie's loud yelp. They looked up. All they could see was Katie's backside wedged between the two closing doors, keeping it open.

"You guys, help!" Katie yelled.

Christy wanted to burst out laughing but swallowed hard and hurried to help Doug pry open the door. They separated it far enough for Doug to yank Katie and her luggage inside the train just before it started to move.

"Katie, are you okay?" Tracy said. "You could have been killed! What were you thinking?"

"I was thinking I didn't want to get separated from you guys. That seems to be the theme of this trip, doesn't it?" Katie dropped her canvas suitcase on the floor at Christy's feet and held onto a long metal bar next to the seat. "I think we need to make a plan B here, Doug. If I hadn't made it on this train, I would have been completely lost. I don't even know where we're staying! How would I ever have found you guys? We need a little more teamwork."

"You're right," Doug said, reaching for the back of Christy's seat to steady himself as the train picked up speed and jostled them from side to side. The four of them huddled closer together, Christy and Tracy in the seats and Katie and Doug standing above them. Christy felt sure they were a humorous spectacle to all the other passengers.

"Okay," Doug said, assuming his coach voice, "we're staying at the Miles Hampton on Seymore Street. We get off at Hyde Park. It's only a few blocks' walk to the hotel. If you guys need help with your luggage, just tell me. And let's make an agreement that we'll all stick together and look out for each other, okay?"

Doug's "few blocks" turned into more like a few miles. Either that, or they were lost.

"Can I look at the map again?" Katie asked, stopping in front of another row of houses that looked just like the row of houses on the last street they had walked up. "Are you sure this place is a hotel?"

"It's a Bed and Breakfast," Doug said, willingly dropping the canvas luggage he held in both hands and reaching for the map. "My parents stayed there a couple of years ago. They said it was easy to find. Look, here's Seymore Street. What street are we on now?"

Christy parked her rolling suitcase and gladly took the heavy black bag off her shoulder. She couldn't believe how tired she was from walking. For the first time since they began their parade through the streets of London, Christy stopped and drew in the sights around her. Tall, narrow brick houses lined the street. Black taxis drove past them on the "wrong" side of the road. Noisy cars and buses honked their horns. A small, furry dog at the end of his owner's leash barked at them as they walked past. From across the street came the merry sound of a little bell clinking as a woman entered a bakery.

"Uh-oh," Christy said, looking up into the thick, gray sky and lifting her open palm heavenward. "I hope we're almost there because it's starting to rain."

That's when she noticed how cold it was. They had been walking so hard and so fast, she hadn't realized the damp cold was creeping up her legs. Her jeans weren't protection enough against the bitter cold, and her legs began to feel prickly and chilled to the bone.

"This way," Doug said, heading down the street with long, deliberate strides. "Only two more blocks."

This time he was right. And it was a good thing. Just as they huddled under the bright blue canopy over the Miles Hampton door, the mist that had been teasing them for the past two blocks turned into a respectable London downpour.

The door was locked, so Katie rang the door buzzer a couple of times. A rosy-cheeked, white-haired woman peeked at them through the lace curtains drawn across the window in the door. "Who's the impatient one?" she said brightly as she opened the door. "Come in, come in! It won't do to have you catching cold your first day."

It took only a few minutes to check in at the quaint "B and B," as the woman called the Bed and Breakfast. Then they lugged their suitcases up four winding flights of stairs to the top floor, where two rooms awaited them. The girls' room had three twin beds and a separate bathroom with the biggest bathtub Christy had ever seen. The house was old, but it had been nicely restored; the room was clean and fresh. Christy noticed how puffy the flowered bedspreads looked, and she flopped down on the nearest bed.

Tracy did the same, face first on the bed next to Christy. "This pillow is calling my name," Tracy said. "It wants me to stay right here with it all day."

Christy heard the rain tap dancing on their window. She couldn't help but agree with Tracy. After all, it was three in the morning back home; none of them had slept on the plane during the ten-hour flight. A little nap would feel so good.

"Ready, gang?" Katie called, bursting through the door with Doug right behind her. "Let's go see London."

Christy and Tracy groaned.

"You guys definitely got the better of the two rooms," Doug said, surveying their wallpapered surroundings. "My room isn't bad. It just feels more like I'm sleeping in an attic. Slanted ceiling. Kind of squishy. You even have a bathroom."

"You don't?"

"I get to use the one at the end of the hall on the floor below us," Doug said. "I don't mind, really. For the money, this is a great place. Besides, we're not going to hang around here. We've got a city to explore!"

"Doug's right, you guys," Katie said, stepping into the bathroom and running some water in the sink to wash her face. "The worst thing we could do would be to sleep now. We have to stay up all day to trick our internal clocks into thinking it's daytime now and not nighttime. Hey, how do you get warm water out of this thing?"

Doug joined her in the bathroom and demonstrated how to use the sink stopper to fill the sink with hot and cold water at the same time, resulting in warm water.

"You mean only hot water comes out of this side and only cold out of this side? How archaic!"

"I hate to break this to you, Toto, but we're not in Kansas anymore," Doug said, sticking his fingers in the water and sprinkling Katie's face. "This is a very old city. This is a very old house. It would follow that the plumbing would be a little on the archaic side."

Doug dipped his fingers in the sink again and took three steps over to Christy's bed where he sprinkled her. "Wake up! It's time to have some fun."

"Tracy," Christy said, "I think the ceiling is leaking. I feel a drip."

"Yeah, I hear a drip," Tracy agreed.

"Oh, yeah?" Doug said. Before Christy or Tracy realized what was happening, Doug had dunked a hand towel into the full sink and began to wring it out over Tracy's head. She screamed, jumped up, and started to laugh. "Doug! We're not at the beach! You can't go around splashing girls with water in London. It isn't proper!"

They all laughed at Tracy's fake British accent, which she

attempted to employ on the last two sentences.

"Besides, Doug, it's raining out there, and it's so cozy in here," Christy said in a pretend whine.

"I can make it rain inside too!" Doug threatened Christy with his wet hand towel.

"Okay, okay. Let me brush my hair first." Christy traded places with Katie in the bathroom and closed the door behind her. Her reflection in the mirror startled her. Her cheeks were red, and her brown hair lay flat against her head, hanging lifelessly a few inches past her shoulders.

She thought of how cute Tracy's short hair looked. She had cut it short, just below her ears, especially for this trip. Tracy's hair had a lot of natural body and had kept its shape with only a quick brushing when they had landed at Heathrow Airport.

Christy wondered if she should have gotten her hair cut short for the trip too. She knew Doug liked it long. She liked it long. It just looked so blah.

After trying to pull it back with a headband, put it in a ponytail, and quickly braid it, she gave up.

"Are you still alive in there?" Katie asked, knocking on the door.

"My hair is driving me crazy!" Christy said.

"You're going to drive us crazy!" Katie yelled.

"Okay, okay." Christy shook out her mane, washed her face, and stuck a scrunchie in her pocket in case she wanted to try a ponytail later. She opened the bathroom door, ready to go. A bright light flashed in her face.

"Thanks, Christy," Katie said. "You've become my first official photo in London. Let's go see what other funny-looking stuff we can take pictures of."

"Oh, thanks a lot," Christy said, reaching for her coat and

following her friends down the long, winding stairs and into the front lobby.

"I want to get a close-up shot of one of those guards who stands in one place all day and never flinches," Katie said. "Maybe I can get him to give me a little smile."

"Food first," Doug said as they stepped outside, all bundled up and holding their umbrellas high. "We must keep our priorities straight."

The first food they found was, of all things, a Kentucky Fried Chicken restaurant.

"I didn't come all the way to England to eat Kentucky Fried Chicken," Katie said, looking down the street for signs of any other kind of restaurant.

"Come on," Tracy pleaded. "It's only a snack. We'll find some fun English place for lunch. I don't think Doug can hold out much longer."

"Thanks, Trace," Doug said, collapsing his umbrella and stepping inside the all-too-familiar-looking fast-food restaurant.

They all ordered from a lit-up menu above the counter that looked just like one from home. The only difference was the currency.

"That's one pound, forty-five 'P,' miss," the man behind the counter told Christy. Christy handed him a ten-pound note and received a handful of change and a five-pound note. She joined the others at a table by the window.

"Isn't this money weird?" Katie said, examining her change.

"Katie," Tracy said, "didn't we already go over the weird money thing?"

Christy was aware that the elderly couple at the table next to them was watching. She was also aware of how quiet it was for a restaurant full of people. Everyone else seemed to be speaking softly and keeping to themselves.

In comparison, Katie was extraordinarily loud. It bothered Christy. She guessed it was bothering Tracy too. Doug seemed unaffected.

He pulled out his handy-dandy map and pocket-size tour book and stated, "Okay, so we'll see Big Ben first, then the crown jewels at the Tower of London. We take bus 16, I think. No, maybe it's bus 11."

"Let me see that," Katie said, snatching the tour book away from Doug. "Oh, Charles Dickens' house. That would be an interesting tour. Let's go there after the Tower of London."

"It's on the opposite side of town, Katie," Doug said.

"No, it's not. Look, it's right here by . . . oh, you're right. Okay, then let's go to St. Paul's Cathedral. That's only two inches away from the Tower of London."

"Let's just go and see what we can see," Tracy suggested, tossing her trash into a bin that was marked "rubbish."

Christy was glad it wasn't up to her to plot their course or decipher how to get there. She was happy being a follower and letting Katie and Doug be the pioneers.

They hopped on a bus near the Marble Arch that took them to Piccadilly Circus. Doug told them to get off and look for bus 12, which would take them to Parliament and Big Ben.

Riding on the top of the double-decker bus was fun, Christy thought, because she had a good view of the bustling streets below and of the statues and monuments everywhere. What she didn't like was getting off, shivering under her umbrella, and listening to Doug and Katie argue. She also hated feeling lost and confused.

It seemed worse when they got off in front of the huge, architecturally intricate Parliament Building and found that the famous old clock, Big Ben, was so shrouded in fog that it hardly seemed worth the effort to take a picture. Christy did, however. Her camera, a gift last year from Uncle Bob, had served her well during her senior year as a photographer on the yearbook staff. She knew when she returned home she would be glad she had the pictures, even if they were all gray and foggy.

"Well, that was a thrill," Katie said, spinning around and blocking Christy's viewfinder with her umbrella. "What's next?"

Without saying anything to Katie, Christy took a few steps to the right and adjusted her zoom again before snapping a picture of Big Ben. "Why don't you guys all stand there by the fence, and I'll take a picture of you with Parliament in the background?"

The three obliged, umbrellas bumping each other and people passing in front of the camera. Christy snapped the picture, then turned around and snapped a shot of the street behind them with a black taxi and a red bus passing each other in the heavy traffic.

"Do you want to see the River Thames?" Doug asked. "According to this map, it's right over there, beyond that park."

"What's to see?" Katie asked.

"It's a famous river," Doug said. "Come on. Have a little adventure, Katie."

"I *did* have a little adventure. I saw Big Ben. Now I want a *big* adventure. I want to see the jewels and the guards in the big furry hats."

"We're so close to the river," Tracy said. "Maybe we should look at it so we can at least say we saw it."

"Whatever we do, could we take a bus?" Christy asked. "My legs are freezing!" She wished she had taken the time to put on a pair of tights when they were at the hotel. She felt cold. Wet cold. Miserable cold.

"It's only a quick walk to the river," Doug said, taking

Christy's hand. "If we walk fast, you'll warm up. Come on."

Off they went to the river. In Katie's words, the wide, gray, fog-mantled water looked "like Big Ben, only horizontal and without numbers."

They were hoofing it back to catch another bus when Tracy noticed an old, interesting-looking building on their left.

"Let's check the tour book, Doug. I'm sure that's something important," Tracy said.

Christy hated standing still in the drizzle. She stomped her feet to get them warm and to shake the chill off her legs. "You guys," Tracy exclaimed, "that's Westminster Abbey!"

"Great," said Katie. "What's that?"

"It's a very old church," Tracy said, scanning the tour book. "It says here this site was first used as a place of worship in the year A.D. 604. Can you even imagine how old that is? And listen to this: 'Since the eleventh century, the church has been the coronation site of English kings and queens.' We have to see it, you guys. There's a bunch of famous people buried there. Charles Dickens is buried there!"

Katie noticed that the drizzle had let up and closed her umbrella while Tracy was reading. With squinting eyes she moved in for a closer look at Tracy. "Are you serious here, girl? You really want to go look at a bunch of old dead people?"

"This is Westminster Abbey. It's famous, Katie!"

"Well, so was Big Ben. And that turned out to be a real dud!"

"Can I cut in here, you two?" Doug said, closing his umbrella and stepping in between them. "I think we're all pretty tired and hungry. Why don't we find someplace to eat and decide what to do next after we've had some food."

"Great idea," Christy said. "I'm freezing. I think my socks got wet. My feet are numb."

"What do you say, ladies? A nice spot of tea, perhaps?"

They couldn't help but release their tension when they heard Doug try a British accent on his last sentence. Then following their trail back up the road toward Trafalgar Square, the four cold, wet, weary travelers went in search of a quiet little restaurant and a hot cup of tea.

# CHAPTER THREE

# A Cup of Tea

"No wonder the English like tea so much," Christy said, holding a white china cup with both hands. She sipped her tea as if it were warming her to her toes. "If I lived here, I'd be looking for something to warm me up several times a day too."

Katie took her last bite of fish and said, "The vinegar was okay on this fish, but I still like good old American tartar sauce. You want the rest of my fries, Doug?"

"Sure, I'll take your chips," he said, using the British word for fries.

"I have a question," Tracy said. "If they call french fries 'chips,' then what do they call potato chips?"

" 'Crisps,' " their waiter said, reaching to clear Katie's empty plate.

They had stumbled into a quaint-looking restaurant and found a table with four chairs as if it were waiting for them. The waiter had turned out to be friendly. The four orders of fish and chips had come in huge portions with the mushiest green peas Christy had ever seen. She ate about half her fried fish, half her chips, and only a reluctant spoonful of the mushy peas. They tasted the same as they looked.

Doug managed to put away whatever food the girls left, including the peas. Christy decided he must have been born without taste buds. Either that or his bottomless stomach was so demanding it left little room for a discerning palate.

Doug stuck the last few cold chips in his mouth and glanced at his watch. "It's a little after four. What do you think? Should we try to make it to the Tower of London to see the jewels now, or wait until tomorrow?"

"We would have more time tomorrow," Tracy suggested.

"Where did this day go?" Christy asked. "And what day is it, anyhow?"

"Wednesday," Doug said. "It's eight in the morning at home right now. Time to start today."

"Isn't that weird?" Katie said. "At home everyone is just starting this day, and we're almost done with it."

Once again Christy could see Tracy cringing at Katie's loud voice and her declaration of something else that was weird. It bugged Christy, too, but not as much as it seemed to irk Tracy.

"So what do you guys want to do? It'll be dark soon," Doug said.

"Let's see as much as we can," Tracy said. "Even if it's dark. We only have today and tomorrow. We've come all this way and there's so much to see. Would you guys be willing to go back to Westminster Abbey? I'd really like to see it."

"Sure," Doug answered for all of them. "Let's figure out this bill and get out of here."

Christy noticed as they walked briskly down the street toward the ancient Gothic church that Katie was unusually quiet. Tension between Katie and Tracy seemed to be growing, and Christy felt uneasy about it.

Over the years, Doug and Katie had experienced plenty of

friendly conflicts, but through all their tumbles, their friendship always managed to land on its feet. Katie and Doug had a brother-sister kind of esteem for each other.

Tracy and Doug had been close friends even longer than Christy and Tracy. As a matter of fact, Doug and Tracy even dated for a while several years ago. The two of them had remained close friends, and Christy couldn't remember ever hearing either of them saying anything unkind about the other. They seemed to get along in any kind of situation.

But Katie and Tracy had never spent an extended amount of time together. Their personalities were so different, yet so alike. They were both strong, determined women: Katie in an outward, aggressive manner, and Tracy in her gentle, firm, uncompromising way.

Then, as if Tracy sensed the same tension with Katie, she fell back a few steps next to Katie, and Christy heard her say, "I really appreciate you being flexible. I'm looking forward to going to the Tower of London tomorrow. We'll have more time then. I'm sure it'll work out and be much better than trying to go now."

Katie didn't respond at first. Then, as they crossed the street to Westminster Abbey, Christy heard Katie say, "Do you always get your way, Tracy?"

Christy wanted to turn around and scold Katie for saying such a thing, but Doug quickly looped his arm around Christy's shoulders and spoke softly in her ear. "Let the two of them work it out, Chris. Trust me. It's the best way for both of them."

Christy had to trust Doug. There wasn't much she could do. She strained to listen as Tracy, in her gentle yet firm way, told Katie they needed to work together as a team and do what was best for the group.

"Right," Katie responded. "It would help, though, if the

group were making more of the decisions and not just you."

"You're right, Katie. After this, we'll all decide what to do next," Tracy said.

They were at the door of the old stone building, and Christy realized she had hardly paid attention to what the church looked like. She entered solemnly. A sign by the door indicated an admission fee of three pounds.

"Three pounds!" Katie blurted out. "I'm not paying to go inside a church! I'm waiting right here. You guys can go in without me."

"I think the charge is only for a tour, Katie," Doug said quietly. "I don't think we have to pay anything to look around this part."

The four entered the tourist-filled sanctuary with Katie lagging behind. They walked around, quietly observing the statues, memorials, and engravings on the stone floor that identified who was buried beneath their feet.

"Look," Doug said to Christy, pointing to the large letters etched on the floor in front of him. "David Livingstone is buried here. He was that famous missionary to Africa. Did you know that they brought his body back here to England, but they took out his heart and buried it in Africa because that's where his heart was—with the African people? Is that awesome or what?"

Christy wasn't sure it was awesome. *Bizarre* might be a better adjective. It sounded like something Todd would do.

*Todd. Where did that thought come from?*

Christy impulsively reached over, took Doug's hand, and squeezed it tight. "Doug, do you want to be a missionary to some far-off place?"

"You mean like Todd?"

*Is he reading my thoughts? Or is he thinking the same things about Todd that I am?*

"I don't know," Doug said thoughtfully, looking down at the floor once more. "That's why I wanted to come on this outreach. To see if I have what it takes. I'm not like Todd."

"I know," Christy said quickly. "And I don't want you to be. I want you to be Doug. And you are . . ." Now her thoughts seemed scrambled, and she felt angry that she hadn't been able to leave thoughts of Todd back on the airplane. Back in California. Back in her collection of high school memories. Todd had followed both of them to England and once again stood between them. ". . . I just wondered if you had thought much about being a missionary." Christy held Doug's hand tighter. She wanted to think of Doug and only Doug.

"Not really. With my business major I've pictured myself being in the American workforce at some big company and sort of being a missionary to all the lost business people. I don't think I could live overseas."

"Me either," Tracy whispered. Christy hadn't noticed her standing on the other side of Doug. "I mean, this is fun to visit, but I do better in familiar surroundings. What about you, Christy?"

"I don't know. That's why I wanted to come on this trip too. I don't know what I want to do with my life. Or, I guess I should say, I don't know what God wants to do with my life." Saying it aloud sounded even scarier than when she had thought it or written it in her diary. It was like admitting she was lost, aimlessly taking general ed. courses at a junior college and trying to come up with answers for the career counselors who asked what she was interested in. She honestly didn't know.

A uniformed gentleman politely asked if they would like to

take a seat because it was time for evening vespers to begin. Katie
was already sitting in one of the folding chairs set up in the section where they were standing. The three of them joined her, with
Doug taking the initiative and sitting next to Katie.

Within a few minutes a line of choir boys wearing white and
red robes with high white lace collars flowed down the center
aisle, two by two. They stepped right over the David Livingstone
engraved stone on their way to the altar at the front of the chapel.

Christy closed her eyes and breathed in the majesty of the moment as the clear, high voices of the choir danced off the rounded
stone ceiling of this ancient place of worship. During the music
and Bible reading that followed, Christy quietly bowed her head
and worshiped the same awesome God whom people had sought
to worship on this site for more than a thousand years. The
thought sobered her and made her feel a reverence she had never
felt in her church at home in California.

She tried to explain it to her friends the next morning as they
ate breakfast together in the small dining room of their Bed and
Breakfast. Christy sat with her back to a huge fireplace where a
cheery fire crackled and warmed her. Doug seemed to know what
she was saying, and Tracy agreed between bites of crisp toast.
Katie ate silently, studying a tour book and not entering into the
conversation.

Things had not been good between Katie and Tracy that
morning. Katie had washed her hair and had asked to borrow
Tracy's hair dryer.

"Be sure to plug in the adapter first," Tracy said.

Katie had plugged the adapter into one electric outlet and the
hair dryer into another. When she turned on the hair dryer, it
sounded like a lawn mower. In less than ten seconds the dryer
started to spit sparks into their room. Then, with a loud pop,

Tracy's hair dryer had burned out.

Tracy's face had turned deep red as she followed the cord from her dead hair dryer to the outlet and said, "Katie, you're supposed to plug the hair dryer *into* the adapter!"

"How was I supposed to know? All you said was to plug in the adapter first, and I did!"

Tracy grabbed her awful-smelling dryer from Katie's hand, threw it in the trash can, and said in a controlled voice, "That's okay. Don't worry about it."

At the time Christy had thought it would have been better if Tracy had hauled off and slugged Katie. Katie could have taken that. Instead, the two of them hadn't spoken one word to each other since.

"You want the rest of your eggs and sausages?" Doug asked Christy, eyeing her half-full breakfast plate.

"No. Go ahead, help yourself." Reaching for the silver teapot in the center of their table, Christy poured herself another cup of hot tea, tempering it quickly with milk and sugar.

"Would anyone else like some tea?" Christy asked.

"No, thanks," Katie said without looking up from the tour book.

"Which bus do we take to the Tower of London?" Doug asked.

"There's a bunch that will take us there once we get on Oxford Street. Do you remember how to get back to Oxford Street?"

Doug thought he knew, and within a half-hour they were bundled, umbrellaed, and armed with their cameras. Christy wore tights and leggings under her jeans today, and two pairs of socks. She could feel the difference when they hit the pavement and marched to Oxford Street in the foggy drizzle. Much warmer.

Today, more than the day before, she felt as if she were in England. And she liked it.

She enjoyed her top-deck perch again on the bus as they slowly edged their way down crowded Oxford Street. It seemed quite a while later when Doug asked Katie for the map and said, "Did that street say 'Bloomsbury'? We're going the wrong way."

"No, we're not," Katie said. "This is bus 8. Bus 8 goes to here," she said, leaning over and pointing to the map. "Then we switch to number 25, and it takes us right there."

"Yeah, but look," Doug said, pointing to the map. "This is the street we just passed. The Tower of London is way down here. We went the wrong way. This where we are now. Way up here."

"I don't believe this!" Katie said.

"Wait," Doug said. "Look here. We're not far from Charles Dickens' house. You wanted to go there, didn't you? We could take a quick tour and then catch bus 25."

"That's a great idea," Tracy said. "I'd love to see Dickens' home."

It turned out to be a good idea, even though they got lost and walked block after block, trying to find 48 Doughty Street, which wasn't well marked. Katie complained when they discovered the admission charge was two pounds. They took off in separate directions to explore the home of this author who had made old England come alive in his *A Christmas Carol, Oliver Twist, Great Expectations*, and dozens of other works.

Christy thought it was pretty interesting, especially the flimsy-looking quill pen displayed under glass that Dickens used to write his stories. She couldn't imagine what it would be like to write with a feather pen. Especially an entire book. Dozens of books. Writing back then must have been hard work.

Tracy and Doug seemed absorbed in all the displays, lingering to read the information cards much longer than Christy had the patience for. She left the two of them on the third floor, examining a huge painting of a lighthouse, and went down the narrow winding stairs in search of Katie. She found her sitting on a small wooden bench near the front door.

"Are you ready to go?" Christy asked.

Katie didn't look up as Christy sat next to her but waited for a group of tourists to meander down to the basement before answering, "Why am I being such a brat?"

"We're all kind of tired, Katie."

"I know, but that shouldn't be an excuse. I like Tracy. I really do. It's just that she's . . . I don't know. She gets to me."

"I think it's because you two are so much alike."

"No, we're not!"

"You each show it differently, but you're both strong and zealous. That's not a bad thing. I think it's a great quality."

Katie seemed thoughtful. She let out a deep breath. "Things somehow aren't the way I thought they would be."

"How did you think it would be?"

"Exciting and interesting and, well . . . much more fun than this. This is a lot of walking, getting lost, being frustrated, and feeling weird. I feel out of place. I'm not into all this ancient museum stuff. And it makes me feel uncultured and ignorant. I'm on new-experience sensory overload. I've never heard of any of these people we've seen statues of. And when Doug was explaining that stuff about the battles and statues at Trafalgar or whatever that square was, he might as well have been talking about life on another planet. I hate being so clueless about everything!"

Christy had always appreciated Katie's honesty and her ability to express her feelings accurately. "I know what you're saying," Christy said, trying to sound as comforting as possible.

"Then why doesn't it bother you? When I saw you holding your little cup of tea at breakfast, you looked as if you belonged here. As if it all came naturally to you. How do you do that?"

"I don't know. I guess it hasn't hit me yet. I like experiencing all these new things."

Just then Doug and Tracy came thumping down the stairs, talking intensely about a photograph they had seen of Hans Christian Andersen when he had come from Denmark to visit Dickens, whose work he admired. They kept their discussion going even after the four of them left and headed back to catch the bus. At least *they* were getting along well.

Katie seemed a little less tense as they boarded the bus and headed for the Tower of London. Christy should have know that Katie would be more relaxed once she had blown off a little steam.

As the bus lurched to a stop at an intersection, Christy caught a glimpse of her reflection in the window. She looked different. Scholarly maybe, with her hair back in a braid, almost no makeup on and wearing a turtleneck. All she needed was a pair of wire-rimmed glasses. It occurred to her that she looked like a person who knew where she was going in life. The thought made her smile. At least she could look the part. And before this trip was over, maybe she would feel the part too.

As she stomped her feet to warm them up, Christy thought how nice a hot cup of tea would taste right now.

CHAPTER FOUR

# *Carnforth Hall*

"Where did our sunshine go?" Christy asked, peering out the window of the train as it sped out of London to the north.

An hour earlier they had made their way, luggage and all, to the Euston train station. Their backs had been teased by a brief stream of welcome sunbeams. But now the sky had pulled up its thick, gray winter blanket and tucked the sun back into bed.

When none of her friends answered her question, Christy switched her attention to the seats and found everyone else was asleep. Doug, sitting next to her, slept with his head tilted back and his mouth half-opened. He looked as if he might start to snore any minute. Christy wondered if she should wake him if he did.

Katie and Tracy, seated across the table and facing Doug and Christy, had each found her own space: Tracy with her head resting on a wadded-up sweater against the cold glass window and Katie, opposite Doug, with her head buried in her folded arms on top of the table.

Christy wasn't sure why she was still awake. It had been a strenuous early morning romp to get to the train on time. Now the train's constant sway and roll should have been enough to lull anyone to sleep, especially someone who had gotten so little rest in the past three days.

But Christy was too excited. This was England! She didn't want to close her eyes and miss anything. The view outside her window changed from city sights, with red brick homes and black wrought-iron fences, to country sights with long stretches of meadow broken by neatly trimmed hedgerows. The bushes were all brown and naked, awaiting the kiss of spring to grace them with a fresh new wardrobe. And the fields looked almost a silver-gray color, with only a hint of the rich green grass that hid beneath the unbroken frost now covering the land.

*I've got to write about this,* Christy thought, searching in her bag for her journal. She remembered Charles Dickens' quill pen as she clicked the top of her ballpoint pen. She was glad she didn't have to try to write with quill and ink on this moving train table.

*We're on a train on our way to Lancashire, which is somewhere in northwest England,* she wrote. *Everyone is asleep but me. I love the countryside, even though it's all shrouded with a winter frost. I'm warm and cozy inside this comfortable train. If we make our connection in Manchester, we should arrive at Carnforth Hall before dinner and in time for the opening meeting of our outreach training.*

*How can I describe London? What a huge, ancient, modern, bustling, polite, quaint, crowded, exhausting city! Two days were not enough to make its acquaintance. We did finally see the crown jewels at the Tower of London, like Katie wanted, and it was pretty interesting. But my favorite part was climbing to the top of St. Paul's Cathedral and looking down on the city. St. Paul's is such an incredible church. I've never been inside a huge church like that before, and it made me feel full of reverence and awe.*

Doug stirred in his sleep and adjusted his large frame so that his left leg stuck out in the aisle and his head bobbed over toward Christy.

"You can lean on my shoulder if you want," she whispered. He must have been too far gone to hear her, because he didn't respond. Christy continued in her diary.

*I also liked the words that were etched in the stone at the front of one of the churches. I think it was Westminster Abbey.* Christy had copied them onto a scrap of paper and now dug for it in her bag.

"May God grant to the living, grace; to the departed, rest; to the church and the world, peace and concord; and to us sinners, eternal life."

Christy wasn't sure why this inscription intrigued her so much, except for the way it focused on grace and peace and "concord," or harmony. Those were not exactly qualities their foursome had experienced so far on this trip. She hoped that would change once their training began at Carnforth Hall.

Just then Doug's head slumped onto Christy's shoulder, immediately waking him. "Oh, I'm sorry. I must have fallen asleep."

"That's okay," Christy said. "Why don't you get some more sleep? You can use my shoulder if you need a pillow."

Doug's little-boy grin spread across his groggy face. "How come you're still awake? Those two look like they fell asleep as fast as I did."

"There's too much to see," Christy said, smiling back at Doug. "This is all so amazing to me. I don't want to miss anything."

Without drawing attention to her actions, Christy closed her diary and slid it back into her shoulder bag. It wasn't that she had anything to hide from Doug. She just didn't have anything she wanted to share. Her diary was her collection of private thoughts, and as much as she liked Doug, she didn't want to let him into those thoughts.

"You hungry?" Doug asked.

Christy let out a gentle laugh. She knew Doug was hungry. He was always hungry. "I could go for a cup of tea."

"You're becoming quite the little tea drinker, aren't you?" Doug yawned and stretched both his long legs into the aisle. "I think I'll go find that snack bar or whatever they call it and see if they have any sandwiches. You want a candy bar or something to go with your tea?"

Christy shrugged. "Doesn't matter." Then with a friendly tease in her voice she said, "I'm sure you'll eat whatever I can't finish."

"I'll get two candy bars then. Maybe three," Doug said, standing in the aisle and reaching for his backpack under the seat.

"Do you need some money?" Christy asked. "Mine is right here."

"No, I've got it." He balanced his way down the narrow aisle and through the doors into the next car on the train.

*What a sweetheart. He really is an incredible guy.* Christy sighed and looked out the window.

The train was slowing to a stop at a small-town train station. On the wooden landing stood a lad wearing a black cap, knee socks, shorts, and a dark blazer. He held a closed umbrella in one hand and a briefcase-looking book satchel in the other. He stood completely still as the train chugged out of the station. Christy watched him through her wide window with a smile. In her imagination, he was Peter, brother of Susan, Edmund, and Lucy in C. S. Lewis' British fantasy series *The Chronicles of Narnia*. Christy was sure "Peter" was about to enter an invisible door into Narnia.

"Your tea, miss," Doug said, startling her back to the real world.

He placed a large paper cup covered with a plastic lid on the table before her and handed her several tiny plastic cream containers and packets of sugar. In his hand was a medium-sized paper bag with a handle.

Doug looked cute. He had swaggered away as a long-legged man and trotted back as a shy boy with a picnic basket in his hand. He sat next to Christy and reached into the lunch bag.

"Ham and cheese," he said, producing two wrapped sandwiches. "And Toblerone." Christy recognized the long, triangular-shaped box that held a candy bar. She had seen some on sale at a newsstand in London.

"They call candy bars 'sweeties' here," Doug informed her. "At least that's what the guy at the lunch window said. It's kind of hard not to crack up when a grown man looks you in the eye and says, 'Would you like a sweetie?' "

Christy giggled and poured her cream and sugar into her hot cup of tea.

"I should have told the guy I already had a sweetie," Doug said.

Their eyes met. Christy smiled her thanks and then looked away.

*Why do I feel embarrassed? This is Doug. My boyfriend. Why does it still feel awkward when he says nice things to me?*

Christy didn't have time to come to a conclusion because just then Tracy woke up and said, "Are we almost to Manchester?" It was as if she had invaded their private moment, and yet somehow Christy felt relieved.

"No. About another hour, I'd guess," Doug said, chomping into his sandwich. "You want a bite, Trace?"

With a yawn she answered, "No, thanks. I could use a bathroom, though. Do you know which way it is?"

"That way," Doug said, pointing in the direction from which he had just come. "Only they call it a 'W.C.' Stands for 'Water Closet,' I think."

"Katie," Tracy said, gently nudging the sleeping redhead. "Sorry, Katie, but I need to get out."

Katie groaned and reluctantly lifted her head. With an annoyed look, she moved to the aisle so Tracy could slide by.

"Thanks," Tracy said before hurrying down the aisle.

"Why don't you slide over by the window so you won't have to move again when she comes back?" Christy suggested.

"All her junk is there," Katie said.

"So? Move it. She won't mind."

With exaggerated movements, Katie plopped Tracy's things onto the top of the table, jiggling Christy's cup of tea and nearly causing it to spill. Then Katie scooted over and curled up with her head against the window, closing her eyes and tuning them out.

Doug and Christy exchanged glances, but neither of them made a comment. Christy hated this feeling. She wished that everyone could just get along and not become upset with each other. But life didn't tend to be like that.

And she wasn't so innocent herself. She had had her share of conflicts with friends and grumpy comments that she had later regretted. Christy decided it would be best to leave Katie alone and pray for grace and peace and concord for the remainder of the trip. It would be great if Katie and Tracy could recognize their similarities and work at using them together, as a team, instead of turning against each other.

"How's the tea?" Doug asked, obviously trying to redirect the focus.

"Good. Really good. Thanks."

Doug looked at his watch. "We should be right on schedule, which means we'll have about an hour to settle into our rooms at the castle before the evening meal."

"Is it a real castle?" Christy asked. "I thought that's just what they called it, but then Tracy said some guy bought it after World War II and turned it into a Christian retreat center for teens."

"That's right. The guy bought this old castle and something like five hundred acres. He wanted the youth of Europe to unite after the war and thought the best way to do that would be to bring them together for summer Bible camps. They would get saved and go back to their countries equipped to share the Gospel."

"That's pretty amazing," Christy said. "This whole outreach program to different parts of Europe amazes me too."

"I'm looking forward to meeting the rest of the group tonight," Doug said in between bites of his second sandwich. "The last I heard, there are going to be about forty students from all over the world. They'll divide us up into groups of eight on a team."

"Do you think the four of us will be together?" Christy asked.

"That's what I requested. I think they'll probably keep us together."

Christy was thinking it might be better if Tracy and Katie were split up. She didn't let her thoughts out in the open, though somehow, by the look on Doug's face, she had a feeling he was thinking the same thing.

Later that evening, at their opening meeting in Carnforth Hall, Doug's prediction was confirmed. When the director read

the team lists aloud, Doug, Tracy, Christy, and Katie were all together with three other guys and one more girl. Their team assignment was Belfast, Northern Ireland.

"I don't believe it," Katie said under her breath to Christy.
"That's exactly where I wanted to go. This is perfect! I feel as if
I already know about Belfast from everything Michael told me
last year."

Christy remained silent as the rest of the assignments were
announced. It was fine for Katie to feel good about the assignment because she had dated a guy from Belfast, but Christy felt
disappointed. Or was she a little frightened? Belfast wasn't where
she expected to go. She didn't know where she expected to go.
Sweden, maybe? Or Spain? Ireland didn't feel right.

"Find the rest of your team members," the director, Charles
Benson, said. "We'll gather back in this room in one hour."

Doug's name had been listed as the team captain, and he immediately began his role as organizer by calling out, "Belfast!
Who's on the Belfast team?"

Other team leaders began to do the same, calling out their cit-
ies. "Barcelona, over here." "Oslo." "Amsterdam." "Edinburgh!"
It sounded like an international train station, as chairs were
shuffled and everyone began to mingle.

Christy felt overwhelmed for the first time on the trip. Perhaps jet lag was finally catching up with her, or maybe it was reality catching up. She was standing in an ornately decorated
drawing room in an old English castle. After a week's training, she
would be on her way to Belfast. It hit her like a gust of wind,
nearly knocking the breath out of her.

"Okay, great! Belfast is all together. Let's grab those chairs
over there by the windows," Doug said.

They weren't just windows. They were castle windows, six

long columns reaching to the high ceiling with ornate woodwork laced along the top. The thick, floral drapes hung to the floor. The blue couch and chairs in front of the window were ordinary enough, which was a good thing. Christy was beginning to feel the way Katie had in Charles Dickens' home: new-experience sensory overload.

"I'm Doug, and this is Christy, Katie, and Tracy. We're all from southern California," Doug said once the eight of them were seated. "Why don't you guys introduce yourselves?"

"I'm Sierra," the girl next to Tracy said. "I'm also from California, but I'm from northern California. Pineville. I know you've never heard of it. No one has. It's a very small mountain community near Lake Tahoe. I grew up there, but while I'm on this trip my family is moving to Portland, Oregon. So I'm sort of from California still."

Christy immediately liked her. She had wild, wavy, caramel-colored hair, a freckled nose, and a natural, approachable demeanor. There was an earthy, honest quality about her that was reflected in her jeans, cowboy boots, and brown leather jacket. Somehow, on her, the outfit worked. Even her unusual name seemed like a perfect fit.

"I'm Gernot," said a tall, thin guy with a definite accent. "I'm from Austria. My home is not far from Salzburg."

"My name is Ian, and I'm from England, but I'm living now in Germany." Ian reminded Christy of a professor, with his thin nose, wire-rimmed glasses, and thick gray wool sweater.

"And I'm Stephen. I also live in Germany, where I am going to school with Ian. And I'd like to say we must have the best team here since all of our girls are from America." He smiled, and his previously somber face turned into a splash of sunshine. His dark hair was combed straight back, and he had a goatee, which made

Stephen seem older than the rest of their group.

For the get-acquainted hour, each of them told why he or she had come on the trip. Katie seemed to come alive, with her animated description of her motivations for coming and why Belfast was the perfect place for their outreach. The two German guys seemed thoroughly entertained.

Christy stammered a bit when it was her turn to share. She said she wanted to find out what God had for her life and if maybe missions should be a part of it. Aside from that, she couldn't give much more of an explanation. The trip seemed like a great idea when Doug suggested it, and the money had come in on time, so she thought she should go.

"My reason is kind of the same," Sierra said. "It all worked out. I guess I needed to get a dose of the big world out there that I've never seen. I don't know what I want to be when I grow up, and I'm hoping this trip will help give me some direction."

Now Christy knew she really liked Sierra. She felt as if she'd just discovered a kindred spirit. Christy smiled at her. Sierra smiled back. Their friendship was sealed.

CHAPTER FIVE

# Knights on White Steeds

It didn't really hit Christy where she was until the next morning. She woke up before the alarm sounded and, through bleary eyes, gazed around the second-floor dorm room. The seven other girls who shared her room were all still asleep.

*I'm in England. I'm in a castle. I'm not dreaming.*

She remembered a wish she had made at summer camp two years ago while in a canoe in the middle of a lake. She had said she wished she could go to England someday and visit a castle. And now, poof! Here she was in England, and for the next week, this castle was her home.

Christy stuck her legs out of bed and padded to the window on stockinged feet. It had been cold last night. Despite her warm sweats and thick socks, she had felt a damp chill while trying to fall asleep. Now, tiptoeing to the frosted windowpane, she caught her first daytime view of the grounds surrounding Carnforth Hall. Even through the frost, the world beyond her window was beautiful. Storybook-like.

She gazed at the acres of icy green meadows stretching out below her. Gnarled trees lifted their leafless branches toward the gray sky, and thick moss clung to the tree trunks and fence posts.

A fine mist enveloped the entire scene, making it look like an impressionist painter's work. It was all so different from the warm beach climate at home. She loved it.

"Beautiful, isn't it?" Sierra whispered over Christy's shoulder. Christy jumped. She hadn't heard Sierra approach. Christy nodded and smiled.

Sierra stood a few inches away. She wore her blanket wrapped around her shoulders like an Indian maiden and stared out the window with a contented look on her face. "I'm so glad I'm here."

"Me too," Christy whispered back. "I'm glad you're here too."

"This is going to be quite an experience, isn't it?"

Just then someone's alarm went off, and a groping arm shot out from under a blanket and slapped at the bedside table several times before hitting its mark.

"What time is it?" Tracy called from her burrow beneath the warm blankets.

"Six-thirty," came the muffled response from the alarm slammer. "Breakfast is in an hour."

"Don't you wish they would serve us hot tea in our rooms?" Sierra asked with a giggle.

"I know," Christy agreed. "That would sure take the edge off this morning chill. I can't bear the thought of having to take off these sweats to get dressed! I just want to add more layers and put on my boots."

"Why not?" Sierra said, her freckled nose scrunching up. "You could start a fashion trend. It sounds pretty practical. It might catch on."

Christy decided against starting a new trend and managed to quickly change into her leggings, her warmest black pants, several layers on the top, and two pairs of wool socks. Castles may look enchanting, but Christy decided they can be freezing!

The group assembled for breakfast, all forty of them, in a small dining room. A large chandelier and three up-to-the-ceiling windows brightened their morning meal. Christy was happy to see a pot of hot tea already placed at the center of each table with a small jug of milk and a bowl of sugar.

Doug sat next to her, wearing his favorite green and blue rugby shirt with a white turtleneck underneath. Tracy joined them, her short hair perfectly holding its shape and her cheeks looking especially pink. She sat across the table from them, and after the prayer and a song, Doug asked Tracy her opinion on how to organize the team, which she gladly gave in her sweet, well-thought-out manner.

It bugged Christy that Doug hadn't asked her opinion. However, if he had, she wouldn't have known what to say. She hadn't thought about it at all. Obviously Tracy had.

Doug used Tracy's ideas when their team met after breakfast. "Before we get going, I wonder if each of you would feel comfortable giving your testimony. You know, say a little bit about how you became a Christian, what God has been doing in your life since then, and what your spiritual gifts are, if you know. Who would like to start?"

Each member of the group told his or her story. All were different and interesting. Christy was the last to share.

"My family always went to church, and my parents are Christians. I guess I knew all about God, only it was as if He were all around me, but not inside me, if you know what I mean."

Christy told about meeting Todd, Doug, and Tracy on the beach the summer she turned fifteen. She explained how Tracy and Todd gave her a Bible for her birthday. It was nice having Tracy right there as sort of a visual aid for her testimony.

"Then the day after my birthday . . . well, some stuff had happened that made me realize I needed God to be more than just someone who was watching me from a distance. So I surrendered my life to Him. I guess that's the best way of saying it. I just gave everything to God and asked for His forgiveness for my sins. I promised Him my heart. My whole heart. Forever."

Christy didn't expect the tears, but suddenly they were there, filling her eyes. Doug reached over and gave her a comforting hug. Her mind flashed back to the night after she had given her life to the Lord. Doug was sitting beside her by the campfire on the beach that night too. He was the first one of their crowd to congratulate her on becoming a Christian, and his hug that night had felt just as warm and reassuring as his hug did this morning.

Something bothered Christy, though. Something deep inside. She knew her tears came from something other than joy. They had been swallowed long ago, maybe not all at once, but slowly. Deliberately. Stuffed deep inside her heart.

She wanted to leave the room, run outside, go for a long walk, and dig to the bottom of her emotional treasure chest until she found where those tears came from.

The rest of the group apparently thought she was moved by the miracle of her salvation, because all of them began to give words of comfort and reassurance. Everyone but Sierra.

Sierra's testimony had been straightforward enough. She grew up in a Christian home, asked Jesus into her heart when she was five one night in her bedroom with her mom, and had been a good girl ever since. Could it be there was something in Sierra's heart that connected with Christy's?

Christy stayed in her seat and participated with the rest of the group in planning out the first stage of their training. Her soul-searching would have to wait. Their preliminary assignment was

a week away, next Saturday. They were to plan a day-long outreach in a small town nearby. In conjunction with the church that
was hosting their team, they were to present a drama, some
music, a program for the children, and an evening message. This
was a miniature version of the kind of ministry they would be
doing in Belfast with a local church.

Katie immediately volunteered to head up the drama, and
Sierra and Stephen jumped in, saying drama was their area of interest as well. Since Doug was the only one who could play a guitar, he accepted responsibility for the music. Tracy offered to help
him. Ian, who looked the part of a professor, wanted to try his
hand at the evening message. Gernot suggested that he head up
a game of soccer with the boys of the town to draw them in for
the evening meeting. All that was left for Christy was the children's program. That was fine. She had worked many hours in the
toddler Sunday school at her church, and she liked little kids.

"That was easy," Doug said, checking his watch. "Well, we
have morning chapel in about fifteen minutes. I'll try to hunt up
an extra guitar around here. Our team has lunch duty, so go to
the kitchen right after chapel."

Christy was glad the chapel was in a different building. It
meant bundling up and taking an umbrella, but the walk helped
clear her head a bit.

Even in the frost, the garden seemed beautiful to her. Neat
rows of trimmed rose bushes lined the walkway. She was sure that
in the spring and summer this would be her favorite place. She
passed under an arched trellis with some kind of barren vine
woven through the latticework. She thought of the fragrant jasmine that climbed up the posts by her front porch at home, and
for the first time, she missed her mom, dad, and little brother. She

had sent them a postcard from London. Today would be a good day to write a real letter.

The chapel was situated at the end of the garden walkway. The fine, old stone building had once served as a church for the castle's household.

Entering the chapel through the thick wooden doors, Christy felt the same reverent awe she had experienced at Westminster Abbey. For hundreds of years this spot had been a place of prayer and worship, and now she was one of the many who had entered in and sought the Lord.

Christy sat alone on a solid wooden pew about halfway toward the front. Instead of an altar at the front, there was a stage with microphones and a keyboard. At first glance it seemed out of place. But within a few minutes the chapel began to fill with other students, and several musicians stepped up on the stage to begin to tune their instruments.

"Are you saving this seat for anyone?" a girl with a big smile and very short, blond hair asked. She wore a sweatshirt that said, *"Aika on kala."* Christy couldn't begin to guess what language that was.

"No," Christy automatically said, not even thinking that Doug might have expected her to save him a seat. "My name's Christy."

"I'm Merja. I'm from Finland. Where are you from?"

"The United States. California."

"Really? Do you surf and drive a convertible?" Merja asked with a teasing smile.

"You've been watching too much TV," Christy said.

"You live in Beverly Hills, don't you?" Merja asked, still teasing.

"Not exactly," Christy said. "However, I do know several guys who surf, and my aunt and uncle used to own a convertible. Does that count?''

"Close enough," Merja said. "We can be friends now. I'm on the team going to Barcelona. Where are you going?''

For the next few minutes, the two new friends enjoyed a lively conversation. Christy was enjoying this opportunity to make friends with people from all over the world.

When she glanced up on the stage, she noticed Doug standing there, guitar in hand, tuning up with the rest of the band.

"Let's start off with some praise choruses," the group leader said. "This first one is from Psalm 5.''

The singing sounded majestic in the small chapel. It was the first time Christy had felt like everyone was part of one group as they sang these familiar choruses, all in English but with a variety of accents.

Doug kept up with the rest of the band. Apparently he knew all the chords to all the songs they played. At one point he looked up and cast his little-boy grin into the crowd. She thought he was smiling at her, but the look seemed to go over her head. Christy slowly looked over her shoulder between songs and noticed Tracy sitting two rows behind her.

*Oh, it's Tracy.*

Now she wondered where Katie was, and if everything was cleared up between the two of them. She guessed it would become evident as the week went on.

She didn't have to wait long to see. After chapel their team assembled in the kitchen. Within two minutes, Katie and Tracy were disagreeing over how the tables should be set.

Mrs. Bates, the white-aproned cook, stepped in and made it clear. "Knife only on the right side. Fork only on the left side. The spoon goes above the plate, like this.''

"But that's not how we do it at home," Katie protested.

"You are *not* at home," Mrs. Bates said firmly. With a twinkle of good humor in her voice, she added, "This is how we do it here. And for this week, this is your home, and I am your mother, so mind your mother!"

Tracy had every right to say "I told you so" to Katie. But she said nothing and calmly went about setting her tables while Katie walked around her table, resetting each place with the spoon above the plate.

Suddenly Katie blurted out, "You guys, I'm sorry. I don't know why I'm being like this. I keep trying to make everything familiar, and it's not. It all seems so weird to me."

*Oh no, there she goes with the weird thing again!*

Christy thought Tracy would arch her back like a cat. She didn't. Instead she quietly stepped over to Katie and said, "I know. It's not easy fitting into another culture, is it?"

"I don't see you having such a problem with it. I don't see anyone else having a hard time." Katie waved her handful of knives around the room. "It's just me. I don't fit in here."

Doug had proven to be a wonderful counselor more than once to Katie. He stepped in and, putting his arm around her, said, "Can we talk in the other room, Katie? I think these guys can set the table without you."

Katie let her knives drop loudly onto the table. "Yeah, they'll do a better job without me." She walked out of the dining room with Doug's arm still around her.

The rest of the team went about their lunch duties without saying much.

Tracy came up to Christy and said, "Could I talk to you sometime?"

"Sure," Christy answered. "Right after lunch."

Lunch was the main meal every day, and today it was sausages, scalloped potatoes, and once again, mushy peas. Doug and Katie had returned to the dining room in time to eat, and even though they sat across the room, Christy could tell Katie had been crying.

As soon as the team had finished their cleanup duties, Tracy and Christy headed for a sequestered nook with a padded bench seat. A tall, arched window beside them opened up a view of the lawn that stretched all the way down to the brook. Beyond that was the forest.

"I wanted to ask you something," Tracy said.

Christy liked Tracy, with her gentle yet direct manner. The two had shared many meaningful conversations over the years, and this felt as if it were going to be one of those heart-to-heart talks.

"What can I do to change things with Katie? I feel awful. I thought London would be so fun with you guys. And it was, in a way. But the whole time I felt as if Katie were mad at me. I don't know what to do."

Christy tried to accurately represent one friend to another. She found it wasn't easy. "I know Katie doesn't want to be acting, well . . . for lack of a better word, 'weird.' I guess this trip is harder for her than she thought it would be. I don't think it's you, Tracy. I think it's everything being so different. This doesn't seem to be Katie's cup of tea, so to speak. I know she's trying, though. I don't think you could do anything differently than you've been doing it."

"Every time I open my mouth, I seem to offend her," Tracy said. "I don't know what the problem is. What do you think I should do?"

"I think you two should talk. You're both special friends to me, and I'll be honest, it has bothered me that things have been tense. I think the two of you should sit down and talk."

"Do you want to be there?"

"I don't think that would help. It would be better if it were just the two of you."

Tracy let out a sigh. "I guess you're right. I'll try to talk to her this afternoon. Pray for us, okay?"

"I will." Christy squeezed Tracy's hand, and the two friends sat silently for a few minutes on the tapestry-covered seat, gazing out the window.

"Can't you just picture some princess sitting at this very seat hundreds of years ago, waiting for her prince to ride up on his white horse and whisk her away to the ends of the earth?" Christy said, swooping her hand through the air in a dramatic gesture.

"You don't have to wait for your prince," Tracy said with temperate, steady words.

"What do you mean?" Christy asked.

Tracy looked at her with disbelief. "You know, Doug? That prince-type of a guy? Your knight on a white steed has already arrived."

"Oh, yeah," Christy said. She felt embarrassed and surprised that she hadn't even been thinking about Doug. "I meant, you know, some princess long ago. I wasn't thinking about you and me and our princes."

The minute the words were out, Christy wished she could reel them back in. There was no prince in Tracy's life. There hadn't been for a long time.

Christy decided to probe a little. "How are things in the prince department for you, anyhow? Did anything ever work out with that guy from college you mentioned at Christmas?"

"No, that fizzled."

"So there's nobody you're interested in?" Christy asked.

Tracy paused. By the expression on her heart-shaped face, Christy could tell she was carefully pondering her answer. Tracy couldn't lie. She always told the truth, which made it difficult for her when she was cornered with a question.

"I didn't say there's nobody I'm interested in. However, I've learned over my vast years of experience that it simply works better when he's interested in me as well."

"Wait a minute," Christy said. "I distinctly remember having this same sort of conversation with you once before. Don't you remember? We were making cookies at my aunt and uncle's house. You liked somebody then, but you wouldn't tell me who it was."

If Tracy did remember the conversation, she didn't appear to be willing to comment on it or on her current interest.

Christy prodded her along. "Don't you remember that afternoon at my aunt and uncle's? You didn't tell me then, but I figured out later that you liked Doug."

Tracy nodded.

"Can you believe you guys used to go out?" Christy asked. "Doesn't that seem like a lifetime ago?"

Tracy's expression changed a little. "I guess it does. That was more than three years ago, and we only dated for a few months."

"Why did you guys break up?"

Now Tracy paused longer. "What has Doug told you?"

"Nothing. We've never talked about it," Christy said.

"Maybe it's best we leave it that way," Tracy said.

"You know," Christy said after a pause, "this thing Doug has about how he's never kissed a girl and how his first kiss will be at the altar on his wedding day? Well, it's made our relationship different because I don't wonder about his past girlfriends or what went on with them. It's really freeing. He's never kissed me, and that takes all the pressure off. I don't wonder if he's going to or not. Do you know what I mean? Of course you know what I mean."

Tracy looked out the window, seemingly lost in thought. "Um-hmm," she agreed.

"It's just different," Christy said. "It makes it easy for us to all be friends."

"Um-hmm," Tracy agreed again.

The two friends sat together silently, each lost in her own world of thoughts and dreams.

CHAPTER SIX

# Communion and Concord

Sunday morning church service was in the chapel. The mission director, Charles Benson, introduced the group doing the music. "And now, Undivided will lead in morning worship."

The name struck Christy as ironic. Tracy and Katie had not yet talked, and in their room this morning it was obvious the tension was growing. Now at the morning service, Christy sat next to Tracy while Katie was on the other side of the chapel with two of the guys from their team. Sierra sat on the other side of Christy, and Doug was on the end of the aisle, next to Tracy. Their team was quickly becoming anything *but* undivided.

The tension made it hard for Christy to concentrate as they sang and even harder to take the message for herself. Everything seemed to apply to Katie, not her.

Dr. Benson spoke on John 17. "Did you know that Christ actually prayed for us? Look at verse 21. Here Christ prayed that we might be one, just as He and the Father are one. This is usually the biggest challenge for ministry teams. Each of you is coming from a different background, with different opinions and points of view. It's not easy to be 'one.' One heart. One mind. One undivided team."

Christy thought Dr. Benson must know what was going on with their team, even though he seemed to speak to the whole group. He then talked about forgiveness and starting over. He urged the teams to learn how to exercise grace and peace.

It made Christy think of the inscription she'd written in her diary on the train. Grace and peace and what was that word for harmony? Concord. That's what they needed. Grace, peace, and concord. At this moment it seemed impossible.

"I'm going to ask you to do something you may never have done before," Dr. Benson said. "We're going to take communion this morning, and we need to come before God with clean hearts. Some of you need to be reconciled with your brothers and sisters in this room. Before we serve communion, we will have ten minutes in which, if you need to ask someone for forgiveness, you should do so. It would be utterly false to take part in communion and then be commissioned for your outreach trips if any of you is harboring unforgiveness in your heart."

Christy closed her eyes and searched her heart. She wanted to make sure she was right with God in every way. Plenty of small things needed to be confessed, things between her and God. But she didn't think she needed to go to anyone and ask forgiveness.

As Christy silently prayed, she heard Katie's voice behind her saying, "Tracy, could I talk to you for a minute?"

Tracy slipped past Doug, and Christy peeked to see the two of them walk to the back of the chapel and speak quietly with each other. She wanted to listen in. She felt thrilled the two of them were patching things up.

Just then Doug slid over on the pew next to Christy and, leaning over to whisper in her ear, he said, "Christy, will you please forgive me?"

She was caught off guard. "For what?" she whispered back.

Doug hesitated and seemed to have a hard time finding the words. "I haven't been, well, I guess I haven't been honoring you the way I should."

Christy wasn't sure what he meant. She looked up at his face for a clue. He looked distraught about something. "Of course I forgive you. Have I done anything that's bothered you?"

"No, no. Of course not." Doug looked relieved. He smiled at her and said, "Life can get complicated sometimes, can't it?"

Christy nodded and returned the smile he was giving her, even though she still wasn't sure what he was talking about. Perhaps he meant complicated with Tracy and Katie, and he felt he should have been more understanding of Christy since she was caught in the middle. Whatever the situation was, it didn't matter.

Tracy and Katie were returning to the pew now, both teary-eyed and with humble expressions. Doug scooted over closer to Christy to make room for the two of them on the end of the bench. Christy let out a tiny sigh of relief and bowed her head, waiting for the communion to be served.

It was the most meaningful communion she had ever partici-pated in. After that, they all stood, and the mission director and several staff members prayed for the forty and commissioned them to go forth on their outreaches next Saturday. When the service was over, Doug asked that their team stick around for a few minutes. Once they were all together, he asked if anyone had anything he or she wanted to say. It seemed as if they were all trying not to look at Katie, or at least to wait until she said some-thing before they looked at her.

"I need to apologize to all of you guys," Katie said.

All eyes quickly focused on her. "I've learned a lot these past few days, and God has been teaching me some stuff I didn't want to learn. I've been trying to hold on to a lot of things. It's like I had this fistful of stuff I didn't want to give to God, and He's been patiently trying to pry back each of my fingers to get the garbage out of there." Katie held out her hand and demonstrated God's imaginary hand pulling at her clenched fingers.

"All I can say is that I'd like to start over, with a new attitude of being open to God and open to you guys. Tracy has forgiven me, and now I want to say to the rest of you, I'm sorry I've been such a jerk. I hope you guys can all forgive me too."

A chorus of yeses responded to Katie.

"You're among friends, Katie," Sierra said. "It's never too late to start over." She gave Katie a hug, and the rest of the group followed.

"I think we should pray," Doug said. "Let's pray right now that our team will be knit together in love, like Dr. Benson was saying. We need to be of one mind and heart."

They all prayed. It was as if a huge breath of fresh air blew over them. They left the chapel with arms around each other, laughing and high stepping their way to the dining room. Christy tried not to think about Doug's comment. It was past. Over. She had forgiven him—for whatever it was.

That afternoon they had four hours of free time, and Christy thought it would be fun to go for a long walk with Doug. She sidled up to him after their meal time. He was talking with Tracy, and Christy asked if either or both of them wanted to go for a walk with her.

"Maybe a little bit later," Doug said. "Tracy and I need to work on our music for the outreach."

"You guys could go now if you want to, Doug," Tracy said quickly. "We can practice another time."

It was silent for an awkward minute before Christy said, "No, that's fine. You guys don't have much time to practice. We can go for a walk later. It doesn't matter, really."

"Are you sure?" Doug asked, turning to face Christy and looking into her eyes.

"Of course, I'm sure. You guys need time to practice. Have fun, okay?" Christy said sincerely. Then she willingly received Doug's hug.

"I'll come looking for you later," he said.

"Okay." Now Christy wasn't sure what to do. She wanted to go for a walk by herself, yet she thought a nap sounded good. What she didn't want to do was feel sorry for herself. Not after that communion service and the way the team had started to come together.

She decided to go to her room and headed down the hallway. The sound of laughter drew her into the great drawing room. Some of the Barcelona team was gathered around the huge marble fireplace, where a great orange fire crackled and warmed the whole room.

Merja spotted Christy and called her over to their group. "We need one more player. Will you be on our team?"

Spread before them on the low coffee table was some sort of word game Christy had seen before but had never played. Joining a group of laughing friends seemed much more appealing than the quiet, close quarters of the chilly dorm room.

"Sure, but I've never played this before." Christy wedged in on the rug next to Merja and tucked her long legs underneath her. Merja made quick introductions of the other players. Christy was teamed up with Merja and another girl from Finland named Satu. She said her name in English meant "fairy tale," and then she burst out laughing.

"It really does," Satu said. "No one here believes me."

"I believe you," Christy said.

"And what does your name mean?" Satu asked Christy.

"It means 'follower of Christ.' "

"How perfect!" Satu flipped her long blond hair behind her right ear and said, "I'm glad to have an American to play this English game with. English is really my fourth language, and it is not my best."

"What other languages do you speak?" Christy asked.

"Finnish, Spanish, Italian, and then English. I know some Russian and some German, but not much." Satu didn't throw her list out in a bragging way. She almost seemed to apologize that her English wasn't better. To Christy's ear it sounded perfect.

The game began, and within five minutes, Christy was laughing so hard the tears were skipping down her cheeks. It was the first time she had laughed that hard since she left home. There had been some funny moments in London, but the tension and exhaustion had made the first four or five days of this trip strained. For the next few hours, she, Merja, Satu, and the others laughed. It was like medicine.

She didn't see Doug again until the evening meal. Christy was sitting next to Satu when Doug and Tracy walked in. She waved at them, but they didn't seem to notice her and slipped into two open seats at a table by the door. After dinner a prayer and praise meeting was held in the chapel. It lasted for nearly two hours, with singing and praying. Christy loved it, but now this growing mysterious feeling about Doug was really bothering her.

After the evening worship, their team went as a group to the dining room for cake and hot chocolate. Doug was standing next to Sierra with a cup of cocoa in his hand when Christy decided it was time to get his attention.

"Could I talk to you a minute, Doug?" she asked, surprised that her voice came out shaky.

"Sure." He turned his full attention to her, looking surprised at her expression. "Is something wrong?"

"May I have your attention, please?" Dr. Benson stood in the doorway. "The hour draws to a close, and you need to be in your rooms in ten minutes."

A group groan leaked out across the room.

"I know, I know," the good-natured Dr. Benson said. "But good soldiers are disciplined, and this is your opportunity to exercise that discipline. Tomorrow is a full day, starting with breakfast at 7:30. I need to see all the team leaders for a moment in the hallway. May you all experience the truth of Proverbs 3:24, 'When you lie down, your sleep will be sweet.' Good night. See you all in the morning."

"We'll talk tomorrow, okay?" Doug said, placing his cup down on the table and making his way to the hallway to meet with the other team leaders.

Christy swallowed her disappointment and walked up the stairs to their room with Sierra by her side. She hated it when these clouds of moodiness hovered over her like the morning mist on the fields outside her castle window. She tried to shake off her thoughts and pay attention to what Sierra was saying.

"Doesn't it seem as if we've been here months and months instead of only a few days?"

"Sort of," Christy answered.

Sierra kept up the friendly chatter even after they were ready for bed. She wrapped herself up in her blanket and curled up at the foot of Christy's bed while the other girls finished their bedtime preparations. It was fun getting to know Sierra. Christy liked her more each day and was glad they were on the same team.

Katie wrapped herself in a blanket and joined them, laughing as she tried to repeat a joke one of the guys from Sweden had told her at dinner. Tracy crawled into her bed, which was directly across from Christy's, and listened in on the conversation.

"I don't get it," Tracy said when Katie finished the joke and laughed joyfully.

Katie repeated the punch line. "She come on a Honda."

Still none of them laughed.

"I guess it was one of those you-had-to-be-there kind of jokes. Leo is really hilarious. I wish he were on our team."

"I think our team is perfect," Sierra said. "Or were you hoping for guys who were a bit more promising as future spouse material?"

Christy liked being all curled up with her friends and having a "boy talk." It felt like a slumber party from her high school days. It was especially good to see Katie back to her old self, relaxed and getting along with everyone.

"Our guys are pretty cool," Katie said. "They're kind of quiet, though. I like guys who are a bit more on the rowdy side."

"Not me," Tracy said. "I prefer the strong, leader type. You know, the kind of guy who tries to make everyone feel welcome and who doesn't draw a lot of attention to himself."

"That sounds like Doug," Sierra said, brushing back a wild curl of hair that had fallen onto her forehead. "Come to think of it, you and Doug would make a perfect couple. Why aren't you going after Doug?"

Katie, Tracy, and Christy greeted the question with silence. "What? What did I say? Is there something wrong with Doug? I think he's a great guy. You two would be good together with your personalities, your gifts, your interests. You would make a cute couple. What's wrong with that?"

"There's only one slight problem," Katie volunteered. "Doug happens to be Christy's boyfriend."

"You're kidding," Sierra said, scanning Christy's face for verification.

Christy didn't say anything. She bit her lower lip. How should she respond?

"I'm sorry," Sierra said quickly. "I just never would have guessed. And maybe that's a good thing. You guys don't exclude anyone else. You act like friends, and he seems to treat you the same way he does the other girls, and well . . . I just didn't know."

"The three of us *are* all good friends," Katie explained. "We've known each other a long time, and Doug did go out with Tracy for a while, but that was a long time ago, right, Tracy?"

Tracy nodded.

"See, Christy used to go out with this surfer named Todd. You know the type, tall, blond, blue-eyed, incredibly strong Christian," Katie said.

"Sounds too good to be true," Sierra said.

"Exactly," Katie agreed. "And Todd just so happened to be best friends with Doug." She adjusted her cross-legged position and proceeded to fill Sierra in on Christy's dating history as if Christy weren't there. It would have bothered Christy, except everything Katie said was true, and somehow it was less agonizing to hear it all from Katie than to try and explain it herself.

Right at the part in the saga in which Todd received a letter from a mission organization last spring asking him to join their staff full-time, a knock at the door reminded the girls it was time for lights out. They switched off the lights. Tracy pulled her bed over next to Christy's, and Katie continued her story, whispering in the dark.

When she finished, Sierra asked, "So Tracy, why did you and Doug break up?"

Tracy didn't answer for a long time. "I don't think it really matters. Like Katie said, that was a long time ago, and Christy and Doug are together now. I know Doug has wanted to go out with Christy for years. That may have had something to do with how he felt about me even while we were dating."

"This is a soap opera, you guys," Sierra said. "I never would have guessed any of this. Where is this Todd guy now?"

"Who knows?" Christy said.

"You really don't know? He never wrote any of you?"

"Doug heard from him once or twice," Tracy said. "But Todd is rather independent. He's doing what he always wanted to do, probably on some South Seas island somewhere. It's not much of a surprise to any of us."

"My next question," Sierra said. "Tracy? Katie? Are either of you interested in any of the guys here?"

"I'll tell you about my interest in guys," Katie said. "I've come to a conclusion after spending so many years of my life trying not to be jealous of Christy because she's always had some guy interested in her. I don't even try anymore. We didn't even tell you about Rick. Now *that* was a bizarre guy. I tried to get Rick interested in me for a while. Boy, was that a mistake. Rick turned out to be such a loser. I heard he moved in with some girl, and he totally fell away from whatever kind of relationship he had with the Lord."

"I still feel bad about that," Christy said.

"It certainly wasn't your fault," Katie said.

"I know, but I still wish he hadn't walked away from the Lord."

"It's hard," Sierra agreed.

"Then there was Michael," Katie continued. "That was another whole era in my life. Michael was from Belfast, so that's one good thing that came from our relationship. I'm probably more interested in Belfast than anyone else on the team. Anyway, my new motto is 'Seek pals only.' I am so far from being ready for a romance, it isn't even funny."

"I feel the same way," Sierra said.

"In a way," Katie said, "I'm trying to go back and make up for all those dumb years I spent in high school trying so hard to get a boyfriend and missing out on some great friendships. I learned a lot about non-romantic friendships with this guy, Fred, that I went to my senior prom with. Of course, Fred was also crazy about Christy for a long time, and he only took me to the prom because she turned him down. Still, Fred is my pal. I'm only interested in finding more pals here and trying to grow up a little bit emotionally before I consider anything more in a relationship with a guy."

"That is exactly how I feel," Sierra agreed. "I couldn't have said it better myself. Isn't it funny how backwards we are? This is what we should have been doing back in middle school, and here we are, half grown up and just now trying to figure out how to be friends with guys. All I can say is I'm sure glad God didn't answer all my prayers regarding some of the guys I've been interested in over the past few years."

"Amen!" Katie said. "If you ask me, Tracy, you're ahead of all of us in the being-friends-with-guys department. You're also older than the three of us."

"I'm also probably more desirous of a romance at this point in my life, and that's not an easy thing to live with." Tracy's whispered confession carried a hint of sadness. "I'd love to get married as soon as I finish college, settle down, and have a couple of kids while I'm still young. And in a way, I feel ready for that phase of my life. However, there does seem to be one thing missing."

"Mr. Right," Sierra answered for her.

"You guessed it," Tracy said.

Sierra leaned forward and said, "Who knows, Tracy. Mr. Right might be here this week, and you had to come all the way to England to meet him. Don't you think God gives us the desires of our hearts? I mean, as long as our desires aren't sinful or anything, which yours sure don't seem to be. This world needs more Christian couples who are raising godly kids. What is that verse about delighting yourself in the Lord and He'll give you the desires of your heart?"

"But His timing isn't always the same as ours," Christy said. "And His way of doing things isn't always the same as ours."

"Yeah, God is weird," Katie said. "That's my philosophy. God is weird, and we are tweaked. He's full of surprises, and we make our lives harder than they need to be. It'd be great if everything always went the way we wanted it to, but it doesn't seem to be like that very often."

"You know what we should do, you guys?" Sierra suggested. "We should pray. Pray for ourselves and pray for our future husbands."

"I write letters to mine," Christy said, and then felt surprised at her own confession. She could feel the penetrating gaze of the other girls.

"What do you write to him?" Sierra asked.

"I don't know. What I'm feeling. Times when I'm thinking about what it will be like to be married to him, whoever he is. I tell him that I'm praying for him, and sometimes I write out my prayers. I've been writing to him for I guess about three years now."

"That is so cool," Sierra said.

"What do you do with the letters?" Tracy asked.

Christy smiled, feeling kind of silly to be revealing her little secret after all these years. "They're in a shoe box under my bed."

"I wish I'd kept my letter locked away," Tracy said almost inaudibly.

"What do you mean?" Christy asked.

"Nothing," Tracy said. "I think your idea is wonderful. I also think it's good to keep your letters a secret until the right time."

It was quiet for a minute, and then Sierra said, "Christy, can you imagine what it's going to be like on your wedding night?" She sniffed as if she might be crying. "Your future husband is going to feel like the most blessed guy in the whole world when you hand him that shoe box full of prayers and promises. What an incredible wedding present!"

Christy fell asleep dreaming of what it would be like to hand her shoe box full of letters to her future husband. She could see strong, manly hands eagerly receiving her gift. But in her dream, as she looked up, where the face of her future spouse should have been, there was only a big, fluffy cloud.

# CHAPTER SEVEN

# The Awesome Team

"You said last night that you wanted to talk?" Doug caught up with Christy and walked with her past the barren rose bushes on their way from the chapel to the castle. The early morning drizzle had turned into a sporadic sprinkling of white snowflakes that collected on Christy's eyelashes.

"It would be better if we had more time," Christy said, not sure what she wanted to say to him and not comfortable with the thought that anyone walking past them might hear.

"Our team meeting isn't for another five or ten minutes. We have training pretty much all afternoon. This is probably our best chance until after dinner. Why don't you tell me what you're thinking and feeling? I'd really like to hear."

Doug had switched into his counselor voice, and Christy wasn't sure she liked it. She wanted to talk to him as one friend to another, like a girlfriend would talk to her boyfriend. Not like a psycho patient to an all-wise counselor.

"Actually, it's nothing."

"Are you sure?"

"Yep, I'm sure." Christy forced a smile and blinked a flutter-ing snowflake from her eyelash. Everything was going so great for their team. The last thing she wanted was to cause division by questioning Doug on why he felt he wasn't honoring her. Or worse, to give in to the insecurities that arose in her last night when Sierra said she would never have guessed they were going together. Her confusion made her want to question Doug about his feelings for her. Her emotions kept chasing themselves around in a circle in her head. It would be best to try to stop her racing feelings long enough for their group to complete their outreach without disunity. She could always sit down with Doug back in California and spend as many hours as she needed to discuss their relationship and their future.

"You said yesterday that you wanted to go for a walk," Doug continued in his counselor voice. "Maybe we could squeeze one in this afternoon."

"Sure. That would be great." They could walk, but they wouldn't have to talk.

Doug and Christy now stood at the large front door of the castle. Christy noticed for the first time a brass lion-head door knocker with a brass ring in its mouth. At that moment, she felt as if she too held a brass ring between her teeth. Like that silent lion, she could hold on. He had apparently held on for centuries. She could hold on for a few weeks.

"Our team is meeting by the big windows in the drawing room," Doug said as he held the door open for Christy. "I'm going to see if I can borrow that guitar again. I'll meet you there."

Christy stopped at the "sweet trolley" as everyone called it, poured herself a cup of tea, and picked up a biscuit before reporting to the drawing room. All the other team members were taking their tea break and milling around the hallway. As Christy walked by, she noticed the variety of accents and the different ways the other students laughed and joked.

Katie stood in the corner with a guy Christy hadn't met yet. They seemed caught up in a serious discussion.

Katie noticed Christy and motioned for her to join them. "Christy, this is Jakobs. He's from Latvia. This is Christy."

Jakobs nodded his head in greeting and warmly shook Christy's hand.

"Jakobs is heading up the drama for the Amsterdam group. He's been giving me some great ideas."

Just then, Sierra, Stephen, and Tracy walked up, and Katie made introductions all around. A few minutes later, when they broke up into their team meetings, Katie grasped Christy by the arm and said, "Jakobs' grandfather spent twenty-five years in Siberia. Can you believe that? He was taken from his home and exiled because he was a pastor. I'm telling you, Christy, we have no clue what it means to be persecuted for our faith."

Katie's words were sobering. It seemed that in the past twenty-four hours she had gone from resisting any kind of cultural change to seeking as much input as she could from the variety of international students at the castle. That was Katie, though. Impulsive. Direct. And one who rarely looked back once she had put her mind to something new.

*Exactly the opposite of me.*

That realization didn't bother Christy, but it did make her admire Katie and inwardly wish she could be more flexible and open.

Christy penned those thoughts in her journal that night. She had retired to the dorm room early and was the only one there. The afternoon walk with Doug had never worked out. He didn't even sit by her at dinner. Right now he and Tracy were practicing their music, and the rest of her roommates were down in the drawing room, socializing for their last free hour before lights out.

Christy wanted to be alone to catch her breath. It was about this time only a week ago that she had been finishing up her packing for this trip and letting her imagination fill with expectations of all the amazing things she would experience. She had never expected the emotional confusion and stress the past week had brought.

Her diary had always served as a useful mirror, a place to put her feelings outside herself and then stand back and take a look. The examination nearly always changed her perspective. Tonight she wanted to do her examining without any roommates peeking over her shoulder. For a full fifteen minutes she had her wish. Then Avril, one of the English girls, came into the room crying.

"Are you okay?" Christy asked.

Avril was crying so much she couldn't answer. Christy put down her diary and went to Avril, opening her arms and offering her shoulder for Avril to cry on. She cried so hard Christy could feel the moist tears through her sweatshirt.

"I'm sorry," Avril said at last, sitting up and wiping her eyes with the back of her hand.

"That's okay," Christy said. "Is there anything I can do?"

"It's my brother. My mum just rang to tell me he's been in an automobile accident. I have to collect my things. Dr. Benson is driving me to the train station."

"Oh, Avril, that's awful! Is he okay?"

"He's still alive, but he's in critical condition." Avril's hands were shaking. "I don't know what to do first."

"Let me find you some tissue," Christy said, getting up and looking around the room. "Here you go. Now you just sit there and tell me where your suitcase is and which drawer is yours."

"It's under the bed. My drawer is the second one down."

Christy pulled out the blue suitcase and began to swiftly,

calmly transfer the clothes from the drawer into the suitcase. Avril fumbled for her bag hanging over the end of the bed and started to stuff her Bible, notebook, and other bedside items into it.

"Do you want me to get your shampoo and stuff from the bathroom?"

"Sure. Mine's the red striped bag with the broken zipper. You don't have to do all this, Christy."

"I don't mind," Christy said.

She found Avril's bag on the counter in the bathroom down the hall and tucked it into the suitcase. "Now what else? Your coat?"

"I have it already. I think that's all. I feel so awful about leaving." Avril stood and looped the bag over her shoulder while Christy snapped the clasps closed on the suitcase. "I hope I can come back in time to participate in the outreach."

"Don't feel bad," Christy said. She wanted to say something comforting. "God is kind of weird sometimes," she said, cautiously echoing Katie's words. "I'm sure it seems hard to understand why this is happening. I'm sorry it's happened. I promise I'll be praying for you and your brother."

"Thanks, Christy," Avril said, giving her a big hug and letting the next round of tears fall. "I'm so glad you were here for me. I'll be praying for you, too."

Avril pulled back and looked at Christy with an expression of fresh pain. "If I can't make it back, I don't know when I'll see you again. Maybe not until heaven."

Christy hugged her again, and in her ear she said, "Then I'll look forward to heaven even more than ever."

Now they were both crying. Without another word, Avril lifted her suitcase and walked across the room. She paused at the door and looked heavenward as if to say "Until then." Christy nodded, and Avril was gone.

That's when Christy fell apart. She threw herself onto her bed and let the tears fall. Tears for saying good-bye until heaven. Tears for the thought of how hard it would be if it were her own little brother who was in an accident. Tears earned over a week of trying hard to be strong, courageous, and understanding of everyone else's problems while her own insecurities had reached the breaking point.

"Did you hear about Avril's brother?" Katie said, bursting through the door. "Oh, I guess you did. Can you imagine how awful that would be? Yeah, I guess you can." Now Katie was crying too. "I can't believe I'm actually saying this, but I miss my family!"

Katie flopped on her own bed and cried out all her own tears while Christy released the rest of hers. A special bond formed as they let each other cry. Christy crawled into bed under her warm blankets and, with only a few more sobs, fell into a deep, exhausted sleep.

The next morning she stayed in bed, hoarsely telling a concerned Tracy that her throat hurt and she needed to sleep another hour or so. It was hard to go back to sleep while the other girls scurried around to get ready. Once they went to breakfast, Christy had no trouble nodding off.

She awoke sometime later. The room was empty. On a chair next to her bed sat a breakfast tray with a glass of orange juice, a pot of tea, white toast, and a tiny jar of orange marmalade. The note on top of the toast said, "Hope you feel better. Love, Tracy."

Christy propped herself up and poured a cup of tea. It was cold. The tray must have been there for quite some time. She drank the juice and crunched on the slice of toast before checking her alarm clock. It was 11:40. Almost time for lunch. Her throat no longer hurt. She felt rested and a little bit guilty about missing the morning meetings. However, she knew she had needed the sleep even more than she had realized. Part of her wanted to float back to dreamland, and another part of her felt she should get up and get going. The responsible side won.

"Christy, are you feeling better?" Sierra was the first one to notice her when she entered the dining room.

Doug noticed too. He got up from his seat, came across the room, and gave her a hug. "How are you doing?"

"I'm fine. It all caught up with me, I guess."

Katie now stood on her other side and said, "Jet lag finally got to you, huh? At least all you did was sleep instead of turn into a brat, like I did."

"I'm glad you're okay," Doug said. "Right after lunch all the people working with children are meeting in the conference room. Do you feel up to going?"

"Sure. I'm fine, really."

The lunch of chicken with some kind of cream sauce tasted bland, but Christy was hungry and gladly ate it all. She noticed then that nearly everything they ate had some kind of sauce or cream over the top of it. Whether it was meat or potatoes or even pie, it all came with cream.

She still felt a little spacey as the meeting for children's ministry started up. But soon she became excited about all the things the leaders were going over. They had adorable puppets available for the team members to use, a whole box of craft materials for each team, and helpful suggestions on how to get the kids to listen during the Bible story time. Christy looked over the handout of Bible stories and felt relieved that she knew them all and had even taught a couple of them to the toddlers at her home church.

At her team meeting later that afternoon, Christy gave a glowing report. "I could use one other person to help me with a puppet show. They gave us a script and everything. It seems pretty easy, and I think it would add a lot to our program this Saturday."

"I'll do it," Katie said. "Maybe we can work the puppets into the drama ministry somehow and get double use out of them."

"This is going to be awesome, you guys," Doug said enthusiastically. "How did your meeting go, Ian? Do you feel you'll be ready to preach it, brother?"

"Well, it's really a short talk more than a sermon, you know." Ian pushed up his wire-rimmed glasses. "I need to practice it in front of our group before Saturday."

"Right," Doug said. "That's what they told us in the leaders' meeting this afternoon. By Thursday everyone is supposed to present to us whatever his or her part of the program is. We'll start with the drama, then do the children's, the message, and then the music. Gernot, it would be great if you could help Christy with the children's program since you're rounding them up for soccer in order to get the kids there. Maybe she could take the little kids, and you could take the ones in grade school."

Gernot nodded.

"Especially the rowdy boys," Christy said. "You can have all of them."

"My specialty," Gernot said with a smile.

Christy found it hard to believe that this tall, slim guy would want to take on a bunch of hooligans.

She saw another side of Gernot that night after dinner, though. For their free time, the Belfast team challenged the Barcelona team to a game of Bible charades in the drawing room. Gernot had to act out Baalam and his talking donkey. Somehow he managed to play the angel, the donkey, and Baalam in lightning-fast time and without a word. They all laughed until their sides ached.

The charades turned out to be the best thing they could have done to relieve the tension of the week. Christy laughed and felt full of life, especially while she watched Doug act out Moses coming down from Mount Sinai with the Ten Commandments. It was like old times. He laughed, and after his performance, he sat next to Christy on the couch and put his arm around her. She felt as if everything was normal, the way life had been for the past few months of her life. Was she really half a world away, in England?

It was a good thing they slid the charades break in when they did, because the rest of the week was nonstop activities. Christy spent all of Wednesday working on her children's program. Katie practiced puppets with her for almost two hours, and then after lunch, Christy and Gernot went over the Bible story. They came up with some good ideas on how to work the puppet show into the middle of the story to make it more interesting and fun for the kids.

By Thursday morning, Christy felt ready and had everything together to practice her part of the program in front of the team. She felt excited, eager, and confident.

Katie, Sierra, and Stephen presented their drama to the group first, and it was amazing. The three of them worked well together, and the point of the drama was clear without being overdone.

"Any suggestions?" Doug asked after they had finished.

"Stephen, you had your back to the audience for a little bit at the beginning," Gernot pointed out. "It was hard to see what you were doing."

"Okay, I'll remember that."

"Anything else?"

"It was really good," Tracy said. "It got me right here," she said, patting her heart. "And I even knew ahead of time what you were going to do."

"It was great!" Christy agreed. She thought of how close the group now seemed and how well everyone was working together.

"Okay, Ian, you're on," Doug said.

When Ian stood in front of them, Christy learned how deceiving appearances could be. Ian looked so quiet and professorlike; yet when he stood before them and presented his message, they all sat still, absorbing every word. In less than fifteen minutes, he powerfully presented the Gospel and offered an invitation to anyone who wanted to know more. The team spontaneously began to clap when he finished.

"This is pretty exciting, you guys," Doug said. "Ian, that was perfect. Don't change a word. Now, do you all remember that we do the message last, and Ian will say if anyone wants to know more about God, they can stick around and talk to any of us."

Everyone nodded.

"Okay, your turn, Christy."

Suddenly she felt unprepared. Everyone else had done such a great job. What if she blew it? She fumbled for her notes, and then realized she had left them in the room because she had felt so confident. "Should we do the puppets first?"

"Sure," Doug said.

Katie joined Christy, and they plunged their hands into the puppets and began their play as practiced. It went okay. Everyone said it was great, and they laughed at all the appropriate times, but Christy felt so nervous, she wasn't even sure she had said all her lines. It did help break the ice for her story, though, and she sailed through that without losing her place. Instead of looking into the faces of her friends as she spoke, she tried to imagine the faces of little kids, and she felt more at ease.

"Good job," Doug praised her when she sat down. "Looks like we're on a roll here, team. Now for the music. I'd like to do one song with the whole group, and we can practice that tomorrow. Tracy and I have a song we'll do right before the message. Ready, Trace?"

Petite Tracy took her place standing next to Doug. He played an intro on the guitar, and they began to sing in perfect harmony. It was a song Tracy had written last summer about God never giving up on us and how He waits for us to invite Him to come in. Even though everyone else had done terrific jobs on their presentations, something about Doug and Tracy's singing was especially moving. They sounded so good together. The words to the song were so powerful. Christy held her breath as they held out the final note.

When they finished, there was a pause for several seconds before anyone responded. Clapping seemed almost irreverent. "That had to be the most beautiful song I've ever heard," Sierra said. "If I weren't already a Christian, I would be ready to make a commitment after that. Have you guys sung together a lot?"

"No," Tracy said, her cheeks flushing.

Doug put his arm around her and gave her one of his hugs. "What did I tell you?" he said. "We're an awesome team."

That night while she was trying to fall asleep Christy ran that scene over and over in her mind. Was Doug saying the whole team was awesome? Then why was he looking at Tracy and hugging her when he said it?

Christy couldn't sing, at least not like Tracy. Sometimes Christy and Doug had sung together in the car for fun, but her voice never sounded the way Tracy's did with Doug's.

Then, like a huge wave breaking over her and pulling her under with its force, Christy felt furious with Tracy. She wanted to reach over the few feet to Tracy's bed, shake her awake, and yell at her that she had no right being so close to Doug. Christy was too mad to cry. And too hurt to think clearly. How could Tracy do this to her?

*Do what? All Tracy and Doug did was sing together. Tracy didn't do anything wrong. What am I thinking?*

Christy rolled over and fought against what she already knew to be true. A still, small voice was speaking to her. She had heard it before. Once, in high school she had heard it when she knew she should give up her place on the cheerleading squad. And once again she had heard it at San Clemente beach when she gave back her ID bracelet to Todd. Both times the voice told her those were the actions she should take. Now she wrapped her pillow around her ears, as if that would make the voice go away.

"Forget it, God," she muttered under her breath. Then she cried bitter, salty tears while murmuring, "I'm sorry. I really don't hate Tracy. I'm sorry."

That was enough to help relieve her hurt and allow her a night of fitful sleep. Her subconscious told her the tears weren't over her anger at Tracy. They were long-ago tears over losing Todd, and they were frightened tears over the thought that she might be about to lose Doug. Then where would she be? There was no one else.

# CHAPTER EIGHT

# Sir Honesty

Christy avoided talking to anyone the next morning, especially Tracy. It wasn't hard, because all the girls in their room overslept, and they all frantically scrambled to make it to breakfast in time. It was the last day before their local outreach, and all of them had much to do to get ready.

Christy sat next to Sierra at breakfast and across from Doug. It was a relief to her when Tracy entered the dining room and sat at another table without making eye contact with any of them.

They had an hour after breakfast for personal quiet time and devotions, which Christy spent scribbling postcards to her family. She wrote surface information, trying to sound cheery and as if everything were going wonderfully. She then gathered her children's materials and made sure she was the first one to their team meeting. The others showed up a few minutes later. Everyone except Tracy.

Doug asked Stephen to open their meeting in prayer. Doug looked unusually solemn and cleared his throat several times before starting the meeting. "I have something to announce," he said.

Christy felt her heart start to pound.

"Tracy has asked to be on another team." Doug just laid out the information without explanation or personal comment.

Christy was shocked. She hadn't said a thing to Tracy. She had asked God last night to forgive her for her anger, and she had made sure she didn't do anything out of the ordinary to give Tracy the impression Christy had ever been mad at her. It couldn't be Christy's fault.

"What's wrong?" Gernot asked. "Why does she want to switch teams?"

Doug shrugged. "All I know is that she does."

"Do we have to meet right now?" Sierra asked. "Could we all take a little break and get back together after lunch?"

"That's a good idea," Ian agreed.

"Okay," Doug said, "we'll meet here right after lunch."

They all went their separate ways, except for Christy and Doug. Doug sat with his head down, and Christy wasn't sure he knew she was standing there.

"Maybe we should go for that walk now," Doug said to her without looking up.

"Sure," she said timidly. Was he mad? Hurt? She couldn't tell.

Christy grabbed her umbrella, pulled on her jacket, and waited for Doug to rise. She felt sick inside. Tracy must be leaving because of her. That was the only explanation she could think of. Obviously something powerful was going on between Tracy and Doug. Christy knew Tracy would rather take all the responsibility and sacrifice on herself than cause conflict for anyone else.

Doug silently walked with Christy through the castle, out the front door, and around to the meadow. He remained silent until they were all the way to the stone bridge that spanned the brook and connected the meadow with the forest.

Christy struggled with what to say, what to think, what to feel.

She wanted Doug to be the first one to speak. He remained silent.

They stopped on the stone bridge. Doug tossed a pebble into the white, foaming water below.

"I haven't been fair to you, Christy," he finally said. No other words followed.

Christy wasn't sure what to think. "What do you mean, Doug?"

It took him a few minutes before he asked, "Did Tracy ever tell you why we broke up?"

"No."

"It was because of a letter she wrote me. Actually, it was a poem."

Christy remembered Tracy's comment a few nights earlier about how it was a good idea Christy had kept all her shoe box letters a secret. Now it was beginning to make sense. Tracy must have liked Doug more than he liked her, and she had revealed her feelings in a letter.

"You see," Doug continued, "that was three years ago, and I wasn't ready to get serious about anyone. Plus, I had this thing about you."

"This 'thing'?" Christy questioned.

"I hope you'll take this the right way, Christy." Doug looked like a little boy. "When something is unattainable, sometimes that makes a guy want it so much that he thinks he can't rest until he conquers it. Does that make sense?"

"You're saying I was unattainable?"

"Yes, in a way. For so long you were only interested in Todd, and the more I watched you guys, the more I thought I'd be better for you than he was. I don't want to hurt your feelings by saying all this, Christy."

Christy drew in a long breath of brisk air through her nostrils and squarely faced Doug. "You don't have to say anything else, Doug. I understand, and I agree with you. We should break up."

"Break up? It sounds so harsh when you say it that way," Doug said. "That's not what I'm trying to say."

"Look," Christy said calmly, "you and I have been good friends for a long time. We should have known that it would be best to stay friends instead of trying to make something more out of it."

"That's my fault," Doug said. "All last summer you were right when you wouldn't agree to go together. I was stubborn. Trying to prove something to myself, I guess. I'm sorry, Christy."

"I don't think you should be sorry, Doug. I mean, when you think about it, even when we started going together, we still acted the same—like we were good friends. I admire you for not kissing me. It makes it easier now to break up."

Doug shook his head. "I don't like saying that we're breaking up."

"Then what are we doing?"

"I don't know. What *were* we doing? I mean, why did I wait so long and pressure you so much to go out with me? I've been a jerk."

"No, you haven't. That's not the way I see it, Doug. I think both of us had to test our relationship and see if there was anything more to it. There wasn't. We're good friends. You're free, Doug. You don't owe me anything. Not even an apology. I admire you, I appreciate you, and I think you're a great guy."

"And I think you're an incredible woman, Christy. That's the problem. I've always admired you, and I've wondered for so long if maybe there might be something more. You know, fireworks."

Christy pressed her lips together and looked down into the water rushing beneath the bridge. She had to admit she liked

Doug, but he had never given her goose bumps. It was humbling to know she apparently had never given him goose bumps either. Still, the honesty helped. A lot. Their feelings were mutual. It was too bad they hadn't been able to confess that to each other earlier.

"I feel as if we're in junior high," Christy said.

"I think when it comes to gut-level emotions," Doug said, "we tend to express them the most accurately and honestly when we're in junior high. As we get older, we only think we're sophisticated because we learn to play some complicated games. I'm sorry I've played this one so long with you, Christy. I never meant to hurt you."

"I know," Christy said, feeling hot tears well up in her eyes. "And as long as we're being so honest, I need to tell you that I've played the game too. It was much easier to keep things the way they were than to let you go, because then I wouldn't have anybody."

Doug, the tenderhearted counselor, put his arm around her and said, "You'll always have me as your friend, Christy. And now as your new, improved, completely honest friend, I feel I can honor you. And you can honor me."

Christy stood for a long moment with her head resting on Doug's shoulder, gazing through misty eyes at the meadow beyond the creek. She recognized it as the same meadow she and Tracy had looked out on from their window seat. This was the meadow Christy had imagined a knight in shining armor riding through on his trusty steed, ready to storm the castle and take his princess. Now here she stood, shivering on this old bridge, letting go of her pretend knight.

"Kneel," she suddenly said, turning toward Doug and startling him. "Kneel!"

He slowly obliged, giving her a confused look as he went down beside her on one knee.

"I knight thee Sir Douglas, the Honest," Christy said, gently tapping him on each shoulder with her closed umbrella. "Arise, fair friend. I believe a true princess awaits you in the castle."

Doug looked up. No words passed between them, only smiles of admiration exchanged by two close friends.

"You ready to go back?" Doug asked, rising to his feet.

"Actually, I think I'd like to be by myself for a while. Why don't you go on back? You and Tracy have some honesty to catch up on."

Doug took off jogging across the meadow. Christy smiled, thinking how this knight didn't even need a white horse.

As she stood listening to the gurgling brook and the far-off, high-pitched twitter of a lone bird in the forest, she felt a rush of contentment. She had done the right thing. There were no more confused, hidden feelings for her to keep buried in her heart. Doug and Tracy were suited for each other and the kind of couple God could use to further His kingdom here on earth.

Then, from out of nowhere, came an overwhelming sense of loss. She had nobody. Katie was right the other night when she told Sierra that Christy had always had a guy in her life. Even when she broke up with Todd, Fred was there, paying attention to her the next day. It didn't matter that she didn't like Fred. What mattered was that for more than four years she had had some guy in her life. Now there was no one. No one she was interested in, and no one interested in her. The hole inside felt bottomless.

It began to drizzle. Christy hid under her umbrella and stomped her feet to warm them up. She felt really cold now, chilled inside and out. Not even a cup of tea would make a difference.

The dismal forest on the other side of the bridge beckoned her to run to it and hide herself among the brambles. She could stay there for days, and no one would ever know.

The intense, cold tingles in her feet made her snap out of her dramatic plotting and walk back to the castle. Thin clouds now hung over the highest of the castle's turrets. It looked cold and gloomy. Just like she felt inside.

When she reached the front door, she spotted the brass lion head. The ring still hung between his clenched teeth. Maybe she was glad she no longer had to hold on to her circle of feelings for Doug. Maybe she was free now.

*Free for what? Free to meet another guy? Free to go on without a guy in my life? What if there's nobody? Ever! What if I never have another boyfriend in my life and I die an old maid?*

Christy gave the lion a sympathetic pat on the nose and shook out her wet umbrella before entering. The smell of lunch greeted her, and she slipped quietly into the dining room, where most of the students had nearly finished the meal.

"Could you pass the tea, please?" She sat in the first open spot she saw, which was right by the door. Doug had his back to her, three tables away, and Tracy was sitting next to him. Christy assumed the two of them had talked. Everything between them would be settled now, and their relationship could move forward. Their team would have its unity back. Everything would be great. Just great.

Christy took a sip of tea and quickly put down her cup. It was lukewarm and too strong. "Excuse me," she said, pushing back her chair.

She left the dining room as quickly as her appetite had left her. Rushing up the stairs, she retreated to the stillness of the dorm room, where she changed her clothes, starting with her damp socks. Being dry and semi-warm helped.

As she was lacing up her boots, Sierra walked in and looked surprised to see her. "There you are! I wondered what happened to you. Did you get any lunch?"

"I wasn't very hungry. I went for a walk down to the creek and got really cold. All I wanted to do was put on some dry clothes."

"Doug canceled our afternoon team meeting. We're supposed to pack up our stuff so we'll be ready to leave at 6:30 in the morning. I'm thinking a nap sounds pretty good."

Christy nodded. "A nap does sound good."

"Oh, and did you hear?" Sierra said, pulling off her shoes and sticking her feet under the blankets on her bed. "Tracy is back on the team. I don't know what the problem was. At lunch, Doug said she changed her mind and was going to stay with our team. That's all he said, and she just sat there smiling. I tell you, Christy, it's a soap opera around here."

"I broke up with Doug," Christy blurted out. "Or actually, we both agreed to break up and go back to being just friends."

"You're kidding! Oh, Christy! I'm sorry. I didn't know."

"He and Tracy belong together," Christy said.

Sierra looked at Christy with admiration on her freckled face. "You have to be the most noble person I've ever met. After all Katie told me the other night, and now here you go and break up with him so he and Tracy can get back together . . ." Sierra paused as the door to their room opened and Tracy and Katie came in.

"I was right," Katie said, her red hair swishing as she turned her head from Christy to Tracy and back to Christy. "I told you she would be hibernating under those covers. That's what I have on my schedule this afternoon."

Tracy walked over to her bed and sat on the edge, facing Christy. Her heart-shaped face looked so delicate. "Mrs. Bates from the kitchen is going into town today. I asked her if you and I could ride with her. There's a little restaurant I heard about, and I thought maybe we could go for tea and have a chance to talk."

Christy was aware of Sierra and Katie's listening ears, even though they pretended to be looking at something on Sierra's bed.

Perhaps it would be better if they went somewhere to talk. "Sure," Christy said. "What time?"

"First I have to meet with some of the people doing music for the other teams. How about if you and I meet Mrs. Bates down in the kitchen at 2:30?"

"Okay, I'll be there."

Tracy grabbed a notebook at the end of her bed and left for her meeting.

"Are you all right?" Katie asked, turning her attention to Christy.

Christy let out a huge sigh. "I feel like a dork. A total dork. Why did I ever start going with Doug? It was so pointless."

"Do you want to join our club?" Sierra asked. "Katie and I are going to start a club called the P.O. Box."

"Right," Katie said with a glimmer in her bright green eyes. "It stands for 'pals only,' and the 'box' is for the shoe boxes we're going to start filling with letters."

Christy smiled and shook her head. "You guys are hilarious."

"So, what do you think?" Sierra said. "Guys are not worth all this grief. It's pals only for us." She and Katie slapped a high five. "P.O." said Sierra.

"Right-o," answered Katie. "P.O. rules forever!"

Christy lifted her right hand into the air. Katie slapped her a high five.

Sierra galloped across the room and did the same. With a whoop, she said, "Member number three! All right, P.O. forever!"

Christy had to laugh. "You guys, it sounds like you're saying 'B.O.' like you want to have body odor forever."

Katie started to crack up. "That's it," she said. "That's our secret weapon to keep the guys away. B.O. forever!"

# CHAPTER NINE

# *Garden of the Heart*

The first thing Christy noticed when she and Tracy scrambled into Mrs. Bates' car was that the steering wheel was on the "wrong" side. She hadn't noticed it so much in the car that had picked them up at the train station the first night, because she was riding in the backseat. Now it felt awkward since she was sitting in the front, in the passenger seat, which was actually where she sat to drive her car at home.

It was even a stranger sensation riding down the narrow country lane on the wrong side of the road, with fast, little cars passing them on the wrong side.

"This is a beautiful drive," Tracy said. "Thanks for taking us."

"Not at all," Mrs. Bates replied. "I'll give you a lift to the tea shop, and then, if it would be agreeable with you, I'll come round to collect you at half-four."

Christy realized she must mean 4:30 and the "coming round to collect" must mean picking them up.

"That would be fine. Thank you," Tracy said.

They continued down the lane, under a bridge, around a winding curve with a moss-covered stone wall, and past two men wearing long black boots, dark jackets, and black riding hats, seated on very tall horses.

For Christy, there was no mistaking where they were. This was exactly how she had always pictured the English countryside. Her only wish was that she could return in the spring, or maybe even in the summer, when the green meadows would be polka-dotted with white lambs and the trees clothed in their proper, leafy attire. It must be absolutely beautiful then.

Once in town, Mrs. Bates edged the car into a narrow wedge of a parking space so the girls could climb out. They stood in front of a quaint building called "The Cheery Kettle Tea Shoppe."

"Half-four, then?" Mrs. Bates said.

"Yes, we'll see you then," Tracy said and waved good-bye.

A bell above the door rang merrily as they stepped into the restaurant. Soothing classical music floated through the air. Five or six round tables stood in the small room, with a vase of bright flowers and a white lace tablecloth atop each of them. Along the walls were lots of pictures and knickknacks. A bookshelf with an ornate rail ran along the top of the wall near the ceiling. The rack held clumps of old books, china plates, and photographs in pewter frames. In the corner stood a majestic grandfather clock that bonged three times as they sat down.

For a minute Christy forgot they had come here for a heart-to-heart talk. She felt intrigued and delighted by the charm of this place.

"Don't you love this?" she asked Tracy. Christy whispered because it seemed everything was hushed and calm around them.

"It's so quaint," Tracy agreed.

A round woman in a blue apron came up to their table just as two older women wearing hats came into the tea room and seated themselves at a table across the room.

"We'd like some tea," Tracy said, ordering for both of them.

"And a nice sweet for you today, miss?" the woman asked. She looked like Mrs. Rosey-Posey, a character from one of Christy's favorite children's books. Christy half expected the woman to offer them some chocolate covered cherries like in one of Mrs. Rosey-Posey's stories. Instead, she offered fresh apple pie or raisin scones.

"I'll have the scones," Christy said. She wasn't exactly sure what they were, but they sounded much more British than apple pie.

"Me too," Tracy agreed.

"Cream for both of you?" the woman asked.

Christy thought she meant cream for the tea and answered yes. The cream turned out to be a small bowl of whipped cream that came with the scones. "What do we do with the whipped cream?" Christy whispered after the woman walked away.

"I guess put it on these. They look like English muffins only flakier, like a biscuit." Tracy broke open her scone and scooped some whipped cream on top. "Oh, this is good!"

Christy prepared her tea the way she liked it, with milk and sugar, and then followed Tracy's lead, putting the whipped cream on the scone. It was yummy. Christy couldn't help but feel like a little girl who was playing dress-up in her mother's clothes and having a tea party. She wondered if Tracy felt the same way.

"I'm glad we could come here," Tracy said. "This is a nice, quiet place for us to talk."

Christy nodded, licking a dab of whipped cream off her top lip and wondering if she should bring up the topic of Doug first. She wasn't quite sure what to say. Tracy obviously knew they were no longer "together" and that he was free to pursue his relationship with Tracy. There wasn't a whole lot to talk about.

"Did Doug tell you why we broke up before?" Tracy asked.

"He told me today you wrote a letter, but he wasn't ready to be serious about anyone. I remembered what you said the other night in the room, and figured you put your heart out on paper, and he rejected it."

"I didn't feel like he was rejecting it," Tracy said cautiously. "He just pulled back. Big time. And then we decided to break up. It was mutual, but we never talked about what I wrote to him."

Tracy took a sip of tea and continued. "You know how Todd was always saying the guy should be the initiator and the girl should be the responder? Well, that's sort of what the problem was. I wrote Doug this poem, and I was initiating way too much. For the past three years I've hung back, wondering if I'd ever get another chance to respond and not initiate."

Christy thought of what Katie had said about Doug: His love was patient. If Doug had been patient, Tracy had been even more so. Obviously Doug had meant a lot to her for a long time, but Tracy had kept it all inside, waiting. What Christy admired most was that Tracy had never shown one speck of jealousy toward Christy while she and Doug were together.

"What I want to know, Christy, if you feel comfortable telling me, is why you broke up with Doug."

"I have a question for you first," Christy said. "Why did you ask to be put on another team?"

Tears began to fill Tracy's gentle eyes. "After Doug and I sang together last night, I knew I couldn't handle it any longer. I couldn't be around him and keep my feelings bottled up. You see, a couple of times on this trip Doug and I have been alone. Like when we were practicing. He said some things that were nicer than the average Doug-type of things, and I got the impression he felt more for me than he had ever let on."

Suddenly Christy felt betrayed. Doug had been two-timing her. Her expression must have reflected her indignation because Tracy said, "He never said anything obvious or anything against you. It was mostly a feeling that maybe he liked me. It felt complicated, and I didn't want to hurt you in any way, Christy, or hurt Doug or myself, for that matter. I thought the easiest thing would be to walk away."

"I was the one who needed to walk away, not you," Christy said. "And to answer your question of why I broke up with him, it was because it had become evident to me, well . . . to both of us, really, that our relationship was never going to grow beyond the level of good friends. It was kind of silly to even say we were going together since neither of us felt or acted that way. I realized that the other night when Sierra was so surprised we were going together. We weren't being completely honest with each other. Neither of us felt like we were going together inwardly, and neither of us acted like it outwardly."

Tracy wrapped her hands around her china teacup as if to warm them. Then, looking up at Christy, she said, "Are you sure? Very, very sure?"

"Absolutely. I think you two belong together. I can't believe it's taken this long for all of us to figure it out."

Tracy smiled. "I can't tell you how happy I feel right now. When Doug came up to me before lunch, I was by the rose bushes, walking back from the chapel. He came running across the green, calling my name. I'll never forget the look on his face. He told me about your talk and how you dubbed him Sir Honesty, and then he asked if I was ready to unlock the garden gate because this time he was ready to come in." Tracy looked starry-eyed.

"Did he mean the rose garden? There's no gate there," Christy said.

"No, you see, he was remembering the poem I had sent him three years ago."

"A poem?" Christy asked.

"Yes, that's what the letter was. Do you want to hear it?"

"You have it memorized?" Christy poured another cup of tea for each of them from the stout silver pot.

"I think I do. Let me try and see how far I get.

> Within my heart a garden grows,
> wild with violets and fragrant rose.
> Bright daffodils line the narrow path,
> my footsteps silent as I pass.
> Sweet tulips nod their heads in rest;
> I kneel in prayer to seek God's best.
> For 'round my garden a fence stands firm
> to guard my heart so I can learn
> who should enter, and who should wait
> on the other side of my locked gate.
> I clasp the key around my neck
> and wonder if the time is yet.
> If I unlocked the gate today,
> would you come in? Or run away?"

Christy sat mesmerized by Tracy's words. "You wrote that?"

Tracy nodded. "Kind of bold, huh?"

"I think it's beautiful," Christy said.

"Well, when I gave it to Doug three years ago, I guess I freaked him out. He ran away. He remembered it, though," Tracy said, the dreamy look returning. "That's why today he said if I unlocked the garden gate this time, he would come in."

Christy sipped at her hot tea and pondered Tracy's words. "This is so hopelessly romantic, I can't believe it. Why did you let me stand between you all this time? I had no idea!"

Tracy leaned forward. "If I had told you about my feelings for Doug, you would have pulled back and never dated him."

"That would have been okay," Christy said.

Tracy shook her head. "No, don't you see? It had to follow its natural course. Doug had to decide for himself if there was anything between the two of you. You had to see if there was anything there. Doug is so pure-hearted and sincere. It wasn't hard to wait. Well, up until last night it wasn't hard. Then after we sang together, I thought I was going to burst!"

The two friends sat sipping the remainder of their tea, pondering the events of the past few days, months, and years. "Katie is right," Christy said. "God is so weird. His way of doing things is bizarre."

A smile crept across Tracy's face. "And I wouldn't want God to be any other way."

"Will you promise me one thing?" Christy asked.

"Sure. What?"

"If, or should I say when, you and Doug get married, can I be a bridesmaid? I want a front-row view of when he kisses you for the first time."

Tracy let a nervous bubble of laughter explode a little too loudly, and the older women across the room gave them a look of mild disapproval. Tracy quickly drew her white linen napkin up to her mouth to muffle her chuckle.

"You really are a true friend, Christy. And if we ever do get married, yes, of course I'd love to have you stand with me as one of my bridesmaids. As long as you promise me that I can be a bridesmaid at your wedding too."

All Christy's feelings of contentment and awe drained from her. Christy couldn't imagine herself ever letting her feelings grow for another guy again. But she could picture herself standing at the gate of her heart's garden, making sure the gate was locked tight. She felt like swallowing the key.

"Hallo, girls!" Mrs. Bates' cheerful voice called out from behind them.

"Oh, is it time to go already?" Christy asked, glancing at the grandfather clock in the corner. "I hope we haven't kept you waiting."

"Not at all. I have to arrange a few things in the boot, so I'll meet you at the car when you're ready."

Tracy and Christy figured out how much they owed for their lovely tea and paid at the cash register. Out front they noticed Mrs. Bates was busily rearranging a variety of boxes and parcels like a jigsaw puzzle in the car's trunk.

"Do you need some help?" Tracy asked.

"These bundles won't quite fit here in the boot."

"The boot?" Christy asked. "You mean the trunk? I thought you were talking about the boots on your feet."

Mrs. Bates looked up. "No, the boot. This is the boot. The front of the car is the bonnet. Why? What do you call it?"

"The trunk and the hood."

With a ripple of laughter, Mrs. Bates said, "Well then, I can't seem to fit these things in the trunk."

"I can hold some things on my lap in the backseat," Tracy volunteered.

"Actually, it's my turn to sit in the back," Christy said. "I'll hold them."

"Brilliant!" Mrs. Bates shut the trunk, or rather, the boot, and handed several packages to Christy for her to balance on her lap once she wedged herself into the already half-loaded backseat.

They drove down the country lane, with Mrs. Bates and Tracy chattering all the way. Christy kept silent in the backseat beneath her packages. She felt this was where she belonged, taking a backseat to Tracy, who for years had taken a backseat to her. It was a humbling experience.

At the castle Christy and Tracy hurried to prepare everything for their early morning departure to Noelsbury.

"Should we pack a change of clothes?" Christy asked.

"We're supposed to be back here tomorrow night," Tracy said. "I think all we need is a jacket and our materials for the outreach."

"I don't know how to pack these huge puppets and all these craft materials," Christy said. Then she had an idea. She forced everything into her suitcase and zipped it shut. With the pullout handle and wheels, she was sure it would be easy to get on and off the train.

"Brilliant!" Tracy said, eyeing the suitcase.

" 'Brilliant,' " Christy repeated. "Isn't that the funniest word? Everyone around here says it. We better watch out, or before we know it, Doug will be replacing his 'awesome' with 'brilliant.' "

Tracy sat on the edge of her bed and pulled a brush through her hair, checking her reflection in a small oval mirror she held in her hand. Christy thought how pretty Tracy was, how sweet and kind and perfect for Doug in every way.

Christy's talk with Doug on the bridge seemed a decade ago. So much had changed in her feelings after the talk and after she understood about the garden in Tracy's heart.

However, one thing hadn't changed—the deep, hollow ache right in the middle of her stomach. The ache of loneliness.

# CHAPTER TEN

# The True Princess

"It *would* be pouring rain," Christy muttered. She stood inside the small train station with her other teammates, waiting for their host pastor to arrive and drive them to the church for their Saturday outreach. The train ride had taken a little more than two hours, and although it was almost nine in the morning, it still felt like the middle of the night.

A bright red minivan pulled up in the parking lot, and a man in a black raincoat got out and ran inside. "You're here!" he said when he spotted the group. "Sorry to keep you waiting. I'm Reverend Allistar."

Doug shook hands with him and introduced everyone.

"Shall we go then?" the pastor said, opening the door to the pouring rain.

"Let me get that for you, Christy," Doug said, offering to carry her suitcase with all the puppets and craft materials tucked neatly inside. He smiled, and she thanked him. It all seemed so normal again, so natural for the two of them to be friends. It also had seemed natural to see Tracy sitting next to him during the train ride this morning and for Doug to have his arm resting across the back of her seat as he listened to her with interest.

The team had to squeeze to fit inside the minivan. Christy was glad the drive to the church was only fifteen minutes. They all tumbled out in the rain when they arrived. Gernot handed Christy's suitcase to her once they were inside the small, stone church and said, "I'll help you with the children since they might not be too keen on soccer in the rain."

"Brilliant!" said Doug, who had overheard Christy and Gernot talking.

Tracy and Christy burst out laughing. "We were afraid this might happen," Tracy said. "You're changing into a 'brilliant' man!"

Doug looked deeply into Tracy's eyes. The two of them seemed to exchange some unspoken message. Christy felt a bit uncomfortable.

"Actually, you've always been a brilliant man," Tracy said.

Doug loved receiving praise. He used to smile whenever Christy complimented him. Now Tracy's words made him glow.

"Where would you like us to set up for the children?" Christy asked the pastor, moving away from Doug and Tracy.

"This way," he said, leading Christy and Gernot down the short hallway to a large, carpeted room. "Please feel free to arrange the room to your liking."

Gernot began to move chairs, creating a clever stage for their puppet show. Christy unzipped her suitcase and lifted out the craft materials. From that moment on, she barely stopped moving all day.

Their first group of children arrived with bountiful energy. Christy and Gernot's job was to keep the young ones occupied while their parents were in the sanctuary meeting. Since it was a small church, Christy wondered if the noisy children could be heard down the hallway. But all in all, the morning program went smoothly. She was glad they had enough crafts to keep the older kids interested and that all of them liked the puppet show.

Gernot saved the day during the last fifteen minutes when the children began to get hungry and tired. He seemed to know an endless number of indoor games, which the children loved.

After their morning session, a cold lunch was served to them in the church kitchen. Doug asked Christy how it went with the children.

"Fine," she said, "thanks to Gernot. We could use some more help in there, though. If anyone else would like to come in during the afternoon program, that would be great."

The next session began at 1:30, and a new flock of kids arrived. There weren't so many at first. Christy thought it might be easier than the morning bunch. Then a few more children arrived, and then a few more, and pretty soon the noise level in the room rose. They decided to move right into the Bible story and the puppet show to see if they could get all the kids to sit down and, hopefully, to quiet down. It seemed to work.

Halfway through the puppet show, Tracy and Sierra entered the room and stood in the back.

"Ian is giving his message first this time," Tracy explained after the puppet show as they gathered the children in groups of five to work on their craft. "So we have some time before we do the drama and music. How can we help out here?"

"We're making paper crowns," Christy said. "These stars don't seem to peel off very easily. You could help with that. And if one of you wants to pass out the crayons, that would be great. The littler kids usually break the crayons, so give them the fat colors or the ones that are already broken."

"You're quite the natural children's ministry woman," Katie said. Then, striking a pose with her arms muscled out like a weight lifter, she added in a low, beefy voice, "I am ministry woman." She flexed her arm muscles again, and Christy laughed. Some of the children noticed Katie's muscle-bound pose and laughed at her too.

"Would you kids like to hear a little song?" Tracy asked. She sat down in a circle of girls busily maneuvering their blunt scissors around the edges of their cut-out paper crowns. With her high, charming voice, Tracy sang a song about a baby bird in its nest and how it trusted its heavenly Father and we should too.

"Sing another!" the children asked.

Tracy sang about how the mountains, the meadows, and even the trees sing out their praise to God, and we should too. Christy was pretty sure these were all songs Tracy had written. She could picture Tracy singing them one day with Doug.

Katie whispered to Christy, "I am song woman." She struck another muscle-flexing pose.

"And what are you, Katie?"

"I am drama woman," she said, readjusting her pose so she could check her watch. "And I must go." She motioned to Sierra, who was sitting on the floor helping a small girl affix her stars in just the right place on her crown.

Sierra hopped up, and on her way to join Katie, she whispered to Christy, "I'll be back. This is fun!"

Tracy left too. As soon as the crowns were finished, the children brought them to Christy so she could measure their head size and staple the crowns in the back.

When the parents came to pick up the kids, one little boy put his crown on his head and cried out, "Mummy, Mummy, look! Jesus is the King of everything!"

The "mummy" smiled and said to Christy, "Thanks so much. I really enjoyed the program. It gave me a lot to think about."

"And Mummy," the boy continued, "Jesus loves me."

Christy felt good knowing that the message had come across clearly for the little guy. She wished his mom didn't look quite so serious and unsure.

"I have something for you," Christy said. She reached in her craft box and pulled out one of the booklets the ministry team was giving to people who said they wanted to know more about Christ. "Here. Maybe this will help you to think through what you've heard. We'll be back tonight at six o'clock it you would like to come again."

She didn't know if she sounded too pushy. The program would be the same as this afternoon, so why would the lady want to come again? Still, Christy was glad she hadn't let the woman walk away empty-handed.

The last child had just left when Doug popped his head in the door and said, "Grab your coats! We're ready to go. You can leave all this."

Christy and Gernot were the last to squeeze into the minivan. The pastor drove fast down the narrow streets of the town to their appointed location at the town square for their four o'clock drama presentation. Christy felt relieved that she didn't have any responsibilities for this portion so she could catch her breath.

The drama team went to work in the van, applying make-up and a few simple costume pieces. Doug and Ian carried the props out to the center of the square and tried to find the driest spot to set up. The good news was that the rain had stopped. The bad news was that the cobblestone square was wet and slippery and only a few people were out and about.

Still, the team stayed on course, and right at four o'clock the drama team began their performance before a gathering of seven local people. A few other people joined them, and by about halfway through the presentation, Christy noticed the crowd had swelled to about thirty.

"Here," Doug whispered to Christy near the end of the play. "Be ready to pass these out." He handed her a bunch of booklets explaining how to become a Christian and another handful of flyers announcing their evening meeting at the church.

As soon as the drama ended, the crowd spontaneously applauded, which Christy thought was a good sign. Several teenagers and older children were in the crowd. Christy went right up to them and offered a brochure before they walked away.

"Where are you from?" a young teenage boy asked her.

"Some of us are from America, some from Germany. We're part of an outreach team," Christy explained.

"Why are you here?"

Before Christy had time to think through her answer, she said, "Because people need Jesus, and we want to tell them about Him."

The boy snickered and walked away. Christy felt foolish. The other people she handed brochures to were polite and thanked her. She wished she hadn't blown it with that boy, though.

To her surprise, the boy showed up at their six o'clock meeting. There were a lot of teenagers, and Reverend Allistar said many of the people were from his congregation. Christy and Gernot had their hands full with more than forty-five children. Tracy, Sierra, and Katie came in later to help out, which was a good thing, because when Christy gave the lesson and told the children how they could become Christians, thirteen of them raised their hands. Gernot and the other team members went right to work, counseling the children while Christy started the craft for the others.

"It was amazing," Christy said when their team scrunched

back in the minivan so the pastor could drive them to the station. "The lesson, the invitation, everything was the same as the two earlier meetings, yet this time thirteen kids responded. Why?"

"That's part of what they told us in training," Doug said. "Our job is to be faithful to present the message of salvation through Christ and then trust God for the results. His Spirit moves sometimes when we're not looking. Altogether in the meetings today, we had eighteen people who wanted more information and four people who prayed with us to give their lives to Christ."

"Did you give me that list of addresses?" Reverend Allistar called over his shoulder as he drove.

"Yes," said Doug, "I think you put it in your office on your desk."

"Right," the pastor responded. He parked the car and turned around with a look of delight on his face. "You have done so much today in helping me to further the ministry in this town. Thank you, thank you."

They each shook hands with him in turn after they got out of the van. Christy felt as if they had really done so little. She had had fun, actually. It was a bit wild at times, but all in all, she thought it had been easy and fun.

As soon as they were on the train, Christy turned to Sierra, who was seated next to her, and asked, "Do you know who the four people were who made commitments to Christ? Was one of them a teenage guy who was at the drama this afternoon?"

"No, they were all women," Sierra said.

Christy silently prayed for the mystery guy and for the children who had said they wanted to be Christians. About twenty minutes into the train ride, when everyone else was involved in a conversation or asleep, Sierra asked Christy, "Do you think you could do this all the time?"

"What, you mean work with kids?"

"Yes, and do outreach work like this."

Christy thought a moment and said, "You know, I think I could. Maybe I've found my niche."

"You did seem quite natural in there," Sierra agreed.

Christy struck a muscle-man pose the way Katie had earlier and said, "I am children's ministry woman."

Sierra laughed. "I don't know what I am yet. I like the drama and everything, but I don't know if that's my strongest point."

"What else do you like to do?" Christy asked.

"I like to write and make up stories."

"Maybe you should be a writer," Christy suggested.

"You know, I was thinking about writing a story about a princess and how she was looked down on because she wasn't very good-looking. Actually, she was ugly. She gets locked outside the castle, and the peasants are all mean to her. Then one person shows kindness to her, and in the end they find out she's a princess, and she rewards the person. What do you think?"

"I like it," Christy said. "You should write it. This sure is the place for inspiration, isn't it? I've been dreaming about knights and princesses while we've been at Carnforth Hall too."

"It's also the place for thinking about marriage," Sierra said. "This P.O. Box stuff is getting harder the more I watch other people pair up. You know, I'm beginning to wonder if there really could be somebody out there for me."

Christy smiled at her freckled-face, clear-eyed friend. "I'm sure there is. You will be a treasure for any guy to discover."

"Thanks for the vote of confidence, Christy. I guess I should just be patient and see what God has in mind, right?"

Christy nodded. But her thoughts were rapidly traveling back in time.

"Hello in there," Sierra said, waving her hand in front of Christy's face. "Where did you go?"

"Oh, I was just thinking about last summer. My family went camping, and we were hiking along this mountain trail that cut through the middle of a forest. My dad was next to me, and he held out his arm for me to hold on to while we walked down this path that was shaded by a canopy of huge trees."

Christy glanced over her shoulder to make sure no one else was listening. She leaned a little closer to Sierra and continued her story. "My dad comes across kind of gruff most of the time, but every now and then his tender side shows through, and he does or says things that just level me emotionally. So here we are, parading arm in arm down this trail, and he says, 'One day I'll be walking like this down the church aisle, and I'll be giving you away.' "

Sierra's eyes opened wide. "What did you do? I would have started to cry right there."

"Well, I almost did. It was so incredibly tender, the way his voice came out all rough and whispery at the same time. And then he said, 'Christina, I know you'll be wearing white on that day. I'll never be able to tell you how proud I am of you.' " Christy blinked away a tear and said, "And then from out of nowhere there came this wind that made all the trees start to shake their leaves. You know how it can sound like applause?"

"I know; I love that sound," Sierra said. "It's like that verse about all the trees in the field clapping their hands for joy."

Christy nodded. "Then my dad said, 'You're surrounded by a crowd of witnesses, Christy. Just listen.' So we stood there together, arm in arm, listening to the wind in the trees. Then my dad said, 'They're clapping for you, honey. They know a true princess when they see one.' "

Now Christy and Sierra were both crying, with slow, silent tears rolling down their cheeks.

"I am so glad I've been saving myself for my future husband," Sierra said softly. "That is, if there *is* a future husband for me somewhere. The peer pressure is for such a short time. And being married is like . . ." Sierra paused, searching for the right word.

"Forever," Christy said.

"Yeah. Forever."

# CHAPTER ELEVEN

# *Missionary Woman*

When Christy and her other teammates arrived back at Carnforth Hall at the end of their outreach, they joined all the other teams in the chapel. Even though it was late, everyone was wide awake, enthusiastically sharing stories of what God had done that day. The room seemed electrified with excitement as, for more than an hour, the team members took turns sharing their stories with the whole group.

They could have gone on for another hour, but Dr. Benson stepped in and closed the meeting by giving final details of when each of the teams was leaving for its ministry destination. Some were scheduled to depart in the morning because they had a longer distance to travel. The Belfast team wasn't leaving until later in the day. Their train ride would take them to Stranraer, where they would board the Sea Cat, a modern, high-speed ferry that would take them directly into Belfast Harbor at six o'clock that evening.

"You'll be met by the Reverend Norman Hutchins and his wife, Ruby." Dr. Benson read from his list while Doug quickly wrote down the names. "They have received a fax from us with your photo, Doug, so they'll be looking for you."

Dr. Benson went on to the next team and read their itinerary. Christy thought perhaps she should have written down some of the details for their trip. All she remembered was that they had to be ready to leave Carnforth Hall at eleven o'clock. From there, she could rely on Doug to lead them to Belfast.

As the meeting drew to a close, Christy's new friends from Finland, Merja and Satu, came over to say good-bye. "Our group leaves for Barcelona at four o'clock in the morning, so we had better say good-bye now. We're so glad we met you."

"Me too," Christy said, returning both their hugs. "Have a great time in Barcelona, and I'll see you back here for the last two days of the conference."

All over the chapel, people were hugging, laughing, crying. Some were gathered in small groups, holding hands and praying for each other. Christy felt sure God was about to do something incredible with each group.

The next morning breakfast was served at seven o'clock. Christy thought it seemed noticeably quieter in the dining room since two of the teams had already left. The Amsterdam team was scheduled to depart right after breakfast. Christy and Sierra had their suitcases packed and were ready to go.

Just as Christy took her last spoonful of porridge, Dr. Benson walked into the dining room and scanned the students' faces until his gaze rested on Christy's. He strode over to her and said, "May I speak with you a moment in my office?"

"Sure." Christy gave Katie and Sierra a shrug of her shoulders and followed him out the door. She couldn't help but feel she was in trouble. Or worse, what if it was bad news about something at home, like Avril's call?

"Is everything okay?" Christy asked as soon as she was seated in the chair in front of his huge wooden desk.

Dr. Benson took his seat and picked up some papers from his desk, which Christy recognized as her application. "Yes, I'd simply like to ask you a few questions."

Christy swallowed, and a bit of oatmeal caught in her throat. She began to cough.

"It says here that you speak Spanish."

Christy nodded and tried to stop her cough. "I . . . I took it for four years in high school." She kept coughing. "But I'm not fluent." The irritating tickle continued.

Dr. Benson rose and poured her a drink of water from a glass carafe sitting on the window sill. "Are you all right, then?"

Christy quickly drank the water, cleared her throat, and said, "Yes, I'm fine now. Thanks."

Dr. Benson continued. "We had an excellent report from Reverend Allistar regarding the children's ministry you led at his church on Saturday. You also have a glowing reference here from the children's ministry director at your home church." Placing the papers on his desk and leaning back in his chair, Dr. Benson said, "Let me come to the point. Perhaps you remember Avril, the young woman who went home last week."

"Yes. I heard her brother is out of the hospital and doing well," Christy said.

"He is, and that is good news. However, Avril has decided to stay home and not participate in the outreach. We completely understand her decision. Our dilemma is that Avril was our children's ministry worker on the Barcelona team."

"Oh," said Christy.

"There's more. Just this morning we received a fax from our missionary in Barcelona that their full-time children's worker had to return to the States. So as you can see, Barcelona is in great need of someone to do the children's ministry, particularly someone who is capable and who has a Spanish background."

Christy wasn't sure what he was getting at until Dr. Benson said, "What I'm asking, Christy, is are you willing to go to Barcelona?"

"Me?"

"Yes," he said. "You're the most qualified. It's up to you, though. Are you willing to trust God in this new way?"

"I . . . don't know. Didn't the Barcelona team already leave this morning?"

"Yes. What we would do is put you on the train with the Amsterdam team. You would travel with them as far as France and then take the train by yourself to Barcelona."

"By myself?"

Dr. Benson smiled. "The Lord will be with you. This is why I'm asking if you're willing to trust God in a new way."

Christy had never expected this. They were asking her to leave all her friends and travel alone to a place she wasn't prepared for and, from the sounds of it, single-handedly carry on the children's ministry. The only comforting thought was that Satu and Merja were on the Barcelona team. Certainly they would help her out.

"I don't know. Is it up to me to decide?"

"Yes, completely. I wish we had more time, but the Amsterdam team is leaving in . . ." he checked his watch, ". . . about ten minutes, and we would like you to travel with them as far as Calais."

"Calais? Where's that?"

"France." Dr. Benson picked up a fax and read the schedule. "You'll change trains at Calais and take an overnight train to Port Bou. We'll arrange for you to have a sleeper car so you'll be quite safe and comfortable. You will arrive in Port Bou on the Spanish side of the border at 11:02 the next morning and change trains to Barcelona at 12:25. You will arrive at Sants, the main train station in Barcelona, at 2:55 that afternoon. From there you'll take a commuter train at 3:15 and arrive at Playa Castelldefels at 3:30. It's really a lovely ride down the Costa Brava."

Christy bowed her head, closed her eyes, and pursed her lips. Perhaps Dr. Benson thought she was praying. She was really trying hard not to cry. It all hit her so hard and fast. His rapid-fire itinerary seemed overwhelming. Plus this was her worst nightmare, having to make split-second decisions that might affect the rest of her life.

She knew the need was great, but what about Belfast? Gernot and the others could carry on in her absence, she supposed. Still, how could she change directions so instantly and go to Barcelona instead of Belfast? She had already written her parents and told them she was going to Belfast.

"Would I be doing the same lessons I prepared for Belfast?" she asked, stalling for time.

"Yes, everything from your training will be exactly the same. They already have the craft materials and puppets with them. You'll be in a small town outside Barcelona, right on the Mediterranean coast and working with our local missionary. It's much warmer there than in Belfast."

Christy wondered if he actually thought the weather would make a difference in her decision. It wasn't the weather; it was the insecurity of leaving her friends and doing something on her own. And the panic of having only a few seconds to decide.

"Okay, I'll go," Christy heard herself blurt out. For a moment she thought it was someone else's voice. Then, as if to make sure she heard herself right, she repeated, "I'll go to Barcelona."

"Wonderful!" Dr. Benson said with a huge smile. "The Lord

will bless your devoted service to Him. This is the essence of genuine missionary work and separates the spectators from the true servants. You have the kind of heart God can use to accomplish great things for His kingdom!''

Christy wished she felt as brave as he made her sound. Before she realized what was happening, a stack of papers was thrust into her hand, and Dr. Benson was explaining how she was to go about buying her tickets when she arrived at Victoria Station in London.

Suddenly she wished she had said no. How could she remember all these details and manage to change trains by herself? She had depended on Doug during the rest of this trip to direct her to the right bus and train.

Maybe this was part of what God wanted to teach her, to be completely independent from any guy—or any human, for that matter—and to trust God alone.

She didn't have time to think of all the reasons for this crazy twist. All she knew was that in less than ten minutes, she had to get all her luggage downstairs and find a way to say good-bye to Katie, Doug, Tracy, Sierra, and the rest of her team.

Christy rose to leave.

Dr. Benson shook her hand warmly and said, ''We'll fax your file to the mission director in Castelldefels. Your photo is on here, so he'll know who to look for at the station. It's a very small station. I'm sure you two will have no difficulty in finding each other. You know how Americans tend to stand out in a crowd.''

Christy's head was spinning with details as she clutched her papers in her hand and, with weak knees, hurried up to her room.

*I'm going to Spain. All by myself. I can't believe this is happening. And I won't even arrive there until tomorrow afternoon!*

Seven minutes later, Christy stood in front of the two

Carnforth Hall vans, which were being loaded with the Amsterdam team's luggage.

"Good-bye," Tracy said, hugging Christy. "I love you. I'll be praying for you. You'll never know how much this past week with you has meant to me."

"I love you too," Christy said to Tracy.

"Okay, my turn to freak out, here," Katie said, giving Christy a quick hug and trying hard to keep the tears in her green eyes from spilling over. "Can I just say one thing?"

Christy had to smile. Katie always used that line, but she always had more than one thing to say.

Katie struck her buff muscle-man pose and spouted, "You are missionary woman!"

They all laughed, which made it easier for Christy to hug Gernot, Ian, and Stephen. But then it was Doug's turn, and she felt herself choking up.

"You're awesome, Christy," he said, wrapping his arms around her in one of his super hugs. "God is awesome. He's going to do awesome things in your life. Thanks for everything. Really. Thanks."

He squeezed her in another hug, and she whispered in his ear, "You're welcome, Sir Honesty. Take care of your princess."

Doug pulled away and smiled at her. "I will," he said. "Thanks, Christy."

Sierra was the last to say good-bye. "I don't know why I'm crying. I'm going to see you again in just a little more than a week when we meet back here." She hugged Christy and said, "I just feel like we really connected, you know? I wish we could have stayed together."

"I know," Christy said. "Me, too. You can come to Barcelona with me if you want." Christy playfully grabbed Sierra by the arm and pretended to push her into the van.

"Hey, wait a minute," Katie said. "Red rover, red rover, send Sierra back over!"

Doug said, "Losing you, Christy, is about as much of a sacrifice as anyone should have to make in one week."

Christy thought his words carried an underlying message aimed at their breaking up. That made it even harder for her to leave. She thought of how close their team had become after their week of training. God had answered her prayers for unity, and now they were becoming divided by her leaving. It didn't make sense.

Katie's phrase echoed in her mind: "God is weird."

"Time to go," the van driver called as he started up the engine.

Forcing a smile, Christy waved to her old teammates and climbed into the van. "Bye. I'll be praying for you guys. Pray for me!"

The van door slid shut, and Christy's seven friends all stood in a line, waving good-bye. Then at Katie's signal, just as the van pulled away, all seven of them assumed a weight-lifter pose and called out, "You are missionary woman!"

She laughed aloud, and one of the guys in the van said, "What was that?"

"A little joke," Christy said, still wavering between smiling and crying.

The train ride to London seemed to go quickly. Christy sat beside Jakobs, the guy from Latvia Katie had introduced her to. Jakobs was several years younger than Christy, but in some ways he seemed more mature, as if he had lived more of life in his sixteen years than Christy would experience in a lifetime. Jakobs wore his very short hair brushed straight up in the front. He was a few inches shorter than Christy.

Several hours into their train ride, Jakobs bought Christy a cup of tea and shared some of his sack lunch with her. Mrs. Bates had handed each of the students a sack lunch and at the same time had promptly planted a kiss on every team member's right cheek. Christy had stuck her lunch into an open corner of her suitcase, which was now nearly impossible to get at. She gladly shared Jakobs's sandwich.

"Are you yet used to the idea of going to Spain?" Jakobs asked.

Something mechanical turned on inside Christy's head, and she said, "Yes, I believe this is God's plan, and so I know He will work everything out. I'm learning to trust God in new ways."

A slow grin crept up Jakobs's face. "I think you are speaking to me through the flowers."

Although Jakobs's English was very good, sometimes his accent made his words sound a little unclear to Christy. She asked what he meant by "speaking through the flowers."

Jakobs looked a bit embarrassed. "It's an expression from where I live in Riga. We use it to mean when a person is making a pretty covering for his words and not saying what he truly feels. You are then 'speaking to me through the flowers.' "

Christy knew Jakobs was right. She was trying to sound brave and spiritual. What she really felt was terrified. Did she dare tell him? He seemed the sort of person she could trust.

"I'm really scared," she said.

Jakobs gave her a look of compassion and said, "Of what?"

"Of getting lost. Of missing my train connections."

"Then you can take the next train," Jakobs answered logically.

"But what if I can't find the right train? What if something happens, and I lose my luggage or my passport?"

"You go to your Embassy, apply for another passport, and wear your same clothes for two days in a row."

Christy couldn't tell if Jakobs was teasing her or if he was trying to be helpful. Earlier that week Christy had overheard Jakobs talking with a Texan about how Americans were overly concerned about their clothes and hygiene. The girl from Texas had to wash and blow-dry her hair every morning, and she never went out in public without her makeup perfectly applied. Jakobs told her she should try wearing the same clothes for more than one day to practice being a good steward of what God had given her. The girl told Jakobs he was crazy.

Christy didn't think he was crazy, but she did think he had a rather simplistic approach to life. "What if I get attacked, or what if I get killed?" Christy said, challenging him with a worst-possible scenario.

Jakobs's grin returned, and he said, "Then you will die and be with the Lord, and perhaps I might envy you getting to heaven before me."

Christy smiled back. Jakobs certainly had an eternal perspective on life. With such heaven-oriented thinking, it made it hard to see anything as bad. In Jakobs's vocabulary, the term "tragedy" didn't seem to exist.

Christy finished her last sip of lukewarm tea and said, "In America we would probably call you a 'Pollyanna.' That means someone who finds the good in every situation."

"In Riga, you would probably tell me to 'find ducks,' " Jakobs said and then chuckled at his own apparent joke.

" 'Find ducks'?" Christy asked.

"It's our way of saying 'go away.' Not everyone says it. Just some of my friends. If you go to Riga, you might not want to try that on just anyone. Especially someone like the officer who stamps your visa."

Christy couldn't begin to imagine what it would be like to visit a country like Latvia. Spain was exotic enough for her.

Spain. The sudden thought of Spain paralyzed her all over again. Her feelings must have shown on her face.

"Are you again worried about the trains?" Jakobs asked.

Christy knew better than to try "speaking through the flowers" to him again. "I guess a little."

"What is your verse?" Jakobs asked.

"My verse?"

"You need a verse. Something from God's Word to plant in your heart for this trip."

"To plant in the garden of my heart?" Christy said, thinking of Tracy's poem.

"Yes. You need a promise to . . . how do you say it?" Jakobs clenched his fist. "Held on with?"

"You mean to hold on to," Christy said. "You think I need a special verse to hold on to."

"Yes, I do."

"Do you have a verse?" Christy asked.

Jakobs nodded, and he rattled off some words in his melodic Latvian tongue. "It is Jeremiah 1:7-8. Sorry, but I do not yet know it in English. May I read it in your Bible?"

Christy dug to the bottom of her bag, pulled out her Bible, and turned to Jakobs's verse. She handed her Bible to him, and in his wonderful accent he read it to her. " 'But the LORD said to me, "Do not say, 'I am only a child.' You must go to everyone I send you to and say whatever I command you. Do not be afraid of them, for I am with you and will rescue you," declares the LORD.' "

"That's perfect!" Christy said. "That's exactly how I feel."

"This is my verse," Jakobs said in a teasing voice, holding Christy's Bible close to his chest. "You need to search until you find your own verse."

"Oh, go find ducks!" Christy said, teasing him right back. "I can have the same verse if I want to. Now give me my Bible back!"

Jakobs laughed and said, "You should do just fine in your new culture. I am not worried for you at all."

Christy hoped Jakobs's words would come true. They seemed true enough when the group made its connection in London. Everything went as planned, nice and smooth. All Christy had to do was follow the other team members to the ticket window and buy her ticket to cross the English Channel. Then she waited in line with them again to buy her train ticket to Barcelona while the others bought their tickets to Amsterdam.

The envelope Dr. Benson had handed her that morning had a little money left over after the purchase of her tickets. With the two pounds and some change, Christy bought herself a candy bar while they waited.

Fortunately, she decided against eating it right away. The ferry ride across the English Channel proved to be a little too rough for her stomach. The candy bar would have come right back up.

About twenty-five minutes into the trip, Christy knew she couldn't postpone the inevitable any longer. Leaving her seat next to Jakobs, she cautiously maneuvered her way to the bathroom. She barely made it into one of the bathroom stalls before she threw up. She hated throwing up. What made it worse was, right when she thought she might be okay, she could hear someone in the stall next to her throwing up, and that made her feel like doing it all over again.

It was a horrible experience. Christy slumped on the

bathroom floor, feeling too weak to return to her seat.

*This is awful; I'm never going to make it. I can't go on! This whole trip was a huge mistake. God, what are you trying to do to me?*

Another overwhelming urge to throw up seized her, and she stumbled to the sink, where her stomach muscles went through their wrenching motions, but she had nothing else to throw up. Rinsing out her mouth and wetting a paper towel to hold against her throbbing head, Christy sank again to the floor next to another sick passenger.

Under her breath she groaned, "I am *not* missionary woman."

# CHAPTER TWELVE

# *Midnight Picnic*

When they arrived in Calais at 6:30 that night, Christy felt as if she could barely walk. Her head pounded, her throat felt raw and clenched, and she was desperate for a drink of cold water. One of the guys on the Amsterdam team watched their baggage while Christy, with the sympathetic assistance of Jakobs, who also had gotten seasick, went in search of a snack bar and some bottled water.

Everything moved in slow motion as Christy and Jakobs had to exchange money, stand in line to pay an outrageous price for the bottles of water, and then find the rest of the group. Christy collapsed onto a bench where the rest of the team had gathered with their luggage and slowly sipped her water. Overhead, train departure times were being announced in French and several other languages. From where Christy sat, she could see a large board that listed train schedules with their departure times.

"We need to get all our luggage to that track down there," the Amsterdam team captain told Christy as their group began to pick out their luggage from the pile next to the bench. "Will you be okay here, Christy?"

She wanted to scream out, "No, don't leave me!" The only

words she mustered were "I'm not sure which track my train leaves from."

"I'm sure you can figure it out," the guy said. He didn't say it in an unkind way; it was just that he obviously had his hands full with four of his team members also feeling sick and their train leaving in less than fifteen minutes. "Just look on that sign over there for the 8:24 overnight train to Port Bou. It can't be that hard. Or ask someone."

With a round of hurried good-byes and a warm handshake from Jakobs, the Amsterdam team moved away like a row of ducks to their train track. Jakobs was about twenty yards away from her when he turned around and called out, "Don't forget to find your verse!" He still looked a little green around the gills and appeared to be using a lot of strength to yell his encouragement to her.

Christy sat still. All around her spun a busy, loud confusion of travelers. She felt cold, and the station suddenly smelled like mildew. Or maybe it was her breath that smelled so bad. Christy tried another swig of water, and then, popping out the handle on her wheeled suitcase, she gathered all her belongings and headed toward the train schedule board, as if she knew exactly what she was doing.

There it was plain as day, the name "Port Bou," and the time listed next to it was "8:24." Track three. How hard had that been? Now where was track three?

Christy had nearly half an hour before the train departed, but she wanted to find the right track. Walking seemed to help her recover from her seasickness, especially since the ground was level and didn't move under her feet the way it had during the English Channel crossing. The ferry ride had taken all afternoon, and although it was the cheapest way to get to France, it certainly didn't seem to Christy to be the best way. Maybe she could persuade the mission director in Barcelona to allow her to personally pay the extra amount, whatever it was, to fly back to England instead of repeating this train and ferry trip.

When she arrived at track three, there was no train. But several people were standing around. They seemed to be waiting, so she thought she must be in the right place.

Rolling her luggage and toting her black shoulder bag over to a vacant spot on a nearby bench, Christy felt as if she were going to faint. Everything in front of her began to get dark, and her vision narrowed to a small circle of bright spinning dots. She sat down just in time.

After she lowered her head and breathed deeply, everything came back into focus. Christy drank some more water and tried to get her pounding heart to slow to a steady pace.

*Everything's okay. You can do this. The Lord is with you.*

Christy had never thought of herself as a weak person. She hated this sensation of losing control. She wanted everything to be normal and calm and right up front where she could see it. She wanted to feel strong and in control again, and yet she couldn't. All she felt was queasy and weak and as if she were barely hanging on with her fingernails.

Just then she heard the loud rumble of her train coming down the track. It even drowned out the sound of the French announcer's voice over the loudspeaker.

Christy reached for her ticket in her bag. It wasn't there. She fumbled through all her junk and couldn't find it. Then, unzipping the bag's side pouch, Christy plunged her hand in. Right next to her butane curling iron, she felt the reassuring forms of her passport and her train ticket.

*Don't panic, Christy! Whatever you do, don't freak out here. You're doing fine.*

Christy was one of the first passengers to board the train. The conductor in a black coat and hat looked at her ticket as she stepped up into the train. He rattled off something to her in French.

"What? I'm sorry. I don't understand you," she said.

The man motioned with his hand toward the back of the train as a stream of French words tumbled from his mouth. "Ze sleeper cars are in ze back of ze train," a woman behind Christy said. She didn't look up at Christy, and she hadn't spoken very loudly—just enough for Christy to hear and understand.

"Oh, I'm sorry. Thank you. Excuse me." Christy tried to turn around on the narrow landing and go down the steps back to the train platform. Her suitcase got caught in the small space, and Christy couldn't budge it. The conductor spoke harshly to her again in French. She used all her might to free the snagged suitcase and get down the steps.

Once on the platform, Christy walked as fast as her wobbly legs would take her to the far end of the train. There she tried to enter the train again with the assistance of another conductor. He looked at her ticket and pointed the other way, toward the front of the train, speaking briskly in French.

"But I just came from there, and they sent me down here!" She felt sure the man could understand her, even though he waved his hand and spoke back to her in French.

Before she could stop them, salty tears filled her eyes, and she felt all the color drain from her face. "Could you please help me?" she said to the conductor.

He looked at her again, and his expression softened a bit. Motioning for her to enter the train, he lifted her suitcase for her and indicated that she should follow him. He lead the way through several train cars that were all linked together, down the narrow hallway of the train lined with windows on one side and compartments with closed doors on the other. Suddenly he stopped in front of a compartment and slid open the door, indicating for her to enter.

"Thank you," Christy said, viewing the empty compartment with the two upholstered bench seats that faced each other. She couldn't wait to lie down and get some sleep.

The conductor entered the small compartment with her and lifted her suitcase to an overhead rack. Then, with a tug on one of the seats, he pulled it out to reveal a sort of Hide-a-Bed already made up. He reached for a blanket from the overhead rack and muttered a few more French words.

Christy thought to reach for some money to tip him. She grabbed everything she had in her coat pocket left over from when she and Jakobs had bought the water. She had no idea if the handful of francs she offered him was a lot or a little.

He glanced at the bills and coins she had dropped into his hand and then looked again. With a tip of his hat he backed out of her train compartment and mumbled something in French.

Christy pulled the shades down on her compartment windows that faced the narrow hallway and then closed the shade on the large window that overlooked the train tracks and the station. Her bed looked so inviting. Slipping off her shoes and pulling back the covers, Christy crawled in and hoped to sleep straight through until the morning light peeked in.

She fell into a deep sleep as the train pulled out of the station, rocking her with its rhythmic motion down the tracks. Unfortunately her sleep lasted only a short time. Someone suddenly slid her compartment door open, spoke loudly in French, and snapped on the overhead light.

It was a conductor, but not the one who had helped her earlier.

*"Passporte,"* he said. Then in exaggerated English, "Passport."

Christy groped for her shoulder bag, which she had tucked under the covers with her as a precaution. She handed him her passport and ticket. He looked it over, seemed satisfied, and jammed the sliding door shut as abruptly as he had opened it. The rude fellow had left on the light.

Christy returned her passport to its safe place in her bag and then crawled out of her burrow to turn off the light. The train slowed to a stop. Apparently they were at another station. A few minutes later the train started up again. The voices of new passengers could be heard in the hallway outside her door. Now Christy couldn't get back to sleep.

At least she felt better. She sat up in bed and finished her bottle of water. Then she realized how hungry she was. It was nearly midnight, and she hadn't eaten for close to twelve hours. Snapping the light back on, she scrounged through her suitcase until she found the sack lunch Mrs. Bates had packed for her. Sitting cross-legged, Christy spread her little picnic out on her bed, folded her hands, and bowed her head to pray.

"It's just You and me, Lord. Thank You for taking care of me and for providing this food for our little midnight picnic. Thanks for making me feel better. I'm sorry I blamed You for this trip back on the ferry. I just hate being sick."

Christy opened her eyes and took a bite of her sandwich, but she continued talking to Jesus as if He were sitting next to her. "I just like everything to be, well . . . comfortable. I guess I like to be in control. But, then, that's supposed to be Your job, isn't it?"

It hit her like a revelation. She pictured herself standing by the gate of her heart's garden. Jesus was definitely in the garden with her, but clearly Christy was the one who held the key to the gate.

She put down her sandwich, and looking into the thin air next to her, she said, "That's what's been missing, huh? I'm still the one making all the decisions, holding the key, and I'm the one deciding who should come in and out of my garden. I've been the one locking and unlocking the gate. I've been the one in control.

"Lord Jesus," Christy whispered, "I want You to hold the key. I want You to decide what should happen in my heart's garden. I want You to let in or send out anything or anybody You want. Especially with guys. I don't want to ever unlock that gate again. I want You to open it only when the right man comes along. Take the key, Lord. Take all my keys. I'll wait for You."

For a moment Christy thought she might be going crazy because a sweet fragrance seemed to be in the cabin after she prayed. Certainly in her heart's garden there was the fragrance of fresh, blooming newness. She felt so free, so completely right with God. She continued their picnic, imagining that she and Jesus were seated together under a plumeria tree in her heart's garden. Beside them a wild patch of daffodils bobbed their heads and a long, trailing vine of jasmine lined the trellis that covered her garden gate.

Christy couldn't remember the last time she had felt so happy. So safe. So completely content. She had never felt this close to Jesus, either.

"Is it because there's always been some guy in my garden with me? Is that why I've never before been so open and sought You so wholeheartedly?" Christy wondered aloud. "I want it to be You and me, Lord. Always. Close, like this. Even if You do bring a guy into my life, I still want to feel this close to You. Forever."

So many things seemed to make sense to Christy. The unsettled feelings she had fought with last week were gone. She knew the weeks ahead of her would be difficult and stretching, yet she wasn't afraid of what might happen. She felt tremendous assurance that she had done the right thing in letting go of Doug.

She even felt a peace about Todd. She had done the right thing in letting him go too. He was serving God, and that was where he belonged. Christy knew she needed to move on, to fully become the woman God created her to be and not to be dependent on any guy. She would be dependent on the Lord alone.

After eating half her sandwich and two of her carrot sticks, Christy put away her lunch, deciding to save the rest for later. It was the middle of the night, and she desperately needed some sleep.

Turning off the light, she thought of one of the evening verses Dr. Benson had quoted, "I will lie down and sleep in peace, for you alone, O LORD, make me dwell in safety."

"Amen," she whispered, and she fell into a deep sleep.

But not for long.

CHAPTER THIRTEEN

# *Forever*

Suddenly the door of Christy's compartment flew open, and a rough, coarse voice blared into the darkness.

"Who's there?" Christy called out, sitting up in bed.

The overhead light flipped on, temporarily blinding her with its flash.

"What do you want?" Christy demanded of the gruff, smelly, obviously drunk man who had entered her compartment. "Get out of here," she yelled. "I mean it! Get out of here right now, or I'll scream."

The confused man stumbled farther into her room, and the door slid shut behind him. As it did, Christy let out the loudest scream she could.

The man covered his ears but didn't move. Christy screamed again, then drew in a deeper breath and screamed again. The door slid open, and two conductors and three passengers all crammed inside, grabbing the man by the arm and ushering him out as quickly as he had found his way in.

The conductor who had helped Christy find her room now stood beside her and in a soothing voice spoke to her in French. She scrambled to remember the word for "thank you" and hoarsely told the conductor, *"Merci."*

He kept talking and pointed to her door. She thought at first he wanted her to leave, and she began to get out of bed. He motioned for her to stay, and then he went out the door. Christy waited a moment and then peeked out the drawn shades into the hallway. The conductor was still standing by her door. Apparently he had appointed himself her personal bodyguard for the remainder of her trip through France.

*I must have tipped him a lot of money*, Christy thought. *Either that, or he's my guardian angel in disguise.*

She swallowed; her throat hurt terribly. She found a cough drop in her bag and tried to sleep. It was an on-and-off endeavor.

Right before sunrise, Christy decided she couldn't wait any longer to go to the bathroom. She put on her shoes and looped her black bag over her arm. Carefully opening her door, she was almost surprised to see that her personal guard wasn't standing there.

Then Christy heard a *"bonjour"* and saw that he had moved to the end of the hallway and was smoking a cigarette by an open window.

*Probably not my guardian angel.* She smiled, said *"Merci"* again, and pointed to the tiny train rest room across the way. When she came out several minutes later, the conductor was still standing there. He pointed to something out the window, and she stopped to see the sun coming up across rolling green hills. An old stone barn stood alone in the distance. The chilly wind from the open window blew her hair back. It was a beautiful scene and a beautiful morning. Christy imagined they must be somewhere in the middle of France, but she had no idea where.

Back in her compartment, she crawled into her warm bed. She lifted the shade on her window just far enough to see outside. For nearly an hour she sat contentedly watching the breathtaking scenery roll past her.

"I'd like to come back someday," she said to her Silent Companion. "I'd like to explore every little village we've passed and experience all kinds of new adventures."

Christy pulled out her journal and recorded the events of the past few days as best she could. It seemed impossible that so much had happened in such a short time.

After bringing her journal entries up to the event of the drunken man and her uniformed bodyguard, Christy wrote, *I think I know what I'd like to be when I grow up. Or should I say, what I think God would like me to be when I grow up. I'd like to be a missionary. Here, in Europe. I like working with children. Surely there's some place that needs a missionary to tell the little kids about Jesus. Whatever it takes in schooling or training, I want to go after it wholeheartedly when I get home.*

Reaching for her sack lunch, Christy opened her bottle of orange juice. She sat back, enjoyed the scenery, drank orange juice, and ate the Toblerone candy bar she had bought before the ferry ride.

The memory of that nightmare of a trip made her shudder. At the same time, she felt as if she had accomplished something grand and glorious. She had made it this far in one piece. She felt she could do anything.

The renewed energy and confidence came in handy at Port Bou when she had to change trains. The train to Barcelona left Port Bou promptly at 12:25. It was an older train and much more crowded. Christy didn't have a compartment to herself, but shared it with five other people. Two women who appeared to be traveling together sat across from Christy and spoke such rapid Spanish that Christy could barely understand what they were saying. A teenage boy sat next to her, reading a paperback book. An elderly woman sat next to him and talked to another woman seated across from her until they both nodded off.

It felt peculiar to share a compartment with these strangers until Christy realized they were ignoring her. Perhaps she shouldn't be so interested in them. This would be a good time to finish her sandwich and the apple left in her lunch.

With her first bite into the sandwich, Christy thought of Jakobs, who had shared his sandwich with her. She wondered if he had gone hungry later in his journey to Amsterdam. Then she remembered his words at the Calais train station about finding her own verse.

She pulled out her Bible and began to skim through the psalms to see if she had underlined any verses that would mean a lot to her now. Every verse she read touched her in a different way. She had never felt so refreshed reading her Bible.

After nearly an hour, Christy found a verse that seemed perfect for her desire to be a missionary and to work with children. She copied Psalm 78:4 into her diary: *"We will not hide them from their children; we will tell the next generation the praiseworthy deeds of the* LORD, *his power, and the wonders he has done."*

That verse stirred within Christy a call to serve God, yet it didn't seem like "her" verse, the way Jakobs's had seemed so personal for him. So she read on.

And then, in Psalm 86:11 and 12, she found it. *"Teach me your way, O* LORD, *and I will walk in your truth; give me an undivided heart, that I may fear your name. I will praise you, O* LORD *my God, with all my heart; I will glorify your name forever."*

"Forever," Christy repeated as she wrote the last word in her journal. "With all my heart forever," she whispered. It felt as if the Lord were sitting right next to her, listening to every word of her promise.

When she heard an audible voice next to her, she jumped.

"Pardon me. May I ask what you are reading?" It was the teenage boy. Christy had thought he was sleeping. To her surprise she realized he had been observing her, and he spoke English.

"It's a Bible," Christy said.

"Do you mean the Holy Bible?" he asked, eyeing her Bible. Perhaps the pink-flowered fabric cover seemed unusual to him.

"Yes, of course. The Bible."

He looked surprised. "And you have been reading it this long? And with such interest?"

Christy nodded. "Do you ever read the Bible?"

"No," the tanned, dark-haired boy said, "I do not have one."

Without thinking, Christy said, "Here, would you like to have mine?"

His eyes grew wide in disbelief.

Christy quickly removed the pink cover. "Really. You can have it. It's in English, but you seem to speak English very well." She placed the Bible in his hand and said, "Here. I want you to have it, really."

"*Muchas gracias*. Thank you."

"You have to read it now," she said with a smile. She was thinking of the teenage boy in England who had scoffed at her after the drama performance.

"I will. Thank you."

"Are you going to Barcelona?" Christy asked.

"Yes," the boy answered, "I surf there sometimes. Sitges has better surfing, though. It's not far."

*Surfing*, Christy thought. *Maybe I will feel at home here.*

"This is Sants now," the boy said as the train began to slow down in a huge station. "You will change here. The train to Castelldefels is very nice. More modern. Go to platform five and get on the Villa Nova train."

"Thank you," Christy said. "By the way, my name is Christy. What's your name?"

"Carlos."

"I'm working with a group of people in Castelldefels who are doing drama and music this week," Christy said. "Maybe you can come sometime, Carlos. I'm sorry I don't know when or where it will be."

"Castelldefels is not a very big place," he said with a smile. "I should be able to find you. Thank you again for your Bible. You are a different woman."

As soon as Christy was situated on the modern commuter train, she reviewed Carlos's words in her mind. *"You are a different woman."* She supposed "different" was meant in a good way. And he had said woman, not girl. Maybe she had grown up so much on this trip that it showed—even to strangers.

Christy could picture herself relating this story to Katie when they gathered back at Carnforth Hall. She would flex her arms and tell Katie, "I am different woman!" Indeed, that's how she felt.

Christy glanced out the window and spotted the ocean. The Mediterranean Sea, to be exact. It was a beautiful, rich blue color. Suddenly she felt at home. She could almost smell the moist ocean air through the closed train windows. A smile grew as Christy thought of how it would feel in a few short minutes to take off her shoes and socks and wiggle her bare feet in the cool sand on the beach.

*This is it, Lord! This is perfect. Thank You for bringing me here; I could stay forever.*

Then it hit Christy that she had no idea who was meeting her at the station. Dr. Benson had said the mission director would have her photo along with her application. She decided to look for a man like Dr. Benson, late forties, hair graying by the temples and wearing . . . wearing what? A flowered surfing shirt? Christy giggled at the thought of a mission director who might know how to surf. For all she knew, this guy would greet her in a sombrero and riding a donkey! Hopefully Merja and Satu would be there too, and they would recognize her right away.

She felt nervous. This was it. She had made it all the way by herself. With the Lord, of course. But here she was. And in less than five minutes, the train would stop, and she would begin her week as a missionary woman.

She decided to make a quick run to the train's rest room and do her best to look presentable. It wasn't an easy task. The eighteen hours of travel had taken their toll on her. But a quick wash of her face and brush of her hair helped her to feel refreshed. She had a sample vial of perfume, which she snapped open and rubbed up and down her arms.

*Much better. Now to get my luggage and stand by the door.*

As soon as the train came to a stop, Christy jumped off, all smiles. She looked around. There was no Satu. No Merja. And no mission director on a donkey. She saw no one who even vaguely looked as if he might be waiting for her.

*I thought this was the right place.*

She glanced around the small, nearly vacant station. There was a ticket booth and what looked like a snack bar. The station itself was old and run-down.

The train pulled away, heading down the coast toward Sitges. Christy wistfully watched it go. That's when she noticed the graffiti on the wall, and with the ocean breeze racing through the corridor came the smell of urine.

*Lord, remember me? What are we doing here?*

All her courage left her. This had to be a mistake. Christy reached into her bag and fumbled for the papers Dr. Benson had given her. Perhaps there was a phone number to call. Was there even a pay phone around this place? And what could she use for money? She hadn't exchanged any traveler's checks into pesetas yet. Where were those papers?

Christy dug her hand deeper into her shoulder bag. Scanning the papers she finally located there, she found no phone numbers or addresses listed. All the plans had been made in such haste. All she knew was that someone was supposed to meet her. She was here and he or she wasn't.

Never in her life had she felt so completely alone. Stranded with nowhere to turn. A prayer came quickly to her lips. "Father God, I'm at Your mercy here. I know You're in control. Please show me what to do."

Suddenly she heard a voice calling to her.

"Kilikina!"

Christy's heart stopped. Only one person in the entire world had ever called her by her Hawaiian name. She spun around.

"Kilikina," called out the tall, blond surfer who was running toward her.

Christy looked up into the screaming silver-blue eyes that could only belong to one person.

"Todd?" she whispered, convinced she was hallucinating.

"Kilikina," Todd wrapped his arms around her so tightly that for an instant she couldn't breathe. He held her a long time. Crying. She could feel his warm tears on her neck. She knew this had to be real. But how could it be?

"Todd?" she whispered again. "How? I mean, what? . . . I don't . . ."

Todd pulled away, and for the first time she noticed the big bouquet of white carnations in his hand. They were now a bit squashed.

"For you," he said, his eyes clearing and his rich voice sounding calm and steady. Then, seeing her shocked expression, he asked, "You really didn't know I was here, did you?"

Christy shook her head, unable to find any words.

"Didn't Dr. Benson tell you?"

She shook her head again.

"You mean you came all this way by yourself, and you didn't even know I was here?" Now it was Todd's turn to look surprised.

"No, I thought you were in Papua New Guinea or something. I had no idea you were here!"

"They needed me here more," Todd said with a chin-up gesture toward the beach. "It's the perfect place for me." With a wide smile spreading above his square jaw, he said, "Ever since I received the fax yesterday saying they were sending you, I've been out of my mind with joy! Kilikina, you can't imagine how I've been feeling."

Christy had never heard him talk like this before.

Todd took the bouquet from her and placed it on top of her luggage. Then, grasping both her quivering hands in his and looking into her eyes, he said, "Don't you see? There is no way you or I could ever have planned this. It's from God."

The shocked tears finally caught up to Christy's eyes, and she blinked to keep Todd in focus. "It is," she agreed. "God brought us back together, didn't He?" A giggle of joy and delight danced from her lips.

"Do you remember what I said when you gave me back your

bracelet?" Todd asked. "I said that if God ever brought us back together, I would put that bracelet back on your wrist, and that time, it would stay on forever."

Christy nodded. She had replayed the memory of that day a thousand times in her mind. It had seemed impossible that God would bring them back together. Christy's heart pounded as she realized that God, in His weird way, had done the impossible.

Todd reached into his pocket and pulled out the "Forever" ID bracelet. He tenderly held Christy's wrist, and circling it with the gold chain, he secured the clasp.

Above their heads a fresh ocean wind blew through the palm trees. It almost sounded as if the trees were applauding.

Christy looked up from her wrist and met Todd's expectant gaze. Deep inside, Christy knew that with the blessing of the Lord, Todd had just stepped into the garden of her heart.

In the holiness of that moment, his silver-blue eyes embraced hers and he whispered, "I promise, Kilikina. Forever."

"Forever," Christy whispered back.

Then gently, reverently, Todd and Christy sealed their forever promise with a kiss.

# Don't Miss These Captivating Stories in
## THE CHRISTY MILLER SERIES

# THE SIERRA JENSEN SERIES

If you've enjoyed reading about Christy Miller,
you'll love reading about Christy's friend Sierra Jensen.

### #1 • Only You, Sierra
When her family moves to another state, Sierra dreads going to a new high school—until she meets Paul.

### #2 • In Your Dreams
Just when events in Sierra's life start to look up—she even gets asked out on a date—Sierra runs into Paul.

### #3 • Don't You Wish
Sierra is excited about visiting Christy Miller in California during Easter break. Unfortunately, her sister, Tawni, decides to go with her.

### #4 • Close Your Eyes
Sierra experiences a sticky situation when Paul comes over for dinner and Randy shows up at the same time.

### #5 • Without A Doubt
When handsome Drake reveals his interest in Sierra, life gets complicated.

### #6 • With This Ring
Sierra couldn't be happier when she goes to Southern California to join Christy Miller and their friends for Doug and Tracy's wedding.

### #7 • Open Your Heart
When Sierra's friend Christy Miller receives a scholarship from a university in Switzerland, she invites Sierra to go with her and Aunt Marti to visit the school.

### #8 • Time Will Tell
After an exciting summer in Southern California and Switzerland, Sierra returns home to several unsettled relationships.

### #9 • Now Picture This
When Sierra and Paul start corresponding, she imagines him as her boyfriend and soon begins neglecting her family and friends.

### #10 • Hold On Tight
Sierra joins her brother and several friends on a road trip to Southern California to visit potential colleges.

### #11 • Closer Than Ever
When Paul doesn't show up for her graduation party and news comes that a flight from London has crashed, Sierra frantically worries about the future.

### #12 • Take My Hand
A costly misunderstanding leaves Sierra anxious as she says goodbye to Portland and heads off to California for her freshman year of college.

# FOCUS ON THE FAMILY®
# $\mathcal{L}$IKE THIS BOOK?